GEORGETTE HEYER

THE TOLL-GATE

Complete and Unabridged

ULVERSCROFT
Leicester

First published in Great Britain in 1954

This Ulverscroft Edition
published 2019
by arrangement with
Penguin Random House UK
London

A catalogue record for this book is available
from the British Library.

ISBN 978–1–4448–4201–2

Published by
F. A. Thorpe (Publishing)
Anstey, Leicestershire

Set by Words & Graphics Ltd.
Anstey, Leicestershire
Printed and bound in Great Britain by
T. J. International Ltd., Padstow, Cornwall

This book is printed on acid-free paper

THE TOLL-GATE

Home from Waterloo, life in peacetime is rather dull for the adventure-loving Captain John Staple. But when he finds himself lost and benighted on the moors, he hardly expects to find a frightened young boy who's been left alone to tend a toll gatehouse. Undercover as the new keeper of the house, John investigates, and begins to unravel a complex mystery. Then he meets the orphaned Nell Stornaway, an outspoken beauty who is an unwitting pawn in a treacherous scheme. Between hiding his true identity from Nell, and the arrival in the neighbourhood of some distinctly shady characters, John finds himself embarking upon the adventure — and romance — of a lifetime . . .

Books by Georgette Heyer
Published in Ulverscroft Collections:

ARABELLA
SPRIG MUSLIN
DEATH IN THE STOCKS
COTILLION
BEHOLD, HERE'S POISON

1

The Sixth Earl of Saltash glanced round the immense dining-table, and was conscious of a glow of satisfaction.

It was an emotion not shared by his butler, or by his steward, each of whom had served the Fifth Earl, and remembered, with a wealth of nostalgic detail, the various occasions upon which the State Dining-room had been used to entertain Royalty, foreign Ambassadors, and *ton* parties of great size and brilliance. The Fifth Earl had been a Public Man. It was otherwise with his son, who had neither the desire nor the ability to fill a great office. Indeed, so little expectation had he of entertaining even the most undistinguished scion of a royal house that the State Apartments at Easterby might have fallen into total disuse had he not, at the age of thirty, become betrothed to the Lady Charlotte Calne.

This, since he was the sole surviving son of the Fifth Earl, he could not but consider to be a matter of considerable family importance; and to mark it he had summoned to Easterby, to meet his prospective bride, every available member of the house of Staple. A rapid review of his maternal relations had been enough to convince him that their presence at this triumphant gathering would be as unnecessary as it was undesirable. To the Staples he was a person of consequence, the head of his family, and not even his masterful sister Albinia would withhold from him (in public) the respect to which his position entitled him. It was otherwise with the Timbercombes, owing him no allegiance; and it did not take him more than a few reflective minutes to decide that his marriage did not concern them.

So twenty persons only sat down to dinner under the painted ceiling in the State Dining-room; and the Earl, seated at the head of a table loaded with plate, and bearing as a centrepiece an enormous epergne, presented by some foreign potentate to the Fifth Earl, looked around him with satisfaction.

It mattered nothing to him that the room was over-large for the company, and that the gentlemen outnumbered the ladies by two: the Staples had responded in the most gratifying way to his invitation, and were behaving — even his formidable Aunt Caroline — just as they ought. He could see that Lady Melksham, his future mother-in-law, was impressed. With most of the Staples she was already acquainted, but she had not until today met his Uncle Trevor, the Archdeacon, who was seated beside her, or his huge cousin John. His unmarried aunt, Maria, who kept house for him, had suffered a little qualm about John's lowlier position at the dining-table, but she had yielded to the Earl's wish. She knew, of course, that an Archdeacon must take precedence over a retired Captain of Dragoon Guards, but the Archdeacon was her younger brother, and it was difficult for her to realize that he had any particular standing in the world. John, on the other hand, was the only son of her second brother, and heir-presumptive to the Earldom, which made him, in her eyes, a person of consequence. She ventured to say as much to the Earl, and he was not displeased: he felt it to be a very just observation.

'However, I daresay dear John won't care where he sits!' had added Lady Maria comfortably.

The Earl felt that this was regrettably true. He was very fond of John, but he thought him far too careless of his dignity. Probably his years of campaigning in the Peninsula had made him forgetful of what was due to himself and the name he bore. His manners were easy to a fault, and he very often behaved in a freakish way which seriously shocked his noble relative. His exploits in the Peninsula had made him a by-word amongst his fellow-officers; and one at least of his actions since he had sold out, in 1814, had seemed to the Earl unbecomingly whimsical. No sooner did he learn that Napoleon was again at large than he returned to the Army as a volunteer; and when the Earl had shown him that duty did not demand such a sacrifice of his dignity, he had burst out laughing, and had exclaimed: 'Oh, Bevis, Bevis — ! You don't suppose I'd miss this campaign, do you? I wouldn't, for a fortune! Duty be hanged!'

So off had gone John to the wars again. But he had not remained for long in the humble position of a volunteer. Colonel Clifton, commanding the 1st Regiment of Dragoons, no sooner heard that Crazy Jack was back than he enrolled him as an extra aide-de-camp. He emerged from the Waterloo Campaign much refreshed, and with no more serious injuries than a sabre-cut, and a graze from a spent ball. The Earl was very glad to see him safe home again, and began to think that it was time he settled down, and married an eligible female. He had inherited a small estate from his father; he was twenty-nine years of age; and he had no brothers.

His lordship, glancing round his table, remembered this, as his eyes alighted on his aunt-in-law, the Honourable Mrs Staple. He wondered that she should not have provided her son with a suitable wife, and thought that perhaps he would broach the matter to her later in the evening. He was not quite two years older than John, but as the head of the family he believed himself to be responsible for his cousins. This helped him to overcome the feeling of inferiority which too often possessed him when he was confronted by these over-poweringly large persons. A big race, the Staples: he was himself a tall man, but narrow-shouldered, and inclined to stoop. John, of course, was a giant; and his sister, Lady Lichfield, who was talking with determined amiability to the Earl's very dull brother-in-law, Mr Tackenham, stood five foot nine inches in her bare feet. Lucius Staple, only child of the Fourth Earl's third son, was a big man, too; and so was Arthur, the Archdeacon's eldest-born, just now striving to entertain his cousin Lettice, who was

4

making sheep's eyes at John, across the table. Even young Geoffrey Yatton, Lettice's brother, though still slightly gangling, bade fair to tower above the Earl; and their mother, Lady Caroline, could only be described as massive.

Lady Charlotte Calne, the Earl's betrothed, had been so much struck by the splendid proportions of the Staples that she had been moved to utter a spontaneous remark. 'How very big your cousins are!' she said. 'They are all very good-looking: exceptionally so, I fancy.'

He was gratified, and said eagerly: 'Do you think so indeed? But Lucius has red hair, you know, and although Geoffrey is well enough, I don't consider Arthur above the ordinary. But John is a fine fellow, isn't he? I hope you will like him: everyone likes John! I have a great regard for him myself.'

'If that is so he must have a claim on *my* regard. I assure you I shall like him excessively,' replied the lady, as one who knew where her duty lay.

Not for the first time he congratulated himself on his choice of bride. Himself a man of no more than mild sensibility he found nothing amiss with his Charlotte's colourless manner; and he would have experienced considerable surprise had he known that she did not meet with universal approbation in his family. But although Lady Maria thought she would make Bevis an excellent wife, the Archdeacon that she was a pretty-behaved girl, and Lady Caroline that her only fault was a lack of dowry, it was noticeable that Mrs Staple refrained from expressing an opinion, and Mr Yatton (though not within his wife's hearing) went so far as to say that she favoured her mother too much for his taste.

The younger generation was more forthright, only the Earl's sister, who had been instrumental in promoting the match, according Lady Charlotte a full measure of approval. Miss Yatton, with all the assurance of a young lady with one successful London Season at her back, pronounced her to be a dowdy; her brother Geoffrey confided to his cousin Arthur that he would as lief, himself, take a cold poultice to wife; and Captain Staple, unaware of Lady Charlotte's amiable determination to like him, answered the quizzical lift of Lucius's sandy brows with an expressive grimace.

They were standing together at one end of the Crimson State Saloon after dinner. Lucius chuckled, and said: 'Oh, she'll suit Bevis well enough!'

'I hope she may. She wouldn't suit me!' said the Captain. He glanced round the ornate room. 'This is a horrid party!' he decided. 'What the devil made Saltash dish up all his relations? Enough to make the girl cry off! Lord, here's my uncle bearing down on us! I wish I hadn't been fool enough to come!'

'Well, my dear boy!' said the Archdeacon, in mellifluous accents, and laying an affectionate hand on one of the Captain's great shoulders. 'And how is it with you? I need not ask, however: you are in a capital way! A happy event this, is it not?'

'Yes, if Bevis thinks so,' replied the Captain.

The Archdeacon thought it best to ignore the implication of this. He said: 'A young female of the first consequence! But come, now! When, you great creature, are we to be celebrating *your* approaching nuptials?'

'Not yet, sir: I'm not in the petticoat-line. And if ever I do become engaged,' he added, his blue gaze wandering thoughtfully round the room, 'I wouldn't celebrate the event in this fashion, by Jupiter!'

'Well!' remarked Lucius, as their uncle, with a sweet, mechanical smile, moved away, 'you do know how to repulse the enemy, don't you, Jack?'

'I didn't mean to. Do you think he was offended?' Captain Staple broke off, his eyes widening in suspicion and dismay. 'Good God, Lucius, just look at that!' he ejaculated.

Lucius, following the direction of his horrified gaze, saw that a footman had entered the Saloon, tenderly bearing a gilded harp. Lady Charlotte was being solicited to display her chief accomplishment, while her mama informed Mrs Staple, with complacency, that her voice had been trained by the first masters. While Lord Saltash, eagerly, and the elder ladies of the party, politely, begged Charlotte to overcome her diffidence, Lord Melksham, the lady's brother, edged his way across the Saloon, and suggested to Lucius that they should (as he phrased it) nabble Ralph Tackenham, and withdraw, with Captain Staple, from the Saloon for a quiet rubber of whist.

'Ay, willingly!' responded Lucius. 'But you'll

find his wife won't permit him to go with us, if I know my cousin Albinia!'

'Nabble him when she ain't looking,' said Lord Melksham hopefully. 'Very partial to a quiet rubber, Ralph!'

'No, it can't be done.' Captain Staple spoke with decision. 'We must — shall! — stay, and listen to your sister's performance.'

'But she'll sing for ever!' objected his lordship. 'Dismal stuff, too: assure you!'

But Captain Staple, with a shake of his head, moved away towards the group gathered about the fair harpist, and, obedient to an inviting smile, sat down on a small sofa beside his cousin Lettice.

'This will be *dreadful!*' Miss Yatton whispered.

'Yes, very likely,' he agreed. He turned his head to look down at her, a smile in his eyes. 'You've grown very fine since I saw you last, Letty. I suppose you've come out, have you?'

'Good gracious, yes! At the beginning of the Season! If you had been in London, you would know that I enjoyed a *considerable* success!' said Miss Yatton, never one to hide her light under a bushel. 'Only fancy! Papa received three offers for my hand! Quite ineligible, of course, but just think of it! *Three*, and in my first Season!'

He was amused, but he checked her, Lady Charlotte having by this time disposed herself at the harp. He covered one of his lively young cousin's hands with his own large one, and gave it an admonishing squeeze. Miss Yatton, who was bidding fair to become an accomplished flirt, obeyed the unspoken command, but cast up at him so roguish a look that his sister, observing it, and the smile with which it was received, took instant fright, and determined at the earliest opportunity to draw her mother's attention to a danger she had perhaps not perceived.

But Mrs Staple, visited by her daughter some two hours later, listened to her warning with unshaken placidity, merely saying: 'Dear me, did you get me to send my maid away only to tell me this, Fanny?'

'Mama, she ogled him throughout dinner! And the way in which he took her hand, and smiled at her — ! I assure you — '

'I observed the whole, my love, and was most forcibly put in mind of the way he has with his puppies.'

'Puppies?' exclaimed Lady Lichfield. 'Letty is not a puppy, Mama! Indeed, I think her an arrant flirt, and I cannot but be uneasy. You will own that she would not *do* for my brother!'

'Do not put yourself in a taking, my love!' replied Mrs Staple, tying the strings of her nightcap under her chin. 'I only hope she may amuse him enough to keep him here over the weekend, though I don't scruple to say that I very much doubt it. My dear Fanny, was there ever such an insipid affair?'

'Oh, there was never anything like it!' readily agreed her daughter. 'But, Mama, how shocking a thing it would be if John were to fall in love with Letty Yatton!'

'I have no apprehension of it,' replied Mrs Staple calmly.

'He seemed to be quite taken with her,' said

Fanny. 'I cannot but wonder, ma'am, if Letty's vivacity may not make dear Elizabeth's *gentler* manners seem to him — well, *tame!*'

'You are making a piece of work about nothing,' said Mrs Staple. 'If he should feel a partiality for Elizabeth I shall be excessively happy. But I hope I am not such a goose as to set my heart upon the match. Depend upon it, your brother is very well capable of choosing a wife for himself.'

'Mama! How can you be so provoking?' exclaimed Fanny. 'When we have both of us been at such pains to bring John and Elizabeth together, and you have actually invited Elizabeth to Mildenhurst next week!'

'Very true,' returned Mrs Staple imperturbably. 'I should not think it wonderful if John were to find Eliza's quiet good sense welcome after three days spent — if the chit can contrive it! — in Letty's company.'

Fanny looked a little dubious, but she was prevented from making any rejoinder by a knock on the door. Mrs Staple called to this late visitor to come in, adding, in an under-voice: 'Take care! This is John: I know his knock.'

So, indeed, it proved. Captain Staple entered, saying: 'May I come in, Mama? Hallo, Fan! Talking secrets?'

'Good gracious, no! Unless you think it a secret that this is the most insipid party that ever was given!'

'Well, that's just it,' said John confidentially. 'If you don't object, Mama, I think I shall be off in the morning.'

'Not remain until Monday!' cried Fanny. 'You can't cry off like that!'

'I'm not crying off. I was invited to meet the bride, and I have met her.'

'But you can't tell Bevis you don't mean to stay!'

'As a matter of fact, I have told him,' said John, a little guiltily. 'Told him I had arranged to visit friends — not having understood that I was expected to remain here above a night. Now, there's no need to pull that face, Fan! If you're thinking Bevis was offended, you're quite out.'

'Very well, my dear,' interposed his mother, before Fanny could speak. 'Do you mean to go home? For I must tell you that although I should like nothing better than to bring *my* visit to an end to-morrow I cannot do it without putting your Aunt Maria into a miff.'

'No, no, I don't mean to drag you off with me, Mama!' he assured her. 'To tell you the truth, I thought I might take a trip into Leicestershire, to see Wilfred Babbacombe. Bound to be there, now cubbing has started.' He read condemnation in his sister's eye, and added hastily: 'It seems a pity I shouldn't do so, now that I'm in the district.'

'In the district! Easterby must be sixty miles from Leicester, and very likely more!'

'Well, now that I'm in the north,' amended the Captain.

'But you will not let Mama return to Mildenhurst without an escort!'

'No, of course I won't. My man shall go with her. You won't object to having Cocking to ride beside the chaise in my stead, will you, Mama? You'll be quite safe with him.'

'By all means, my dear. But had you not better take him with you?'

'Lord, no! I'll take what I want in a saddle-bag, and shan't have the least need of him.'

'When,' demanded Fanny, a look of foreboding in her eyes, 'do you mean to return to Mildenhurst?'

'Oh, I don't know!' said her maddening brother. 'In a week or so, I daresay. Why?'

Fanny, prohibited by a quelling glance from her mama from answering this question, merely looked her disapprobation. Mrs Staple said: 'It is not of the smallest consequence. I have friends coming to stay at Mildenhurst next week, so you are not to be thinking that I may be lonely, John.'

'Oh, that's famous, then!' he said, relieved. 'You know, Mama, I don't know how it is — whether it's my uncle, with his bamboozling ways, or Aunt Caroline, or Lucius's laugh, or Ralph Tackenham prosing on for ever, or young Geoffrey aping the dandy-set, or just the devilish propriety of Easterby — but I can't stand it here!'

'I know just what you mean,' his mother assured him.

He bent, giving her a hug and a kiss. 'You are the best mother in the world!' he said. 'What's more, that's a very fetching nightcap, ma'am! I must go: Melksham wants to start a faro-bank now, and Bevis don't like it above half. Poor old fellow! he'll never be able to handle Melksham

12

— not when Melksham's muddled, which he is, six days out of the seven. Christened with pump-water, that lad! He'll be as drunk as an artillery-man before morning.'

With this ominous prophecy, the Captain then took himself off, leaving his parent unperturbed, and his sister seething. Hardly had the door closed behind him, than she exclaimed: 'I think John is the most vexatious creature alive! How could you let him go, Mama? You know what he is! I daresay you won't set eyes on him again for a month! And now he won't even meet Elizabeth!'

'It is unfortunate, but I don't despair,' replied Mrs Staple, smiling faintly. 'As for letting him go, a man of nine-and-twenty, my love, is not to be held in leading-strings. Moreover, had I *obliged* him to come home to meet Elizabeth I am persuaded he would have taken her in aversion from the outset.'

'Well,' said Fanny crossly, 'I think he is odiously provoking, ma'am!'

'Very true, my dear: all men are odiously provoking,' agreed Mrs Staple. 'Now I am going to bed, and you had best do the same.'

'Yes, or Lichfield will wonder what has become of me,' Fanny said, getting up from her chair.

'Not at all,' responded her mother coolly. 'Lichfield, dear child, is no less provoking than any other man, and is at this moment — I have no doubt — playing faro downstairs.'

Fanny acknowledged the probable truth of this pronouncement by bidding her parent a dignified good-night.

2

Captain Staple was not destined to leave Easterby at an early hour on the following morning. Thanks to the nocturnal habits of Lord Melksham, it was daylight before he went to bed. That amiable but erratic peer, dissuaded from opening a faro-bank, had challenged the company to a quiet game of loo; and since the elders of the party, who included besides the Archdeacon, his brother-in-law, Mr Yatton, and Mr Merridge the Earl's chaplain, had retired soon after the ladies, and the Earl was plainly unable to keep the situation within bounds, Captain Staple had not the heart to desert him. The Earl was grateful, but he would not permit him to break up the party, which he was perfectly willing to do. He said: 'No, no! If Melksham is determined — He is my guest, you know, and, besides — Well, you will understand how it is!'

'No, I don't,' said John bluntly. 'And if I were you, old fellow, I would order things as I liked in my own house!'

No one, after as much as one glance at the Captain's good-humoured but determined countenance, could doubt this. The Earl said fretfully: 'Yes, but you don't understand! It's all very well for you — However, that don't signify! The thing is, you know what Lucius is, and that stupid brother-in-law of mine! And here's my Uncle

Yatton taken himself off, and left young Geoffrey to do as he pleases! I wish you will stay, and help me to see that they keep the line!'

So Captain Staple, no gamester, stayed; and if he failed to keep the stakes as low as his noble cousin would have wished he did contrive to prevent the quiet game of loo from becoming an extremely noisy game of loo. By the time Lord Melksham had wearied of this sport, and inaugurated a game of brag, young Mr Yatton had succumbed to his potations, which, as the Captain cheerfully informed the Earl, was a very happy circumstance, since it cut his losses short.

Having carried Geoffrey up to bed, he presently held his own brother-in-law's head under the pump in the scullery, guided his cousin Arthur's wavering steps up the stairs, and gently but firmly convinced Lord Melksham that it would be better to retire to bed than to try the power of a hunting-horn discovered in the Great Hall.

After so strenuous a night it was not surprising that the Captain should have slept far into the morning. He did not leave Easterby until past noon, and had he attended to the representations made to him by his host and his sister he would not have left it at all that day. It was pointed out to him that the sky threatened bad weather, that he could not hope to achieve more than a few miles of his journey, and that he would do well to abandon the whole project of riding to Leicestershire. But the probability of rain did not much trouble any man who was accustomed to bivouacking under the worst of conditions in the

15

Peninsula and the Pyrenees; and the possibility of having to rack up for the night at some wayside inn seemed to him infinitely preferable to another of Lord Melksham's convivial evenings. So at noon, Cocking, the private servant who had been with him through all his campaigns, brought his big, Roman-nosed bay horse up to the house, and strapped to the saddle a heavy frieze cloak, and the bag which contained all that the Captain considered to be necessary for his journey. The rest of the Captain's luggage consisted of a couple of portmanteaux, and these he instructed Cocking to despatch by carrier to Edenhope, Mr Babbacombe's hunting-box in Leicestershire. The sight of two such modest pieces caused Lord Melksham's man, a very superior person, to wonder that any gentleman should care to travel about the country so meagrely provided for. His own master, he said, never stirred from home without several trunks, a dressing-case, and himself: a highly talented valet. However, the bubble of his conceit was swiftly pricked, Cocking replying without hesitation that there was nothing for him to hold his nose up at in that. 'If the Captain was a tallow-faced twiddle-poop, mounted on a pair o' cat-sticks, I dessay he'd need a snirp like you to pad his calves out, and finify him,' he said. 'Only he ain't! Would there be anything more you was wishful to say about the Captain?'

Lord Melksham's man prudently decided that there was nothing more he wished to say, explaining this forbearance later to his colleagues as being due to his reluctance to bandy words with a vulgar make-bait. Cocking, left in possession of the field, carefully loaded the Captain's pistols, placed them in the saddle-holsters, and led the bay up to the house. The Captain, attired in buckskin breeches and top-boots, and a coat of slightly military cut, gave him a few last instructions, and mounted the big horse. Keeping a hand on the bridle, Cocking looked up at him, and asked if he was to join him at Edenhope, when he had escorted the mistress safely home.

'No, you might not find me there. Besides, I shan't need you.'

'Well, sir, that's as maybe, but what I *should* like to know is who's going to clean them leathers?' demanded his henchman.

'I don't know. Mr Babbacombe's man, I daresay.'

'Ho!' said Cocking. 'That'll put Mr Babbacombe's man in prime twig, that will! Howsever, it's just as you wish, sir, out of course!'

He then watched his master ride off down the avenue, slowly shaking his head. A sparrow, hopping about within a few yards of him, was the recipient of his next cryptic confidence. 'Resty, very resty!' he said, staring very hard at the bird. 'If you was to ask me, I should say we shall have him up to some kind of bobbery in just a brace o' snaps!'

The Captain, although he had not the smallest intention of getting up to bobbery, was heartily glad to escape from Easterby. There was nothing but Lord Melksham's mild excesses to

17

break the tedium; and he did not find these amusing. His cousin's life was hedged about by all the proprieties which had driven the Captain, eight years earlier, to persuade his father to buy him a pair of colours. He had had a strong notion that the Army in time of war would suit him, and events had proved him to be right. Life in the Peninsula had been uncertain, uncomfortable, and often haphazard, but it had offered almost every kind of adventure, and John had refused none of these. He had enjoyed himself enormously, and never so intensely as when engaged upon some dangerous enterprise. But when the war ended, in 1814, although he rejoiced as much as any man in the downfall of Bonaparte, he knew that the life he liked had ended too. Not for John Staple, the boredom of military life in peace-time! He yielded at last to his mother's solicitations, and sold out. She thought that he would find plenty to occupy him in the management of his estate, his father having died a year previously. The elder John Staple had been an indolent man, and for some months his son was busy enough. Then had come the news of Bonaparte's escape from Elba, and a brief period of exciting activity for John. But Bonaparte had been a prisoner on St Helena for two years now, and everyone seemed to feel that it was time John settled down to a life of civilian respectability. He felt it himself, and tried to be content, but every now and then a fit of restlessness would seize him. When that happened his subsequent actions would be

18

unpredictable, though, as his brother-in-law gloomily said, it was safe to assume that they would be freakish, and possibly outrageous. Lord Lichfield had every reason to believe that he had once wandered for a couple of weeks with a party of gypsies; and not readily would he forget John's sudden arrival at his house in Lincolnshire, at midnight, by way of an open window, and clad in strange and disreputable garments. 'Good God, what have you been doing?' he had exclaimed.

'Free trading!' had replied John, grinning at him. 'I'm glad I've found you at home: I want a bath, and some clean clothes.'

Lord Lichfield had been too much shocked to do more than goggle at him for a full minute. It wasn't, of course, as bad as John made it sound: the whole affair had been the result of an accident. 'But what I say is this, Fanny!' had complained his lordship later. 'If I go sailing, and run into a squall, and have to swim for it, do I get picked up by a smuggling-vessel? Of course I don't! No one but John would be! What's more, no one but John would finish the voyage with a set of cut-throat rascals, or help them to land their kegs! And if it *had* happened to me, I shouldn't be alive to tell the tale: they'd have knocked me on the head, and dropped me overboard.'

'I cannot conceive how it comes about that he was spared!' Fanny had said. 'Oh, I *wish* he would not do such things!'

'Yes,' agreed her lord. 'Though, mind you, he's very well able to take care of himself.'

'But in the power of a whole crew of smugglers!'

'I expect they liked him.'

'*Liked* him?'

'Well, you can't help liking him!' pointed out his lordship. 'He's a very charming fellow — and I wish to God he'd settle down, and stop kicking up these larks!'

'Mama is right!' declared Fanny. 'We must find him an eligible wife!'

Candidate after candidate for this post did Fanny and her mama find, and cunningly throw in John's way. Apparently he liked them — all of them. This one was a most conversible girl, that one seemed to him a very lively girl, another a remarkably pretty girl. But he asked none of them to marry him. When his sister ventured to ask him once if he had ever been in love, he had replied quite seriously, Yes: he rather thought he had been desperately in love with the lodge-keeper's wife, who used to regale him with brandy-snaps, and allowed him to keep in a hutch outside her kitchen-door the ferrets Mama had so much disliked. Was that all? had demanded an exasperated sister. No, there had been a girl in Lisbon, when he first joined. Juanita, or was it Conchita? He couldn't remember, but at all events she was the loveliest creature you ever saw. Dark, of course, and with the biggest eyes, and *such* a well-turned ankle! Had he been in love with her? 'Lord, yes!' replied John. 'We all were!'

He admitted that it was time he was thinking of getting married: not, of course, to Fanny, but to Mama. 'Well, I know, Mama,' he said apologetically. 'But the thing is I've got no fancy for one of these dashed *suitable* marriages, where you don't really care a fig for the girl, or she for you. I don't mean to offer marriage to any girl who don't give me a leveller. So I daresay I shall remain a bachelor, for they don't — any of 'em! And if one *did*,' he added thoughtfully, 'it's Lombard Street to a China orange you wouldn't take to her!'

'Dearest boy, I should take to any girl whom you loved!' declared Mrs Staple.

He grinned his appreciation of this mendacity, and gave her shoulders a hug, saying: 'That was a whisker!'

She boxed his ears. 'Odious boy! The fact of the matter is that it is a thousand pities we are not living in archaic times. What *you* would have liked, my son, is to have rescued some female from a dragon, or an ogre!'

'Famous good sport to have had a turn-up with a dragon,' he agreed. 'As long as you didn't find yourself with the girl left on your hands afterwards, which I've a strong notion those fellows did.'

'Such girls,' his mother reminded him, 'were always very beautiful.'

'To be sure they were! Dead bores too, depend upon it! In fact, I shouldn't be at all surprised if the dragons were very glad to be rid of 'em,' said John.

Not very promising, this. But Fanny had discovered Elizabeth Kelfield, and Mrs Staple had acknowledged, after careful and critical study of Miss Kelfield, that here was a lady who might well take John's fancy. She was dark; she was decidedly handsome; her fortune was respectable; and although she was not quite twenty years of age she seemed older, the circumstance of her having taken from an invalid mother's shoulders the burden of household cares having given her an assurance beyond her years. Mrs Staple thought she had quality, and began to cultivate the ailing Mrs Kelfield.

And now, when mother and daughter had been coaxed to Mildenhurst, off went John into Leicestershire, so that all the scheming so painstakingly undertaken on his behalf seemed likely to be wasted.

In happy ignorance of this, Captain Staple, climbing the slopes of the Pennines, found himself in a wild, moorland country, and liked it. Having a good sense of direction, he had left the pike road at the earliest opportunity, and with it, in a very short space of time, all signs of civilization. This exactly suited his mood, and he rode over the moors, at an easy pace and in a south-easterly direction. He had meant originally to have spent the night in Derby, but his late start made this impossible. Chesterfield became his objective. That was before the bay cast a shoe. When this happened, the Captain had ample time in which to regret having left the pike road, for he appeared to be in the centre of a vast desert. The only habitations to be seen for miles were an occasional cottage, and a few rough sheds dotted about the moors for the protection of shepherds. It was dusk when the Captain, leading Beau, dropped off the moor into a small village, which boasted not only a forge, but an alehouse as well. The smith had gone home, and by the time he had been fetched from his cottage, and the fire had been blown up again, not only had the last of the daylight vanished, but the rain, which had held off all day, had begun to fall. There was no possibility of racking up for the night at the alehouse, but bait was forthcoming for man and beast. Captain Staple ate a hearty meal of ham and eggs, lit one of his Spanish cigarillos, and went out to see what hope there might be of the weather's clearing. There was plainly none. The rain was falling with persistent steadiness, and not a star was to be seen. The Captain resigned himself to a wet ride, and sought counsel of the landlord. This was his undoing. The worthy man not only knew of a comfortable inn a few miles distant, but, anxious to be helpful, directed the Captain to it by what he assured him was the shortest route. He said that the Captain could not miss it, and no doubt the Captain would not have missed it if the landlord had not omitted to tell him that when he bade him take the first lane on the right he did not mean the track which, as every native of those parts knew, led winding upwards to the moor, and ended at a small farmstead. It was an hour later when the Captain, trusting his instinct, and riding steadily southward, found a lane which, rough though it was, seemed likely to lead to some village, or pike road. He followed this, noting with satisfaction that it ran slightly downhill, and within a short space of time knew that his guess had been correct. The lane ran into a broader road, which crossed it at right angles. Captain Staple had no very certain idea where he was, but he was reasonably sure that Sheffield lay to the east, probably at no great distance, so he turned left-handed into the larger road. The rain dripped from the brim of his hat, and mud generously splashed his top-boots, but the heavy frieze cloak had so far kept him fairly dry. He leaned forward to pat Beau's streaming neck, saying encouragingly: 'Not much farther now, old chap!'

A bend in the road brought into view an encouraging sight. A small light glowed ahead, which, from its position, the Captain judged to be the lantern hung upon a toll-gate. 'Come, now, Beau!' he said, in heartening accents. 'We're on the right track, at all events! If this is a pike road, it must lead to *some* town!'

He rode on, and soon saw that he had indeed reached a pike. The light, though very dim, enabled him to see that it was shut, and guarded, on the northern side of the road, by a gatehouse. No light was visible in the house, and the door was shut. 'Cross-country road, not much used,' the Captain informed Beau. He raised his voice, shouting imperatively: 'Gate!'

Nothing happened. 'Do I dismount, and open it for myself?' enquired the Captain. 'No, I'll be damned if I do! *Gate*, I say! Gate! Turn out, there, and be quick about it!'

The door in the centre of the gatehouse opened a little way, and a feeble glimmer of lantern light was cast across the road. 'Well,

24

come along!' said the Captain impatiently. 'Open up, man!'

After a moment's hesitation, this summons was obeyed. The gatekeeper came out into the road, and revealed himself, in the light of the lantern he carried, to be of diminutive stature. The Captain, looking down at him in some surprise, as he stood fumbling with the gate-tickets, discovered him to be a skinny urchin, certainly not more than thirteen years old, and probably less. The lantern's glow revealed a scared young face, freckled, and slightly tear-stained. He said: 'Hallo, what's this? Are you the gatekeeper?'

'N-no, sir. Me dad is,' responded the youth, with a gulp.

'Well, where is your dad?'

Another gulp. 'I dunno.' A ticket was held up. 'Frippence, please, your honour, an' it opens the next two gates.'

But the Captain's besetting sin, a strong predilection for exploring the unusual, had taken possession of him. He disregarded the ticket, and said: 'Did your dad leave you to mind the gate for him?'

'Yessir,' acknowledged the youth, with a somewhat watery sniff. '*Please*, sir, it's frippence, and — '

'Opens the next two gates,' supplied the Captain. 'What's your name?'

'Ben,' replied the youth.

'Where does this road lead to? Sheffield?'

After consideration, Ben said that it did.

'How far?' asked the Captain.

'I dunno. Ten miles, I dessay. Please, sir — '

'As much as that! The devil!'

'It might be twelve, p'raps. I dunno. But the ticket's frippence, please, sir.'

The Captain looked down into the not very prepossessing countenance raised anxiously to his. The boy looked frightened and overwatched. He said: 'When did your dad go off?' He waited, and added, after a moment: 'Don't be afraid! I shan't hurt you. Have you been minding the gate for long?'

'Yes — no! Dad went off yesterday. He said he'd be back, but he ain't, and please, sir, don't go telling no one, else Dad'll give me a proper melting!' begged the youth, on a note of urgent entreaty.

The Captain's curiosity was now thoroughly roused. Gatekeepers might have their faults, but they did not commonly leave their posts unattended except by small boys for twenty-four hours at a stretch. Moreover, Ben was badly scared; and to judge by the furtive glances he cast round he was scared by something besides the darkness and his loneliness.

The Captain swung himself to the ground, and pulled the bridle over Beau's head. 'Seems to me I'd better stay and keep you company for the night,' he said cheerfully. 'Now, where am I going to stable my horse?'

Ben was so much astonished that he could only stand staring up at the Captain with his mouth open and his eyes popping. The Captain knew that the generality of country gatehouses had small gardens attached to them with, often enough, rough sheds erected for the storage of hoes, swap-hooks, and wood. 'Have you got a shed?' he demanded.

'Ay,' uttered Ben, still gazing, fascinated, at this enormous and fantastic traveller.

'What's in it?'

'Cackling-cheats.'

The Captain recognized the language. His troop had contained several of the rogues of whom his Grace of Wellington, in querulous humour, had more than once asserted that his gallant army was for the most part composed. 'Hens?' he said. 'Oh, well, no matter! Take me to it! Is it big enough for my horse?'

'Ay,' said Ben doubtfully.

'Lead the way, then!'

Apparently Ben felt that it would be unwise to demur, which he seemed much inclined to do, for after giving another gulp he picked up his lantern, and guided the Captain to a wicket-gate behind the toll-house.

The shed proved to be surprisingly large; and when the lantern was hung up on a protruding nail its light revealed not only a collection of fowls, perched on a roost, but also some straw, and a truss of hay in one corner. There were unmistakable signs that Beau was not the first horse to be stabled there, a circumstance which John found interesting, but which he thought it wisest not to comment upon. Ben was regarding him with a mixture of awe and suspicion, so he smiled down at the boy, and said: 'You needn't be afraid: I shan't hurt you. Now, my cloak's too wet to put over Beau here:

have you got a blanket to spare?'

'Ay. But if Mr Chirk was to come — But I dessay he won't!' said Ben. 'Coo, he is a big prancer!'

He then took the saddle-bag which John had unstrapped, and went off with it. When he returned it was with a pail of water, and a horse-blanket. He found that the Captain, having shed his coat, was rubbing Beau down, and he at once collected a wisp of straw, and set to work on the big horse's legs. He seemed to have decided that his uninvited guest, though alarmingly large, really did mean him no harm, for he looked much more cheerful, and volunteered the information that he had set the kettle on to boil. 'There's some rum left,' he said.

'There won't be presently,' replied John, watching the boy's fearless handling of his horse. The mild jest was well-received, a friendly grin being cast up at him. He said casually: 'Do you work in a stable?'

'Some days I does. Others it's all sorts,' replied Ben. 'Mr Sopworthy hires me mostly.'

'Who is he?'

'Buffer, at Crowford. Blue Boar,' said Ben, beginning to wipe the stirrups with a piece of sacking.

'Innkeeper?' hazarded John.

'Ay.'

'Does your dad keep a horse?'

The wary look came back into Ben's face. 'No.' He eyed John sideways. 'That horse-cloth ain't me dad's. It — it belongs to a friend. He comes here sometimes. Maybe he wouldn't like you using of it, so — so you don't want to go saying anything about it, please, sir! Nor about him, acos — acos he don't like meeting no strangers!'

'Shy, is he? I won't say anything,' promised John, wondering if this were perhaps the man of whom Ben was afraid. He was by this time convinced that some mystery hung about the toll-house, with which, no doubt, the disappearance of its custodian was connected; but he was wise enough to keep this reflection to himself, since it was plain that Ben, in the manner of a colt, was uncertain of him, ready to shy off in a panic.

When Beau had been covered with the blanket, and left to lip over an armful of hay, Ben led the Captain up the garden to the back of the toll-house, where a central door opened into a small kitchen. The house, as John quickly saw, was of the usual pattern. It consisted of two tolerable rooms with another between them, which had been divided into two by a wooden partition. The rear half was the kitchen, and the front the toll-office. The kitchen was small, over-warm, and extremely untidy. Since it was lit by a couple of dip-candles in tin holders, an unpleasant aroma of hot tallow hung about it. But the Captain knew from past experiences in the more primitive parts of Portugal that the human nose could rapidly accustom itself to even worse smells, and he entered the room without misgiving. Ben shut and bolted the door, set down the lantern, and produced from the cupboard a black bottle, and a thick tumbler. 'I'll mix you a bumper,' he offered.

The Captain, who had seated himself in the Windsor chair by the fire, grinned, but said: 'Much obliged to you, but I think I'll mix it myself. If you want to make yourself useful, see if you can pull off these boots of mine!'

This operation, which took time, and all Ben's strength, did much to break the ice. It seemed to Ben exquisitely humorous that he should tumble nearly heels over head, clasping a muddied top-boot to his chest. He began to giggle, forgetting his awe, and looked all at once much younger than John had at first supposed him to be. He disclosed, upon enquiry, that he was going on for eleven.

Having found a pair of pumps in his saddle-bag, John mixed himself a glass of hot rum and water, and sat down again with his legs stretched out before him, and his boots standing beside the hearth to dry. 'That's better,' he said, leaning his fair head against the high-back of the chair, and smiling sleepily across at his host. 'Tell me, are we likely to be called out very often to open that gate?'

Ben shook his head. 'No one don't come this way after dark much,' he said. ''Sides, it's raining fit to bust itself.'

'Good!' said John. 'Where am I going to sleep?'

'You could have me dad's bed,' suggested Ben doubtfully.

'Thank you, I will. Where do you think your dad may have gone to?'

'I dunno,' said Ben simply.

'Does he often go away like this?'

'No. He never done it afore — not like this. And he ain't gone on the mop, because he ain't no fuddlecap, not me dad. And if he don't come back, they'll put me on the Parish.'

'I expect he'll come back,' said John soothingly. 'Have you got any other relations? Brothers? Uncles?'

'I got a brother. Leastways, unless he's been drownded, I have. He was pressed. I shouldn't wonder if I was never to see him no more.'

'Lord, yes, of course you will!'

'Well, I don't want to,' said Ben frankly. 'He's a proper jobbernoll, that's what he is. Else they wouldn't never have snabbled him. Me dad says so.'

If Ben possessed other relatives, he did not know of them. His mother seemed to have died some years before; and it soon became apparent that he clung to his father less from affection than from a lively dread of being thrown on the Parish. He was convinced that if this should befall him he would be sent to work at one of the foundries in Sheffield. He lived near enough to Sheffield to know what miseries were endured by the swarms of stunted children who were employed from the age of seven in the big manufacturing towns; and it was not surprising that this fate should seem so terrible to him. There was only one worse fate known to him, and this, before long, he was to confide to John.

While he talked, and John sat sipping his rum, the wind had risen a little, bringing with it other sounds than the steady dripping of the rain. The wicket-gate for the use of travellers on foot creaked and banged gently once or twice, and when this happened Ben's face seemed to sharpen, and he broke off what he was saying to listen intently. John noticed that his eyes wandered continually towards the back-door, and that the noises coming from the rear of the house seemed to worry him more than the creak of the gate. A gust of wind blew something over with a clatter. It sounded to John as though a broom, or a rake, had fallen, but it brought Ben to his feet in a flash, and drove him instinctively to John's side.

'What is it?' John said quietly.

'*Him!*' breathed Ben, his gaze riveted to the door.

John got up, and trod over to the door, ignoring a whimper of protest. He shot back the bolts, and opened it, stepping out into the garden. 'There's no one here,' he said, over his shoulder. 'You left a broom propped against the wall, and the wind blew it over, that's all. Come and see for yourself!' He waited for a moment, and then repeated, on a note of authority: 'Come!'

Ben approached reluctantly.

'Weather's fairing up,' remarked John, leaning his shoulders against the door-frame, and looking up at the sky. 'Getting lighter. We shall have a fine day tomorrow. Well? Can you see anyone?'

'N-no,' Ben acknowledged, with a little shiver. He looked up at John, and added hopefully: 'He couldn't get me, could he? Not with a big cove like you here.'

'Of course not. No one could get you,' John replied, shutting the door again, and going back to the fire. 'You may bolt it if you choose, but there's no need.'

'Yes, 'cos he might come to see me dad, and I mustn't see him, nor him me,' explained Ben.

'Lord, is he as shy as all that? What's the matter with him? Is he so ugly?'

'I dunno. I never seen him. Only his shadder — onct!'

'But you've rubbed his horse down for him, haven't you?'

'No!' Ben said, staring.

'Wasn't that his blanket that you brought me for Beau?'

'*No!* That's Mr Chirk's!' said Ben. 'He's a — ' He stopped, gave a gasp, and added quickly: 'He's as good as ever twanged, he is! You don't want to go telling nobody about him! *Please,* sir — '

'Oh, I won't breathe a word about him! Are *all* your friends so shy?'

'He ain't shy. He just don't like strangers.'

'I see. And does this other man — the one you're afraid of — dislike strangers too?'

'I dunno. He can't abide boys. Me dad says if he was to catch me looking at him he'd have me took off to work in the pits.' His voice sank on the word, and he gave so convulsive a shudder that it was easy to see that coal-pits were to him a worse horror than foundries.

John laughed. 'That's a fine Banbury story! Your dad's been hoaxing you, my son!'

Ben looked incredulous. 'He *could* have me

took off. He'd put a sack over me head, and — '

'Oh, would he? And what do you suppose I should do if anyone walked in and tried to put a sack over your head?'

'What?' asked Ben, round-eyed.

'Put a sack over *his* head, of course, and hand him to the nearest constable.'

'You *would?*' Ben drew an audible breath.

'Certainly I would. Does he come here often?'

'N-no. Leastways, I dunno. After it's dark, he comes. I dunno how many times. Onct, there was two on 'em. I woke up, and heard them, talking to me dad.'

'What were they talking about?'

Ben shook his head. 'I didn't hear nothing but just voices. I got right under me blanket, 'cos I knew it was Kim.'

By this time it seemed fairly certain to John that the gatekeeper's disappearance was connected in some way with Ben's mysterious bugbear; and it seemed still more certain that he was engaged upon nefarious business. What this might be John had not the remotest conjecture, and it was plainly useless to question Ben further. He got up, saying: 'Well, it's high time you were under your blanket again. If anyone shouts gate, I'll attend to it, so you show me where your dad's bed is, and then be off to your own.'

'You can't open the gate!' said Ben, shocked. 'You're a flash cove!'

'Never mind what I am! You do what I tell you!'

Thus adjured, Ben escorted him into the

34

toll-office, from which access to the two other rooms was obtained. One of these, where Ben slept on a truckle-bed, contained stores, but the other was furnished with some degree of comfort, the bed even being provided with cotton sheets, and a faded patchwork quilt. The Captain, having no fancy for the gatekeeper's sheets, coolly stripped them off the bed, rolled them into a bundle, and tossed them into a corner of the room. He then stretched himself out on top of the blankets, pulled the quilt over himself, and blew out the candle. For a few minutes, before falling asleep, he wondered what he was going to do if the gatekeeper did not return that night. The proper course, which would be to report the man's absence, would seem unpleasantly like a betrayal of Ben; yet no other presented itself to him. But the Captain was never one to meet troubles halfway, and he very soon stopped frowning over this problem. After all, it was probable that before morning the gatekeeper would be back at his post. Stale-drunk, too, thought John, setting little store by Ben's assurance that his dad was not one to go on the mop.

3

The Captain slept soundly, and awoke to daylight, and the sound of voices. On getting up, and looking out of the little latticed window, he saw that Ben was holding open the gate for a herd of cows to pass through, and exchanging courtesies with the boy who was driving them. A fine autumn day had succeeded the night's downpour, and the mist still lay over the fields beyond the road. A glance at the watch which he had laid on the chair beside the bed informed John that it was half-past six. He strolled into the toll-office just as Ben shut the gate, and came in.

With the daylight the worst of Ben's fears were laid to rest. He looked a different boy from the hag-ridden urchin of the previous evening; walked in whistling; and greeted the Captain with a grin.

'Your dad not back?' John asked.

The grin faded. 'No. Likely he's piked.'

'Run away? Why should he?'

'Well, if he ain't piked, p'raps he's gorn to roost,' temporized Ben. ' 'Cos when he loped off, he told me to mind the gate for an hour, and he'd be back. What'll I do, guv'nor?'

This question was uttered, not in a tone of misgiving, but in one of cheerful confidence. Ben looked enquiringly up into John's face, and John realized, ruefully, that his small protégé was reposing complete trust in his willingness and ability to settle the future satisfactorily for him.

'Well, that's a problem which seems to hang in the hedge a trifle,' he said. 'We shall have to talk it over. But first I want a wash, and breakfast.'

'I got some bacon cut, and there's eggs, and a bit of beef,' offered Ben, ignoring the first of the Captain's needs as a frivolity.

'Excellent! Where's the pump?'

'Out the back. But — '

'Well, you come and work it for me,' said John. 'I want a towel, and some soap as well.'

Considerably surprised (for the Captain looked quite clean, he thought), Ben collected a piece of coarse soap, cut from a bar, and a huckaback towel, and followed his guest into the garden. But when he discovered that the Captain, not content with sousing his head and neck, proposed to wash the whole of his powerful torso, he was moved to utter a shocked protest. 'You'll catch your death!' he gasped.

The Captain, briskly rubbing the soap over his chest, and down his arms, laughed. 'Not I!'

'But you don't need to go a-washing of yourself all over!'

'What, after sleeping all night in my clothes? Don't I just!' John glanced critically down at Ben, and added: 'It wouldn't do you any harm to go under the pump either.'

Ben stepped out of reach instinctively, but was summoned back to work the pump-handle. He would then have beat a hasty retreat, but was frustrated. A large hand caught and held him; he looked up in alarm, and saw the blue eyes laughing. 'I had a wash Sunday last!' he said

37

imploringly. 'I ain't cutting no wheedle! *Honest,*
I did!'

'Did you, by Jupiter? Then it's a week since
you were clean, is it? Strip, my lad!'

'No!' said Ben tearfully, wriggling to be free of
the grip on his shoulder. 'I won't!'

The Captain dealt him one hard, admonitory
spank. 'You'd better!' he said.

His voice was perfectly good-humoured, but
Ben was no fool, and, with a despairing sniff, he
capitulated. It was doubtful if ever before he had
been obliged to scrub his skinny person so
thoroughly; and certainly no well-wisher had
ever held him remorselessly under the pump,
and worked it with such a will. He emerged
spluttering and shivering, and eyed his persecu-
tor with mingled respect and resentment. John
tossed the towel to him, saying: 'That's better! If
you own another shirt, put it on!'

'What, clean mish too?' gasped Ben.

'Yes, — and comb your hair!' said John.
'Bustle about, now! I'm hungry.'

Half an hour later, surveying Ben across the
kitchen-table, he professed himself satisfied. He
said that Ben looked much more the thing, an
observation which caused that young gentleman's bosom to swell with indignation. His eyes
were red-rimmed and watering from contact
with the soap, and his skin felt as though it had
been scoured. He still thought the Captain a
fascinating and an awe-inspiring personage, but
having watched him vigorously brushing his
teeth he now suspected that he must be queer in
his attic. When a hearty breakfast had been

disposed of, and the Captain insisted not only that all the crockery should be washed, but that the floor should be swept clean of mud, crumbs, scraps of bacon-rind, and some decayed cabbage-stalks, he was sure of it. He explained that Mrs Skeffling, from down the road, came to clean the place every Wednesday, but the Captain paid no heed, merely telling him to fetch a broom, and to be quick about it. He himself, having discovered some blacking and a brush in the cupboard, took his boots into the garden, and set about the unaccustomed task of removing the dried mud from them. He also tried, not very successfully, to get rid of the travel stains from his buckskin breeches. He recalled, as he worked on them, Cocking's words, and realized that there was more to the care of leathers than he had supposed. In fact, the upkeep of a gentleman's wardrobe seemed to entail a great deal of unforeseen labour, not the least arduous of which was the removal of Beau's hairs from the skirts of his coat, where they obstinately stuck, resisting all efforts to brush them off.

When this was accomplished, there was Beau to be watered, fed, and groomed, his bit to be cleaned, the saddle-girths to be brushed free of mud, by which time the morning was considerably advanced. While he performed all these labours John tried to think of some solution to Ben's problem. He thought of several, but not one that was likely to meet with any sort of approval. It began to seem as though he would be obliged, instead of continuing his journey to

Leicestershire, to spend the day in making discreet enquiries into the gatekeeper's possible whereabouts.

He went back into the gatehouse, a crease between his brows. This did not escape Ben's notice. He made haste to point out that he had thoroughly swept the kitchen; and as this was productive of nothing more than a nod ventured to ask if the Captain was angry.

John, who was rather absently ladling water into the iron kettle which hung from a hook above the old-fashioned fireplace, paused, dipper in hand, and looked down at him. 'Angry? No. Why should I be?'

'I thought you looked as if you was in a tweak — a bit cagged, like,' explained Ben.

'I was wondering what's to be done with you, if your dad doesn't come back today. Can you think of any place where he might have had business? Did he ever visit anyone in Sheffield, for instance?'

'He don't visit nobody, me dad don't. And if he was going to town, he'd put his best toge on, and a shap on his head, and he didn't,' replied Ben shrewdly. 'He loped off just like he was going down to the Blue Boar. P'raps he's been pressed, like Simmy!'

Since this solution did not seem in any way to disturb Ben, the Captain refrained from trying to convince him that the Press Gang neither operated in remote inland districts, nor pressed such persons as gatekeepers. He went on ladling water into the kettle; and Ben, suddenly remembering that he had not fed the pig, which led a somewhat restricted life in a sty at the bottom of the ground, took himself off to repair this omission.

As soon as the kettle began to sing the Captain poured some of the water into a tin mug, and bore it off to the gatekeeper's bedroom. He had just set out his shaving-tackle, and was about to lather his face, when he heard the sound of a vehicle approaching down the road. A shout of Gate! was raised, and John was obliged to put down his brush. Collecting the tickets on his way, he strolled out of the toll-house, and saw that a gig had drawn up to the east of it. A cursory glance showed him that the reins were being handled by a woman, and that a middle-aged groom sat beside her; and a rapid scrutiny of the list of tolls set up on a board beside the house informed him that the charge at this pike for a one-horse vehicle was threepence. He walked up to the gig, and the groom, who had been looking at him in some surprise, said: 'Well, shake your shambles, can't you? Who are you? What are you doing here?'

John raised his eyes from the book of tickets. 'Gatekeeping. The charge is — '

The words died on his lips. He stood perfectly still, gazing not at the groom, but at the girl beside him.

A very tall girl, and nobly-proportioned, she was dressed in a green pelisse that was serviceable rather than fashionable. A pair of tan gloves, not in their first youth, covered her capable, well-shaped hands; and a plain bonnet with no other trimming than a bow of ribbon

41

was set on a head of thick chestnut hair, which showed tawny gleams in the sunlight. Humorous gray eyes looked down into John's, the arched brows above them lifting slightly; an amused smile hovered about a mouth too generous for beauty. But this faded as John stood looking up at her. She stared down at him, seeing an unshaven young giant, in stained leathers and a shirt unbuttoned at the throat, with curly fair hair ruffled by the breeze, and the bluest of eyes fixed unwaveringly on her face.

'Church!' said the groom impatiently. 'Open up, my lad!'

If John heard him he paid no heed. He stood as though stunned, for he had received his leveller at last.

A flush crept into the lady's cheeks; she said, with an uncertain laugh: 'I suppose you must be Brean's elder son. You are certainly a big fellow! Please open the gate! Churchgoers, you know, are exempt from tax.'

Her voice recalled John to his senses. Colour flooded his face; he uttered an inarticulate apology, and made haste to open the gate. It was a single one, and he stood holding it at the side of the road while the gig passed beyond it. The lady nodded to him, quite kindly, but in the manner of one immeasurably his superior; and drove away at a brisk trot.

John remained where he was, still holding the gate, and looking after the gig until it passed round the bend in the road, and was gone from his sight.

He became aware of Ben, who had emerged

from the toll-house, and was regarding him in mild surprise. He shut the gate, and said: 'Did you see that gig, Ben?'

'Ay. I give that big prancer of yours a carrot. Coo, he is — '

'Who was the lady driving it? Do you know?'

' 'Course I does! When I gives a carrot to Mr Chirk's Mollie, she — '

'Well, who is she?'

'I'm a-*telling* of you! She's Mr Chirk's mare, and she shakes hands for carrots! You arsts her what she'll do for it, and she lifts up her right fore — '

'The devil fly away with Mr Chirk's mare! *Who was the lady in that gig?*'

'Oh, her!' said Ben, losing interest. 'That was only Miss Nell. She'll be going to Church.'

'Where does she live? Will she be coming back?'

'Ay, out of course she will! There ain't no other way she can get home from Crowford, not with the gig there ain't.'

'Where is her home?'

Ben jerked his chin, vaguely indicating an easterly direction. 'Over there. Mr Chirk's learnt Mollie to do all sorts of tricks. She — '

'He had best sell her to Astley, then. Does Miss Nell live nearby?'

'I *telled* you!' said Ben impatiently. 'At the Manor!'

'What Manor? Where is it?'

It was plain that Ben thought poorly of persons who were so ignorant that they were unaware of the locality of the largest house in the vicinity. 'Everyone knows where Squire's house is!' he said scornfully.

'The Squire, eh? Is he Miss Nell's father?'

'*Squire?* No! He's her granfer. He's an old gager. No one ain't set eyes on him since I dunno when. They do say he's as queer as Dick's hatband, ever since he was took bad all on a sudden. He can't walk no more. Folks say it's Miss Nell as is Squire these days.'

'How far is it from here to the Squire's place?'

'Kellands? A mile, I dessay.'

'Who is he? What is his name?'

Tired of this catechism, Ben sighed, and answered: 'Sir Peter Stornaway, out of course!'

'Do you see her — do you see Miss Nell often?'

'Ay, most days,' replied Ben indifferently.

The Captain drew a breath, and stood for a few moments gazing down the road to where he had last seen the gig. Emerging suddenly from this trance, he ejaculated: 'Good God, I must shave!' and strode into the toll-house.

Miss Stornaway, returning homewards, was not obliged to summon the new gatekeeper to open for her. Captain Staple was on the watch, and came out of the toll-house as soon as he heard the sound of carriage-wheels. He was still in his shirt-sleeves, but he now sported a neatly tied neckcloth, and had pulled on his top-boots. He had recovered from his stupefaction, too, so that Miss Stornaway, pulling up, found herself looking down, not at a gigantic hobbledehoy, as tongue-tied as he was handsome, but at a perfectly assured man who smiled up at her

44

without a vestige of shyness, and said: 'Forgive me for having unlawfully demanded toll of you! I'm a new hand — shockingly green!'

Miss Stornaway's eyes widened. She exclaimed involuntarily: 'Good heavens! you can't be Brean's son!'

'No, no, I fancy he's at sea. The poor fellow was pressed, you know.'

'But what are you doing here?' she demanded.

'Keeping the gate,' he replied promptly.

She was bewildered, but amused too. 'Nonsense! How could you be a gatekeeper?'

'If you mean that I'm a bad one you must remember that I'm a novice. I shall learn.'

'Nothing of the sort! I mean — Oh, I believe you're hoaxing me!'

'Indeed I'm not!'

'Where is Brean?' she demanded.

'Well, there you have me,' he confessed. 'Like Ben — are you acquainted with Ben? — I dunno! That's why I'm here.'

She wrinkled her brow. 'Do you mean that Brean has gone away? But why should you take his place? Are you doing it for a wager?'

'No, but now that you come to suggest it I see that that might not be at all a bad notion,' he said.

'I wish you will be serious!' she begged, trying to frown and succeeding only in laughing.

'I am very serious. On the whole, I believe I shall do better to announce myself to be a cousin of Brean's.'

'No one would credit such a tale, I assure you!'

45

'Don't you think so? I can talk cant with the best, you know.'

She made a despairing gesture. 'I don't understand a word of this!'

The groom, who had been staring very hard at John, said: 'Seems to me there's something smoky going on here. If you ain't playing a May-game, sir, nor cutting a sham — '

'I'm not, but I agree with you that there's something smoky going on,' John interrupted. 'The gatekeeper went off two nights ago, and hasn't been seen since.'

'Well, that's very bad,' acknowledged Miss Stornaway. 'But I do not see why you should take his place!'

'But you must see that Ben is a great deal too young to remain here alone!' John pointed out.

'You are the oddest creature! How do you come here? Why — Oh, I wish you will explain it to me!'

'I will,' he promised. 'It is quite a long story, however. Won't you step down from your gig? I shan't invite you to come into the toll-house, for although I have induced Ben to sweep out the kitchen it is not at all tidy, but we could sit on the bench.'

Her eyes danced; it seemed as if she were half inclined to fall in with this suggestion, but at that moment the groom said something to her in a low voice, directing her attention to the road ahead.

Coming towards the gate, on a showy-looking hack, was a thickset man, rather too fashionably attired for his surroundings. He wore white hunting-tops, a florid waistcoat with several fobs and seals depending from it, a blue coat with long tails and very large buttons, and a beaver hat with a exaggeratedly curled brim.

The laughter went out of Miss Stornaway's eyes; she said rather hurriedly: 'Some other time, perhaps. Please to open the gate now!'

John went to it immediately. It had a fifteen-foot clearance, and the man on the gray hack reined in short of its sweep towards him. He looked rather narrowly at John for a moment, but rode forward as soon as the gate stood wide enough, and reined in alongside the gig. The beaver was doffed with a flourish, revealing exquisitely pomaded and curled black locks.

'Ah, Miss Nell, you stole a march on us, did you not?' challenged the gentleman jovially. 'But I have found you out, you see, and come to meet you!'

'I have been to Church, sir, if that is what you mean,' Miss Stornaway replied coldly.

'Sweet piety! You will allow me to escort you home!'

'I cannot prevent you from doing so, sir, but I am sorry you should have put yourself to the trouble of coming to meet me. It was unnecessary,' said Miss Stornaway, whipping up her horse.

John shut the gate, and went back into the toll-house. A strong aroma of onions assailed him, from which he inferred that Ben considered it was time to start cooking dinner. He went into the kitchen, and said abruptly: 'Ben, did you tell me that there is a woman who comes here to clean the place?'

'Ay, Mrs Skeffling. She comes Wednesdays. She washes the duds too,' replied Ben. 'We has a roast, Wednesdays, and a pudden, and all. Coo, she's a prime cook, she is!'

'We must have her every day,' John said decidedly.

'Every day?' gasped Ben, nearly upsetting the pan he was holding over the fire. 'Whatever for, guv'nor?'

'To keep the house clean, and cook the dinner, of course. Where does she live?'

'Down the road. But she has to have a sow's baby every time!'

'In that case, I shall have to go to market and buy a litter of pigs,' said John. He perceived that Ben was looking quite amazed, and laughed. 'Never mind! How much is a sow's baby?'

'A half-borde — sixpence! Properly turned-up we'd be!'

'Don't bother your head about that!' recommended John.

Ben eyed him with considerable respect. 'You got a lot of mint-sauce, guv'nor?'

'I'm tolerably well-blunted,' responded John gravely. 'Now, listen, Ben! I'm going to remain here — '

'You are?' cried Ben joyfully.

'Until your dad comes back, or, at any rate — '

'Coo, I hope he don't never come back!'

'Quiet, you unnatural brat! If he doesn't come back — lord, I'm dashed if I know what I'm to

48

do with you, but I won't throw you on the Parish, at all events! The thing is, if I'm to stay here I must make some purchases. How far off is the nearest town, and what is it?'

After reflection, Ben said that he thought Tideswell was only a matter of five miles or so. He added that his dad had bought the pig there, and a new coat for the winter. This sounded promising. 'I'll ride there tomorrow,' John said. 'You won't be scared of minding the gate while I'm away, will you?'

'*I* ain't scared — leastways, not in the day time I ain't,' said Ben. 'But I got to muck out Mr Sopworthy's hen-house, mind! He'll tip me a meg, and likely want me to lend a hand at summat else. I dunno when I'll be back.'

'Well, you must tell him that you're needed here. What kind of a man is this Mr Sopworthy?'

'He's a leery cove, he is, me dad says. He ain't one as'll squeak beef on you, but it's pound dealing with him, else he goes up in the boughs — proper, he does!'

'If that means that he's an honest man, I fancy I had best make his acquaintance. I gather you don't think he'd be likely to inform against your dad, so we shall tell him that your dad's been called away for a few days, and left me to take his place. I'm a cousin of yours,' said the Captain.

'He won't never swallow a rapper like that!' objected Ben. 'He ain't no chub! He'd know you was a flash cull, sure as check!'

'Not he!' grinned John.

'Soon as you opens your mummer, he will!'

49

insisted Ben. "'Cos you *talks* flash, and you got a lot of cramp-words, like all the gentry-coves.'

'I'll take care not to use 'em,' promised John.

'Yes, and what about that mish you got on, and them stampers?' demanded Ben, quite unconvinced.

'If you mean my shirt, I am going to buy some others, in Tideswell, and a stout pair of brogues as well. Don't shake your head at me! I've been discharged from the Army, understand? Trooper, 3rd Dragoon Guards — and batman (that means a servant) to an officer. That's how I come to talk a trifle flash. You remember that, and we shall come off all right!'

Ben looked dubious, but all he said was: 'What'll I call you, guv'nor?'

'Jack. What I must have is decent stabling for Beau. He can't remain cooped up in a hen-house, and it seems to me that the Blue Boar's the best place for him.'

'Why couldn't you stable him in Farmer Huggate's barn?' asked Ben captiously.

'I could, if I knew where it was,' John retorted.

'It's nobbut a step, back of here,' Ben said. 'Farmer Huggate and me dad's as thick as hops. If you was to grease him in the fist, likely he'd let you have fodder for Beau, too, 'cos he's got two big prads of his own.'

This suggestion pleased the Captain so well that he sent Ben to see Farmer Huggate as soon as he had eaten his dinner. He himself remained on duty, but was only twice called upon to open the gate. Whatever might happen during the week, the road seemed to be very little used on

Sundays. Having discovered some clean sheets in a chest, John was able to make up his bed. He did some energetic work with the broom, drastically tidied the kitchen, and then sat down to compile a list of the various commodities which were needed to make life in a toll-house tolerable. He was engaged on this task when an imperative voice summoned him to the gate. He got up rather quickly, for he recognized the voice, and strode out.

Miss Stornaway, mounted on a good-looking hack, and unattended, said, with a slight smile: 'Well, sir, I've come to hear that long story, if you please! You must know that they call me the Squire in these parts: *that* must serve as an excuse for my curiosity!'

'You need none,' he said, opening the gate a little way.

She touched her horse with her heel, saying as she went past John: 'Do you mean to demand toll of me? I warn you, I shall inform against you if you do! I don't go above a hundred yards from the gate: not as much!'

'Is that the rule?' he asked, going to her horse's head.

'Of course!' She transferred the bridle to her right hand, brought one leg neatly over the pommel, and slipped to the ground. Shaking out the folds of her shabby riding-dress, she glanced up at John. 'Heavens, how big you are!'

He smiled. 'Why, yes! You told me so, this morning!'

She laughed, blushed faintly, and retorted: 'I did not know how big until now, when I find

51

myself on a level with you. You must know that in general I look over men's heads.'

He could see that this must be so. She did not seem to him to be an inch too tall, but he realized that she was taller even than his sister, and built on more magnificent lines. Hitching her horse to the gatepost, he said sympathetically: 'It's a trial, isn't it? I feel it myself, and my sister tells me it has been the bane of her existence. Do you always ride unattended, Miss Stornaway?'

She had seated herself on the bench outside the toll-house, under the fascia board, which bore, in staring black capitals, the name of Edward Brean. 'Yes, invariably! Does it offend your sense of propriety? I am not precisely a schoolgirl, you know!'

'Oh, no!' he replied seriously, coming to sit down beside her. 'I like you for it — if you don't think it impertinent in me to tell you so. I've thought, ever since I came home, that there's a deal too much propriety in England.'

She raised her brows. 'Came home?'

'Yes. I'm a soldier — that is to say, I *was* one.'

'Were you in the Peninsula?' He nodded. 'My brother was, too,' she said abruptly. 'He was killed.'

'I'm sorry,' he said. 'Where?'

'At Albuera. He was in the 7th.'

'You should be proud,' he said. 'I was at Albuera, too. I saw the Fusiliers go into action.'

She lifted her chin. 'I am proud. But he was my grandfather's heir, and — Oh, well! What was your regiment?'

52

'3rd Dragoon Guards. I sold out after Toulouse.'

'And your name?'

'John Staple. I have told Ben to set it about that I was a trooper — an officer's batman. He says I talk flash, you see.'

She laughed. 'Perfectly! But how do I address you?'

'In general, my friends call me Jack.'

'*I* cannot be expected to do so, however!'

'Well, if you call me Captain Staple you will undo me,' he pointed out. 'I'm only a gatekeeper. Don't be afraid I shall encroach! I won't — Miss Nell!'

'You are certainly mad!' she said. 'Pray, how do you come to be a gatekeeper?'

'Oh, quite by chance! I had been staying with one of my cousins, up in the north — the head of my family, in fact, and a very dull dog, poor fellow! There was no bearing it, so I made my excuses, and set out to ride into Leicestershire, to visit a friend of mine. Then my horse cast a shoe, up on the moors, I lost my bearings, became weather-bound, and reached this gate in darkness and drenching rain. Ben came out to open it for me. That seemed to me an odd circumstance. Moreover, it was easy to see he was scared. He told me his father had gone off on Friday evening, and hadn't returned; so I thought the best thing I could do would be to put up here for the night.'

'Ah, that was kind!' she said warmly.

'Oh, no! not a bit!' he said. 'I was deuced sick of the weather, and glad to have a roof over my head. I'm curious, too: I want to know what has become of Edward Brean.'

'It *is* odd,' she agreed, knitting her brows. 'He is a rough sort of a man, but he has been here for a long time, and I never knew him to desert his post before. But you surely don't mean to continue keeping the gate!'

'Oh, not indefinitely!' he assured her. 'It's not at all unamusing, but I expect it would soon grow to be a dead bore. However, I shall stay here for the present — unless, of course, the trustees find me out, and turn me off.'

'But your family — your friends! They won't know what has become of you!'

'That won't worry 'em. I've done it before.'

'Kept a gate?' she exclaimed.

'No, not that. Just disappeared for a week or two. I don't know how it is, but I get devilish bored with watching turnips grow, and doing the civil to the neighbours,' he said apologetically.

She sighed. 'How fortunate you are to be able to escape! I wish I were a man!'

He looked at her very kindly. 'Do you want to escape?'

'Yes — no! I could not leave my grandfather. He is almost helpless, and very old.'

'Have you lived here all your life?'

'Very nearly. My father died when I was a child, and we came to live with Grandpapa then. When I was sixteen, my mother died. Then Jermyn went to the wars, and was killed.' She paused, and added, in a lighter tone: 'But that is all a long time ago now. Don't imagine that poor Grandpapa has kept me here against my will! Far

54

from it! Nothing would do for him but to launch me into society — though I warned him what would come of it!'

'What did come of it?' John enquired.

She made her mouth prim, but her eyes were laughing. 'I did not *take*!' she said solemnly. 'Now, don't, I beg of you, play the innocent and ask me how that can have come about! You must see precisely how it came about! I am by far too large. Grandpapa compelled my Aunt Sophia to house me for a whole season, and even to present me at a Drawing-room. When she saw me in a hoop, we were obliged to revive her with hartshorn and burnt feathers. I cannot love her, but indeed I pitied her! She can never have enjoyed a season less. It was so mortifying for her! I had no notion how to behave, and when she took me to Almack's not all her endeavours could obtain partners for me. I don't know which of us was the more thankful when my visit ended.'

'I expect I must have been in Spain,' he said thoughtfully. 'I never went to Almack's till after I had sold out, and my sister dragged me there. To own the truth, I found it devilish dull, and there wasn't a woman there, beside my sister, whose head reached my shoulder. It made me feel dashed conspicuous. If you had been there, and we had stood up together, it would have been a different matter.'

'Alas, I'm more at home in the saddle than the ballroom!'

'Are you? So am I! But my sister can keep it up all night.'

55

'Is your sister married?'

'Yes, she married George Lichfield, a very good fellow,' he replied.

'I think I met him once — but I might be mistaken. It is seven years since my London season. Do you feel that Lady Lichfield would approve of your present occupation?'

'Oh, no, not a bit!' he said. 'She and George don't approve of any of the things I do. I shan't tell her anything about it.'

'I think I am a little sorry for her. And still I don't understand why you mean to remain here!'

'No,' he said, 'I don't suppose you do. I didn't mean to, last night, but something happened today which made me change my mind.'

'Good gracious! What in the world was it?'

'I can't tell you that now. I will, one day.'

'No, that's too provoking!' she protested. 'Is it about Brean? Have you discovered something?'

'No, nothing. It wasn't that,' John replied.

'Then what, pray — '

'I must own I should be glad if I could discover what has happened to the fellow,' he remarked, as though she had not spoken. 'If he had met with an accident, one would think there would have been news of it by now. He must be pretty well known in the district, isn't he?'

She nodded. 'Yes, certainly. He is red-haired, too, which makes him easily recognizable. You don't think, I collect, that he can have gone off, perhaps to Sheffield, and drunk himself into a stupor?'

'I *did* think so,' he admitted, 'but Ben assures me his dad don't go on the mop. He is quite positive about it, and I imagine he must know. According to his story, Brean went out on Friday evening, saying that he would be back in an hour or two. He was not wearing his hat, or his best coat, which, in Ben's view, precludes his having had the intention of going to town.'

'He would scarcely set out for Sheffield after dark, in any event. It is more than ten miles away! How very odd it is! Are you sure that Ben is telling you the truth when he says he doesn't know where his father went?'

'Oh, yes, quite sure! Ben is excessively frightened — partly by the thought that he may be thrown on the Parish, much more by a mysterious stranger who seems to have formed the habit of visiting the toll-house after dark, and with the utmost secrecy.'

She looked startled. 'Who — ?'

'That I don't know. But I have a strong suspicion that he is in some way concerned in Brean's disappearance,' John said. 'And I have another, even stronger, that there's something devilish havey-cavey going on here!'

4

'What makes you say that?' she asked quickly, her eyes fixed with great intentness on his face.

He looked a little amused. 'Well, ma'am, when a man does his visiting at night, and takes the most elaborate precautions against being seen, he's not commonly engaged on honest business!'

'No. No, he cannot be, of course. But what could he be doing *here?* It is absurd! — it must be absurd!'

He turned his head. 'That sounds as though you have been thinking what I have said,' he remarked shrewdly.

She glanced at him, and away again. 'Nonsense! You must let me tell you that you are a great deal too fanciful, Captain Staple!'

He smiled very warmly at her. 'Oh, I would let you tell me anything!' he said. 'You are quite right, of course, not to confide in strangers.'

She gave a little gasp, and retorted: 'Very true — if I had anything to confide! I assure you, I have not!'

'No, don't do that,' he said. 'I don't mean to tease you with questions you don't care to answer. But if you think, at any time, that I could be of service to you, why, tell me!'

'You — you are the strangest creature!' she said, on an uncertain laugh. 'Pray, what service could I possibly stand in need of?'

'I don't know that: how could I? Something is

troubling you, I think I knew that,' he added reflectively, 'when that would-be Tulip of Fashion put you so much out of countenance this morning.'

Her chin lifted; she said, with a curling lip: 'Do you think I am afraid of that counter-coxcomb?'

'Lord, no! Why should you be?'

She looked a trifle confounded, and said in a defiant tone: 'Well, I am not!'

'Who is he?' he enquired.

'His name is Nathaniel Coate, and he is a friend of my cousin's.'

'Your cousin?'

'Henry Stornaway. He is my grandfather's heir. He is at this present staying at Kellands, and Mr Coate with him.'

'Dear me!' said John mildly. 'That, of course, is enough to trouble anyone. What brings so dashing a blade into these parts?'

'I wish I knew!' she said involuntarily.

'Oh! I thought I did know,' said John.

She threw him a scornful look. 'If you imagine that it was to fix his interest with me, you're quite out! Before he came to Kellands, I daresay he did not know of my existence: he had certainly never seen me!'

'Perhaps he came into the country on a repairing lease,' suggested John equably. 'If he teases you, don't stand on ceremony! Give him his marching orders! I'm sure his waistcoat is all the crack, but he shouldn't sport it in the middle of Derbyshire.'

'Unfortunately, it is not within my power to give him his marching orders.'

'Isn't it? It is well within mine, so if you should desire to be rid of him, just send me word!' said John.

She burst out laughing. 'I begin to think you have broken loose from Bedlam, Captain Staple! Come, enough! I am sure I do not know how it comes about that I should be sitting here talking to you in this improper fashion. You must be thinking me an odd sort of a female!'

She rose as she spoke, and he with her. He did not reply, for Ben chose that moment to appear upon the scene, with the announcement that Farmer Huggate said he was welcome to stable Beau in the big barn.

'Well, that's famous,' said John. 'You shall show me where it is presently, but first go and see if you can prevail upon Mrs Skeffling to come up to the toll-house tomorrow. Promise her as many pig's babies as you think necessary, but don't take no for an answer!'

'What'll I say?' demanded Ben. 'She'll think it's a queer set-out, guv'nor, 'cos what would anyone want with her coming to clean the place every day?'

'You may tell her that your cousin, besides being the worst cook in the Army, has picked up some finical ways in foreign parts. Off with you!'

'Wait!' interposed Miss Stornaway, who had been listening in considerable amusement. 'Perhaps I can help you. I collect you wish Mrs Skeffling to come to the toll-house each day. Very well! I daresay I can arrange it for you. Go and ask her, Ben, and if she says no, never mind!'

'Admirable woman!' John said, as Ben went

60

off down the road. 'I'm much in your debt! What will you tell her?'

'Why, that you seem to be a very good sort of a man, but sadly helpless! Have no fear! She will come. Did I not tell you that they call me the Squire? I shall ride down the road directly, to visit her, which is a thing I frequently do. She will tell me, and at length, of your summons, and certainly ask my advice. You may leave the rest to me!'

'Thank you! Will you assist me in one other matter? I must contrive somehow to ride to Tideswell tomorrow, to make some necessary purchases, and the deuce is in it that I've no notion of what, precisely, I should ask for. I must have some tolerable soap, for instance, but it won't do just to demand soap, will it? Ten to one, I should find myself with something smelling of violets, or worse. Then there's coffee. I can't and I won't drink beer with my breakfast, and barring some porter, the dregs of a bottle of rum, and a bottle of bad tape, that's all I can find in the place. Tell me what coffee I should buy, I'll make a note of it on my list.'

Her eyes were alight. 'I think I had better take a look at your list,' she decided.

'Will you? I shall be much obliged to you! I'll fetch it,' he said.

She followed him into the toll-house, and he turned to find her standing in the kitchen doorway, and looking critically about her. 'Enough to make poor Mrs Brean turn in her grave!' she remarked. 'She was the neatest creature! However, I daresay Mrs Skeffling will

61

set it to rights, if she is to come here every day. Is this your list?'

She held out her hand, and he gave it to her. It made her laugh. 'Good heavens, you seem to need a great deal! Candles? Are there none in the store-cupboard?'

'Yes, tallow dips. Have you ever, ma'am, sat in a small room that was lit by tallow dips?'

'No, never!'

'Then take my advice, and do not!'

'I won't. But wax candles in a kitchen! Mrs Skeffling will talk of it all over the village. Soap — blacking — brushes — tea — ' She raised her eyes from the list. 'Pray, how do you propose to convey all these things from Tideswell, Captain Staple?'

'I imagine there must be a carrier?'

'But that will not do at all! Conceive of everyone's astonishment if such a quantity of goods were to be delivered to the Crowford gatekeeper! Depend upon it, the news would very soon be all over the county that an excessively strange man had taken Brean's place here. It must come to the ears of the trustee controllers, and you will have them descending on you before you have had time to turn round.'

'I am afraid I am quite corkbrained,' said John meekly. 'What must I do instead?'

She glanced at the list again, and then up at him. 'I think I had best procure these things for you,' she suggested. 'That, you see, will occasion no surprise, for I very often go shopping in Tideswell.'

'Thank you,' he said, smiling. 'But I must buy

some shirts, and some shoes and stockings, and you can hardly do that for me, ma'am!'

'No,' she agreed. She considered him anew, and added candidly: 'And it will be wonderful if you can find any to fit you!'

'Oh, I don't despair of that! There are bound to be plenty of big fellows in the district, and *somebody* must make clothes for 'em!' said the Captain cheerfully. 'As a matter of fact, I saw a fine, lusty specimen not an hour ago. Cowman, I think. If I'd thought of it, I'd have asked him the name of his tailor.'

She gave a gurgle of laughter. 'Oh, if you can be content with a flannel shirt — or, perhaps, a smock — !'

He grinned at her. 'Why not? Did you take me for a Bond Street beau? No, no! I was never one of your high sticklers!'

'I take you for a madman,' she said severely.

'Well, they used to call me Crazy Jack in Spain,' he admitted. 'But I'm not dangerous, you know — not a bit!'

'Very well, then, I will take my courage in my hands, and drive you to Tideswell tomorrow, in the gig — that is, if you can leave the gate in Ben's charge!'

'The devil's in it that I can't,' he said ruefully. 'The wretched boy has informed me that he must muck out Mr Sopworthy's hen-houses tomorrow!'

'Oh!' She frowned over this for a moment, and then said: 'It doesn't signify: Joseph — that's my groom! — shall keep the gate while you are away. The only thing is — ' She paused, fidgeting with

63

her riding-whip, the crease reappearing between her brows. Her frank gaze lifted again to his face. 'The thing is that it is sometimes difficult for me — now — to escape an escort I don't need, and am not at all accustomed to! But I fancy — I am not perfectly sure — that my cousin and Mr Coate have formed the intention of driving to Sheffield tomorrow. You will understand, if I should not come, that I could not!' He nodded, and she held out her hand. 'Good-bye! I will ride to Mrs Skeffling's cottage now. Oh! Must I pay toll? I have come out without my purse!'

He took her hand, and held it for an instant. 'On no account!'

She blushed, but said in a rallying tone: 'Well for you it is not thought worth while to post informers on this road!'

She picked up her skirts, and went out into the road. Captain Staple, following her, unhitched her horse from the gatepost, and led him up to her. She took the bridle, placed her foot in his cupped hands, and was tossed up into the saddle. As the hack sidled, she bent to arrange the folds of her skirt, saying: 'I mean to visit one of my grandfather's tenants, so don't look for me again today! My way will take me over the hill.'

A nod, and a smile, and she was trotting off down the road, leaving John to look after her until the bend hid her from his sight.

She was not his only visitor that day. Shortly before eight o'clock, the wicket-gate clashed, and a heavy knock fell on the toll-house door. Ben, who was engaged in whittling a piece of wood into the semblance of a quadruped, in which only its creator could trace the faintest resemblance to the Captain's Beau, jumped, but showed no sign of the terror which had possessed him during the previous evening. Either he did not connect his father's mysterious visitor with an open approach to the office-door, or he placed complete reliance on Captain Staple's ability to protect him.

John went into the office. He had left the lantern on the table, and by its light he was able to recognize the man who stood in the open doorway. He said: 'Hallo! What can I do for you?'

'Jest thought I'd drop in, and blow a cloud with you,' responded Miss Stornaway's groom. 'Stretching me legs, like. The name's Lydd — Joe Lydd.'

'Come in!' invited John. 'You're very welcome!'

'Thank'ee, sir!'

'The name,' said John, pushing wide the door into the kitchen, 'is Jack.'

Mr Lydd, who was both short and spare, looked up at him under his grizzled brows. 'Is it, though? Jest as you please, Jack — no offence being meant!'

'Or taken!' John said promptly. 'Sit down! Saw you this morning, didn't I?'

'Now, fancy you remembering that!' marvelled Mr Lydd. 'Because I didn't think you noticed me, not partic'lar.'

John had gone to the cupboard, but he turned at this, and stared across the kitchen at his guest. Mr Lydd met this somewhat grim look with the utmost blandness for a moment or two, and then transferred his attention to Ben. 'Well, me lad, so your dad's hopped the wag, has he? What sort of a fetch is he up to? Gone on the spree, I dessay?'

'Gone up to Lunnon, to see me brother,' said Ben glibly. ''Cos he heard as Simmy ain't in the Navy no more.'

'Fancy that, now!' said Mr Lydd admiringly. 'Made his fortune at sea, I wouldn't wonder, and sent for his dad to come and share it with him. There's nothing like pitching it rum, Ben!'

John, who was drawing two tankards of beer at the barrel beside the cupboard, spoke over his shoulder, dismissing his imaginative protégé to bed. Ben showed some slight signs of recalcitrance, but, upon encountering a decidedly stern look, sniffed, and went with lagging step towards the door.

'That's right,' said Mr Lydd encouragingly. 'You don't want to take no risks, not with your guv'nor looking like bull-beef. *I* wouldn't!'

John grinned, and handed him one of the tankards. 'Is that what I look like? Here's a heavy wet for you! Did you come to discover where Brean is? I can't tell you.'

Mr Lydd, carefully laying down the clay pipe he had been filling, took the tankard, blew off the froth, and ceremoniously pledged his host. After a long draught, he sighed, wiped the back of his hand across his mouth, and picked up his pipe again. Not until this had been lit, with a screw of paper kindled at one of the smouldering logs, did he answer John's question. While he alternately drew at the pipe, and pressed down the tobacco with the ball of his thumb, his eyes remained unwaveringly fixed on John's face, in a meditative and curiously shrewd scrutiny. By the time his pipe was drawing satisfactorily, he had apparently reached certain conclusions, for he withdrew his stare, and said in a conversational tone: 'Properly speaking, Ned Brean's where-abouts don't interest me. If you like to set it about he's gone off to visit young Simmy, it's all one to me.'

'I don't,' John interrupted.

'Well, it ain't any of my business, but what I say is, if you're going to tell a bouncer let it be a good 'un! However, I didn't come here to talk about Ned Brean.'

'What did you come to talk about?' asked John amiably.

'I don't know as how I came to talk about anything in partic'lar. Jest dropped in, neigh-bourly. It's quiet up at the Manor, these days. Very different from what it used to be when I was a lad. That was afore Sir Peter ran aground, as you may say. A very well-breeched swell he was, flashing the dibs all over. Ah, and prime cattle we had in the stables then! Slap up to the echo, Squire was, and the finest, lightest hands — ! Mr Frank was the same, and Master Jermyn after him — regular top-sawyers! Dead now, o' course. There's only Miss Nell left.' He paused, and took a pull at his beer, watching John over the top of the tankard. John met his look, the hint of a smile in his eyes, but he said nothing. Mr Lydd transferred his gaze to the fire. 'It's not so far off forty years since I went to Kellands,' he said reminiscently. 'Went as

67

stable-boy, I did, and rose to be head-groom, with four under me, not counting the boys. Taught Master Jermyn to ride, and Miss Nell too. Neck-or-nothing, that was Master Jermyn, and prime 'uns Squire used to buy for him! He wouldn't look at a commoner, not Squire! 'Proper high bred 'uns, Joe!' he used to say to me. 'Proper high bred 'uns for the boy, if I drown in the River Tick!' Which he pretty near did do,' said Mr Lydd, gently knocking some of the ash from his pipe. 'What with his gaming, and his racing, it was Dun Territory for Squire, but he always said as how he'd come about. I dessay he would have, if he hadn't took ill. He had a stroke, you see. Mr Winkfield — that's his man, and has been these thirty years — he will have it it was Master Jermyn being killed in the wars that gave Squire his notice to quit. I don't know how that may be, because he wasn't struck down immediate: not for some years he wasn't. But he wasn't never the same man after the news came. He don't leave his room now. Going on for three years it is since I see him on his feet. A fine, big man he used to be: not as big as you, but near it. Jolly, too. Swear the devil out of hell, he could, but everybody liked him, because he was easy in his ways, and he laughed more often than he scowled. You wouldn't think it if you was to see him now. Nothing left of him but a bag of bones. He sends for me every now and then, just to crack a whid over old times. Mr Winkfield tells me he remembers what happened fifty years ago better than the things that happened yesterday. Always says the same thing to me, he does. 'Not booked yet, Joe!' he says, for he likes his joke. And, 'Take good care of Miss Nell!' he says. Which I always have done, of course — so far as possible.'

John rose, and carried both empty tankards over to the barrel. Having refilled them, he handed one to Mr Lydd again, slightly lifted his own in a silent toast, and said: 'You're a very good fellow, Joe, and I hope you will continue to take care of Miss Nell. I shan't hinder you.'

'Well, now, I had a notion that maybe you wouldn't,' disclosed Mr Lydd. 'I've been mistook in a man, in my time, but not often. You *may* be what they call a flash cull, or you *might* have come into these backward parts because you was afraid of a clap on the shoulder, but somehow I don't think it. If I may make so bold as to say so, I like the cut of your jib. I don't know what kind of a May-game you're playing, because — not wishing to give offence! — you can't slumguzzle me into thinking you ain't Quality. Maybe you're kicking up a lark, like. And yet you don't look to me like one of them young bucks, in the heyday of blood, as you might say.'

'In the heyday of blood,' said John, 'I was a lieutenant of Dragoon Guards. I came into these parts by accident, and I am remaining by design. No shoulder-clapper is on my trail, nor am I a flash cull. More than that I don't propose to tell you — except that no harm will come to your mistress at my hands.'

Mr Lydd, after subjecting him to another of his fixed stares, was apparently satisfied, for he nodded, and repeated that there was no offence meant. 'Only, seeing as I've had me orders to mind the pike tomorrow, while you go jauntering off to Tideswell with Miss Nell — let alone Rose getting wind of it, and talking me up to find out what your business is till I'm fair sick of the sound of her voice — '

'Who is Rose?' interrupted John.

'*Miss* Durward,' said Mr Lydd, with bitter emphasis. 'Not that I'm likely to call her such, for all the airs she may give herself. Why, I remember when she first came to Kellands to be nursemaid to Miss Nell! A little chit of a wench she was, too! Mind, I've got nothing against her, barring she's grown stoutish, and gets on her high ropes a bit too frequent, and I don't say as I blame her for being leery o' strangers — Miss Nell not having anyone but Squire to look after her, and he being burned to the socket, the way he is.'

It was by this time apparent to John that orphaned though she might be Miss Stornaway did not lack protectors, and it came as no surprise to him when, shortly after eight o'clock next morning, he sustained a visit from Miss Durward. He was enjoying a lively argument with a waggoner when she came walking briskly down the road, this ingenious gentleman, recognizing in him a newcomer, making a spirited attempt to convince him that the proper charge for the second of his two vehicles, which was linked behind the first, was threepence. But Captain Staple, who had usefully employed himself in studying the literature provided by the Trustees of the Derbyshire Toll-gates for the perusal of his predecessor, was able to point out to him that as the vehicle in question was mounted on four wheels it was chargeable at the rate of two horses, not of one. 'What's more, it's loaded,' he added, interrupting an unflattering description of his personal appearance and mental turpitude, 'so it pays double toll. I'll take a borde and tenpence from you, my bully!'

'You'll take one in the bread-basket!' said the waggoner fiercely.

'Oh, will I?' retorted the Captain. 'It'll be bellows to mend with you if you're thinking of a mill, but *I've* no objection! Put 'em up!'

'I seen a man like you in a fair onct,' said the waggoner, ignoring this invitation. 'Leastways, they said he was a man. 'Ardly 'uman he was, poor creature!'

'And now I come to think of it,' said the Captain, 'didn't I see you riding on the shaft? That's unlawful, and it's my duty to report it.'

Swelling with indignation, the waggoner spoke his mind with a fluency and a range of vocabulary which commanded the Captain's admiration. He then produced the sum of one shilling and tenpence, defiantly mounted the shaft again, and went on his way, feeling that his defeat had been honourable.

The Captain, shutting the gate, found that he was being critically regarded by a buxom woman who was standing outside the toll-house, with a basket on her arm. Her rather plump form was neatly attired in a dress of sober gray, made high to the throat, and unadorned by any ribbons or flounces. Over it she wore a cloak; and under a

71

plain chip hat her pretty brown hair was confined in a starched muslin cap, tied beneath her chin in a stiff bow. She was by no means young, but she was decidedly comely, with well-opened gray eyes, an impertinent nose, and a firm mouth that betokened a good deal of character. Having listened without embarrassment to John's interchange with the waggoner, she said sharply, as he caught sight of her: 'Well, young man! Very pretty language to be using in front of females, I must say!'

'I didn't know you were there,' apologized John.

'That's no excuse. The idea of bandying words with a low, vulgar creature like that! What have you done to your shirt?'

John glanced guiltily down at a jagged tear in one sleeve. 'I caught it on a nail,' he said.

She clicked her tongue, saying severely: 'You've no business to be wearing a good shirt like that. You'd better let me have it, when you take it off, and I'll mend it for you.'

'Thank'ee!' said John.

'That's quite enough of that!' she told him, an irrepressible dimple showing itself for an instant. 'Don't you try and hoax me you're not a gentleman-born, because you can't do it!'

'I won't,' he promised. 'And don't you try to hoax me you're not Miss Stornaway's nurse, because I wouldn't believe you! You put me much in mind of my own nurse.'

'I'll be bound you were a rare handful for the poor soul,' she retorted. 'If you *are* going to town this morning, see you buy a couple of stout shirts! A sin and a shame it is to be wearing a fine one like this, and you very likely chopping wood, and I don't know what beside! What your mother would say, if she was to see you, sir — !'

Concluding from this speech that he had been approved, John said, with a smile: 'I will. I'll take good care of your mistress, too. You may be easy on that head!'

'Well, it's time someone did, other than me and Joseph — though what good he could do it queers me to guess!' she said. 'I don't know who you are, nor what you're doing here, but I can see you're respectable, and if you *did* happen to fall out with a nasty, bracket-faced gentleman, with black hair and the wickedest eyes I ever did see, I don't doubt he'd have the worst of it. With your good leave, sir, I'll step inside to have a word with Mrs Skeffling, if that's her I hear in the kitchen. I've got some of our butter for her, which Miss Nell promised she should have. And I was to tell you, Mr Jack — if that's what you're wishful to be called — that Miss Nell will be along with the gig just as soon as those two *gentlemen* have taken themselves off to Shef-field!'

With these words she marched through the office to the kitchen, where she found Mrs Skeffling, a widow of many years' standing, zestfully engaged in turning out the contents of the cupboard, and scrubbing its shelves: a thing which, as she informed Miss Durward, she had long wanted to do. After both ladies had expressed, with great frankness, their respective opinions of the absent Mr Brean's dirty and disorderly habits, Mrs Skeffling paused from her labours in order to enjoy a quiet gossip about the new gatekeeper.

'Miss Durward, ma'am,' she said earnestly, 'I was that flabbergasted when I see him, which I done first thing this morning, Monday being my day for lending Mrs Sopworthy a hand with the washing, and Mr Jack stepping up to the Blue Boar to buy a barrel of beer! Even Mr Sopworthy was fairly knocked acock when Mr Jack says as he was Mr Brean's soldier-cousin, come to mind the gate for him for a while. 'Lor!' he says, 'I thought it was the Church tower got itself into my tap!' Which made Mr Jack laugh hearty, though Mrs Sopworthy was quite put out, thinking at first it was a gentleman walked in, which Landlord shouldn't have spoke so free to. Then they got to talking, Mr Jack and Landlord, and I'm sure none of us didn't know what to think, because he didn't talk like he was Quality, not a bit! And yet it didn't seem like he was a common soldier, not with them hands of his, and the sort of way he has with him, let alone the clothes he wears! Miss Durward, ma'am, I've got a shirt of his in the wash-house this moment, with a neckcloth, and some handkerchers, and I declare to you I've never seen the like! Good enough for Sir Peter himself, they are, and whatever would a poor man be doing with such things?'

'Oh, he's not a poor man! Whatever put that into your head?' said Rose airily. 'Didn't Mr Brean ever tell you how one of his aunts married a man that was in a very good way of business? I

74

forget what his name was, but he was a warm man, by all accounts, and this young fellow's his son.'

Mrs Skeffling shook her head wonderingly. 'He never said nothing to me about no aunts.'

'Ah, I daresay he wouldn't, because when she set up for a lady she didn't have any more to do with her own family!' said the inventive Rose. She added, with perfect truth: 'I forget how it came about that he mentioned her to me. But this Mr Jack — being as he's got his discharge, and not one to look down on his relations — took a fancy to visit Mr Brean. He's just been telling me so.'

'But whatever made Mr Brean go off like he has?' asked Mrs Skeffling, much mystified.

'That was where it was very fortunate his cousin happened to come to visit him,' said Rose, improvising freely. 'It seems he was wanting to go off on some bit of business — don't ask me what, because I don't know what it was! — only, being a widower, and not having anyone fit to mind the gate for him, he couldn't do it. So that's how it came about — Mr Jack, being, as you can see, a good-natured young fellow, and willing to do anyone a kindness.'

This glib explanation appeared to satisfy Mrs Skeffling. She said: 'Oh, is that how it was? Mr Sopworthy took a notion Mr Jack was gammoning us. 'Mark my words,' he says, 'it's a bubble! It's my belief,' he says, 'he's one of them young bucks as has got himself into trouble.' What he suspicioned was that maybe there was a fastener out for him, for debt, very likely; or p'raps he up and killed someone, in one of them murdering duels.'

'Nothing of the sort!' said Rose sharply. 'He's a very respectable young man, and if Mr Sopworthy was to set such stories about it'll be him that will find himself in trouble!'

'Oh, he wouldn't do that!' Mrs Skeffling assured her. 'What he said was, however it might be it wasn't no business of his, and them as meddled in other folks' concerns wouldn't never prosper. Setting aside he took a fancy to Mr Jack. 'Whatever he done, he ain't no hedge-bird,' he says, very positive. 'That I'll swear to!' Which I told him was sure as check, because Miss Nell knows him for a respectable party, and said so to me with her own lips. So then,' pursued Mrs Skeffling, sinking her voice conspiratorially, 'Mr Sopworthy stared at me very hard, and he says to me, slow-like, that if so be Mr Jack was a friend of Miss Nell's it wouldn't become no one to start gabbing about him, because anyone as wished her well couldn't but be glad if it *should* happen that a fine, lusty chap like Mr Jack was courting her, and no doubt he had his reasons — the way things are up at the Manor — for coming here secret. Of course, I don't know nothing about that, which I told Mr Sopworthy.'

She ended on a distinct note of interrogation, her mild gaze fixed hopefully on her visitor's face. Miss Durward, who had been thinking rapidly, got up with a great show of haste, and begged her not to say that *she* had ever said such a thing. 'I'm sure I don't know what Mr

76

Sopworthy can have been thinking about, and I hope to goodness he won't spread such a tarradiddle! Now, mind, Mrs Skeffling! I never breathed a word of it, and I trust and pray no one else will!'

'No, no!' Mrs Skeffling assured her, her eyes glistening with excitement. 'Not a *word*, Miss Durward, ma'am!'

Satisfied that before many hours had passed no member of a small community affectionately disposed towards the Squire's granddaughter would think the presence in her gig of the new gatekeeper remarkable, and reckless of possible consequences, Miss Durward took leave of Crowford's most notable gossip, and departed. She found John passing the time of day with the local carrier, and concluded, from such scraps of the dialogue as she was privileged to overhear, that he was making excellent progress in his study of the vulgar tongue. She told him, as soon as the carrier had driven through the gate, that he should think shame to himself, but rightly judging this censure to be perfunctory he only grinned at her, so endearing a twinkle in his eye that any misgivings lingering in her anxious breast were routed. She then put him swiftly in possession of such details of his genealogy as her fertile imagination had fabricated, and adjured him to drum these well into Ben's head.

'I will,' he promised, enveloping her in a large hug, and planting a kiss on one plump cheek. 'You're a woman in a thousand, Rose!'

'Get along with you, do, Mr Jack!' she commanded, blushing and dimpling. 'Carrying on like the Quality, and you trying to hoax everyone you're Brean's cousin! You keep your kisses for them as may want them!'

'I don't know that anyone does,' he said ruefully.

'Well, I'm sure I can't tell that!' she retorted tartly. 'Now, don't forget what I've been telling you!'

'I won't. What is my father's name, by the by?'

'Gracious, I can't think of everything!'

'Didn't you give him one? Then I think I'll keep my own. I daresay there are many more Staples in England than ever I heard of. Tell me this! In what way can I be of service to your mistress?'

The dimple vanished, and her mouth hardened. She did not answer for a minute, but stood with her gaze fixed on the gatepost, her face curiously set. Suddenly she brought her eyes up to his face, in a searching look. 'Are you wishful to be of service to her?' she demanded.

'I never wished anything so much in my life.'

He spoke perfectly calmly, but she was quick to hear the note of sincerity in his deep, rather lazy voice. Her lip quivered, and she blinked rapidly. 'I don't know what's to become of her, when the master dies!' she said. 'She and Mr Henry are the last of the Stornaways, and it's him that will have Kellands, not her that's looked after it these six years past! Long before the master was struck down it was Miss Nell that was as good as a bailiff to him, and better! It was she that turned off all the lazy, good-for-nothing servants that used to eat master out of house and

78

home, let alone cheating him the way it was a shame to see! Scraping, and saving, breeding pigs for the market, leasing this bit of land and that, and bargaining for the best price her own self, like as if she was a man! And when master took ill, she sold the pearls her poor mother left her, and every scrap of jewelry she had from Sir Peter in the days when he was still in his prime, and there wasn't one of us knew how deep he was in debt. Everything she could she sold, to keep off the vultures that came round as soon as it got to be known Sir Peter was done for! All Sir Peter's lovely horses — and I can tell you he had hunters he gave hundreds of guineas for, and a team he used to drive which all the sporting gentlemen envied him — and her own hunters as well, with her phaeton, and Sir Peter's curricle, and the smart barouche he bought for her to drive in when she went visiting — everything! There's nothing in the stables now but the hack she rides, and the cob, and a couple of stout carriage-horses which she kept for farm-work mostly. There wasn't a soul to help her, barring old Mr Birkin, that lived out Tideswell way, and was a friend of the master's, and he's been dead these eighteen months! Mr Henry never came next or nigh the place. He knew that there was nothing but the title and a pile of debts to be got out of it! But he's here now, Mr Jack, and it seems he means to stay! If he'd more heart than a hen, I'd call him a carrion-crow — except that I never saw a crow hover round where there was nothing more to be picked over than a heap of dry bones! I don't know what brings him here, nor I wouldn't care, if he hadn't got that Mr Coate along with him! But that's a *bad* one, if ever I saw one, sir, and he's living up at the Manor like he owned it, and casting his wicked eyes over Miss Nell till my nails itch to tear them out of his ugly face! Miss Nell, she's not afraid of anything nor of no one, but I am, Mr Jack! I am!'

He had listened in silence to what he guessed to be the overflowing of pent-up anxieties, but when she paused, unconsciously gripping his shirt-sleeve, he said quietly, lifting her hand from his arm, and holding it in a warm clasp: 'Why?'

'Because when the master goes she'll be alone! And not a penny in the world but the little her mother left her, and that not enough to buy her clothes with!'

'But she has other relatives, surely! She spoke to me of an aunt — '

'If it's my Lady Rivington you're meaning, sir, it's little she'd trouble herself over Miss Nell, and nor would any of poor Mrs Stornaway's family! Why, when she was a bit of a girl, and the master persuaded her ladyship to bring her out, it was him paid for all, and *I* know the way her ladyship, and the Misses Rivington, looked down on her, because she was so tall, and more like a boy than a girl!'

'I see.' John patted her hand, and released it. 'You go home now, Rose, and don't you fret about Miss Nell!'

She thrust a hand into her pocket for a handkerchief, and rather violently blew her nose. 'I shouldn't have said anything!' she uttered, somewhat thickly.

'It's of no consequence. I should have discovered it.'

She gave a final sniff, and restored the handkerchief to her pocket. 'I'm sure I don't know what possessed me, except for you being so *big*, sir!'

He could not help laughing. 'Good God, what has that to say to anything?'

'You wouldn't understand — not being a female,' she replied, sighing. 'I'll be going now, sir — and thank you!'

5

An hour later, Miss Stornaway's shabby gig drew up at the toll-gate, and her henchman, jumping down, tendered three coins to John, with a broad wink, and demanded a ticket opening the only other gate that lay between Crowfold and Tideswell. But John had already provided himself with this, and he waved away the coins, which made Nell exclaim against him for cheating the trustees.

'Nothing of the sort!' he replied, climbing into the gig. 'I'm not one of those who are able — as the saying goes — to buy an Abbey, but I was born to a modest independance, and I would scorn to cheat the trustees!'

'But you should not be obliged to buy the ticket for my carriage!' she objected.

'Oh, there was no obligation! I hoped to impress you by making such a handsome gesture,' he said gravely.

'Sporting the blunt!' she retaliated, casting a challenging look at him to see how he took this dashing phrase.

'Exactly so!' he said.

A gurgle of laughter escaped her. 'How absurd you are! Are you never serious, Captain Staple?'

'Why, yes, sometimes, Miss Stornaway!'

She smiled, and drove on for a few moments without speaking. She was not, he thought, shy, but there was a little constraint in her manner, which had been absent from it on the previous day. After a pause, she said, as though she felt it incumbent upon her to make some remark: 'I hope you do not dislike to be driven by a female, sir?'

'Not when the female handles the ribbons as well as you do, ma'am,' he replied.

'Thank you! It needs no particular skill to drive Squirrel, but I was always accounted a good whip. I can drive a tandem,' she added, with a touch of pride. 'My grandfather taught me.'

'Didn't your grandfather win a curricle-race against Sir John Lade once?'

'Yes, indeed he did! But that was long ago.' A tiny sigh accompanied the words, and as though to cover it, she said, in a rallying tone: 'I had meant to pass you off as the stable-boy, you know, but you are so smart today I see it will not do!'

He was wearing his riding-coat and top-boots, and his neckcloth was arranged with military neatness. There was nothing of the dandy in his appearance, but his coat was well-cut, and, in striking contrast to Henry Stornaway's buckish friend, he looked very much the gentleman.

He stretched out one leg, and grimaced at it. 'I did my best,' he admitted, 'but, lord, how right my man was about these leathers of mine! He gave me to understand no one could clean them but himself. I don't know how that may be, but I certainly can't! My boots are a disgrace to me, too, but that might be the fault of Brean's blacking.'

She laughed. 'Nonsense! I only wish Rose might see you! You have met Rose, so you will not be surprised to learn that she cannot approve of a gentleman's being seen on the highway in his shirt.'

'Torn, too, but she has promised to mend it for me. I am very much obliged to her, and not only for that cause. She came to see whether I was a fit and proper person to be permitted to go with you to Tideswell, and she decided that I was.'

'Yes, she did. I beg your pardon! but she was used to be my nurse, you know, and nothing will persuade her that I am twenty-six years of age, and very well able to take care of myself. She is the dearest creature, but she is for ever preaching propriety to me.'

'I should think she has some pretty strong notions of propriety,' he agreed.

'Alas, poor Rose, she has indeed, and they have all been overset!'

He was watching her profile, thinking how delightfully she smiled, and how surely her expressive countenance reflected her changing moods. 'Have they? How did that come about?' he said.

She looked mischievous, chuckling deep in her throat. 'She is in love with a highwayman!'

'*What?* Oh, no, impossible!'

'I assure you! She won't admit it — never speaks of it! — but it's quite true. I know nothing, of course! If I dare to question her I get nothing for my pains but a tremendous scold, and when I was saucy enough to ask her if he does not come secretly to Kellands to see her she would have boxed my ears, could she but have reached them! But I am very sure he does. And the ridiculous thing is that she is the most respectable creature alive, and very nearly forty years old! I daresay no one could be more shocked than she is herself, but make up her mind never to see him again she cannot! Mind, not a word of this to her!'

'Good God, I should not dare! But how came it about?'

'Oh, he held us up, rather more than a year ago! It was the most farcical adventure imaginable. She had gone with me to Tinsley, which is beyond Sheffield, you know. It was all to do with a heifer I had a mind to purchase, and since Joseph was laid up with the lumbago, Rose accompanied me in his stead. In this very gig! But owing to a number of circumstances we were detained for longer than I had thought for, so that I was obliged to drive home after dark. Not that I cared for that, or Rose either, for it was moonlight, and I don't think it ever came into our heads that we might be held up. But we were, and by a masked figure, with a couple of horse-pistols in his hands, all in the style of high melodrama! He commanded me to stand and deliver. You may depend upon it that I obeyed the *first* of these commands, but what I was to deliver, beyond the few shillings which I had in my reticule, I knew no more than the man in the moon, which I ventured to tell him. *That* was where we descended from melodrama to farce! He seemed to be a good deal taken aback, and rode up quite close to peer at me. Well! Rose has a temper, and impertinence she will *not* brook! She said, 'How *dare* you?' not a bit afraid! Then she told him to put his guns away *this instant*, and, when he didn't obey, demanded to know whether he had heard her. If it had not been so absurd I should have been in a quake! But there was not the least need: he did put his guns away, and began to beg her pardon, saying he had mistaken me for a man! She was not in the least mollified, however. She scolded him as though he had been a naughty child, and instead of seizing our reticules, or riding off, he stayed there, listening to her, and trying to make his peace with her. He did it, too, in the end! Rose can never remain in a rage for long, and he was so very apologetic that she was obliged to relent. Then he was so obliging as to make us a present of a password, if ever we should be held up again, which I thought excessively handsome of him! *The Music's paid!* that's what you must say if you should be held up. I own, I have never had occasion to put it to the test, but I believe it to be a powerful charm. After that, we drove home, and I never knew, for many weeks, that he followed us all the way, just to discover where Rose lived! It was a case of love at first sight. What do you think of *that* for a romance?'

'Admirable!' he replied, a good deal amused. 'I have only one fault to find with it: I don't see the happy ending. What is the name of this Knight of the Road?'

She shook her head. 'I don't know that.'

'I fancy I do.'

She looked quickly at him, surprise in her face. 'You do? How is this?'

'I think it may be Chirk. I also believe him to ride a mare called Mollie,' he said coolly.

'But how did you discover this?'

'Ah!'

'No, don't be so provoking, pray!'

He laughed. 'Well, when I arrived at the toll-gate, two nights ago, I stabled my horse in the hen-house. It was evident that a horse had been stabled there before, and at no very distant date. My predecessor owns no horse, but he does own a horse-blanket, and fodder. These, Ben informed me, are, in fact, the property of Mr Chirk. Of course, Mr Chirk may be a most estimable character, but as I have been given to understand that he very much dislikes strangers, and would not at all like it to be known that he was in the habit of visiting the toll-house, I take leave to doubt that.'

'Good heavens!' She drove on for a few moments, her eyes on the road ahead. 'Do you mean that Brean may have been in league with footpads?'

'The suspicion had occurred to me,' he admitted. 'To what extent, however, I have no idea. I should imagine that he does no more than afford shelter to this Chirk, for although I can readily perceive that a dishonest gatekeeper on a busy road might be of invaluable assistance to the fraternity, for the information he could give them, I can't believe that such a little-frequented road as ours is a haunt of highwaymen.'

'No, certainly not: I never heard of anyone's being held up on it.' Her eyes sparkled. 'How *very* shocking, to be sure — and how *very* exciting! Of course, if this Mr Chirk of yours is indeed poor Rose's admirer, his presence in the district is readily explained. But if he is *not*, what can bring him here? Is it possible that Brean's disappearance is in some way connected with him?'

'That thought had occurred to me too,' he acknowledged. 'Also that some link may exist between him and the unknown stranger of whom Ben stands in such dread. If it does, however, Ben has no notion of it. He esteems Chirk most highly: in fact, he says he is good as ever twanged, which I take to be praise of no mean order! What I hope is that I may be privileged to meet Chirk. I think he has been quite a frequent visitor. But if Brean is working with him, he must know very well where he is, and he won't come to the toll-house while I am there.'

'And the other? the mysterious man?'

'I've seen no sign of him.'

There was a pause. She was looking ahead, frowning a little. Suddenly she drew a sharp breath, and said abruptly: 'Captain Staple!'

He waited, and then, as she appeared to be at a loss, said encouragingly: 'Yes?'

'It is of no consequence! I forget what I was about to say!' she replied, in rather a brusque tone. The constraint, which had vanished while she recounted Rose's romance, returned; and after an uncomfortable silence, she asked him, as one in duty bound to manufacture polite conversation, whether he admired the Derby-shire scene. His lips twitched; but he answered with perfect gravity that he had been much struck by the wild beauty of the surrounding countryside. He then said that having approached Crowford from the north-west his way had led him across some rough moorland, whence magnificent views had been obtained. This provided Miss Stornaway with a safe topic for discussion. She supposed he must have passed close to the Peak, and was sorry to think he should not have visited the cavern there. 'There are a great many caves in the hills,' she informed him. 'Many more, I daresay, than are generally known, but that one, in particular, is quite a curiosity. You should visit it before you leave Derbyshire. Only fancy! — in its mouth, which is enormous, there is actually a village built! The rock is limestone, you know, and if you penetrate into the cave you will find it worn into the most fantastic shapes. There is a stream running through it, and the guide takes one in a small boat along it. It is most romantic, I assure you — but shockingly cold!'

He responded with great civility; and Miss Stornaway, searching her mind for further matters of topographical interest, recalled that the spring, in Tideswell, which had an uncertain ebb and flow, was also reckoned amongst the wonders of the Peak.

This subject lasted until the turnpike was reached. Tideswell lay not far from this, and the rest of the way was beguiled in discussing the exact nature of the commodities to be purchased in the town. Miss Stornaway, informing the Captain that it was her custom to stable Squirrel at the Old George while she transacted her business, would have driven there immediately; but as soon as the outlying buildings of the town came into sight John stopped her, saying that it would be best if he were to be set down there. 'You may overtake me on the road when we have each of us done all this shopping,' he said. 'It won't do for you to be seen driving a gatekeeper, you know.'

'Good heavens, I don't care for that!' she said scornfully.

'Then I must care for you,' he replied.

'Nonsense! You don't look in the least like a gatekeeper! Besides, no one knows you!'

'They soon will. One of the disadvantages of being bigger than the average, ma'am, is that one is easily recognizable. No, don't drive on!'

Except for a lift of her obstinate chin she gave no sign of having heard him. After a moment, he leaned forward, and, taking the reins above her hand, pulled Squirrel up. She flamed into quick wrath, exclaiming: 'How dare you? Understand me, sir, I am not accustomed to submit to dictation!'

'I know you are not,' he said, smiling at her. 'Never mind! You may very easily punish me by refusing to take me up again presently. Will an hour suffice us, do you suppose?'

He jumped down from the gig, and for a moment she eyed him uncertainly. There was so much amused understanding in his face that her little spurt of temper died, and she said: 'Oh, if you choose to be so nonsensical! Yes, an hour — and you will be well served if I make you trudge all the way to Crowford!'

She drove on, and he followed her on foot into the town.

By a stroke of good fortune, he found a pair of serviceable brogues in a warehouse that catered for the needs of farm-labourers, but not all his endeavours could discover a coat into which he could squeeze his powerful shoulders. He was obliged to abandon the search, and to purchase instead a leather waistcoat. By the time he had acquired coarse woollen stockings, a supply of flannel shirts, and several coloured neckcloths, only a few minutes were left to him in which to write and to despatch a letter to the Hon. Wilfred Babbacombe, at Edenhope, near Melton Mowbray. This missive was necessarily brief, and requested Mr Babbacombe, in turgid ink and on a single sheet of rough paper, to ransack two valises consigned to his guardianship and to wrench from them such shirts, neckcloths, nightshirts, and underlinen as they might be found to contain, and to despatch these, in a plain parcel, to Mr (heavily underscored) Staple, at the Crawford Toll-gate, near Tideswell, in the County of Derbyshire.

Having sealed this communication with a wafer, and deposited it at the receiving-office, Captain Staple gathered together his various packages, and set out on the homeward journey.

He had not proceeded very far along the road out of the town before Miss Stornaway overtook him. She pulled up, and he was soon seated beside her again, bowling along in the direction of Crowford.

'I must tell you at once that I have exceeded your instructions, and bought for you, besides wax candles, a lamp which you may set upon the table, and which will be very much more the thing for you,' she told him. 'You informed me that you were in the possession of an independance, so I did not scruple to lay out another six shillings of your money. Did you contrive to procure raiment more fitted to your calling than what you are wearing now?'

'Yes, but I had a great fancy for a frieze coat, and I could not find one to fit me!'

'You mean, I collect, into which you might squeeze yourself!' she retorted. 'Well! I warned you how it would be! Tideswell is not, after all, a large town.'

'No,' he agreed. 'And sadly lacking in historic interest. Apart from its spring there really seems to be nothing to say about it, which leaves me quite at a loss.'

'Oh?' she said, puzzled, and slightly suspicious.

'We could talk about the weather, of course,' he said thoughtfully. 'Or I could describe to you some of the places I have visited abroad.'

She bit her lip, but when he began, in the blandest way, to expatiate upon the grandeur of the Pyrenees, she interrupted him, exclaiming impetuously: 'I wish you will not be so foolish! I don't care a button for the Pyrenees!'

'You would care even less for them, had you

ever been obliged to winter there,' he observed. '*You* choose what we are to talk about! Only don't say, *Captain Staple!* and then decide that I am not, after all, a trustworthy confidant.'

Quite unused to such direct dealing, she stammered: 'I d-didn't! Why should I — How can I know that you are to be trusted? I never set eyes on you until yesterday!'

'There, I am afraid, I can't help you,' he said. 'It would be of very little use to tell you that I am entirely to be trusted, so perhaps we had better continue to discuss the Pyrenees.'

There was an awful silence. 'I beg your pardon!' said Nell stiffly.

'But why?' asked John.

'I did not mean to offend you.'

'Of course not. I'm not offended,' he said pleasantly. 'On the contrary, I am very much obliged to you for having done my marketing for me. By the by, how much did you expend on my behalf, ma'am?'

A flush mounted to her cheek; she said: 'You need not continue to slap me, Captain Staple!'

That made him laugh. A quick, indignant glance at him informed her, however, that the expression in his eyes was one of warm kindness. No one had ever looked at her just like that before, and it had the effect upon her of making her feel, for perhaps the first time in her life, a strong desire to lay the burden of her cares upon other shoulders. Captain Staple's were certainly broad enough to bear them.

'That, at least, is something I should never do to you, Miss Stornaway,' he said. 'I think life has dealt you too many slaps.'

'No — oh, no!' she said, in a shaken voice. 'Indeed, I have been very much indulged!'

'Yes, possibly, when your grandfather was a hale man. Too much depends upon you now, and I cannot discover that there is anyone to support or to advise you.'

She said, with the flash of a wry smile: 'Captain Staple, if you continue in this vein you will induce in me a mood of self-pity that will very likely cause me to burst into maudlin tears! And that, I am persuaded, you would dislike excessively!'

'I own I would prefer you not to burst into tears on the high road,' he admitted. 'Some other vehicle would be bound to come into sight just at that moment!'

A gurgle of laughter escaped her. 'Very true! I won't do it.'

'I've a notion you are not prone to shed tears,' he said smilingly.

'I'm more prone to swear!' she confessed. She added apologetically: 'It comes from having lived always with my grandfather, and being about the stables a great deal.'

'Don't guard your tongue on my account!' he begged, his eyes dancing.

'Ah, *you* don't provoke me to swear!'

'Who does? The gentleman in the natty waistcoat?'

She hesitated.

'Now is the moment for *Captain Staple*!' he murmured. 'Give me the reins!'

She transferred them without protest to his

hand, and the cob, obedient to a light signal, dropped to a walk. 'That's better,' said John. 'What's the fellow doing here, if he didn't come to dangle after you?'

'I don't know. I don't know what brought either of them here! Since my grandfather was taken ill it is very quiet at Kellands. We don't entertain, and — and there are no longer hunters in the stables. Not that my cousin would care for that: he is not a hunting man; but Coate talks a great deal about the runs he has enjoyed with all the best packs. I don't know how that may be.'

'Nor I, indeed, and it would be unjust to hazard a guess, I expect,' the Captain said cheerfully.

'Well, he hasn't the look of a Melton man, has he?'

'No. How came your cousin to make a friend of him?'

Her lip curled. 'I daresay he could find no one better. Henry is the most miserable creature! My grandfather was used to call him a park-saunterer. Jermyn told me once that he was a pretty loose fish besides.' She saw a muscle twitch in the Captain's cheek. 'Don't laugh at me! I warned you my language is unladylike!'

'Just so! In what way is Henry a loose fish? If he is a miserable creature, I take it he don't go raking round the town?'

'Oh, no! But the people he knows are not at all the thing, and Jermyn said it was too bad he should be known to be *his* cousin, because he suspected him to be not over-particular in matters of play and pay.'

95

'That's bad,' said John. 'Does he pursue any gainful occupation, or is he a gentleman of means?'

'Well, I don't think he's very plump in the pocket, but he must have a competence, I suppose, for my uncle married a lady of moderate fortune, and he was their only child. At all events, he was never bred to any profession.'

'Hangs on the town, eh? Gamester?'

'Oh, yes, and that was what Jermyn disliked so much! He thought him the most paltry fellow to spend his days being ear-wigged at Tattersall's, when he knows so little about horses that whenever he buys one you may depend upon it it will be found to be touched in the wind, or for ever throwing out a splint! Then, too, he does not play at the clubs, but at houses in Pall Mall, where one *never* sees the real Goes! In fact,' said Miss Stornaway, summing the matter up in a word, 'the fellow's a skirter!'

'I see,' said John, only the very slightest tremor in his voice.

'Until Jermyn was killed, I scarcely knew him, because Grandpapa quarrelled with my uncle upon the occasion of his marriage,' Nell pursued. 'She was the daughter of a Cit, and, I believe, rather a vulgar person. Not,' she added, in a reflective tone, 'that Grandpapa ever liked him above half — according to what Huby has told me. Huby is our butler, and he has been at Kellands for so long that he knows far more about Grandpapa than I do. But when Jermyn died, Henry became the heir, and Grandpapa thought himself obliged to receive him. He used to come here now and then, because in those days he was afraid of Grandpapa, but you could see that he thought it a dead bore. When Grandpapa had that dreadful stroke, Henry ceased to come, which I was very glad of. I never heard anything more of him until ten days ago, when he suddenly arrived at Kellands.' Her eyes smouldered. 'He had the effrontery to tell me that he thought it his duty! You may guess how I liked *that*!'

'I imagine you must have told him how soon he might pack his bags again?'

'I did,' she said bitterly. 'Then — then I was made to see that it is not in my power to be rid of him! He is sly enough to know that I would not, for any consideration you might offer me, permit him to agitate my grandfather. I was obliged to acquiesce in his remaining, particularly when he talked of rusticating for a while, because he was scorched. For Grandpapa to be succeeded — as might happen at any moment — by a man imprisoned for debt would be too much! Besides, I am very well able to deal with Henry. But then, you see, Coate arrived at Kellands, and to my astonishment Henry informed me that it was by his invitation! Since that day there has been no doing anything with Henry: he is ruled entirely by that creature, and I think — I am sure — that he is afraid of him. Coate orders all as he pleases — or he would do so, if I were not there to check him!'

'Are you able to do that?'

'Yes, in general, because I have the good fortune to take his fancy,' she said disdainfully. 'I have been the object of his gallantry this past week. He has even done me the honour to inform me that he likes a female to be spirited: it affords the better sport, you see.'

She was interrupted at this point, Captain Staple expressing a strong desire to make Mr Coate's acquaintance. She laughed, but shook her head. 'No, no, I beg you will not! I am well able to take care of myself, and if I were not I have Joseph and Winkfield at hand. If I chose to disclose the whole to my grandfather, he would have both Coate and Henry turned out of doors: he is still master at Kellands! I don't choose to. Dr Bacup considers that any agitation might prove fatal, and my chief concern is to shield him from any knowledge of what is going on.'

'Very well, but you have no need to keep that knowledge from me. What *is* going on?' asked John.

'I don't know.' She clasped and unclasped her hands. '*That* is what alarms me — not, I give you my word, Coate's encroaching fancies! He and Henry are here for some purpose, and I cannot discover what it may be. It's nothing good! Henry is afraid of something, and Coate is afraid of what Henry may divulge when he's in his cups. He watches him like a cat, and once I heard him threaten to break his neck if he didn't keep his mouth shut.'

'Did he, by Jove! Can you discover nothing from your cousin?'

'No. When he is sober, it would be useless to question him, and when he's foxed, Coate takes good care not to let him out of his sight. He

98

becomes a trifle fuddled nearly every night, but he doesn't say anything to the purpose.'

'Am I to understand by that that you are present at these — er — carouses?' demanded John.

'Of course I am not! It is what Huby tells me. He is very old, and he pretends to be deaf, for he was quite sure Coate could be up to no good, as soon as he laid eyes on him. Only he cannot conceive, any more than I can, what it could be that should bring him to the Peak district, or why he should ally himself with such a poor creature as Henry.'

'I haven't met Henry, but I apprehend you don't think it possible that he might have hired Coate for some nefarious purpose? The fellow sounds to me very like a paid bravo.'

She considered this for a moment, but gave a decided negative. 'For Coate is the master, not Henry. Besides, what use could he find for a bravo *here*?'

'Well, if your Cousin Henry is indeed the snirp you think him, I can only suppose that he is useful to Coate for some reason as yet hidden from us. Perhaps he is in possession of some vital secret necessary to the success of Coate's plans.'

She looked at him sceptically. 'You don't believe that!'

'I don't know. There must be some reason for such an ill-assorted alliance!'

'I think you must be quizzing me! Such a notion is fantastic!'

'Very likely, but I might say the same of your apprehensions. Oh, no! don't eat me! I haven't said it, and I swear I don't think it!'

She cast him a fulminating look. 'Perhaps, sir, you believe me to be suffering from the merest irritation of the nerves?'

'Not a bit of it! I believe you to be a woman of admirable commonsense, and I place the utmost reliance on what you tell me. If you were the most vapourish female imaginable, I must still lend an attentive ear to your story: do not let us forget that a gatekeeper, stationed almost at your door, has disappeared under circumstances which one can only call mysterious! That is quite as fantastic as anything you have told me, you know!'

Slightly mollified, she said: 'It seems absurd, but do you suppose Brean's disappearance may be connected in some way with whatever it is those two are plotting?'

'Certainly I do — though in *what* way I must own I have not the smallest conjecture! However, it will not do to be applying the principles of commonsense to a situation which we clearly perceive to be something quite out of the ordinary, so do not tell me, ma'am, that it is fantastic to suppose that your cousin and his friend can have anything to do with a gatekeeper!'

She smiled, but absently, saying, after a moment: 'I thought I was indulging my fancy only, but — the thing is, Captain Staple, that I am persuaded my cousin is suspicious of you! I don't know who told him that there was a new gatekeeper at the Crowford pike, but he knows it, and has been asking me who you are, and

100

what has become of Brean.'

'Well, that does not encourage us to think that Brean is working with him,' John admitted. 'On the other hand, he might be cutting a sham — making it appear, you see, as though he knew nothing of Brean. Or even being afraid of what Brean may be doing.'

'No, I don't think it is that,' she replied, knitting her brows. 'Coate seems not to care about it. He came into the room when Henry was questioning me, and all he said was that he had fancied you were not the man who had opened to him before, but for his part he had paid very little heed to you.'

'Well, before he is much older he will be paying a great deal of heed to me,' observed John. 'However, you were very right not to tell him so! He is too set in his ways, and a surprise will be good for him. For anything we know, of course, he and Brean may have decided to tip Cousin Henry the double. Or — But the possibilities stretch into infinity!'

'Are you funning again?' she demanded. 'I collect that you think it all incredible!'

'Not a bit of it! You will allow, however, that in this prosaic age it is certainly unusual to find oneself suddenly in the middle of what promises to be an excellent adventure! I have spent the better part of my life looking for adventure, so you may judge of my delight. The only thing is, I wonder if I was wise to turn myself into a gatekeeper? I can't but see that it is bound to restrict my movements.'

'I must say, I can't conceive what should have

induced you to do anything so whimsical!' she said frankly.

'Oh, it wasn't whimsical!' he replied. 'After I had seen you, I had to provide myself with an excuse for remaining at Crowford, and there it was, ready to my hand!'

She gave a gasp. 'C-Captain Staple!'

'On the other hand,' he went on, apparently deaf to this interruption, 'I could scarcely hope to escape remark, were I to revert to my proper person, and that might put our fine gentlemen on their guard. No: setting the hare's head against the goose-giblets, things are best as they are — for the present.'

'Yes,' she agreed uncertainly, stealing a sidelong look at him.

He urged the cob to a trot again. 'What I must first discover is the precise nature of Coate's business here. To tell you the truth, I can't think what the devil it can be! If this were Lincolnshire, or Sussex, I should be much inclined to suspect the pair of them of being engaged in some extensive smuggling, and of using your house as their headquarters; but this is Derbyshire, and sixty or seventy miles from the coast, I daresay, so that won't answer.'

'And hiding kegs of brandy in the cellars?' she asked, laughing. 'Or perhaps storing them in one of our limestone caverns?'

'A very good notion,' he approved. 'But my imagination boggles at the vision of a train of pack-ponies being led coolly to and fro, and exciting no more interest than if they were accommodation coaches!' They had come within sight of Crowford village, and he gave back the reins and the whip into her hands, saying: 'And we shall excite less interest, perhaps, if you drive, and I sit with my arms folded, groom-fashion.'

In the event, this precaution was superfluous, since the only two persons to be seen on the village street were a short-sighted old dame, and Mr Sopworthy, who was standing outside the Blue Boar, but seemed to recall something needing his attention, and had disappeared into the house by the time the gig drew abreast of it. Miss Stornaway was still wondering why he had not waited to exchange a greeting with her when she drew up before the toll-gate.

The Captain alighted; the merchandize was unloaded, and his debts faithfully discharged. Joseph Lydd reported that only strangers had passed the gate during his absence, and got up beside his mistress. The Captain went to hold open the gate, and Miss Stornaway drove slowly forward. Clear of the gate, she pulled up again, for he had released it, and stepped into the road, holding up his hand to her. Hesitating, she transferred the whip to her left hand, and put the right into his. His fingers closed over it strongly, and he held it so for a moment while her eyes searched his face, half in enquiry, half in shy doubt. There was a little smile in his. 'I meant what I said to you,' he told her. Then he kissed her hand, and let it go, and with considerably heightened colour she drove on.

6

Mr Lydd, observing these proceedings out of the tail of his eye, preserved silence and a wooden countenance for perhaps two minutes. Then, as the gig, rounding a bend, passed the entrance to a rough lane, leading up to the moors, he gave a discreet cough, and said: 'Fine young fellow, our new gatekeeper, miss. I disremember when I've seen a chap with a better pair of shoulders on him. Quite the gentleman, too — even if he *is* Ned Brean's cousin.'

'You know very well that he is not, Joseph,' said Miss Stornaway calmly. 'He is a Captain of Dragoon Guards — or he was, until he sold out.'

'A Captain, is he?' said Joseph, interested. 'Well, it don't surprise me, not a bit. He told me himself he was a military man, miss, and that didn't surprise me neither, him having the look of it. In fact, I suspicioned he might be an officer, on account of the way he's got with him, which makes one think he's used to giving his orders, *and* having 'em obeyed — and no argle-bargle, what's more!'

'When did he tell you he was a military man?' demanded Nell.

Under the accusing glance thrown at him, Mr Lydd became a little disconcerted. He besought his young mistress to keep her eyes on the road.

'Joseph, when has Captain Staple had the

opportunity to tell you anything about himself, and *why* did he?'

'To think,' marvelled Mr Lydd, 'that I should have gone and forgotten to mention it to you, missie! I'm getting old, that's what it is, and things slip me memory, unaccountable-like.'

'If you have been at the toll-house, prying into Captain Staple's business — '

'No, no!' said Joseph feebly. 'Jest dropped in to blow a cloud, being as I was on me way to the Blue Boar! Yesterday evening, it was, and very nice and affable the Captain was. We got talking, and one thing leading to another he jest happened to mention that he was a military man.'

'You went there on purpose!' said Nell hotly. 'Because he — because you thought — I wish to heaven you and Rose would remember that I am not a child!'

'No, Miss Nell, but you're a young lady, and seeing as Sir Peter can't look after you no more, like you ought to be — and Rose being an anxious sort of a female,' he added basely, 'it seems like it's me duty to keep me eye on things, as you might say!'

'I know you only do it out of kindness,' said Nell, 'but I assure you it is unnecessary! You have no need to be anxious about me!'

'*Jest* what I says to Rose, missie! Them was me very words! 'We got no need to be anxious about Miss Nell,' I tells her. 'Not now, we haven't.' That, out of course, was after I come home from the toll-house.'

Miss Stornaway, fully and indignantly conscious of the unwisdom of attempting to bring to a sense of his presumption a servitor who had held her on the back of her first pony, extricated her from difficulties in an apple-tree, and, upon more than one occasion, rescued her from the consequences of her youthful misdeeds, accomplished the rest of the short journey in dignified silence.

Kellands Manor was an old and a rambling house, standing at no great distance from the pike road, which, in fact, ran through the Squire's land. Its pleasure gardens, though well laid-out, were neglected, the shrubbery being overgrown, the flower-beds allowed to run riot, and the wilderness to encroach year by year on lawns once shaven and weedless. Miss Stornaway, unlike the one remaining gardener, looked upon this decay with indifference. Behind a crumbling stone wall an extensive vegetable plot was in good order; new trees had been planted in the orchard; and the home farm was thriving.

Miss Stornaway, walking up from the stables with her rather mannish stride, the tail of her worn riding-dress looped over her arm, entered the house through a side-door, and made her way down a flagged corridor to the main hall. From this an oaken staircase rose in two graceful branches to the galleried floor above. She was about to mount it when a door on one side of the hall opened, and her cousin came out of the library. 'Oh, there you are, cousin!' he said, in the peevish tone which was habitual with him. 'I have been in these past twenty minutes, and desirous of having a word with you.'

She paused, a hand on the baluster-rail, and one booted foot already on the first step of the stairway. 'Indeed!' she said, looking down at him from her superior height, her brows lifting a little.

His was not an impressive figure, and he was never so conscious of this as when he stood in his magnificent cousin's presence. He had neither height nor presence, and a strong inclination towards dandyism served only to accentuate the shortcomings of his person. Skin-tight pantaloons of an elegant shade of yellow did not set off to advantage a pair of thin legs, nor could all the exertions of his tailor disguise the fact that his narrow shoulders drooped, and that he was developing a slight paunch. His countenance was tolerably good-looking, but spoilt by a sickly complexion and the unmistakable marks of self-indulgence; and his rather bloodshot eyes seemed at all times incapable of maintaining a steady regard. He sported several fobs and seals, wore exaggerat-edly high points to his collars, and fidgeted incessantly with snuff-box, quizzing-glass, and handkerchief.

'I'm sure I don't know where you can have been,' he complained. 'And Huby and that woman of yours quite unable to tell me! I must say, I don't consider it at all the thing.'

'Perhaps they thought my whereabouts no concern of yours,' suggested Nell. 'I have been transacting some business in Tideswell. What is it that you wish to say to me?'

Instead of answering, he embarked on a rambling censure of her independant manners. 'I can tell you this, cousin, you present a very odd appearance, jauntering all over the country as you do. I wonder that my grandfather should suffer it, though I suppose the old gentleman is in such queer stirrups he don't realize what a figure you make of yourself. Nat was saying to me only this morning — '

'Pray spare me a recital of Mr Coate's remarks!' she interrupted. 'If my odd ways have given him a distaste for me, I can only say that I am heartily glad of it!'

'There you go!' he exclaimed bitterly. 'I should have supposed you might have taken pains to be civil to a guest, but no! You behave — '

'Let me remind you, Henry, that Mr Coate is a guest in this house neither by my wish nor my invitation!'

'Well, he's here by mine, and if you weren't such an unaccountable girl you'd be glad of it! Handsome fellow, ain't he? Slap up to the mark, too, as you'd say yourself!'

'I should never describe Mr Coate in such terms.'

'Oh, don't put on those missish airs with me, Nell! Lord knows I've heard you using all sorts of sporting lingo!'

'Certainly! I trust, however, that I am in general veracious!' she retorted.

'*I'm* not surprised that fine aunt of yours couldn't nabble a husband for you!' he said, nettled. 'You've a damned nasty tongue in your head! I can tell you this, a Long Meg like you

108

can't afford to put up the backs of people as you do!'

'That is the second thing you have been so obliging as to tell me, and no more interesting to me than the first. Have you anything more to say?'

'Yes, I have! I wish you will accord Nat a little common civility! It's no very pleasant thing for me to have my cousin behaving like a shrew! One would have thought you would have been pleased with the very flattering distinction he accords you! I don't know what you think is to become of you when the old man slips his wind! You needn't look to me to provide for you, for if he has more to leave than the title and an estate mortgaged to the hilt — '

'Are you having the effrontery to suggest that I — I, Nell Stornaway! — should encourage the advances of *Coate?*' she demanded. 'Perhaps you think he would make a suitable match for me?'

'Oh, well!' he muttered, his eyes shifting from hers. 'You might do worse, and you're not likely to do better. I don't say — I never spoke of marriage, after all! All I care for is that you should make his visit agreeable. You don't give a fig for the awkwardness of *my* position! If you open your mouth at the dinner-table, ten to one it is only to say something cutting to Nat — '

'Yes, indeed! You would fancy that he must be sensible by now, would you not, that his presence at Kellands is only less distasteful to me than the extremely improper style of his advances? But, no!'

'A woman of address would know how to turn

it off without flying into a miff!'

'Yes, and some women, no doubt, are more fortunate than I in those male relatives whose duty it might be thought to guard them from such unwanted attentions!'

He coloured, and shot her a resentful glance. 'What a piece of work you make about a trifle! I suppose you expect Nat to toad-eat you, though how you should when you wear a gown with a darn in it — the shabbiest thing! puts me to the blush, I can tell you! — and serve such plain dinners — only one course, and that ill-dressed! And then, to crown all, go off afterwards, and never come into the drawing-room, as you should! No tea-tray brought in: nothing as it should be! — 'pon my soul, I don't know why you should look to be treated with any extraordinary civility!'

'Good gracious, does Mr Coate desire *tea* in the evening?' she exclaimed. 'I thought it was the *brandy* he wanted! I will not fail to tell Huby that between us we have quite mistaken the matter; and a tray shall be brought to you. My presence, however, you must dispense with: I sit every evening with my grandfather.'

'Yes! If Nat had the good fortune to please you, you wouldn't choose to spend your time with an old dotard who's had his notice to quit!'

She took a swift step towards him. He shrank back instinctively, but not quickly enough to escape a swinging box on the ear, which made him stagger. 'You will speak of my grandfather with respect in this house, Henry! Understand that!'

110

A burst of hearty laughter, coming from the direction of the front door, made her turn, at once startled and mortified. Nathaniel Coate stood upon the threshold, laughing, and waving his hat like a huntsman capping hounds to a scent. 'Bravo, bravo! That was a wisty one, by God! It's bellows to mend with you, Henry: she'll give you pepper, by God, she will!' He tossed his hat and his whip on to a chair, and came forward, saying: 'What have you been about, you stupid fellow? Why don't you take that Friday-face of yours away before Miss Nell slaps it again?'

Henry, taking this broad hint, retired again into the library, shutting the door behind him with a vicious slam, which made his friend give another of his loud laughs, and say: 'Silly ninny hammer! Now we shall have him in the sullens! Ah, don't be in a hurry to slip off, Miss Nell! Damme if this ain't the first time I've laid eyes on you today!'

Since he had contrived to step between her and the staircase she was unable to slip off. He was looking her over in a way that gave her the unpleasant sensation of having been stripped of her clothing; and although she was not at all afraid of him she would have been glad to have been able to escape. She said coolly: 'You might have seen me at the breakfast-table, but you are not an early riser. Now, if you please, I must go to my grandfather!'

He did not move from the stairs. 'Ah, that's a slap for me, ain't it? I shall have to mend my ways, shan't I? Why don't you take me in hand,

111

eh? Blister me if I wouldn't enjoy being schooled by you! I don't know when I've taken such a fancy to a girl as I have to you, and that's the truth! Ay, you may look down that high-bred nose of yours, lass, and try to bam me you're a stone statue, but I know better! Full of spirit, you are, and that's how I like women to be — women and horses, and devilish alike they are! You're a beautiful, stepper, and a ginger besides, and that's the metal for my money!'

'If we are to employ the language of the stables, Mr Coate,' she replied, rigid with wrath, 'I will inform you that having lived all my life with a nonpareil I have nothing but contempt for mere whipsters! Now, if you will be so obliging as to permit me to pass — !'

She had the momentary satisfaction of knowing that she had touched him on the raw, for he flushed darkly, but she regretted it an instant later. He strode up to her, an ugly look in his face, and said in a thickened voice: 'Contempt, eh? We'll see that!' He flung his arms round her before she could evade him, chuckling deep in his chest.

She was a strong woman, and as tall as he, but found herself helpless. He was immensely powerful, and seemed to control her struggles without any particular effort. 'Kiss and be friends, now!' he said, his breath hot on her face.

A dry cough sounded from the staircase; a voice devoid of all expression said: 'I beg pardon, miss: might I have a word with you, if convenient?'

Coate swore, and released Nell. For a moment

she confronted him, still unafraid, but white with anger, her eyes blazing. Then she swept past him, and went up the stairs to where her grandfather's valet stood awaiting her. He stepped aside, bowing politely, and followed her to the gallery off which her own and her grandfather's apartments were situated.

'Thank you!' she said curtly. 'I'm much obliged!'

'Not at all, miss,' said Winkfield, as though such interventions were an accustomed part of his duties. 'It was fortunate that I happened to be at hand. If I may say so, I feel that Mr Coate would feel himself more at home in a different class of establishment. Perhaps, a hint to Mr Henry — ?'

'Quite useless! Don't disturb yourself, Winkfield! I'll take good care never to be alone with him again!'

'No, miss, it *would* be wiser, I expect. But if Sir Peter knew — '

'Winkfield, most earnestly I forbid you to breathe one syllable to him!'

'No, miss, and indeed I have not! But he knows more than we think for, and it's my belief he's fretting over it. He keeps asking me things, and wanting to know where you are, and the day he sent for Mr Henry to come to his room he was too much like his old self — if you understand me!'

'We should not have allowed it. It put him in a passion, didn't it?'

'Well, miss, he never could abide Mr Henry, but you know as well as I do that it won't do to cross Sir Peter. What I didn't like was the way seeing Mr Henry seemed to make Sir Peter feel his own helplessness more than he has done for a long time now. Several times he's said to me that he'll make us all know who's master at Kellands before he's booked. Then he gets restless, and testy, and I know he's been brooding over it, and raging in his mind because he hasn't the power to do so much as get up out of his chair without he has me to lift him.'

She said in a breaking voice: 'Oh, if he had but died when he had that stroke!'

'Yes, miss, I've often thought the same. It comes hard on a gentleman like Sir Peter to be as he is.'

'Winkfield, you have not told him that my cousin has a friend staying here?'

'No one has told him that, miss, unless Mr Henry did, but he knows it well enough.'

'On no account must he be permitted to set eyes on the creature! We must — we *must* get rid of the pair of them!'

'Yes, miss, that's what I have been thinking myself. But without we tell Sir Peter the whole there's not much we can do. If it was only Mr Henry, it would be enough for Sir Peter to tell him to be off: we could do the rest — if I may make so bold as to say so, Miss Nell! But that other! I don't doubt Sir Peter would have him out, if he had to send for a law-officer to do the trick, but, by what Dr Bacup says, it would bring on another stroke if he was to get agitated.'

'No, no!' Nell said, dashing a hand across her eyes.

'No, miss, that's my own feeling. I couldn't do it — not after all these years. We must hope that we can send Mr Coate off without bringing Sir Peter into it.' He added thoughtfully: 'Betty forgot to put a hot brick in his bed last night, but he made no complaint. It won't do to damp the sheets, as I have told Rose, because we don't want him laid up on our hands; but I'd say he was one as is partial to good-living, and that mutton you had for dinner yesterday, Miss Nell — *well*! Let alone Mrs Parbold scorching it on the spit, which she did, and the tears running down her face, Rose tells me, because we all have our pride, and no one can send up a better dressed dinner than she can!'

'*Winkfield!*' Nell choked, between tears and laughter. 'It was *shocking*! I was never so mortified!'

'No, miss, I'm sure! But Sir Peter had the wing of a chicken, poached just as he likes it, and a curd pudding with wine sauce,' said Winkfield consolingly. 'And Huby has been busy in the cellar all the morning, and no doubt he will warn you, miss, not to touch the burgundy at dinner. If you should be at liberty now, Sir Peter has been asking for you this hour past.'

'I will come to him directly. I must put off this old riding-dress: you know how much he dislikes to see me shabbily gowned!'

She hurried away to her own bedchamber, to strip off the well-worn habit in which she spent the greater part of her days, and to put on instead a morning-gown of green velvet, not perhaps fashioned in the latest mode but not yet

115

showing such signs of wear as would be perceptible to her grandfather. Ten minutes later she entered the dressing-room which formed an antechamber to Sir Peter's big bedroom, and tapped on the door between the two. It was opened to her by Winkfield, who gave her a significant look, but said nothing, and at once went away, leaving her alone with her grandfather.

'Nell?'

She crossed the floor to the wing-chair that stood beside the wide fireplace. 'Yes, sir. Now, don't, *don't* scold me, for I have passed the most amusing morning!' she said, bending to kiss Sir Peter's brow.

He did not raise his head, which was sunk forward on his breast, but he glanced up at her under his brows, and lifted his right hand. The other was almost powerless, and lay lightly clenched on his knee. 'Well?' he said.

His utterance was a little slurred, and he seemed to speak with a slight effort. He was the wreck of a once big man, the flesh having wasted away from large bones. His left side was semi-paralysed, and it was only with his valet's assistance that he could move from his bed to a chair. He wore always a brocade dressing-gown, but every day it was Winkfield's duty to arrange a freshly laundered neckcloth round his neck in the style he had adopted years earlier.

Nell took the hand held up to her, and sat down beside him. 'Well! I conveyed our new gatekeeper to Tideswell, as you know, while

Joseph took care of the pike.'

'H'm! I trust he behaved himself!'

'With all the propriety in the world, sir! You need not look so suspiciously: he is most truly the gentleman.'

'Much you know!' he grunted. 'Playing off the airs of an exquisite, I daresay.'

'Oh, no! nothing of the kind! He's a soldier, not a fribble, dearest! I thought his coat was very well cut, but it was quite plain, and put me in mind of the coats Jermyn used to wear.'

'Scott,' said Sir Peter. 'If he *was* a Captain, and ain't hoaxing you! Most of the military men go to him — or they did, in my day.'

'Very likely. At all events, there was no fault to be found with his air, or address, and I think you would say that he has a well-bred ease of manner. I found him excellent company, and I am sure he must have great delicacy of principle, for he was most steady in refusing to drive with me into the town! He said that it would not *do*, and obliged me to set him down before we reached it.'

Sir Peter grunted again. 'What did you talk of?' he demanded.

'Oh, all manner of things!' she replied easily. 'He told me many — many interesting things about the Pyrenees, for instance!'

'He did, did he? Fellow sounds to me like a damned nin-compoop!' said Sir Peter irascibly.

She laughed, but blushed too. 'Oh, no! In fact, I fear he must cause his family the gravest anxiety with these whimsical starts of his! You, I think, would like him, sir. I have not, of course, seen him with a team, but I fancy he has good, even hands.'

'That's as may be. But what the devil's he doing at the toll-house?'

'Oh, diverting himself! I think he finds life sadly flat.'

He said no more, and she picked up a newspaper, and glanced through it, knowing that although he might weary soon of conversation he liked to feel that she was in the room. She thought he had fallen into a light sleep, but he startled her suddenly by saying in an abrupt tone: 'Who is the fellow you have staying in the house?'

'Henry, Grandpapa?'

'Don't be a fool, girl — or think me one! I want none of your bamboozling! Who is he?'

'Oh, Coate!' she said indifferently. 'A friend of my cousin's.'

'Why hasn't he been brought to see me?'

'Because I am persuaded you would give the poor man one of your famous set-downs, sir,' she replied, with great coolness. 'He is not quite up to the trick, you know.'

'Then what the devil does Henry mean by bringing him to my house? Henry's half flash and half foolish, and any friend of his is bound to be a loose fish!'

She was alarmed, for his colour was considerably heightened, and there was a note in his voice which warned her of rising temper. She said: 'Oh, pray don't send him away, sir! To be obliged to entertain my cousin would not suit me at all! I am grateful to Coate for bearing him

118

company, and never see either of them, except at dinner.'

'What brought Henry here? What is going on in my house, Nell? By God, I will not be hoaxed and humdudgeoned! Do you take me for a child, or a lunatic?'

'No, sir, but indeed I don't know what should be going on! You know that we settled it between us that Henry is escaping from his creditors! That was your notion, do you remember? and I am pretty sure you were right.'

He stared at her, his eyes fierce under the jutting brows. 'Don't lie to me, Nell! don't lie to me! You're on the fidgets — blue-devilled! They've cut up your peace between the pair of 'em, eh? Damme, I should have seen to it you had a respectable female to keep you company!'

'Now, that would indeed cut up my peace!' she said, laughing. 'My dear sir, I cannot decide which of us would most deserve pity — me, or your respectable female! A widow, of course, and elderly, with the strictest notions of propriety! I should be the death of her!'

He beat his hand against the arm of his chair, in a gesture of fretting impotence. 'There is no one to look after you. I might as well be coffined!'

She managed to possess herself of his hand, and held it between both of hers. 'Dearest, this is the merest irritation of the nerves! I am beset by protectors!'

He moved his head impatiently. 'Servants, servants! That won't fadge!'

She said coaxingly: 'You must not be so cross,

sir: indeed, there is no reason for you to be vexed! If I needed a protector — which I assure you I do not! — I should send a message to the toll-house, and desire my military giant to come to my aid! I daresay he would be very happy to hurl out of your house anyone you chose to indicate.'

He seemed to be diverted. He looked at her intently, and she was thankful to see that the angry spots of colour in his face were fading. 'He would, would he?'

'Certainly! He is a very obliging person, and has expressed his willingness to serve me at any time!' she said, with a saucy look. 'And if we should feel the need of a man capable of ridding our house of invaders — which, however, I do not at all anticipate — he would be the very one for the task! I am persuaded, my dear sir, that he would *mill cannisters, darken daylights, and draw corks* with all the *gaiety* in the world! Like Hotspur, you know, in that passage which always makes you laugh! *Fie upon this quiet life! I want work!* is what he would say!'

He smiled rather grimly. 'Baggage!' he said. 'Did *I* teach you that language?'

'Yes, to be sure you did, and a great deal more beside!' she said merrily. This drew a laugh from him, and an adroit question putting him in mind of a contest he had once witnessed she soon had the satisfaction of seeing him restored to tranquillity. He dropped into a doze presently, and the knowledge that his memory was erratic encouraged her to hope that when he awoke he would have forgotten the episode.

It seemed as though it had indeed faded from his mind. He did not speak of it again, and she had the comfort, when she went away to change her dress for an evening-gown, of seeing him settle down to his dinner in quiet good spirits.

The relief was short-lived. Her own dinner was partaken of in the company of her cousin and Mr Coate. She sat at the head of the big table, entirely mistress of the situation, maintaining with quelling composure a conversation of such inane propriety as must, she hoped, lead her unwanted admirer to revise his opinion of her charms. He was apparently conscious of a little awkwardness in meeting her again, and seemed anxious to reinstate himself in her good graces; but before very long he was ogling her, and paying her broad compliments expressed in terms that could only disgust. She was almost glad when these were interrupted by an outcry from her cousin against the burgundy, which he declared, with an angry look at Huby, to have been watered; but civility obliged her to desire Huby to fetch up a fresh bottle, which was not at all what she had wished to do. Then she caught sight of the butler's face, and her vexation yielded to an almost overmastering wish to burst out laughing. Every feeling had been offended: he was looking as outraged as though he had not, in fact, committed just that crime.

The uncomfortable meal dragged on; she rose at last from the table, and was about to retire to the sanctuary of Sir Peter's room when the hopes she had been cherishing were shattered by the entrance of Winkfield into the room, with a message from his master. Sir Peter, he announced, begged that Mr Coate would do him the honour of drinking a glass of brandy with him.

Nell gazed aghast at the valet, but he very slightly shook his head. She knew her grandfather well enough to guess that Winkfield judged it to be more dangerous to oppose his will than to permit Coate to be seen by him. She turned her eyes towards Coate, and said as calmly as she could: 'I must beg you, sir, not to linger in my grandfather's room. I need not remind you, I daresay, that he is a sick man.'

'Oh, don't fear me!' he said, with one of his loud laughs. 'I shall be very happy to visit Sir Peter — famous sportsman, wasn't he? We shall deal capitally!'

In an agony, she watched him precede Winkfield out of the room. Her cousin's voice broke into her agitated thoughts. 'I must say I'm deuced glad the old gentleman's sent for Nat!' Henry said, refilling his glass. 'I wonder he shouldn't have done so before, for it's only civil, after all. What's more, it'll do him good. He'll like Nat: you see if he don't! Nat's devilish good company — just the man to cheer the old gentleman up!'

'Just the man to kill him!' she said, in a shaking voice. 'One look at him will be enough to throw him into a passion! How could you bring such a creature into this house? how *could* you?'

'Oh, pooh, you know nothing of the matter! My grandfather likes a good sportsman, and

Nat's a buck of the first head! Up to every rig and row in town, too. They'll go along like winking!'

She could not trust herself to answer him, but hurried out of the room, bent on warning Rose of what might at any moment befall. Her way led her past her grandfather's apartments, and, after hesitating for a moment, she softly opened the door into the dressing-room, and looked in. Winkfield was there, and greeted her with a smile of reassurance. He said in a low voice: 'You need not be afraid, miss. I fancy Sir Peter does not mean to lose his temper with that person. Remarkably calm, he is.'

'It must do harm!' she whispered. 'You know how much he dislikes men of Coate's stamp! I am fearful of what the consequences may be! Could you not have prevented it?'

'It seemed to me, miss, that once the master had formed a determination to see Mr Coate it would be wiser to do as he bade me. He will not be opposed. And to fob him off with excuses would be to set up the very irritation to his nerves which Dr Bacup has particularly warned us against.'

She sighed, listening anxiously to the sound of voices in the room beyond. 'You will not go out of earshot, Winkfield?'

'I shall not leave this room, miss. We cannot but be uneasy, but I fancy Mr Coate is comporting himself as well as he knows how, besides being set a little in awe of the master.'

It was true. Coate, ushered formally into Sir Peter's room, was indeed a trifle over-awed. He had a disconcerting feeling that he had been granted an audience, and the immobility of the gaunt figure in the wing-chair did nothing to dispel this. As he stood for a moment on the threshold, unusually uncertain of himself, he was aware of being scanned from head to foot by a pair of eyes, deep-sunken, but as hard and as fierce as an eagle's. He began, without knowing it, to fidget with the elaborate folds of his neckcloth. A hand the colour of parchment found, and raised to one eye, a quizzing-glass. It was levelled at him; he thought all at once that the room was overheated. The glass was allowed to fall. 'How do you do?' Sir Peter said courteously. 'You must forgive my inability to rise from this chair, Mr Coate.'

'Oh, not at all! don't give it a thought! Never one to stand upon ceremony! Sorry to find you in queer stirrups, sir!'

'Thank you,' said Sir Peter, in a thin voice. 'Pray be seated! I regret that circumstances should have prevented my making your acquaintance before, Mr Coate. I apprehend that I have had the honour of entertaining you for some days. I trust my people have attended to your comfort?'

Mr Coate thought fleetingly of unaired sheets, underhung mutton, and watered wine, and said that he had no complaint to make. A slight lifting of his host's brows then made him wish that he had phrased this assurance differently.

Sir Peter made a sign to his valet, and said: 'Do you mean to make a long stay in Derbyshire, sir?'

124

'Oh, as to that — !' said Coate, watching Winkfield pour brandy into two glasses. 'Daresay you know how it is! One needs to go into the country on a repairing lease every now and then, and my friend Stornaway having begged me to bear him company — well, the long and the short of it was that I told Mawdesley — you are acquainted with his lordship, I daresay: capital fellow! one of the Melton men! — he must not look for me immediately. 'Why, how is this?' he cried. 'You do not mean to miss the cubbing! Here am I depending upon you to give us all a lead!' But I was adamant. 'My friend Stornaway has a claim upon me,' I said. 'I am promised to him, and there is no more to be said.''

'Ah, you hunt in the Shires?' said Sir Peter.

'Oh, lord, where else should a man hunt? No *humbug* country for Nat Coate! Neck-or-nothing Nat: that's what they call me! No fence you can't get over with a fall, I say!'

Sir Peter, who had thought it one of Mr Assheson Smith's sayings, smiled, and sipped his brandy. He encouraged his guest to talk, and when he saw his guest's glass empty, he begged him to refill it. Under this genial influence Mr Coate expanded like a peony on a hot summer's day, and thought he had achieved so excellent an understanding with his host that he was fatally emboldened to compliment him upon his granddaughter's looks and high spirit. He said that he did not mind owning that he had not expected to find his friend's cousin such a dashing chipper, and wound up this tribute by giving Sir Peter to understand that although he

125

had steered clear of marriage and was not to be thought a fellow that was hanging out for a wife, he was damned if he wasn't beginning to change his mind.

It was at this point that Winkfield entered the room. He said that he fancied that Mr Henry was waiting for Mr Coate in the library; and since he stood holding the door in the evident expectation of ushering his master's guest out of the room immediately, there was nothing for Coate to do but to bid Sir Peter good-night, and take himself off. This was not accomplished without his shaking Sir Peter's hand, and saying, with a wink, that he was happy to have met him, for he rather thought that they had reached a very tolerable understanding.

Having closed the dressing-room door behind the guest, Winkfield returned to the bedchamber, and began quietly to clear away the glasses.

'Winkfield!'

'Sir?'

'You may get me to bed!' Sir Peter said harshly.

He did not speak again until he lay between the sheets, and the valet was drawing the curtains round his bed. Then he said, in quite a strong voice: 'Send Joseph up to me in the morning!'

'Very good, sir,' Winkfield said, carefully lowering the wick of the lamp he had carried into the room.

Sir Peter watched him, a grim smile curling his mouth. 'I've had notice to quit, Winkfield, but I can stick to my leaders still, by God!'

7

Captain Staple, having been set down by Miss Stornaway at the toll-house, lost no time in changing his raiment for garments more suited to his new calling. He found the shirts he had bought a trifle harsh to the skin, but by the time he had removed his boots with the aid of the jack he had purchased (and which, he knew well, would rapidly ruin them) and exchanged them for coarse gray stockings and a pair of brogues; and had knotted one of the coloured neckcloths round his throat, in tolerable semblance of a Belcher-tie, he was very well-pleased with his appearance. He was inclined to think he looked his part, but this view was not shared by Ben, who, returning from his labours at the Blue Boar, made no secret of his disapproval. He said that flash coves didn't wear coloured shirts or leather waistcoats.

'I'm not a flash cove,' replied John.

'Yes, you are!' Ben insisted. 'Everyone knows that!'

'Who is everyone?' demanded John.

'Well — everyone! Mr Sopworthy, and Mrs Skeffling, and Farmer Huggate!'

'Did you tell them so?'

'No! I says as you was me cousin, but Farmer Huggate says as Beau's a proper high-bred 'un, which me cousin wouldn't have come by honest.'

'The devil!' ejaculated John.

'It's all rug!' Ben said consolingly. 'Mr Sopworthy told Farmer Huggate as mum's the word, 'cos *I* heard him.'

'Oh, he did, did he?' said John, somewhat taken aback.

'Ay, 'cos of Miss Nell.'

'Because of — What did he mean by that?'

'I dunno,' said Ben, uninterested.

John did not pursue the subject; and, the grating of cartwheels coming to his ears a few minutes later, went out to attend to his duties. A heavily laden tumbril, drawn by an enormous cart-horse, was slowly approaching from the direction of the village, the driver strolling beside his horse. At sight of John, he called out: 'Open up, mate, will 'ee? There ain't nothing to pay: I got a load o' manure.'

John lifted a hand, in token that he had heard the request, but addressed himself to a stocky, middle-aged man who was seated on the bench outside the toll-house, puffing at a short clay pipe. 'Hallo!' he said. 'Aught I can do for you?'

'Thank 'ee, I'm just having a bit of a set-down on this here bench of yours — if so be as you've no objection?'

'You're welcome,' John said, going to open the gate.

'Fine day!' remarked the driver of the tumbril, with great affability. 'Newcomer, ain't you? It weren't you opened to me when I was along last week — leastways, I disremember that it was.'

'That's right,' John replied, his eyes on the tumbril, 'What's your load?'

'Why, I told ye! Manure!'

128

'I know you did, but it looks to me like lime.'

'Lord bless us, wherever was you reared?' exclaimed the driver, with a fine show of astonishment. 'Lime's manure, cully, all right and tight!'

'Yes, and also it ain't exempt from paying toll!' retorted John, grinning at him. 'What kind of a knock-in-the-cradle do you take me for, dry-boots? You hand over the half of a fiddle!'

'How was I to know you was a downy one?' demanded the driver, philosophically accepting defeat. 'I thought you was a cawker.'

'You go and milk a pigeon!' recommended John, handing him a ticket, and accepting in exchange three greasy coins.

He shut the gate again behind the cart, and walked back to the house. The man on the bench, removing the pipe from between his teeth, said: 'I dessay you get a good few coves trying to chouse you out of the toll.'

John laughed. 'Yes, when they think I'm a green-head.'

'Been at the gate long?'

'I'm only taking charge of it while the true man's away. Gatekeeping's not my trade.'

'I suspicioned it weren't. What might your calling be, if I'm not making too bold to ask?'

'Trooper,' John replied briefly. He had come to a halt a few paces from the bench, and was looking down at the stocky man, wondering who and what he might be. He had the accent of a Londoner, but the wide-brimmed hat he wore, the short, full coat of frieze, and the gaitered legs suggested that he might well be a bailiff, or a farmer. 'Native of these parts?' he asked.

The man shook his head. 'Never been in this here county afore. It's too full of hills for my taste. I'm here on a matter o' business. There's a certain party as I'm acting for as has a fancy to buy a property hereabouts, if he could find what might suit him. I seen one or two, Buxton-way, but I dunno as any of 'em are just what I'm after, and the prices certainly ain't. You know of anyone wanting to sell a decentish place, with a bit o' land, not too dear?'

'No, but I'm not a native either.'

'Ah, pity! What's your monarch — if you ain't this cove?' enquired the man, with a jerk of his thumb up at the fascia-board.

'Jack Staple. What's yours?'

'Stogumber — Gabriel Stogumber.' He glanced round, as Ben came out of the toll-house, and said: 'Hallo! Didn't I see you at the Blue Boar this morning? What are *you* a-doing of here?'

'I lives here!' said Ben indignantly.

'Oh, you *lives* here! Beg parding, I'm sure, Master Booberkin!'

'He's Brean's son,' interposed John. 'I'm his cousin.'

'Oh, that's how it is, is it?' said Mr Stogumber, looking from one to the other. 'To be sure, I did think you was too young to be his pa, and yet again too old to be his brother. How do ye like it in these parts? You seen a bit of service, I dessay?'

'Ay, several years.'

'I should think it must seem a dull sort of a

place,' observed Mr Stogumber. 'I'm from Lunnon meself, and it looks to me like nothing ever happens here, nor ever will. I been setting on this here seat close on half an hour, and I seen one dung-cart go through the pike. Meself, I like a bit o' bustle — mail-coaches, and stages, and such. It's all according to taste, o' course. By the way they all stare at me in the village, back yonder, it's easy to guess you don't see a stranger here above once in ten years.'

This slur cast upon his birthplace aroused Ben's pugnacity, and he at once began to enumerate all the unexpected vehicles which had passed the pike during the foregoing twelve months; and to reckon up on his fingers every newcomer to the district, from a bagman, detained in Crowford by a heavy fall of snow, to Mr Coate, the Squire's guest. Mr Stogumber, apologizing with exaggerated humility for his error, added that Ben had forgotten to include his large cousin in the list. 'And I'm sure he's big enough for two,' he said. 'What part of the country do you come from, Mr Staple?'

'Hertfordshire,' responded John.

'Now, that's a part I *do* know,' said Mr Stogumber.

He then proceeded to discourse amiably on this topic. His manner was that of a naturally loquacious man, willing to fall into conversation with any stranger, but it appeared to John that the casual questions which fell from time to time from his lips were all directed to one end: he wanted to know the exact locality of John's home, and what he had been doing since his supposed discharge from the Army. He seemed interested also in the whereabouts of the official gatekeeper, but Ben, bored by his idle chat, had drifted away, and John was able to evade his questions. He suspected Mr Stogumber of being an informer, and thought that it would not be long before he received a visit from the trustees. But Mr Stogumber, taking his leave presently, was still very affable, and said, somewhat surprisingly, that he expected to remain in the district for a day or two, and would no doubt see John again.

The rest of the day passed without incident. Nightfall brought on a slight recurrence of Ben's dread of his father's unknown visitor, but since the Captain had thoughtfully provided himself with a pack of playing-cards during his expedition to Tideswell he was very soon diverted by being initiated into the mysteries of cassino. The Captain, good-naturedly instructing an eager if not very apt pupil, was glad to see that sundry sounds from outside the house went unnoticed. But just as Ben, with a squeal of triumph, succeeded in lurching him, an owl hooted from somewhere close at hand, twice. This brought the boy's head up in a flash. He sat listening intently, and when the cry sounded again, jumped up from his chair, and ran to the door, shooting back the bolts, and pulling it open. John heard the creak of the wicket-gate into the garden, and a minute later soft, swift footsteps.

''Evening to you, bantling!' said a crisp voice. 'Is all bowman?'

'Ay! Me dad ain't here, but it's all rug!' Ben said eagerly. 'Can I take Mollie? Can I, Mr Chirk?'

He stood back, to allow a thin man in a long coat with several shoulder capes to enter the kitchen. Mr Chirk stepped over the threshold, and checked, his keen, bright eyes staring at Captain Staple, who had not risen from his chair, but sat idly shuffling the cards, and looking with considerable interest at the newcomer. Mr Chirk, a wiry man of medium height, wore, besides his great-coat, a wide-brimmed and greasy hat, a muffler knotted about his throat, and a pair of spurred boots. The coat was stained and frayed, and the boots showed slight cracks, but he contrived in spite of these defects to give the impression of being a trim figure.

'Come in!' John invited him.

'What's this?' There was a note of menace in the voice; Mr Chirk shot a quick, suspicious look at Ben.

'It's only Jack: he's a Trojan! He's got a bang-up prancer, too. A big, rum prancer, he is, but he don't know how to shake hands for a carrot, not like Mollie. Oh, Mr Chirk, can I show Jack the way Mollie — '

'Stubble it!' said Chirk briefly.

'Ay, but — '

'Dub your mummer, will you?' Chirk growled. 'If Ned's away, I'll brush!'

'Don't lope off on my account!' said John, putting the pack of cards on the table, and rising to his feet. 'Go and stable the mare, Ben!'

Chirk, whose right hand had sought a pocket

133

lost in the folds of his coat, stepped back a pace. His hand came up with a jerk, a serviceable pistol in its grasp. 'Stand fast, cull!' he said softly. 'Seems to me young bottlehead here has been talking a trifle too free!'

'I ain't, I *ain't!*' asseverated Ben, distressed to perceive that his most valued friend was displeased with him. 'I ain't whiddled nothing, only as how Mollie shakes hands for a carrot! You don't want to brush, Mr Chirk! Honest, he's a bang-up cove, else I wouldn't ha' dubbed the jigger! And we got some rum peck and booze, Mr Chirk! There's a round o' beef, and a whole cheese, and — '

'Ben, go and stable the mare!' interrupted the Captain. 'You can put up your pistol, friend: I'm not a police-officer! God save the mark, do I look like one?'

Mr Chirk's left hand had shot out to grasp Ben by the shoulder, but it relaxed its grip. 'I'm bound to say you don't,' he replied, keeping his eyes on the Captain's face, and his pistol levelled. 'Maybe you're a swell-trap: I dunno that. What might you be doing here, if you ain't a trap?'

'That's a long story. Let the boy go!' said the Captain, walking over to the cupboard which served the toll-house as a larder, and collecting from its depths the beef which Mrs Skeffling had roasted on the spit that morning, and a large cheese. Setting these on the table, he glanced at Chirk, on whose lean countenance a smile was hovering, and said: 'You'll find a loaf of bread in the bin over there.'

Chirk slipped the pistol back into his pocket. 'You're a cool hand, ain't you?' he remarked curiously.

The Captain, emerging from the cupboard again with a jar of pickles and a pipkin of butter, said: 'Do you expect me to break into a sweat because you point a gun at me? I've been hoping you might come here sooner or later.'

'Oh, you have, have you?' said Chirk. 'And why — if I'm not making too bold to ask?'

'Well, as far as I can discover,' said John, holding a large jug under the spigot of his new barrel of beer, and watching the ale froth into it, 'you may be the only person who can tell me where Ned Brean may have gone to.'

'Ain't he here?' demanded Chirk.

'No, and hasn't been, since Friday evening.'

'Well, may I be stuck in the nitch!' exclaimed Chirk, considerably astonished. 'What should have taken him to lope off?'

'Don't you know?'

Chirk shook his head. 'Don't young Ben know?'

'No. He went out, telling Ben he would be back in an hour or so, and he hasn't been seen or heard of since.'

'Strike me lucky!' said Chirk blankly. 'Wonder what his lay is? He ain't one as suffers from windmills in the head neither. Nor he wouldn't pike on the bean without he took Ben along with him — leastways, not to my way of thinking.'

The Captain laid a plate and a knife and fork before him. 'Help yourself! Is he fond of Ben?'

'Well, I wouldn't say that,' temporized Chirk.

135

'He's a hard sort of a cove, if you take me, but he done his duty by the boy, so far as he was able.' He picked up the carving-knife, but lowered it again, looking in a puzzled way at his host. 'I don't know where Ned is, nor what lay he's on, and another thing I don't know is what *your* lay is! And nor I don't know what the likes of you are doing in this ken, because from the way you talk you're a nib-cove!'

'Oh, I'm here by accident!' replied John, pouring the beer into two mugs. 'I came to the pike on Friday night, and found Ben alone, and scared out of his wits, so as I had had enough of the weather, and *he* was afraid to be alone, I racked up for the night — thinking that his father would very likely return before morning. But he didn't, so here I am still.'

'So here you are still!' agreed Chirk, looking at him very hard. 'I suppose you're minding the gate, what's more!'

'That's it.'

'Well, if it is, you must be dicked in the nob!' said Chirk frankly.

John grinned at him. 'No, I'm quite sane. I've several reasons for remaining here. Besides, I don't know what the devil to do about the boy. He's scared of being sent to work in Sheffield, if his father don't return, and I've promised he shan't be thrown on the Parish.'

'Scared of that, is he?' Chirk gave a short laugh. 'Ay, he might well be! That's the way I started, when my old dad tipped off. By the time my mother had buried him decent we were properly dished-up. A couple of bordes — what

136

you call shillings, Mr Nib-Cove! — a groat, and three grigs was all she had left in the stocking. So I went to work in a factory. Not here: up north, it was. Just about Ben's age, I must ha' been. Three years I stayed, and I ain't forgotten, though I'm turned forty now, nor I never will, not if I reach fourscore! I loped off when my mother went to roost.'

'Was that when you took to the bridle-lay?' John asked.

'A peevy cove, ain't you?' Chirk said. 'What d'ye want to do? Cry rope on me? Who told you I was on the bridle-lay?'

'Who told you I was a green 'un?' retorted John.

Chirk smiled reluctantly, and applied himself to the beef. 'Danged if I know *what* you are!' he said. 'But I wasn't a rank-rider all them years ago. Lordy, when you get to be that you're top-o'-the-trees! I started on the dub-lay, and worked my way up.'

'Is it worth it?' John asked curiously.

Mr Chirk smiled a little wryly. 'It's all according to the way you look at it,' he replied. 'You might be lucky, and end up with the dibs in tune, but I ain't met many as did. It's a free life, and if you've a taste for excitement there'll be plenty o' that. The chances are you'll go up the ladder to bed — at York Gaol, with a Black-coat saying prayers, and the nubbing-cheat ready to top you. It's well enough when you're young, but when you get to my time o' life, and maybe have a fancy to settle down — well, that's where the rub comes, and no remedy! If I could lay my

137

hands on a bit o' balsam — and I don't mean a truss with six or seven goblins in it, and a couple o' diamond rings which turn out to be Bristol stone! — no, some real mint-sauce: a monkey, in some old gager's strong-box, or even a couple o' plums: why, I don't know but what I wouldn't turn to pound dealing! A tidy little farm, maybe. But I'm not a lucky cove: never have been!'

John got up to refill the ale-jug. 'What's Brean's lay?' he asked.

'I don't know.'

John laughed. 'A stupid question, Mr Chirk! You wouldn't tell me, if you did. But I want to find the man.'

'Hark 'ee!' said Chirk. 'If you was thinking, because I stable the mare here now and then, and maybe have a bite o' supper with Ned, he's a fence, or a baggage-man, you're going beside the cushion! He ain't — not to my knowledge! This ain't my beat, and I don't come here in the way o' business. What brings me here is another matter: private, you may say! If you're willing I should leave the mare for an hour, well! If you ain't — well again! I'll brush!'

'Oh, quite willing!' John said. 'I'm even willing to believe you don't know what may have befallen Brean, or where to get news of him — if you tell me so, man to man!

Chirk looked at him with, narrowed, searching eyes. 'What's in your mind?' he asked abruptly.

'Who is the man who visits Brean secretly, after dark? The man Ben is afraid of?'

Chirk pushed his chair back from the table. 'What's this? Trying to gammon me, guv'nor?

138

You'll catch cold at that!'

'No, it's the sober truth. That's what had Ben in such a sweat of fear, the night I came to this place. Some stranger he's never seen, nor been allowed to see. Brean pitched him a Canterbury tale to keep him from spying on the pair of them: told him if this mysterious visitor saw him he'd send him to work in the pits. If a tree so much as rustled out there — ' he jerked his head towards the back-door — 'the boy turned green with fear.'

'Sounds to me like a bag o' moonshine!' said Chirk incredulously. 'Why, he went off, happy as a grig, to put Mollie through her tricks! *He's* not scared!'

'Oh, not now! I told him no one could harm him while I was here, and he believed me.'

A gleam of humour lit Chirk's eyes, as they ran over his host. 'I should think he might,' he agreed. He stroked his chin thoughtfully. 'Wonder why the bantling never said a word to me about it? Him and me's good friends, and he tells me most things. Ned's a hard man, like I said, and he's not one to take notice of brats, even when they're of his own get. A monkey's allowance is what he gives Ben: more kicks than ha'pence!'

'How long is it since you were here last?' John asked.

'Matter of three weeks.'

'I've a shrewd suspicion it's happened since then. A pity! I had hoped you might know something. I've a notion there's something devilish queer afoot here, but what it is, or how

Brean came to be mixed up in it — *if* he is — I can't guess. I shouldn't think it could be what you call pound dealing, however: this visitor of his seems to be uncommonly anxious he shan't be seen, or recognized.'

Chirk dived a hand into his pocket, and drew forth a snuff-box. It was a handsome piece, as its present owner acknowledged, as he offered it, open, to John. 'Took it off of a fat old gager a couple o' years back,' he explained, with engaging frankness. 'Prigged his tatler, too, but I sold that. I'm a great one for a pinch o' merry-go-up, and this little box just happened to take my fancy, and I've kept it. I daresay I'd get a double finnup for it, too,' he added, sighing over his own prodigality. 'It's worth more, but when it comes to tipping over the dibs there ain't a lock as isn't a hog-grubber. Now, look 'ee here, Mr Nib-Cove — '

'I wish you will stop calling me that!' interrupted John. 'If it means, as I suspect it may, that you take me for some town-tulip, you're out! I'm a soldier!'

'Oh!' said Mr Chirk, helping himself to a generous pinch of his snuff. 'No offence, Soldier! Now, maybe I could drop in at one or two kens which I knows of, and where I might get news o' Ned Brean; but he never spoke a word to me about this cull which comes to see him secret. I'm bound to say it sounds to me like a Banbury story, but you ain't no halfling, nor you don't look like one o' them young bloods kicking up a lark, and I don't misdoubt you. I don't twig what any boman prig should be doing in a backward

140

place like this, but I'll tell you that there's ways a gatekeeper might be useful to such — if you greased him well in the fist! If so be as you was wishful to take a train o' pack-ponies through the pike, and no questions asked nor toll paid, for instance!'

'Yes, I'd thought of that,' John agreed. 'I've seen it done, but not here. Dash it, man, this is Derbyshire!'

'Just what I was thinking myself,' nodded Chirk. 'In the free-trading business, Soldier?'

John laughed. 'No, only for a week or two! I was picked up at sea once by a free-trading vessel, and made the voyage in her. A famous set of rascals they were, too, but they treated me well enough.'

'I should think,' said Chirk dryly, 'them coves at Bedlam must be looking for you all over! You ain't got a fancy to go on the rum-pad for a week or two, I s'pose?'

'Not I!' John grinned. 'It's pound dealing for me! Try it yourself! — I might be able to help you.'

'Thanking you kindly, I'd as lief stand on my own feet! Nor I don't see why you should want to help me.'

'As you please! When you see Rose Durward, give her a message from me!'

This brought Chirk up on to his feet, with a scrape of his chair across the floor, and a dangerous look in his eye. 'So that's it, is it?' he said softly. 'A man o' the town, are you, Soldier? Would that be why you're being so obliging as to keep the gate for Ned? Quite in the petticoat-line, I daresay! Well, if you're to her taste, she's welcome!'

'Tell her,' said the Captain, carefully trimming the lamp, which had begun to smoke, 'that I'll be hanged if I know what she finds to take her fancy in a damned, green-eyed, suspicious, quarrel-picking hedge-bird, but I'll stable his mare for him — if only to please her!'

Considerably taken aback, Chirk stood staring at him, his humorous mouth thinned, and a challenging frown in his eyes. 'There's not a soul but her knows why I come here,' he said. 'Not a soul, d'ye hear me? So if you know it, it looks uncommon like she told you, Soldier! P'raps you'll be so very obliging as to tell me how that came about?' He had thrown off his greatcoat when he sat down to the table, but his pistol lay beside his plate, and he picked it up. 'I'm a man as likes plain-speaking, Soldier — and a quick answer!' he said significantly.

'Are you?' said the Captain, a hint of steel in his pleasant voice. 'But I am not a man who likes to answer questions at the pistol-muzzle, Mr Chirk! Put that gun down!' He rose to his feet. 'You'll get hurt, you know, if you make me go to the trouble of wresting it away from you,' he warned him.

An involuntary grin lightened the severity of Chirk's countenance. He lowered the pistol, and exclaimed: 'Damme, if you don't beat all hollow, Soldier! It ain't me as would be hurt if I was to pull this trigger!'

'If you were to do anything so mutton-headed, you'd be an even bigger gudgeon than I take you for — which isn't possible!' said John. 'I've a strong liking for Rose, but I don't dangle after women ten years older than I am, however comely they may be!'

'You're Quality, and they're not particular where they throw out their damned lures — just for a bit o' sport to while away the time!' muttered Chirk.

'I shan't be particular where I throw *you* out, if you make me lose my temper!' said the Captain grimly. 'What the devil do you mean by talking of a decent woman as if she were a light frigate?'

Mr Chirk flushed, and pocketed his pistol. 'I never thought such!' he protested. 'It just put me in a tweak, thinking — But I see as I was mistaken! No offence, Soldier! The thing is, I get fair blue-devilled! There's times when I wish I'd never set eyes on Rose, seeing as she's one as is above my touch. She's respectable, and I'm a hedge-bird, and no help for it! But I did set eyes on her, and the more I make up my mind to it I won't come here no more, the more I can't keep away. Then I knew she'd whiddled the whole scrap to you — '

'Nothing of the sort! She never mentioned you,' interrupted John. 'It was her mistress who told me the story!'

Much abashed, Chirk begged his pardon. He then eyed him sideways, and said: 'A regular Long Meg *she* is, but a mort o' mettle, that I will say! Much like yourself, Soldier! Not scared of my pops! Did she tell you how it chanced that I met Rose?'

'She did, and it seemed to me that hedge-bird though you are you're a good fellow, for you didn't take their purses from them. Or were you afraid of Rose?'

Mr Chirk chuckled reminiscently. 'Ay, fit to tear the eyes out of my head she was! And her own sparkling that pretty as you never did see! But, lordy, Soldier, I never knew it was only a couple o' morts in the gig, or I wouldn't have held 'em up!'

'I believe you wouldn't indeed. Does Rose know that you come to this house?'

'No. Only you, and Ned, and young Ben knows that — and only you knows what my business is!'

'Never mind that! Tell Rose you've met me! There have been changes up at the Manor since you were last here!'

'Squire been put to bed with a shovel?' asked Chirk. 'Sick as a horse, he was, by what Rose told me.'

'Not that. But his grandson is at Kellands, with a friend. Name of Coate. What brings him into Derbyshire, no one knows: nothing good, I fancy!'

'Flash cove?' said Chirk, cocking an intelligent eyebrow.

'I'll cap downright!' said John, in the vernacular.

The eyebrows remained cocked; Chirk patted his pocket suggestively.

'No, no!' John said, laughing. 'Just try if you can discover what brought him to Kellands, and whether Ned Brean was concerned in it!' He saw

144

a quizzical look in Chirk's face, and added: 'Don't gammon me you can't do it! If there's havey-cavey business afoot, you can get wind of it more easily than another!'

At that moment, the door opened, and Ben slid somewhat warily into the kitchen. Aware of having incurred his friend's displeasure, he did not venture to address him; but Chirk said encouragingly: 'Come here, Benny!' and stretched out a hand. Much relieved, he bounded across the room. 'It's all right and tight, ain't it?' he asked anxiously. 'And I give Mollie — '

'Never you mind about Mollie! You tell me this, son! Where's your dad loped off to?'

'I dunno. She knows me, Mollie does! She — '

'Don't you tell me no lies!' said Chirk sternly. 'Your dad never loped off without telling you when he'd be back!'

'Well, he did!' said Ben, wriggling to shake off the grip on his shoulder. ''Leastways, he said he'd be back in an hour, but he never said no more. It don't matter, Mr Chirk! I got Jack instead, and we has a bang-up dinner *every* day, and he's learnt me to play cards. I like him better than me dad, much! He's a swell cove!'

'There's a young varmint for you!' said Chirk, with some severity. 'Now, you stand still, Benny, else you don't give Mollie another carrot as long as you live! Did you ever know your dad go off like this before?'

Ben shook his head vigorously, and once more proffered the suggestion that his dad had been pressed.

'And all the same to you if he was, I suppose!'

said Chirk. 'Think, now! Didn't he ever leave you to mind the gate before?'

'Ay. He did when he went to market, or the Blue Boar.'

'Did he leave you all night?'

'No,' Ben muttered, hanging his head.

'Benny!' said Chirk warningly. 'You know what'll happen to you if you tell me any more bouncers, don't you?'

'Me dad said I wasn't to tell no one, else he'd break every bone in me body!' said Ben desperately.

'Well, I won't squeak on you, so he won't know you whiddled the scrap. And if you don't, *I'll* break every bone in your body, so you won't be any better off,' said Chirk calmly. 'This ain't the first time your dad's loped off, is it?'

'Yes, it is!' Ben asseverated. 'Only onct, before, he went off and told me to mind the gate in the night, and if anyone was to ask where he was he said to tell 'em he was laid down on his bed with a touch o' the colic! And he come back before it was morning, honest he did!'

'Where did he go to?'

'I dunno! It was dark, and he woke me up — 'least, he didn't, 'cos there was a waggon, or something, went through the gate, and *that* woke me. And me dad said as I was to sit by the fire in here till he come back, and to keep me chaffer close, 'cos he was going out.'

'How long was he gone, Benny?'

'A goodish while. All night, I dessay,' replied Ben vaguely. 'Nobody comed through the gate, and I went to sleep, and when me dad come in

146

the fire was gone out.'

Chirk let him go. He glanced up at John, slightly frowning. 'Queer start!' he remarked.

'Which way did that waggon go, Ben?' asked John.

After a moment's reflection, Ben said that he thought it was going Sheffield-way. He added that they didn't often get them along the road after dark; and then, feeling that the subject was exhausted, begged for a sugar-lump to give to the mare. John nodded permission, and he sped forth once more, leaving the two men to look at one another.

'It *is* a queer start,' said Chirk, rubbing his chin. 'Danged if I know what to make of it!'

'What had the waggon to do with it? What was on it?'

'It don't make a ha'porth o' difference if there was a cageful o' wild beasts on it, I don't see what call Ned had to go along with it!' said Chirk. 'If a party o' mill-kens have been and slummed Chatsworth, and loaded the swag on to that there waggon, they might grease Ned in the fist to keep his mummer shut, but they wouldn't want him to go along with them!' He pulled out a large silver watch, and consulted it. 'Time I was brushing, Soldier! I don't take the mare up to Kellands, so if you'll let her bide in the shed till I come back, I'll be obliged to you.'

The Captain nodded. 'She'll be safe enough. Think it over, Chirk! — and give my message to Rose!'

8

It was some two hours later when Chirk came back to the toll-house, and he found the Captain alone, Ben having been sent, protesting, to bed an hour before. The very faintest clink of spurred heels was all that warned John of the highwayman's return; he caught the sound, and looked up from his task of applying blacking to his top-boots, just as the door opened, and Chirk once more stood before him. In answer to the questioning lift of an eyebrow, he nodded, and, setting the boot down, lounged over to the cupboard, from which he produced a couple of bottles. Whatever suspicions had still lurked in Chirk's mind, at parting, seemed to have been laid to rest. He cast off his coat, without taking the precaution of removing his pistol from its pocket, and, leaving it over the back of a chair beside the door, walked to the fire, and stirred the smouldering logs with one foot. 'Where's the bantling?' he asked.

'Asleep,' John replied, lacing two glasses of port with gin. 'He wanted to wait for you to come back, but I packed him off — as soon as he'd shown me your Mollie.' He handed one of the glasses to his guest. 'A neatish little mare: strong in work, I should think.'

Chirk nodded. 'Ay. Takes her fences flying and standing. Clever, too. She's the right stamp for a man of my trade. She wouldn't do for a man of your size. What do you ride, Soldier?'

'Seventeen stone,' John said, with a grimace.

'Ah! You'll need to keep your prancers high in the flesh, I don't doubt.' He lifted his glass. 'Here's your good health! It ain't often I get given flesh-and-blood: it's to be hoped I don't get flustered.' He drank, smacked his lips, and said approvingly: 'A rum bub! Rose said as I was to tell you she'd be along in the morning to fetch your shirt. Proper set-about she was, when I told her I'd made your acquaintance: combed my hair with a joint-stool, pretty well!' He smiled reminiscently, looking down into the fire, one arm laid along the mantelshelf. Then he sighed, and turned his head. 'Seems I'll have to put a bullet into that Coate, Soldier. Rose is mortal set on getting rid of him.'

'She's not more set on it than I am, but if you go about the business with your barking-iron I'll break your neck!' promised John genially. 'As good take a bear by the tooth!'

'The old gager — the Squire — saw him tonight,' said Chirk. 'Sent for him to go to his room, which has put them all in a quirk, for fear it might send him off in a convulsion. It hadn't — not while I was there, anyways.' He drained his glass, and set it down. 'I'll pike off now, Soldier, but you'll be seeing me again. Maybe there's one or two kens where I might get news of Ned.' A wry smile twisted his mouth. 'I'm to take my orders from you, unless I'm wishful to raise a breeze up at Kellands. So help me bob, *I* don't know why I don't haul my wind before that dimber mort of mine's turned me into a regular nose!'

John smiled, and held out his hand. 'We shall do!' he said.

'*You* may do! *I'm* more likely to be nippered!' retorted Chirk; but he gripped John's hand, adding: 'No help for it! Fall back, fall edge, I've pledged my word to Rose I'll stand buff. *Women!*'

Upon this bitterly enunciated dissyllable he was gone, as noiselessly as he had come.

The Captain's first visitor, the following morning, was Rose, who stepped briskly into the toll-house soon after nine o'clock, cast a critical eye over Mrs Skeffling's handiwork, wrested from her clutches the torn shirt, and sallied forth into the garden in search of Captain Staple. She found him chopping wood. He greeted her with his disarming smile, and a cheerful good-morning. He then listened with becoming meekness to a comprehensive scold, which, although apparently aimed at the unsuitability of his occupation and his attire, was, as he perfectly understood, a punishment for having dared to discover the trend of her maidenly affections.

'But chopping wood is capital exercise!' he said.

'Capital exercise indeed! I'm sure I don't know what the world's coming to! And I'll thank you, Mr Jack, not to go sending messages to me that you'll stable Mr Chirk's mare to please me! I never did! I declare I was never so mortified! I should be a deal better pleased if Mr Chirk would take himself off, and not come bothering me any more, for I'm a respectable woman, and keep company with a highwayman I will not!'

'No, I do think he must abandon that way of life,' agreed John.

'It's nothing to me what he does!' said Rose. 'Poor Chirk!'

Her face puckered. She whisked out her handkerchief and rather fiercely blew her nose. 'It's no manner of use, Mr Jack!' she said, in a muffled tone. 'You ought to know better than to encourage him! I can't and I won't marry a man who might be carried off to gaol any moment!'

'Certainly not: you would never know a day's peace! Besides, it's not at all the thing. But he doesn't expect you to marry him under such circumstances as that, does he?'

She sat down on the chopping-block, and wiped her eyes. 'No, he says he'll settle down, and live honest, farming. But talking pays no toll, sir, and where is the money to come from to buy a cottage, let alone a farm?'

The Captain refrained from telling her that Mr Chirk proposed to found his career as an honest farmer on the theft of some traveller's strong-box, and merely said: 'Would you marry him, if he were not a highwayman?'

She nodded, and disappeared into the handkerchief again. 'To think, after all these years, and the offers I've had, I should take and fall in love with a common vagabond!' she said, into its folds. 'Enough to make my poor mother turn in her grave! For I was brought up respectable, Mr Jack!'

'So was I, and devilish dull I found it! But Chirk's a good fellow: I like him. He's head over

151

ears in love with you, too.'

A convulsive sniff greeted this. 'Well, if he wants to please me, he'll stop holding people up, and so I've told him. Let him find Brean, like you want him to, and see if he can't get rid of that Coate out of our house! But I'll never marry any man while Miss Nell needs me — and need me she will, poor lamb, when the master goes! And that day's not far distant.'

'I hope she won't need you.'

This brought her head up. She looked very hard at him for a minute; and then got briskly to her feet, and shook out her skirts. 'I hope she won't, Mr Jack — and that's the truth!' She saw his hand held out, and clasped it warmly. 'I have that torn shirt in my basket, and Mrs Skeffling's ironing your other one,' she said, reverting to her usual manner. 'You won't find she's starched the points as they should be, but she's done her best, and I hope, sir, it'll be a lesson to you not to go jauntering about the country with only two shirts to your name!'

With these valedictory words, she took her departure; and John returned to his task of chopping wood. He was called from it by a shout of 'Gate!' and went through the house to answer it, picking up the book of tickets on the way. A phaeton was drawn up on the Sheffield side of the gate; and holding the reins was Henry Stornaway, wearing a drab coat whose numerous shoulder-capes falsely proclaimed his ability to drive to an inch. A pair of showy, half-bred chestnuts, which the Captain mentally wrote down as bone-setters, were harnessed to the vehicle; and Mr Stornaway was unable to produce any coin of less value than five shillings to pay for his sixpenny toll. He said, as John pulled a handful of coins out of his pocket: 'Hallo! Don't know you, do I? Where's the other fellow?'

'Away, sir,' replied John, handing him his change.

'Away? Ay! But where's he gone to?'

'Couldn't say, sir,' said John, holding up the ticket.

'Nonsense! If you're taking his place, of course you know where he is! Come on, now: no humbug!'

Several travellers had asked John what had become of Brean, but none had evinced more than a cursory interest in his where-abouts. He had not previously encountered Henry Stornaway, but he began to have a suspicion of his identity, and did his best to school his features to an expression of stolid stupidity. To every question put to him he returned evasive answers, and noted, with interest, Mr Stornaway's patent dissatisfaction with these. For some unexplained reason, Brean's disappearance had discomposed this would-be blood of the Fancy. Abandoning the lofty tone, he descended to cajolery; said, with a wink, that he and Brean were old acquaintances; and invited John, with one hand significantly jingling coins in his pocket, to tell him where Brean might be found.

'I don't know, sir. He went off sudden-like,' John answered. 'Leaving me to mind the pike,' he added. 'I ain't seen him since, nor heard of him.'

The pale eyes stared down into his; it struck him that there was less colour than ever in cheeks naturally sallow. 'When did he leave his post? You know *that*, at all events!'

'Now, when would it have been?' pondered John, the very picture of bucolic stupidity. 'Was it Friday night, or Saturday night?'

'Come, come, he didn't go off in the night!'

'Oh, yes, sir! 'Deed he did! After dark it was,' John asseverated truthfully. He glanced at the chestnuts, reacting to an unquiet hand on the reins. 'Horses on the fret, sir!' he suggested.

'Damn the horses! Who are you? How do you come to be here?'

'Name of Staple, sir: cousin of Ned Brean's!'

'Oh! Well, it's no concern of mine!' Henry said, and drove on, calling over his shoulder: 'I'm only bound for the village, and shall be back in a few minutes! See you don't keep me waiting!'

John shut the gate, looking thoughtfully after him. He found that Ben was at his elbow, and glanced down at him. 'Who was that, Ben?'

'That rasher o' wind?' said Ben disparagingly. 'That was Mr Stornaway, that was. He's a slow-top. Drives a couple of puffers.'

John nodded, as though this confirmed his suspicion; and, leaving Ben to look after the gate, went off across the field which lay behind the toll-house to the barn where Beau was stabled.

He was engaged in grooming the big bay when a shadow darkened the doorway, and he glanced over his shoulder, and saw Nell Stornaway standing on the threshold. He put the brush down quickly, and moved to meet her, saying

154

involuntarily: 'You! I dared not hope I should see you today!'

Her colour was a little heightened, but she replied in a rallying tone: 'No, indeed! I don't wonder at it, and am only surprised you can look me in the face after *such* treachery!'

He was standing immediately before her, smiling down at her, a fair young giant, in stained buckskins and a coarse shirt, open at the neck, and with the sleeves rolled up to show his powerful forearms. 'What treachery?' he asked.

'Dissembler! Did you not betray to Rose that I had divulged her story?'

'No, only to Chirk!'

'I shall not allow you to excuse yourself on that head! Such a scold as I have had! You deserve I should lay an information against you with the trustees of the tolls!'

'Oh, no! For I have had a scold too, you know! Only Rose forgave me!'

'You made up to her quite scandalously, I daresay! Ah, is this your Beau?' She moved towards the horse as she spoke, looking him over with an appraising eye. 'Oh, you are a very fine fellow: complete to a shade!' she said, patting the arched neck. 'Yes, I have some sugar in my pocket, but who told you so, sir? There, then!' She looked round at John. 'Did you call him Beau for his good points, or for his Roman nose? My brother told me that Beau was the name given to the Duke of Wellington, in the Peninsula.'

'For his nose, of course. Do you like him?'

'Very much. I should think he can go well upon wind?'

'Yes, and best pace for thirty minutes — with me up!'

'That is something indeed! I am glad to have made his acquaintance. I must go now. I came this way, you know, because I had an errand to Mrs Huggate; and by riding across this field, and through the spinney, I evade the toll-gate!'

'Is that what you wished to do?'

She said lightly: 'To be sure! Everyone desires to evade toll-gates! You must be aware of *that*!'

'Of course. I could not help hoping that you came this way to see me. Now tell me what a coxcomb I am — but I know it already!'

The smile wavered on her lips; she looked away. 'No, indeed! I — that is, Ben told me — and there *is* something I have been meaning to speak to Mrs Huggate about!'

'Nell! My love!'

She lifted her head, looking wonderingly up into his face. The next instant she was in his arms, crushed against his great chest. He spoke magical words: 'Little love! My dear one!'

No one had ever called Miss Stornaway little before, and never had she felt so little, or so weak. Captain Staple was holding her with his left arm only, his right hand being employed in pushing up her chin, but it was far too strong a hold to admit of any possibility of escape. She attempted none, but lifted her face in the most natural way, like a child asking to be kissed. Captain Staple, tightening his hold on this vital, yielding armful in a manner as gratifying as it

156

was uncomfortable, responded to the mute invitation promptly and thoroughly, and forgot the world until Beau, possibly affronted by such behaviour, or perhaps hopeful of further largesse, nudged him with sufficient force to recall him to a sense of his surroundings.

'Damn the brute!' said Captain Staple, removing himself and his love to a bench over against the wall. 'My darling, my darling!'

The masterful Miss Stornaway, discovering suddenly the advantages of a large shoulder, snuggled her cheek into it, and heaved a deep sigh. She also clutched a fold of that coarse shirt, but Captain Staple detached her hand, and carried it to his lips. She was moved to expostulate. 'This is only the fifth time we have met!'

'I knew the instant I set eyes on you,' he said simply.

'Oh, was it so with you, too?' She pulled his hand to her exposed cheek, and nursed it there. 'You stood there, staring at me — such a great stupid! — and I could think of nothing else, all through the Service in Church! And when I stood beside you, I looked up, not down, and felt myself not overgrown in the least, but quite small!'

''Just as high as my heart,'' quoted Captain Stable.

Her fingers tightened on his. 'John, John!'

From the other end of the barn Beau snorted, and tossed up his head. This drew a gurgle from Miss Stornaway. 'I don't think Beau was ever more shocked in his life!'

157

'On the contrary! If only I had had the forethought to teach him how to do it, he would bend the knee to you, my treasure!'

She sighed again. 'He is too wise. I think I must have become infected with your madness. It will not do! I am sure it will not do! I have no fortune — not a penny!'

He sounded amused. 'What made you think I was hanging out for a rich wife, my love?'

'Oh, no! But your mother — your sister — '

'Will adore you! I am more afraid of what your grandfather may say to my pretensions. My fortune I should rather call an independance; and I have no expectations worth the name. Tell me when it will be most convenient for me to visit Sir Peter!'

But at that she drew herself out of his arm, trouble in her face. 'No, you must not! Please, John, don't try to see him!'

'But, my darling — !'

'Yes, yes, I know what you would say, and indeed I want more than anything that you and he should be acquainted! But I dare not present you to him yet! You see, he insisted on sending for Coate last night, and we are in the greatest anxiety! He seemed not to be disturbed, but Winkfield — his valet — could not be easy about him. He knows him so well, you understand: better than anyone, I think! He thought him too quiet. He has told me since that had Grandpapa but flown into one of his old rages he would not have felt so apprehensive — though Dr Bacup has warned us never to provoke him! He did not go to bed, and he thinks Grandpapa scarcely closed his eyes all night. He desired Joseph to ride over to Dr Bacup's as soon as it was light, but before the doctor could reach Kellands my grandfather had sent for my cousin to go to him. Winkfield dared not oppose him: he will never tolerate opposition! We don't know what he said to Henry — or what Henry may have said to him, but he scarcely spoke to Winkfield or to me afterwards, and he looked so old and so white that we were cast into alarm. He is laid down upon his bed now, for Dr Bacup gave him some drops of laudanum, which sent him to sleep. The doctor has charged us most straitly not to vex or to agitate him, but to keep him as quiet as we may, and above all not to permit him to tease himself with worry. We mean to tell him, if he should ask, that Coate has gone away, though Winkfield doubts he will not believe us. Dr Bacup considers he may well rally — he is so strong, you know! — and if he does so, *then* I will tell him that my absurd gatekeeper is so foolish as to wish to marry me, and ask him if you may come to visit him. You must not try to see him yet!' She saw that he was looking grave, and laid her hand shyly on his knee. 'Please, John — !'

He took her hand at once, and held it comfortingly. 'You must know that I should do nothing to injure your grandfather, Nell. I was only wondering — But you are the judge! My poor girl! I wish I could help you!'

She smiled at him. 'Oh, if you knew the happiness of knowing you are close, and would come to me, if I called to you! I must go now: I left Rose to watch by my grandfather while Winkfield rests.'

He made no effort to detain her, but got up, saying: 'You have your horse?'

'Tethered outside — was not that indiscreet of me? What a ramshackle wife you have, chosen, Captain Staple! Good gracious, how comes my hat to be lying on the ground?'

He picked it up, and dusted it. 'I think it fell off,' he said. 'It was confoundedly in the way, you know!'

'Wretch! You pushed it off, as though I had a dozen hats to my name!' she said merrily, stretching out her hand for it.

He gave it to her, but before she could put it on again, took her back into his arms. 'If you must go, kiss me goodbye!'

She drew his head down. 'Stoop, then, my giant! You are out of my reach!' There was a pause; she said uncertainly: 'Let me go now! John, I *must* go!'

'Yes,' he said, releasing her. 'You must, of course. Come! I'll put you up in the saddle!'

They went out into the autumn sunlight. He went to fetch her hack from the sheep-fence, to which she had hitched the bridle, and led him up to her, testing the girths before he threw her into the saddle. As she arranged the folds of her skirt, he said: 'When shall I see you again?'

'Tomorrow, unless Grandpapa should be ill, or — or there was some other impediment. Henry, by the by, has been asking me the most searching questions about you. I almost fear that he may suspect me of having a *tendre* for a mere gatekeeper, but I think I fobbed him off.'

'I don't think it's that. He passed the gate this morning, and tried his best to discover what has become of Brean.'

'What did you tell him?'

'Nothing: I was the very picture of bovine stupidity! He is frightened of something — and I wish I knew what it may be!'

'What can Henry have to do with Brean?' she wondered.

'When we know that we shall perhaps know the whole. Go, now, my love! And remember that I *am* close to you!'

'I could not forget that,' she said simply, and touched her horse with her heel, and rode away.

Captain Staple watched her canter across the field, and went slowly back to finish grooming Beau.

Half an hour later, when he re-entered the toll-house, he found Joseph Lydd in possession of the kitchen. Mr Lydd's coat hung over the back of a chair, and he was engaged in polishing Beau's bit. He looked up when the Captain came in, and grinned at him. ''Morning, guv'nor! I was coming to look for you, but seeing as how I happened to catch sight of this here bridle, which you brought in to clean — and not before it needed it, if I may make so bold! — I thought I might as well rub it up for you. You'll find your stirrup-irons over there.'

'Thank you! I'm much obliged to you!' John said. 'Draw yourself a glass of beer, and one for me, too! Is Ben on the gate?'

'In a manner of speaking, he is. He was giving

young Biggin pepper ten minutes ago: regular mill they was having, and the claret flowing very free, which it gen'rally does, when a couple of boys get to sparring,' said Lydd, collecting two glasses and a jug from the cupboard. 'Howsever, I dessay they've thought of something else to do by this time, for they was both blowing when I saw 'em.'

'Up to mischief, I expect,' said John, vigorously scrubbing his hands at the sink. 'What brings you here this morning?'

'You're wanted up at the Manor, guv'nor, that's what.'

John looked quickly over his shoulder at him. 'Who wants me?'

'Squire,' said Lydd, filling the jug. 'Sent for me first thing, he did. His compliments, and he'll be happy to see you this evening, if you'll be so kind as to give him the pleasure of your company. Which, begging your pardon, sir, you better do, because he ain't taking no for an answer.'

John rinsed the soap from his hands, and turned to pick up the towel. 'There's nothing I should like better, but — I have seen your mistress this morning, and she tells me that he must not be worried by visitors.'

'He won't be worried,' responded Lydd calmly. 'The only thing as 'ud worrit him 'ud be if we wasn't to obey orders. What's more, Miss Nell don't know as he wants to see you, guv'nor, because he ain't told her, nor no one's got to tell her.'

'What does his valet say?' John asked abruptly.

'He says as Squire's got something on his

162

mind, and he'd as lief have it took off. He did take the liberty of suggesting to Squire as p'raps he hadn't better have no visitor today, but he got his nose snapped off for his pains, Squire being on his high ropes, and telling the pair of us he ain't burnt to the socket yet. Damned our eyes proper, he did,' said Lydd, with simple pride.

'If he is well enough to see me this evening, I'll come,' John said. 'But I can't leave the boy alone here after dark: he's scared. Will you mind the gate for me?'

'That's all right and tight, guv'nor. The way Mr Winkfield and me has it planned, I've sent the stable-lad off home, and told him he needn't come back till the morning, so there won't be no one in the stables, them two beauties of Mr Henry's and Mr Coate's, which calls themselves grooms, taking themselves off regular to the boozing-ken up the road each evening. If they're back afore midnight it'll be for the first time, nor it wouldn't matter if they was, because they'll be too muddled to notice a strange horse — even if they was to go into the stables, which I never knew them do yet, not at that time o' night. You don't catch *them* making sure all's right afore they turns in!' said Lydd, with bitter scorn. 'If Squire's still of the same mind, I'll come along here when he's had his dinner, and I'll tell you the way. It ain't difficult, and the moon'll be up. All you got to do, guv'nor, is to turn in the first gate you come to, right-handed, a matter of a mile up the road. It'll take you to the stables: it don't go past the house. There's a path which leads up to the side-door: you can't mistake it.

163

Mr Winkfield will be there to take you to Squire.'

Thus it came about that when Ben, released after his dinner from attendance on the gate, returned at dusk after an afternoon of illicit adventure with Master Biggin, he was surprised to find the Captain's horse stabled once more in the shed. When he slid, somewhat guiltily, into the kitchen, he was startled to perceive that his protector was wearing the shirt ironed that morning by Mrs Skeffling, a well-tied cravat, and his top-boots. He had not put on his coat or his waistcoat, and he was engaged in the homely occupation of frying eggs in a pan over the fire, but those gleaming top-boots filled Ben with foreboding. In patent dismay he stood staring up at the Captain, his ruddy cheeks whitening.

John turned his head, surveying him with the hint of a smile in his eyes. 'I suppose, if I did my duty by you, I should send you supperless to bed, shouldn't I?' he remarked. 'What devilry have you been up to, you young rascal?'

'Guv'nor — you ain't going away?' Ben blurted out, his lip trembling.

'No, I'm not going away, but I have to go out this evening. You needn't look so scared, you silly little noddy! Mr Lydd is coming to mind the gate, so you won't be alone.'

'You're going to tip the double!' Ben said, his face sharp with suspicion. 'Don't go, guv'nor, don't go! You *said* you wouldn't leave me, not till me dad comes back!'

'Listen, Ben! Whatever happens, I shan't go away without telling you! You'll find me here when you wake up in the morning: that's a promise! Mr Lydd will stay here till I come back. Now, you wash all that dirt off your face and hands, and set the plates out!'

Ben, whose experience had not taught him to place any degree of reliance on the promises of his elders, burst into tears, and reiterated his conviction that he was to be left to his fate.

'Good God!' exclaimed John, setting the frying-pan down in the hearth. '*Come* here, you wretched little goosecap!' He picked up a candle, took Ben by the ear, and led him to Brean's bedroom. 'Does that look as though I meant to run away?'

Ben stopped knuckling his eyes. When he had assimilated the fact that the Captain's ivory brushes still graced the chest of drawers, together with his shaving-tackle, and the knife he used for paring his nails, he became very much more cheerful; and by the time Joseph Lydd arrived at the toll-house, soon after eight o'clock, he was able to greet him with perfect equanimity.

Lydd, who was riding the cob, slid from the saddle, and winked broadly at the Captain. 'You're looked for, sir,' he said. 'Pretty bobbish he is — considering!'

'Bring the cob round the back, to the shed, then,' John said. 'Beau's there. I must saddle-up.'

'Begging your pardon, guv'nor, that's *my* trade! Come on, booberkin! You show me this big prancer I've heard so much about!'

Half an hour later, Captain Staple trod up the path which led from the stables at Kellands to the eastern wing of the house. As he approached it, a door was opened, and lamp-light showed

165

him the silhouette of a man, who stood aside, and bowed, saying, in a quiet, precise voice: 'Good-evening, sir. Will you be pleased to step this way?'

Captain Staple, entering the house, found himself in a flagged passage. An old chest stood against one wall, and he laid his hat and whip on this. As he straightened his cravat, he glanced down at Winkfield, seeing an elderly man, with grizzled hair, a pair of steady gray eyes set in an impassive countenance, and the unmistakeable stamp of the gentleman's gentleman. 'You're Sir Peter's man? How is your master?'

Some flicker of emotion crossed Winkfield's face. He replied: 'He is — as well as can be expected, sir. If you will follow me — ? You will excuse my taking you up this staircase: it is not desirable that I should conduct you to the main hall.'

'No, I know. I am quite ready.'

He was led up to the gallery where the Squire's rooms were situated, and ushered into the dressing-room. 'What name should I say, sir?' enquired Winkfield.

'Captain Staple.'

'Winkfield bowed again, and opened the door into the big bedchamber. Sir Peter was seated in his wing-chair, motionless; and beside him, reading to him a sporting article in one of the weekly journals, was his granddaughter. She looked up as the door opened.

'Captain Staple!' said Winkfield.

9

The journal was cast aside; Nell rose swiftly, her face a study of conflicting emotions. Astonishment, incredulity, anger were all there. She looked magnificent, her eyes flaming, her colour suddenly heightened, and her breast, very white against the green of her old velvet gown, heaving with her quickened breath. Captain Staple, pausing on the threshold, met the challenge and the reproach in her eyes with the ghost of a rueful smile, and the slightest shake of his head.

'Pray come in, Captain Staple!'

The words, which were uttered by her grandfather, made Nell look quickly down at him, a still greater astonishment widening her eyes. He had raised his head, and was holding his quizzing-glass up. Through it he unhurriedly surveyed the Captain from head to foot. Then he let it fall, and held out his hand. 'How do you do? I am glad that you have found yourself able to visit me, sir. You will forgive me for not rising to greet you: it is not, I regret to say, within my power to get up without assistance.'

The Captain came across the room, and took the hand in his. 'How do you do, sir? It is I, rather, who should ask your pardon for coming to you so improperly dressed. Indeed, I have never more regretted being parted from my baggage!'

Sir Peter sought his quizzing-glass again, and

levelled it. 'Just as I thought: Scott!' he remarked.

The Captain smiled. 'Why, yes, sir!'

'Schultz used to make my coats, but you military men always go to Scott. I fancy, Captain Staple, that you need no introduction to my granddaughter?'

'No, sir.' John turned to shake hands with Nell. His fingers gripped hers reassuringly. 'I made Miss Stornaway's acquaintance three days ago.'

'Just so!' said Sir Peter, regarding them from under drooping eyelids. 'You must know, Nell, that Captain Staple is here in response to my invitation. I have had a great curiosity to meet him.'

'Miss Stornaway knows, sir, that it has been my earnest wish to visit you. Had it not been for your indisposition, I must have requested permission to do so.'

'Ah! I am, unfortunately, beset by persons who, from folly and good-will, seek to spare me the least excitement, and succeed only in vexing me beyond bearing!' said Sir Peter acidly.

John laughed. 'It is too bad, sir! But I perceive that you contrive, in spite of anything they may do, to get your own way!'

As he spoke, he gently compelled Nell to seat herself again, and himself went to the chair on the opposite side of the fireplace to his host's. Winkfield came back into the room, carrying the tea-tray. He shot one look at his master, and appeared to be satisfied, for he did not look at him again, but instead permitted himself to smile

168

primly at Nell, as he set the tray down on a small table in front of her.

She began to pour out. Sir Peter said: 'Don't be alarmed! When my granddaughter has retired, you shall try my brandy.'

'To own the truth, sir,' said John, getting up, and going to the tea-table to receive from Nell's hands a cup and saucer, 'the sight of a tea-tray is most welcome!' He glanced round the room, saw a small table, and brought it to Sir Peter's chair, and set the cup and saucer down on it, within reach of his right hand. 'In my present — er — employment, such niceties are unknown. Such guests as I have prefer to take their refreshment out of a barrel or a bottle.' He took his own cup from Nell, and went back again to his chair.

Sir Peter gave a dry chuckle. 'No doubt! Do you find your present employment congenial?'

'Not entirely,' returned the Captain. 'I think it would soon grow to be excessively irksome. One's movements are so restricted! I must own, however, that there is more to gate-keeping that I had previously supposed. I had no notion how many people there were in the world bent on cheating the tolls, for instance!'

Nell saw that her grandfather was looking amused. Her inward agitation grew less; she found herself able to put in a word, encouraging the Captain to continue on these lines. Her meetings with him had all been informal; she now realized that his manners, on more conventional occasions, had just that well-bred ease which she knew must please Sir Peter. He talked like a sensible man, and with a great deal of humour; and she soon saw that there was no need for her to feel anxious lest he should let fall some remark which would perturb her grandfather. Her heart did indeed take a jump into her mouth when Sir Peter asked him what he supposed had become of Brean; but he replied without hesitation, and with a twinkle in his eye, saying: 'I'm much afraid, sir, that he may be languishing in gaol, and I trust, for his sake, it won't come to the ears of his employers. It seems pretty plain that he went off on the spree, dipped rather too deep, and ended the night by falling foul of the watch. I expect there was a lively mill: four out of five of my troopers were always fatally ready to sport their canvases as soon as they became top-heavy!'

'You were in the cavalry, Captain Staple?'

'3rd Dragoon Guards, sir. I sold out in '14.'

'You should be a hunting-man. Shires?'

The Captain shook his head. 'Above my touch. I've had a day or two with the Quorn, but the most of my hunting is provincial. My home is in Hertfordshire. I find I get very good sport there with a modest stable. A friend of mine, who hunts regularly with the Quorn, assures me that a minimum of ten horses is necessary to him — and, having ridden over his country, I can readily believe it.'

'Twelve! Better, fourteen!' said Sir Peter, roused to animation. 'I remember . . . '

His granddaughter, calling down silent blessings on her lover's head, leaned back in her chair, and was content to listen to Sir Peter enjoying himself. His stories, which she had heard many times, she did not much attend to: it was enough to know that he was happy, forgetting present trouble in memories of bygone and better days. Had he shown clumsiness in his dealings with Sir Peter, she must still have loved Captain Staple; but his tact, which sprang, she knew, from kindliness, could not but enhance his value in her eyes. She fell into a pleasant reverie, from which she was aroused presently by hearing Sir Peter say: 'Staple . . . There was a Staple up at Oxford in my time. Are you related to Saltash?'

'I'm his cousin, sir.'

'You are, are you?' Sir Peter picked up his snuff-box, and placed it in his enfeebled left hand, flicking it open. 'The man I knew must have been his grandfather. We made the Grand Tour at much the same time. I remember meeting him in Rome, in '63, or '64 — I forget. He had some kind of a tutor in tow, but he was getting his education from a charming little barque of frailty. Called herself a Contessa. No such thing, of course, but nobody cared for that. First and last, she cost him a pretty penny, but he used to be very well blunted. Gave capital parties, too: all the bucks and the Cyprians used to go. Iced champagne punch: he had a way of mixing it he learned from some fellow in Frankfurt: made you devilish castaway, if you weren't accustomed to it. Staple was, of course: carried his wine very well. Never saw him really shot in the neck, though he wasn't often stone-sober, in those days. Believe he settled down when he came into the title.'

Captain Staple, who had listened with great enjoyment to these engaging reminiscences, said: 'From anything I've ever heard of him, that sounds very like my grandfather, sir. Didn't they call him Mops-and-Brooms?'

'Mops-and-Brooms!' echoed Sir Peter. '*That* was it! So you're his grandson!'

It was plain that his relationship to this erratic peer did Captain Staple no disservice in the eyes of his host. Sir Peter, saying regretfully that there were few men of his stamp alive today, lapsed into a silence charged with memory, and sat staring into the fire until Winkfield came into the room to remove the tea-tray. John, who had been watching him, exchanged a glance with Nell, nodded in response to the message in her eyes, and rose to his feet.

The movement seemed to bring Sir Peter back with a jerk to the present. He raised his head from his breast, and said authoritatively: 'Time you were off to your bed, Nell! Captain Staple will excuse you.'

'I think it is time I too was off, sir,' John said.

'Nonsense! Sit down! Don't humbug me you go to bed at this hour!'

'May I not come to see you again tomorrow?' John suggested.

'You might not find me, young man,' Sir Peter said, with a grim smile. 'I don't know how much time I have left to me, and I can't afford to waste it. Set out the brandy, Winkfield, and then take yourself off! I'll ring when I want you.'

'I shall be in the dressing-room, sir,' said Winkfield.

He appeared to address his master, but his eyes were on John's face. John nodded, and he bowed very slightly.

'You may kiss me good-night, Nell, and then be off to Rose. You will not go downstairs: do you hear me, girl?'

She bent over him, and kissed his brow. 'Very plainly, dearest! Indeed, I do not mean to go downstairs. Pray do not keep Captain Staple too long from his gate!'

He waved her away impatiently. She crossed the room to the door, which John was holding open, and paused, holding out her hand. 'Good-night — Captain Staple!'

He carried her hand to his lips. 'Good-night — Miss Stornaway!' he returned, smiling down at her.

She went out, and he closed the door behind her, and turned to see Sir Peter's quizzing-glass raised again.

'H'm! Pour yourself out some brandy!'

'Later, perhaps, sir, if I may.'

'Well-primed, eh? Think if *you* drink it, *I* shall — and damn the doctor!'

'No, I've not been primed. Am I to pour some for you, sir?'

'No. There's some damned cordial or other: Winkfield will bring it, if I ring — or even if I don't. Sit down! Now then, young man! We'll have the gloves off, if you please! I was never one to stand on ceremony, and there's too little time left — perhaps not even enough for what I must

173

do. But, by God, I'll make a push to see it out! What do they say of the Squire in the village? Queer as Dick's hatband, eh?'

'They speak of you with affection, sir.'

'Don't you bamboozle me! I know 'em! I'm baked, but not backed yet, and not queer in my attic, I assure you! Did you think I sent for you out of an idle curiosity? I didn't.'

'I think you sent for me to see what kind of a man it might be who had fallen in love with your granddaughter,' said John.

'Here's a high flight! In three days?' said Sir Peter, on a jeering note.

'No, in three seconds.'

'Do you fall out of love as easily as you fall into it?' demanded Sir Peter.

'I can't tell that, sir, for I never did it before,' John replied, laughter in his eyes.

'Good God, boy, are you telling me you were never in love before?'

'Oh, no! I have thought myself in love, but I never before met a woman whom I knew to be the one above all others I wanted to call my wife.'

'How old are you?'

'Twenty-nine, sir.'

'Well, you *ought* to know your own mind — and you look as though you did, in all conscience!'

'I do.'

'Then you had better know that she has not a penny to her name!' said Sir Peter harshly.

'I am not a wealthy man, sir, but my father left me in the possession of a small estate. I believe I can convince you that I am sufficiently beforehand with the world to be able to support a wife.'

'When I die, Captain Staple, I shall leave behind me my name, my title, and my estates. My estates are encumbered; my title will embellish the snirp who is my grandson. A skirter like his father before him, and a damned loose-screw! I shall be dead before he drags my name through whatever mire he's wading in, but he'll do it, as sure as check! I would remind you that it is also Nell's name!'

'I hope the case may not be as desperate as you fear,' John said. 'I am not acquainted with your grandson, but I have seen him, and I should judge him to be a weakling rather than a villain. May I say that one loose-screw can't disgrace an honoured name?' He smiled, and added: 'By all accounts my grandfather was one, but we think our name a good one, in spite of him!'

'Your grandfather! Ay, he was a rake and a gamester, but it was play or pay with him, and he rode straight at his fences! There was no bad blood in him, but in Henry there is more bad than good!' He lifted his hand, and let it fall again, in an impotent gesture. 'I knew that years ago, when I pulled him out of that first, damnable scrape — But Jermyn was alive then. It never occurred to me that Jermyn would be killed, or that I should become the helpless wreck I am — so helpless that I can neither protect my granddaughter from the gallantry of the vulgar rogue my heir has introduced into my house, nor fling the pair of them out of it!'

'Don't distress yourself, sir!' John said. 'With or without your leave I shall take care of Nell; and as for your grandson and his bacon-fed crony, you have only to say the word, and I shall be happy to throw them out of the house for you! Now, if you choose!'

Sir Peter shook his head. He looked up at John under his brows, a smile twisting his lips. 'No. No. Better not. There's something afoot. That rogue has Henry under his thumb, and Henry's afraid. While I live he has no right here, but when I die the place will be his — and I might die tomorrow.'

'I hope not, sir, but I'm at one with you in thinking that we shall do better to keep these gentry where we can watch what they are about. I don't fear for Nell. She at least is no weakling, and she has very faithful guardians in Rose and Joseph.'

'She's safe while I live,' Sir Peter said. His hand worked on the arm of his chair. 'I did my best!' he said suddenly, as though in answer to a challenge. 'Sent her up to her aunt for a season! A damned, insipid woman — nothing but pride and consequence, but she goes to all the *ton* parties! Sulky as a bear she was — but not too stiff-necked to pocket a handsome fee for her services! She had the infernal impudence to tell me my girl was a hoyden! Ha! Nell has too much force of mind for my lady's taste! I could have dowered her then, but she didn't *take*! No! And none of the town fribbles took *her* fancy! It was left for a libertine and a coxcomb — a Captain Sharp, if ever I saw one! — to tell me that he

176

would be pleased to marry her! By God, if I could have my strength back for one minute — !'

John interposed, his eyes watchful on Sir Peter's face, but his deep voice very calm. 'Do I indeed seem to you to be a libertine and a coxcomb, sir? But I'll swear I'm not a Captain Sharp!'

The fierce old eyes stared across at him. 'Not you, fool! Coate!'

'What, does he offer marriage? There must be better stuff in the fellow than I guessed. But why tease yourself, sir? To be sure, it is an impertinence, but persons of low breeding, you know, have such encroaching ways! I wish you will leave me to deal with Coate, and tell me I have your permission to marry Nell!'

There was the glimmer of a smile in Sir Peter's eyes. He said: 'Does my permission count for so much with you?'

'No,' replied John frankly. 'But with her it might! I should prefer, I must own, to address myself to her with your consent, but I won't deceive you, sir! — With or without your consent I mean to marry your granddaughter!'

The smile was growing. 'Joe told me you were a fellow after my own heart, and for once in his life the rascal was right! I wish you well: you may be crazy, but you're not a damned adventurer!' His hand relaxed on the chair-arm: his head sunk on to his breast again, but he lifted it, with an effort, when John rose to his feet, and said sharply: 'Don't go! Something else I have to say to you!'

'I'm not going, sir.' John waited until the head

177

drooped again, and then walked quietly to the door which led into the dressing-room.

Winkfield was dozing in a high-backed chair by the table, but he got up quickly, an anxious question in his face.

'I think your master would be the better for his cordial,' John said. 'He is tired, but he will not permit me to leave him until he has told me something that seems to be on his mind. I think it will be best to let him have his way. Give me the cordial! I'll see he drinks it.'

The valet nodded, and turned to measure it into a wine glass. 'If you could set his mind at rest, sir — !'

'I can at least try to do so. Tell me this! Does that hang-gallows fellow below-stairs force himself upon Miss Nell's notice?'

'Once, sir — but I happened to be at hand. Since then, no. Not yet.'

John nodded, taking the glass from him. 'Send me word if he should become troublesome!' he said, and went back into the bedchamber.

Sir Peter's eyes were closed, but he opened them as John came across the room, and said irritably: 'I wasn't asleep! What's this?'

'Your cordial, sir.'

'I don't want the stuff!'

'Very well, sir. I'll take my leave, then.'

'Damned, managing fellow!' snapped Sir Peter. 'Sit down!'

John put the glass into his groping hand, and guided it to his mouth. Sir Peter drank a little, and was silent for a few moments. Then he said, in a stronger voice: 'Do as you're bid! I'm not so feeble I have to be spoon-fed!'

John obeyed him, drawing up the chair lately occupied by Nell, but he did not say anything. Sir Peter slowly drank the cordial. He made no demur when the empty glass was gently removed from his clasp; he appeared to be lost in thought, his eyes staring straight before him. Presently he turned them towards John, and said: 'They think they can hoax me, but they can't. All of them! — treating me as if I were a child, or an imbecile! I can't get the truth from one of them — not even from Winkfield, though he's served me for thirty years! Bacup is as bad! Thinks it would send me to roost if I knew what was going on in my house, I don't doubt! Bottle-headed old woman! They've all gone, the men I knew and could trust. Birkin was the last of them, and he slipped his wind two years ago. It's a bad thing to outlive your generation, my boy.'

'Will you tell me what's in your mind, sir? If I know the answer to whatever it is you wish to be told, I'll give it you.'

'I believe you will: you haven't a cozening face. You're a gentleman, too. I haven't seen one for months — barring old Thorne, and he's a parson, and not a man of *my* kidney. But *you* may believe I know when I'm being gulled, so don't play off any cajolery! What brought my grandson and that Greeking fellow to Kellands?'

John met the searching eyes squarely. 'I can't answer you, sir, for I don't know.'

'Henry didn't come here out of affection for me, nor Coate to ruralize!'

'Extremely unlikely, I fancy.'

179

'They're up to no good. It isn't debt. No, not that. He'd have told me, if that was all. If there were a warrant out for his arrest, this is the first place where he'd be looked for. Are the pair of them using my house as a shield to cover some piece of filthy knavery?'

'Gently, sir! This is nothing more than conjecture. The truth may prove to be less serious than you fear. Whatever it may be, only harm can come from your vexing yourself like this.'

'Are you telling me you think that pair are here for any honest purpose?' demanded Sir Peter.

'No, I'm not. I think there's something devilish smoky afoot, and that's the truth!' John said bluntly. 'It's my intention to discover just what it is. That's why I'm remaining at that damned toll-house! It has its drawbacks, but it's not such a bad ambush, you know.'

Sir Peter regarded him intently. 'Is the gatekeeper mixed up in it?'

'That again I don't know, though I suspect he may be. I have some hopes of discovering his whereabouts at least, and if I can find him trust me to find out the rest! Until we know a little more, it seems to me it might not serve our purpose to turn these fellows out of doors. If it should turn out to be a hanging matter, you want it scotched, not exposed.'

'I want my name kept clean!' Sir Peter said.

'I give you my word I will do my utmost to do that, sir,' John said steadily.

'You may find it beyond your power.'

'If I do, it will not be beyond my power to see to it that no slur attaches to you, or to Nell.'

'It's Nell I'm thinking of. If we're plunged in scandal — ' He broke off, his hand clasping and unclasping.

'Good God, sir, you cannot suppose that it would make the least difference!' exclaimed John. 'Are you imagining that I might *cry* off?'

'No: that she would!' retorted Sir Peter.

'*Would* she?' said John, a light in his eye. 'We'll see that!'

Sir Peter looked queerly at him, but was silent. After a minute, John got up. 'I think I should leave you now, sir. There is no reason why you should trust me: I might be the shabbiest of impostors! But I wish you will be content to leave this mystery to me to solve!'

This drew a slight smile from Sir Peter. 'An odd sort of an impostor! Shouldn't have told you all this if I didn't trust you.' He held out his hand. 'It's done me good, seeing you. You'll take care of my girl.'

'You may be very sure of that, sir,' John said, clasping the frail hand warmly.

'Jermyn would have liked you,' said Sir Peter abruptly. 'You put me a little in mind of him. He was a big fellow, too. I'm obliged to you for coming here. I shall be seeing you again. Send my man in to me, will you?'

In the dressing-room, John found Nell, talking in a low voice to the valet. She looked up, and smiled, but whispered: 'You have been so long with him!'

'I don't think it has harmed him. I hope it has

not. Winkfield, he desired me to send you to him: I'll let myself out of the house. Good-night!'

'Good-night, sir, and thank you!'

As the door into the bedchamber closed behind the valet, Nell moved towards John, the half-train of her gown hushing on the floor. He opened his arms to her, and she walked into them, as though she found it natural to be there. 'Oh, I was so angry, so very angry!' she murmured.

He put his hand on her head, smoothing the thick locks. 'I know you were! *Such* a look as you cast at me! I thought myself betrothed to a cockatrice!'

'Oh, no!' she protested. 'How infamous of you to say so! I was startled — in a flash, I knew that you would not have come if you had not been summoned. Winkfield told me how it was. How sly of Grandpapa! He breathed not a word to me. I was never more embarrassed in my life, for he was watching us so closely. Oh, and you were so good! You talked to him just as you ought. I know he liked you!' She looked up into his face. 'What did he say to you, when I had gone away?'

'He gave me permission to pay my addresses to you, my heart, so now I will ask you, most formally, if you will do me the honour of accepting my hand in marriage, ma'am?'

'How absurd you are! What should I say? You must know that I have no experience in these matters, and I should not wish to answer with the least impropriety!'

'You should say, Yes, sir, I will!'

'I am sure I ought to display a little confusion, put on an air of surprise, perhaps trifle with you for a while!'

'Thank God you have no such missish ways! And I must remind you, ma'am, that we met each other earlier in the day!'

She pinched his chin. 'What a very unhandsome person you are to remind me of *that*! It was quite shocking!'

'Exactly so! Unless you wish me to think you an outrageous flirt, you must promise to marry me!'

'John, how do you contrive to laugh with your eyes, while you keep your face so grave?'

'I don't know, and you haven't answered me!'

'Ah, you know I will! But not yet! Not while my grandfather needs me! You must not ask that of me, dearest! I *could* not leave him!'

'No, I see that you could not. Don't fear me! I don't mean to tease you. Kiss me once more, and then I must be off!'

She would have escorted him to the side-entrance, but he would not permit it. They parted at the head of the stairs, he to let himself quietly out of the house, she to retire to her own room, to be alone with her happiness.

Winkfield, looking covertly at his master, as he entered his bedchamber, was satisfied that the Captain's visit had done him no harm. He had expected to find him very tired, but he saw that he was wide awake, looking fixedly at the fire, and slightly drumming his fingers on his chair-arm. The valet began to remove the quilt from the bed, and to lay out his master's night-shirt, and his cap. He was startled by Sir Peter's saying suddenly: 'Not yet! Bring me a pen and ink and some paper!'

'Sir?' Winkfield said, blinking at him.

'Don't pretend you're deaf! I must write a letter.'

Considerably dismayed, Winkfield said: 'It's very late, sir. Now, won't you — '

'I know it's late. The letter must be written at once, if it is to catch the mail. What time does it leave Sheffield for London?'

'At six in the morning, I believe, sir, but — '

'Joseph must ride in to catch it. Tell him!'

The valet almost wrung his hands. 'I *beg* you, sir, don't ask me to bring you pen and ink at this hour! The doctor particularly desired you not to sit up, and it's past ten o'clock now!'

'Damn the doctor! And you, too! Do as I bid you!'

'Sir — '

Sir Peter put up his hand and grasped the valet's arm, shaking it feebly. 'Winkfield, old friend, I have no time — no time! Do you want me to sleep peacefully tonight?'

'God knows I do, sir!'

'Then don't thwart me! I know what I'm about. I'm well, too — very well!'

The valet gave a despairing sigh, and went over to where a court-cupboard stood, and opened it. 'You'll kill yourself, sir,' he said bitterly.

'Very likely. Do you think I care for that? Let me but tie one knot tight, and the sooner this

184

miserable existence ends the better I shall be pleased! I shall see it out: I always do what I mean to, don't I?'

'Yes, sir — more's the pity!'

Sir Peter gave a dry chuckle. He waited until a tray had been laid across the arms of his chair, and the standish set upon it. Then he said abruptly: 'That was a very different visitor from the other I received last night.'

'Yes, indeed, sir!'

'Cutter-rigged! nothing queer or yawl-like about *him*! knew his grandfather.'

'You did, sir? It seems a strange thing for him to be keeping the gate, but he's very much the gentleman, of course.'

Sir Peter dipped the pen in the standish. 'Impudent dog! He's courting Miss Nell!'

'So I have been given to understand, sir.'

Sir Peter shot a look up at him. 'It will do, won't it?'

'I think so, sir. If I may say so, I never saw Miss Nell in such a glow. It quite took me aback, the way she looked at the Captain. Rose will have it he was sent by Providence.'

'Maybe. He comes in the very nick of time, at all events. What's the name of my attorney? It ain't Raythorne — he died years ago. Who's the fellow that succeeded him?'

'Mr Marshside, sir,' said Winkfield wonderingly.

'Marshside! Ay, that's it! Hold this damned paper steady for me!'

He began to write, slowly, and with a little difficulty. 'When does the mail reach London?'

'I'm told they do the journey in sixteen-and-a-half hours now, sir. It should reach the General Post Office at about ten in the evening, though it hardly seems possible.'

'Glad I don't travel by it!'

'No, sir, very uncomfortable it must be, racing along at such a pace.'

Sir Peter grunted, and dipped his pen in the ink again. By the time he had scrawled his signature at the foot of the single sheet, he was a good deal exhausted, and his hand was shaking. Winkfield took the pen from between his fingers. 'There, sir, you don't need to do any more. I'll seal it up, and direct it for you.'

'Marshside — somewhere in Lincoln's Inn Fields,' Sir Peter muttered.

'Yes, sir, I know.'

'It must catch the mail!'

'I promise it shall, sir.'

Sir Peter seemed satisfied, and said no more. He let Winkfield do what he wished with him. Only when his head lay on the pillow did he revive a little, and open his eyes. They were surprisingly bright, even rather impish. 'I can still keep my horses well together!' he said. '*I'll* show you!'

10

Captain Staple found no one stirring in the stables, when he left the house, and was soon trotting down the road towards the toll-gate. The light was dim, gathering clouds obscuring the moon, and a little chill wind was bringing a few leaves fluttering down from the trees. He encountered nobody on the road, and in a few minutes saw ahead of him the yellow glow of the storm-lantern hanging on the gate. He dismounted when he reached it, and, before opening the gate, trimmed the lamp, which was flaring too high. Having done this to his satisfaction, he turned, and went to pull back the gate a little way, to enable Beau to pass. As he set his hand on it, the fitful wind blew towards him the unmistakable smell of burning tobacco. Faint though it was, his nostrils caught it, and while he pretended to be fumbling for the fastening on the gate, keeping his head bent, his eyes searched the shadows cast by the overgrown hedge which flanked the road, beyond a rough grass verge and a ditch. Almost immediately he saw the tiny thread of smoke, creeping upward from the faintest red glow just discernible in the long grass not six feet from where he stood. Someone had knocked out a pipe within the last few minutes, and the dottle was still smouldering.

The Captain flicked over the staple that held the gate to the side-post, and stepped back a few paces, pulling the gate with one hand, and with the other, holding Beau's bridle, imperceptibly manoeuvring that sagacious animal into presenting his haunch instead of his head to the opening. Beau, who knew very well that his stable lay beyond the gate, snorted, and threw up his head, as though he were jibbing (which indeed he was), and the Captain backed him a little, saying soothingly: 'Steady, now, you old fool! What's the matter with you? Come along! You know a gate when you see one!'

Beau certainly knew a gate when he saw one, and would have passed through the narrow opening without the smallest hesitation had his master permitted him to do so. But the hand on his bridle was acting in direct contradiction to the voice, and was forcing him back. Fretted, he tried to jerk his head away, presenting all the appearance of a horse unwilling to approach an obstacle. Meanwhile, the Captain, still talking gently to him, was rapidly scanning the hedge. It was difficult to see more than its ragged outline, but a rift in the clouds disclosed the moon for a few seconds, and in the faint lightening of the scene he thought he could detect a movement in the shadows, as though a man, crouching in the ditch, had shifted his position slightly.

Beau found that the extremely irksome hand on his bridle had relaxed its pressure, and at once stepped forward.

'That's more like it!' said the Captain encouragingly, and led him through the aperture. He fastened the gate again, and walked past the toll-house, and down the road, to where, fifty yards away, a white farm-gate gave access to the big meadow at the top end of which was situated the barn that stabled Beau. Opening it, he turned Beau into the meadow, and pulled the gate shut with a clap behind him. Then he strode back to the toll-house, along the grass verge, keeping in the shadow of the hedge, and treading noiselessly over the soft ground. There he took up a position, just round the corner of the house from the road, and waited.

He had not long to wait. In a minute or two the wicket-gate creaked, and an unhurried footstep sounded. Heavy cloud again hid the moon, but there was light enough to see, when the footsteps drew abreast of John, that the figure which passed was that of a stocky man of medium height.

'Waiting for me?'

These pleasantly spoken words made the stocky man stop, and wheel about, grasping the thick stick he carried. Before he had time to raise it (if such had been his intention), he found himself enveloped in an unloving embrace from which it was quite impossible to escape. He seemed to realize this, for he stood perfectly still, merely saying in a mildly ex-postulatory tone: 'Lor' bless you, big 'un, you don't have to squeege the puff out of me!'

'It's you, is it?' said John, removing the stick from his grasp, and casting it aside. 'I thought it might be! Let me tell you, Mr Stogumber, that it is unwise to smoke your pipe when lying in ambush!'

'So that's how you boned me!' said Mr

Stogumber, apparently pleased to have this point explained. 'A very leery cove, ain't you?'

'No, but I don't care to be spied upon!' said John.

'Spied upon! What, *me?*' said Stogumber, in astonished accents. 'Seems to me as it's you as laid in wait for me, Mr Staple! *I* wasn't meaning no harm! *I* didn't jump out on you sudden enough to give anyone a spasm! All I done was to come out to stretch my legs. What's put you in such a pelt?'

'Were you stretching your legs in the ditch?' asked the Captain sardonically.

'I won't try to slumguzzle you, big 'un,' responded Stogumber. 'I wasn't. But this being a very lonely road, d'ye see, and me a peaceable man, I didn't want to run into no trouble. How was I to know you wasn't a bridle-cull?'

'You knew well enough who I was when you heard me speak to my horse! Why didn't you show yourself then?'

'What, and have you laughing at me for being cow-hearted, which I won't deny I am — very!'

'Coming it too strong!' said John. 'What kind of a flat do you take me for, to be flammed by such gammon as that?'

'Since you ask me, Mr Staple, I don't know as how I take you for a flat at all, not by any manner o' means!'

'Then stop trying to turn me up sweet, and tell me what the devil you mean by spying on me!'

'Down to every move on the board, ain't you? Seems to me as how a cove as is as knowing as what you are didn't ought to be minding a pike,' remarked Stogumber. 'What's more, I couldn't hardly believe you could be the pikekeeper, not when I clapped my ogles on that beautiful-stepping tit o' yours! If I was a peevy cove I should suspicion you must have prigged him, but I ain't. I daresay you come by him honest, though what you want with a bang-up bit of blood and bone — you being what you are — I *don't* know! Howsever, it ain't none of my business — '

'None at all!' John interrupted. 'I told you yesterday I'm not a gatekeeper, but a soldier!'

'So you did! And a very handsome trooper you've got! In fact, I was mistook in him: I thought he was a prime 'un!'

'Mr Stogumber,' said John, a grim note in his deep voice, 'my horse is not a trooper, as you very well know; and I am only minding the pike to oblige Brean! Now perhaps you'll tell me — '

'Your cousin,' nodded Stogumber.

'Now perhaps you'll tell me,' continued John, 'why you are so interested in my movements?'

'There you go again!' complained Stogumber. 'I'm a cove as is interested in most things — not you partic'lar!'

'Are you indeed? Well, I, Mr Stogumber, am a cove as is interested in *you* extremely particular!'

'You're bamming me!' said Stogumber.

'No,' said John. 'Nor am I flattering you!'

'Well, even if you ain't, you don't have to look so bluff, nor to grip my arm so as I can't feel my fingers no more! That's the worst of you big 'uns: you don't know your strength.'

'I know mine to the last ounce, and so will you very shortly! I'm interested in you because it seems to me that some business you're mighty anxious to conceal has brought you to these remote parts. Don't spin me any more nacky tarradiddles about this property you have been commissioned to purchase, because we have agreed, have we not? that I am not a flat! You tried yesterday to discover who I am, and how I come to be here; and tonight I find you watching the toll-house. Why is it so important to you to know where I may be going, or what I may be doing, Mr Stogumber? Just what kind of an undergame are you playing?'

There was a pause. John had the impression that his question had taken Stogumber by surprise, but it was impossible, in the darkness, to read his face. After a moment he said: 'You must have had a shove in the mouth, big 'un, though I'm bound to say I never suspicioned it! P'raps you're just betwattled! Did you ever hear tell of the Wansbeck ford?'

'No, and I don't want to hear of it! If you provoke me into losing my temper, Stogumber — '

'Now, don't go for to do that!' begged Stogumber. 'I ain't a match for a man of your size! Besides, it wouldn't do you no good if you was to mill me down. O' course, it wouldn't do me much good neither, but it's you as 'ud catch cold — in the long run! If you never heard tell of the Wansbeck ford, p'raps you never heard tell of a signpost being changed round so as to mislead folks?'

'I didn't. And if you're trying to hoax me into believing that you're here by accident tonight, spare your breath! There is no signpost between this gate and the village! Try another fling!'

'Never heard of that neither!' said Stogumber. 'That's queer!'

Considerably mystified, John demanded: 'Why?'

''Cos I thought you had,' replied Stogumber cryptically. 'Either I've been mistook — which ain't likely — or you're as fly a cove as ever tapped a shy one on the shoulder! Which again ain't likely, seeing the size you are, and big 'uns not being, in general, the slyest things in nature! One thing I'm not mistook about is that there's a horse and cart, or maybe it's a carriage, coming down the road. You'll have to leave go of me, Mr Staple. And if you're going to open the gate, I'd take off that flash shap, if I was you!'

There was indeed a vehicle approaching from the direction of Sheffield. The Captain released Stogumber, and, accepting his advice, removed his hat. But he said somewhat sternly: 'You use too much thieves' cant for my taste!'

'Ah!' said Stogumber, stooping to pick up his stick. 'And you understand too much of it for mine, big 'un!'

That drew a reluctant laugh from John; he allowed Stogumber to go on his way, and himself went to open the gate.

The vehicle, which proved to be a gig, carried Farmer Huggate and his wife. If this worthy couple thought it peculiar to find the gatekeeper nattily attired in a riding-coat of expensive cloth and fashionable cut, and with a modish cravat arranged in intricate folds about his neck, they admirably concealed their surprise. The farmer had only to hand in his ticket, purchased at the first toll-gate out of Sheffield, but he lingered to explain chattily that he and his rib (as he designated the stout lady beside him) had been out on the spree to celebrate the anniversary of their wedding-day. John replied suitably, and Mrs Huggate ventured to say that she hoped it would not be long before he was celebrating his own wedding-day. John was spared the necessity of answering this sally by the farmer's telling her severely not to talk so free, bidding him a cheery good-night, and driving off down the road.

The Captain, walking across the field to where his horse stood patiently awaiting him, outside the barn, was forced to the conclusion that the secret of his matrimonial hopes was shared by most of the inhabitants of the village, and certainly by the entire staff of servants employed at the Manor.

He entered the toll-house presently to find Lydd snoring gently beside the dying fire in the kitchen. He shook him awake, saying: 'Well, you're a fine gatekeeper! I wonder how many people have opened the pike for themselves, and cheated us of the tolls?'

'Lor' bless you, sir, I'd rouse up at the least thing!' Lydd assured him.

'What do you call the least thing? A regiment with a full military band? Tell me, Joseph! Can you watch that pair up at the Manor without their knowing it? Young Stornaway, and Coate?'

Lydd looked at him, stroking his chin. 'I can

— and I can't, guv'nor. It all depends. It might be that I'd have to go off somewheres with Miss Nell, you see. And, if you was to ask me, I should say as there's three of 'em as needs watching. Holt — he's Mr Henry's man — ain't no better than a clunch — and oyster-faced at that! — but Roger Gunn, which calls himself Coate's groom, is a regular ding-boy, or I never see one! Whatever it is them pair o' shog-bags is up to, he's in it, to the chin!'

'Do what you can!' John said. 'Keep your eye on Mr Henry, and don't fail to let me know if he does anything you think smoky! Particularly watch where he goes, and tell me!'

But it was not, in the event, Joseph who saw where Henry Stornaway went, but the Captain himself, and that by the merest accident. With no other thought in mind than to exercise his horse, and to do it at an hour when it was not only unlikely that any vehicle would wish to pass the gate, but when few people would be abroad to see the gatekeeper bestriding a horse of his quality, he got up shortly after dawn on the following morning, and walked through the dank mist to Farmer Huggate's barn. Not wishing either to ride through Crowford, or to branch off short of the village up the very uneven lane which had led him down from the moors on Saturday night, he set off in an easterly direction, following the line Nell had taken on the previous morning. An easy jump over the hedge brought him into the spinney, and through this he was obliged to wend his way circumspectly, until he came to a ride, which led, after a short distance, to a rotting gate. He remembered seeing this when he rode to Kellands, and knew that he had reached the pike road. It was not precisely what he wanted, but if nothing better offered there was at least the broad grass verge along which Beau could stretch his legs in a canter. The mist was lifting momently, and the gate could be seen quite clearly, so that he had no hesitation in putting Beau at it. The big horse, pulling a little, seemed almost to take it in his stride, and, landing neatly on the verge, gave the Captain to understand that after so many idle hours he would like to be allowed to have his head. But the Captain had no intention of galloping down an unknown road while the mist made it impossible for him to see what lay more than fifty yards ahead, and he held him in to an easy canter. He recalled that he had noticed, the night before, that a narrow lane led from the road to the north; it seemed probable that it ran upward to the moors; and he determined to ride along it, in the hope of coming within a few miles to open country, where Beau could have a chance to gallop the fidgets out of himself.

The lane was halfway between the toll-gate and Kellands Manor, and was soon reached. John turned Beau into it, and found it to be no more than a deeply rutted cart-track, separated on either side by a ditch and a bank from fields under cultivation. Between the ruts the ground was grass-grown, and sufficiently level to make it possible for John to let Beau break into a canter again. The big horse had a formidable stride, and he was impatient, trying to lengthen it more and still more. The pace, John knew, was not really very safe on an unknown track, which might, for anything he knew, contain bad pot-holes; it was too swift for him to be able to detect possible dangers ahead, in the chill white mist; and too swift for a solitary pedestrian, making his way towards the pike road, to do more than jump off the track almost into the ditch as he saw Beau looming ahead of him. He had plenty of time to do this, however, and John, perceiving him some thirty yards away, had the impression that if there had been a hedge he would have dived into it for cover. There was something in his aspect which was panic-stricken rather than merely startled; he looked round, as though seeking shelter, and, finding none, seemed almost to cower on the brink of the ditch. John had no time to wonder what there was to alarm anyone in the appearance of a horse and rider, however unexpectedly encountered, before he was abreast of the man. He had made Beau check his pace a little, and he turned his head, intending to shout an apology for having discommoded this early pedestrian, whom he supposed to be a farm labourer. Then he realized that the man was wearing a coat with a superfluity of shoulder-capes; had a glimpse of pale, blood-shot eyes glaring up at him out of a white face; and rode on, without uttering a word. The head had been ducked almost immediately, but he had recognized Henry Stornaway.

It was only for a moment that he saw him plainly, but the Captain was not slow-witted, and his powers of observation were acute. He noticed two things about Mr Stornaway: the first, that in his face had been an expression of starting horror; the second, that he carried an unlit lantern. For the look of horror, no explanation presented itself: something more dreadful than dismay at having been seen had inspired it; the lantern seemed to indicate that he had set forth from the Manor in darkness. Yet even though the night had been overcast, it had not, John thought, been so dark as to have made a lantern necessary for a traveller on foot.

He rode on, keeping a sharp look-out for any house which might have been Stornaway's objective. He saw nothing but two small cottages, and a cluster of farm buildings; beyond them, the country became more wooded, and the lane began to ascend sharply towards the tangled hills which loomed dimly through the mist. These were typical of the district: wild shapes tossed up in confusion, with crags of outcropping limestone, and deep gorges cut in their precipitous sides. The track wound steadily upwards through a pass; one or two sheep, straying across it, scurried away at the approach of a rider; but of human habitation there was no sign. The sharp, sweet tang of the moors came to John's nostrils; the road became level again, dipped slightly, rose again, so that he knew he must have reached the summit, and was now wending his way across the undulations of the moor to whatever town or village the track served.

It began after a mile or two to descend again, and presently ran through a small village, huddled on the northern slope of the hill. John halted there, for the place was awake, and housewives were already shaking mats out of doors, and one or two men were to be seen on the single street, plodding off to work. Enquiries elicited the information that the road went to some town, of which John had never heard, seven miles to the northwest, serving on its way only one house of any size, which appeared, from the somewhat unintelligible description vouchsafed, to be situated only a couple of miles short of the town. It seemed extremely improbable that Henry Stornaway could have walked as far; and John, feeling that it was useless to go on, turned Beau, and rode back the way he had come.

By the time he reached the foot of the pass the mist had cleared appreciably, and he was able to see that besides the farmstead and the two cottages there were no houses within sight. The farm lay some two hundred yards back from the lane, and just as John was wondering whether it would serve any useful purpose if he were to ride up to it, on some pretext or another, he saw an immensely stout man in the garb of a farmer, leaning on an ash-plant, and surveying with a ruminative eye a small mixed herd of cows. He turned his head when he heard the sound of hooves. John pulled up, and, after a minute, the farmer began to walk ponderously towards the gate. As he drew nearer he was seen to have a large, ruddy, and cheerful countenance; and when he came within earshot he called out, in a deep, wheezy voice:

"'Morning, sir! Anything I can do for you?'

He did not look to be at all the sort of man to be engaged on any nefarious enterprise, and within a very few moments John was satisfied that his farm had not been Henry Stornaway's objective. He was of a chatty and an expansive disposition, only too pleased to enter into conversation with strangers, of whom he saw very few. He was one of the Squire's tenants, and shook his head sadly over Sir Peter's illness, saying that things would be very different when he died. It was an easy matter to get him to expatiate on this theme; and it soon became apparent that although he had a great regard for Miss Nell, he didn't (as he put it) reckon much to Mr Henry, whom he scarcely knew, and who didn't (if the half of what he heard tell were true) take any interest in the estate. Yes, he had been told that Mr Henry was staying at Kellands, and a fine London friend with him, but you wouldn't catch Mr Henry coming in to pass the time of day with his grandpa's tenants, not he! No, he had never seen the London friend, and he didn't know as he much wanted to, for he had seen another Londoner that week, and a regular leather-head he was! He was wishful to buy a property in the district, but from the silly questions he asked it was easy to see as he was a chap as would be nailed, sure as check! What was he like? He was a muffin-faced chap, a little on the squat, and precious wide in the boughs.

The Captain, recognizing, from this pungent description, Mr Gabriel Stogumber, rode on his way, a frown knitting his brow. He failed to perceive what object Stogumber could have had in questioning the farmer; and he was still puzzling over this problem when he reached the toll-house. He had been away from it for longer than he had intended, and he found Ben in a mood of considerable disquiet, flatteringly overjoyed to behold him again.

No one visited him from the Manor that day. He spent the morning in the expectation of seeing Nell; but she did not come; and by the time it became apparent that something had prevented her, Mrs Skeffling had gone home, and there was no one in whose charge John could leave the gate, Ben having been engaged by Farmer Huggate for the whole day, to assist in taking livestock to market. Gatekeeping had never been more irksome, for there were certain questions John wished to ask either of Nell, or of Joseph, who, he supposed, must be even more familiar with the district. Thinking over his strange encounter with Henry Stornaway, and cudgelling his brains to hit upon some solution to account for his presence upon a lonely lane at such an unseasonable hour of the morning, there had flashed across his memory an echo of something Nell had talked of during their drive to Tideswell. If her idle words did indeed hold the key to the mystery, he was still far from understanding it, but it might well be within his power to discover it. Then he remembered the look of sick horror in Stornaway's face, and he thought it might be wiser to address his questions to Joseph rather than to Nell. But Joseph did not come, and a certain anxiety was added to the Captain's impatience. When Ben returned from Tideswell, pleasantly weary, and full of all that he had seen and done in the town, John made an attempt to convince him that he had no longer anything to fear in being left for an hour to mind the pike after dark. But Ben, who, while he knew his large protector to be at hand, seemed almost to have forgotten his alarms, no sooner realized that he was in danger of being left alone than he became slightly tearful, and with the utmost urgency begged John not to leave him. It was useless to point out to him that his father's visitor must by this time know that he would no longer find Brean at the toll-house; he merely said, in considerable agitation, that if John went out he himself would run away, and spend the night with Beau in Farmer Huggate's big barn. It was plainly useless to argue with him, and the Captain, suppressing exasperation, promised not to leave the toll-house, and commanded him to stop whining. As it happened he was forced to realize that he could scarcely have done so, had Ben been never so willing. After the unaccustomed excitement of the day, the boy was so sleepy that he dropped off before he had finished his supper, and could not be roused. When picked up, and carried off to his truckle-bed, he did no more than stir, and murmur something unintelligible: it seemed unlikely that anything less than a coach-horn blown in his ear would waken him.

Scarcely an hour later, John had reason to be glad that he had not, after all, gone to Kellands, for he heard the owl's hoot, twice repeated, which had previously heralded Jeremy Chirk's arrival at the toll-house. He walked over to the back-door, and opened it. Chirk's voice, lowered, but sufficiently penetrating, reached him. 'Lend a hand here, Soldier!'

John stepped out into the untidy garden, looking towards the wicket-gate. He saw that Chirk, on his feet, was holding it open for Mollie to pass through; and that seated astride the mare was a thick figure which swayed perilously and seemed only to be held in the saddle by Chirk's hand gripping him. 'Now what?' he demanded, striding forward.

'Bear a bob, Soldier!' Chirk adjured him. 'I've got a cove here as is as sick as a horse. Lift him down, will you? If I was to let go of him, he'd fall, and he's had one ding on the canister already.'

'Good God, is it Brean?' John exclaimed, hoisting the burly figure out of the saddle.

'Lord love you, no! I dunno who it is. I found him trying to mill his way out of a row, couple o' miles back — and a well-plucked 'un he seems to be! Else I wouldn't have meddled. I doubt I'll regret it yet: it don't become a man of my calling to meddle in other folks' business. But I don't like to see a game fighter set on from behind, and that's the truth!'

'Stable the mare!' said John briefly.

A few minutes later, Chirk entered the kitchen to find the victim of the late assault slumped in a chair, with the Captain, a somewhat grim look in his face, forcing brandy down his throat.

'Not hopped the twig, has he?' Chirk asked, shutting the door.

'Oh, no!'

'I didn't think he had. He cast up his accounts, back there along the road, but he didn't swoon off till a minute or two before I got him to the gate. Someone knifed him in the back.'

'I know that. Help me to strip off his coat!' John said, withdrawing his arm from behind the inert form, and showing his shirt-sleeve stained with blood. 'He's lost a good deal of blood, from the look of things, but I should say it's not serious.'

Coat and waistcoat were expeditiously removed, and tossed aside. The Captain then ripped up the shirt, and disclosed a long gash down one shoulder, which was still sluggishly bleeding.

'Nothing but a cut. I've seen many worse,' said John, going over to the sink, and pouring some water from the pail that stood under it into a tin bowl.

'Ah!' said Chirk, with satisfaction. 'I rather suspicioned I spoilt the cull's aim! I saw the chive he had in his famble flash in the moonlight, so I loosed off one of my barking-irons over his head, because chives I don't hold with! They showed their shapes quick then! — him and the other cove.'

'Who were they? Did you see their faces?'

'It would have queered me to do that, Soldier: they were muffled up to the eyes. Well, I was wearing a mask myself, but I don't go winding scarves round my phiz!' He shifted the heavy body he was supporting so that John could more easily bathe the gash. 'If they were foot-scamperers, I don't know what they were doing on this road, nor what they hoped to prig, nor why they set on a chap like this, that wouldn't have anything in his pockets worth the taking. Sticking a chive into a cove for the sake of a coachwheel or two, and maybe a silver tatler, is nasty work, Soldier, and I don't hold with it. Blubberheaded, too,' he added thoughtfully. 'That's the way to get snabbled, sure as a gun! I wonder who this cove is?'

'So do I wonder!' replied John, competently swabbing the wound. 'I can tell you his name, however: it's Stogumber — and I should say he has come by his deserts!'

As though the sound of his own name had penetrated to his consciousness, Mr Stogumber stirred, and opened his eyes.

'Keep still!' John said, as he winced.

Mr Stogumber surveyed him vaguely. His dulled gaze then travelled to Chirk's face. He blinked several times, as though in an effort to clear his sight; and then, the colour beginning to come back into his face, struggled to sit upright. 'Thank 'ee!' he uttered.

'Take a candle, and go and fetch the basilicum powder from my room,' John said to Chirk. 'You'll see it amongst my shaving-tackle: it'll do as well as anything else to put on the wound.'

'Stuck me in the back, did they?' remarked Stogumber, trying to squint over his own shoulder.

'Be still, will you?' said John. 'It's no more than a graze. A case of rogues falling out, eh, Mr Stogumber?'

A faint, wan smile crossed Stogumber's face. He sat leaning his elbows on his knees, his head propped in his hands. 'I wouldn't say it was that, not exactly. I'm mortified: that's what I am — fair mortified! However, I'm obliged to you, Mr Staple, mortal obliged to you!'

'You'd better keep your gratitude for the man who brought you here,' replied John, pulling some cloths out of a chest, and beginning to rip them up. 'If it hadn't been for him, you'd be dead.'

'I'm much beholden to him,' agreed Stogumber, speaking with a perceptible effort. 'And a rare set-out that is! Loosed off his pop, didn't he? I remember seeing him, a-sitting on his horse like a damned statue. What I thought was that the cat was in the cream-pot proper, but I see I was mistook. *I* dunno what the world's coming to! *Me* being beholden to a bridle-cull!'

'Stubble it!' said John, borrowing from Chirk's vocabulary.

Mr Stogumber gave a chuckle, which changed to a groan. 'Oh, my head! I dunno when I've took such a wisty crack on it! I ain't unmindful, Mr Staple. I'm precious hard to kill, but I don't deny I was shook up.'

At that moment, Chirk came back into the kitchen with the basilicum powder. Between them, he and John applied it to the wound, placed a pad over it, and bound it in place with the knotted strips of cloth.

206

'That's the dandy!' said Chirk encouragingly. 'In a brace o' snaps you'll be in prime twig, covey!'

'Take and put my noddle under the pump!' begged Stogumber. 'It's going round like a whirligig! What's more, I'm a-going to shoot the cat again!'

He made a great effort, and hoisted himself to his feet. With commendable promptness Chirk guided his wavering steps to the sink, and held his head over it while this prophecy was fulfilled. The Captain, taking only a cursory and quite unsympathetic interest in his agony, threw the bloodstained water from his bowl out into the garden, and turned to pick up his patient's coat and waistcoat from the floor. As he stooped to pick up the coat, he saw that a small notebook had fallen out of one of its pockets, and lay open, face downwards, on the floor. He shot one quick glance towards the sink, satisfied himself that Mr Stogumber's attention was fully occupied with his stomach's revolt, and picked up the notebook. Standing with his back to the sink, he inspected it. Rather more than half its pages had been inscribed in an illiterate hand; and a great many entries had been made in some kind of primitive cipher. But on the fly-leaf its owner's name was written; and, under it, the revealing words: *Occurrence Book*.

Captain Staple, putting the book back on the floor as he had found it, now knew what Mr Stogumber's real profession was. He knew also that Mr Stogumber was a far more dangerous man than he had supposed him to be, and one whom it might be hard to outwit. He regarded his heaving shoulders thoughtfully, glanced at Chirk's profile, and turned away, his lips twitching. Captain Staple, faced with a desperate problem, found one aspect at least of the situation irresistibly amusing.

11

Chirk, supporting Mr Stogumber's wilting frame back to the chair beside the fire, gave it as his opinion that what was needed to put him to rights was another nip of brandy.

'You're mistaken,' replied John, restoring the bottle to the cupboard. 'If he didn't cast it up again, it would very likely throw him into a fever. Put a wet cloth round his head, and leave him alone! I'll make him some strong coffee presently.'

He went away to his bedroom, and came back in a minute with one of the pillows from his bed. With this, and a soaking towel bound tenderly about his brow, Mr Stogumber was made moderately comfortable. He opened his eyes, achieving a lopsided smile. 'Damme, if I remember when I was so crop-sick!' he muttered. 'Fair shook up I must have been! *Me!*'

'Now, don't you go falling into a fit of the dismals, covey!' said Chirk, in a heartening tone. 'There's no call for you to be hipped. They tapped your claret, and you lost a lot of it, see? It's my blame. The thing was, while you was playing at singlestick with one of them Captain Hackums it didn't seem as I'd any call to interfere; and when t'other jumped out from behind the hedge I was took by surprise, same as you was.'

'I'm in your debt,' Stogumber said, closing his

eyes again. 'I've been near to cocking up my toes afore this, but I doubt it's the closest-run thing I ever stepped into. I take it very kind in you. What's more, I shan't forget it.'

The Captain, who was standing by the door leading into the office, made an imperative sign with his head, and, upon Chirk's going to him, led him out of the room, and softly shut the door. 'He'll go to sleep, if we let him alone,' he said. 'Now then, Jerry! What news?'

Chirk shook his head. 'I've got nothing to tell you, Soldier. They ain't seen nor heard anything of Ned in the kens where he might be looked for.' He jerked his thumb over his shoulder. 'What do ye make of this set-out? Queer fetch, ain't it? What's he been up to?'

'Making enemies, apparently,' John replied. 'Never mind him for the moment! I want you to go up to the Manor. Try if you can to see Rose, and find out from her if there are any caverns in the hills immediately north of Kellands! If she knows of any, get her to tell you where they are; but particularly warn her to say nothing of this to Miss Nell! Or, indeed, to anyone! But she won't! You may tell her also, if you please, that I fancy I may have chanced upon what concerns Henry Stornaway and Coate nearly, but that I do not wish to add to Miss Nell's anxieties, and so would prefer she should know nothing about it.'

Chirk's bright, keen eyes were fixed on his face. 'And have you, Soldier?' he asked.

'I don't know, but I believe it to be possible. Do you know the lane that leads up to the moors, half a mile to the east of the gate?' Chirk nodded. 'Very well! I rode up it, soon after dawn today — exercising my horse. I met Henry Stornaway on it. If he could have hidden from me, he would have done so, but there's no cover: I saw him as plainly as I see you! Whether he knew that I had recognized him, I can't say. He was making his way back to Kellands on foot: I was cantering up the lane, Beau has a long stride, and there was too much mist for either of us to see the other until we were almost abreast. For one instant I saw his face, and I can tell you this, Jerry Chirk! — he had the look of a man who had seen a ghost! Also — and mark this! — he carried a lantern! It was not alight, and for a time I supposed he must have used it only to show him the road, hours earlier. To be sure, the sky was overcast last night, but there was light enough for one to see one's way! It had me in a puzzle to know what he should have wanted with a lantern until I remembered suddenly something Miss Nell said to me once, about the caverns that are to be found amongst these limestone hills. If you meant to penetrate into one of those, you would need a lantern, of course.'

'I daresay you would,' agreed Chirk. 'But — lor' bless you, Soldier, what kind of a rig do you think a couple of flash coves like Stornaway and that Coate have got on hand?'

'I can't tell that, but I've reason to suspect that whatever it is, it's a damned serious business! Be a good fellow, now, and go up to Kellands! And discover, if you can, if all's well there!'

'What about that cove?' Chirk asked, with

211

another jerk of his thumb towards the kitchen.

'He's putting up at the Blue Boar. I'll get rid of him somehow. There's nothing much amiss with him but a splitting head, but if necessary, I'll mount him on the mare, and lead him to the village. You be off to Kellands before Rose has gone to bed!'

'You won't be satisfied till you see me in York Gaol, will you, Soldier?' said Chirk, with a wry smile. 'What with one thing and another, it seems to me I'm getting out of my depth — and I was never much of a swimmer. It's to be hoped that cove in there didn't twig what my lay is.'

'He knows that well enough, but he don't know your name, and in any event I believe he wouldn't cry rope on you. If it hadn't been for you, he'd be cold meat now, and that he knows too! You go to Kellands!'

Mr Chirk, not as loth to obey this command as he chose to pretend, allowed himself to be thrust out of the toll-house; and the Captain, first satisfying himself that Ben was still sunk in the heavy sleep of weary youth, softly opened the door into the kitchen. Mr Stogumber, his head fallen a little sideways, was breathing stertorously, his legs stretched out before him, and one arm hanging limply outside the chair, its hand almost touching the floor. The Captain shut the door again, and went to sit on the bench outside the house. Heavy snores presently assailed his ears. He got up, and went to collect a cigarillo from his bedroom, and, having kindled it at the lamp burning on the table in the office, retired again to the bench, and for a long time sat smoking, and gazing with slightly knit brows at the star-scattered sky.

It must have been three-quarters of an hour later when the snores ceased; and the Captain had twice struck a light from his tinderbox to enable him to read his watch. He waited for a minute, for once or twice the snores had stopped with a choking snort, only to start again almost immediately, but this time there was no recurrence of the rhythmic sounds. He went back into the kitchen, and found Stogumber yawning, and tenderly feeling his head.

'Well, you look a degree better,' he remarked, going over to the fire, and stirring the logs to a blaze. 'How's your head?'

'Setting aside it's got a lump on it the size of your fist, it ain't so bad,' responded Stogumber. 'It's a mighty hard head, d'ye see? I been asleep. Where's t'other cove?'

'Gone,' said John, pouring the cold coffee, carefully saved by Mrs Skeffling from his breakfast-table, into a pan, and bringing it to the fire.

'I'm sorry for that,' said Stogumber, rising rather stiffly from the chair. 'I disremember that I thanked him for what he done.'

'You did, but it's no matter: he wanted no thanks. He's a very good fellow. Keep quiet till you've drunk this coffee: it'll make you feel more the thing.'

'If it's all the same to you, big 'un, I'd as lief put my coat on again: I've got a bit chilly.'

'As you please,' John said indifferently. 'I'm afraid it's done for, however: you bled like a pig,

213

you know! I threw it somewhere — ' he glanced over his shoulder — 'ay, there it is! Don't stoop! I'll get it for you!' He set the pan down in the hearth as he spoke, and walked over to where the coat and waistcoat lay. He had thrust the notebook under the skirt of the coat, and as he picked the coat up it was revealed. He said: 'Hallo! This yours?'

'That's right,' Mr Stogumber said, holding out his hand, but keeping his eyes on John's face.

But the Captain, casually giving him the notebook, seemed to be more interested in the condition of the coat. He showed the rent in it, and the wide patch of drying blood, to its owner, grimacing expressively. 'You won't wear this again,' he remarked.

'It'll serve to keep the cold off till I get back to the Blue Boar,' said Stogumber, rather painfully inserting his arms into his waistcoat, and beginning to do up its buttons. 'I got another. Not but what it fair cags me to have a good coat spoilt the way that is.'

'Who were they that set on you?' asked John, easing him into the ruined garment.

'Ah, that's the question!' said Stogumber, resuming his seat by the fire. 'A couple of ding-boys, that's certain! I never got a chance to tout their muns, 'cos I only saw one, and he had his muns all muffled up so as his own ma wouldn't have known him. Where was you, while I was asleep, big 'un?'

'Outside, blowing a cloud,' replied John, knowing that the hard little eyes were fixed on his face, and not raising his own from the pan he was holding over the flames. The coffee was sizzling round the edges, and after a moment he removed it from the fire, and poured it into an earthenware mug, still conscious of that unwavering scrutiny. 'Do you want me to lace this?' he enquired, looking up with a smile. 'You don't seem to have a fever, so I daresay it won't harm you if I add a dash of brandy to it.'

'It won't,' said Stogumber, with conviction. 'I'm bound to say coffee ain't a bub as I'm in the habit of drinking, but I won't deny it smells good — and I dessay it'll smell better if you drop a ball o' fire into it.'

John laughed, and went to fetch the brandy bottle from the cupboard. Having poured a measure into the coffee, he handed the mug to his guest, and said, untruthfully, but in the most natural manner: 'I'm damned if I know what your lay is, Stogumber, but I'll go bail it wasn't pound dealing that brought you here! I've no wish to offend you, but you seem to me a curst rum touch! It's my belief you know who set on you tonight, and why they did so.'

'Maybe I got a notion who they was,' admitted Stogumber, cautiously sipping the laced coffee. 'But when a man has a lump on his noddle the size of this here one of mine, it don't do for him to set much store by his notions, because his brains is addled for the time being. What's more, I've been mistook before, and I might be again, easy! The first time as I ever clapped my ogles on you, big 'un, I thought you was Quality.' He paused, and directed a look upwards at John, under his brows. 'Then I heard as you was the gatekeeper's cousin, so, out of course, I see as I was mistook *there*.' He sighed, and shook his head. 'Betwattled, that's what I am! What with owing my life to a bridle-cull, and you — which wasn't so very friendly last time I see you — taking me in, and patching me up, like you have done, I'm danged if I know what to think! And when I don't know what to think, it's my way to keep me chaffer close, Mr Staple, see?'

'I'm not Brean's cousin, and you may call me Quality if you choose. Since you are putting up at the Blue Boar, I fancy you've a fair notion of what *my* lay is!'

'Maybe,' agreed Stogumber, drinking some more coffee. 'Maybe! And another notion I got, big 'un, is that you're a dangerous sort of a cove, which would take the wind out of my eye if you could do it! Maybe I'm wrong, maybe I ain't.' He drained the mug, and set it down. 'I'm beholden to you, and I don't deny it. I wouldn't want to do you a mischief. But if you was to try to tip me the double, Mr Staple, or to come crab over me, you want to bear in mind I'm up to slum, and I ain't a safe cove to cross!' He got up. 'Thanking you kindly for all you done, I'll brush now. You remember what I said to you!'

'I'll remember it,' promised John. 'Are you able to walk as far as to the village, or shall I mount you, and go with you?'

'No, no, I'll beat it on the hoof!' Stogumber replied. 'I'm feeling pretty stout now, and there's no call for you to leave the gate.'

'Would you like a pistol?'

'Much obliged to you, no! Gabriel Stogumber

216

ain't caught napping twice in one night.'

He then took his leave, and went off, leaning on his ash-plant. John watched him until he passed out of sight round the bend in the road, and then went back into the toll-house to await Chirk's return.

This was not long delayed. In a very few minutes, the highwayman was tossing his hat and coat on to a chair, and saying: 'I'm to tell you, Soldier, the Squire's not so stout today, which is why Miss Nell ain't left the house. Seems there was a bit of a kick-up this morning, which threw Squire into some kind of convulsion. Howsever, he's been sleeping pretty well all day, and they say as he's middling well now.'

'What happened?' John demanded.

'The butler-cove had back-words with Coate's man,' replied Chirk, accepting a tankard, and blowing the froth from it expertly. 'By all accounts, he mistook one of the wenches for a light-skirt, and acted according, and she, not having a fancy for a stub-faced cull — and wapper-eyed at that, so Rose tells me! — set up a screeching fit to burst anyone's listeners. So this old cove tells Gunn that what with him being in the habit of prigging the drink, and never coming into the house but what he's ale-blown and uncommon full o' bounce, he won't have him there no more, and if he sets his foot over the threshold again, he'll have up Squire's groom, and the stable-boy, which is a fine, lusty lad, to take and throw him out. Then in walks Mr Henry Stornaway, and he flies into his high ropes in a brace o' snaps, and tells the butler-cove he's as good as master at Kellands, and things will be as he wants 'em to be. Which the butler-cove says they won't, not while Squire's above ground. So off goes this Henry in a twirk, and as soon as Squire's own man is out o' the way he goes in to see his granfer. What he said to him no one don't know, but Squire's man come back to find Squire fair foaming at the mouth, and trying to get out of his chair to give this Henry a leveller. Which his man was so obliging as to have done for him, which, so far as anyone could tell, Squire not being able to speak, pleased the old gager considerable. Then Miss Nell goes off and dresses Coate down like you never heard, and tells him if him or Henry goes next or nigh Squire, or Gunn sets foot in the house, she'll have in the constable from Tideswell to heave 'em out, the whole scaff and raff of 'em. Rose had her ear to the door, misdoubting there might be a turn-up of some sort, but by what she tells me Coate did his best to come over Miss Nell with a lot o' bamboozling talk, saying as Henry was a buzzard, and Gunn a worse 'un, and he'd see as she wasn't troubled no more. Then she tells him to his teeth that the sooner he pikes the better pleased she'll be, and he says as she'll do well to take care, 'cos if she meddles with him it'll be very much the worse for her, and Squire, and Henry too. Rose says he sounded as wicked as if he was the Black Spy himself, and gives a laugh which makes the blood curdle in her veins. But I don't set much store by that,' he added indulgently, 'women's blood being remarkable

218

prone to curdle. So that's how it is, Soldier — excepting that Henry's took to his bed with a chill, which Rose says is true enough, him sneezing fit to bring the roof down.'

John was silent for a moment, frowning over this intelligence. He looked up at last, and asked curtly: 'Did you ask Rose if she knew of a cave near the Manor?'

'I did, and in a manner o' speaking she does, only it would queer her to tell us where it is, because she ain't ever seen it. There's a couple of small caves in the hills north o' Squire's place, and one big 'un, very like the one at the Peak, she says, but Squire closed up the entrance to that afore ever Rose went to the Manor, Henry's pa having broke his leg in it. It's on his land, you see, but there ain't no road to it, and Squire never took a fancy to show it to folks, like they show the one at the Peak. Miss Nell's pa, which was Squire's eldest son, Mr Frank, was with Henry's pa when he broke his leg, the pair of 'em being no more than shavelings, and he run off to get help, which was just as well, seemingly 'cos there's water in the cavern, and when it rises it don't take more than five or six hours to flood it. So Squire wouldn't let no one go in it no more, and Rose says she doubts the lads nowadays even know where it is, nor nothing about it. She says she'll take her oath Miss Nell and her brother never knew there was a big cave, 'cos Squire laid it on everyone they wasn't to be told, them being the kind of young 'uns as 'ud think it rare sport to go getting drownded in a cavern.'

'But Henry might have known!' John said. 'No doubt his father told him of his adventure in it! I'm much obliged to you, Chirk!'

Chirk eyed him shrewdly. 'You're welcome. What might you be meaning to do?'

'Find the cavern, and discover what the secret of it is. If it's being used to serve some purpose — why, that would explain what brought Coate to Kellands, and what made him ally himself with such a creature as Henry Stornaway!'

'*If* it is,' agreed Chirk sceptically.

'The more I think of it, the more convinced I am that nothing could be more likely,' declared John. 'Jerry Chirk, I've a strong notion I am going to enjoy myself!'

Mr Chirk noticed that there was a sparkle in his eyes, and a queer little upward tilt to the corners of his mouth, but since his acquaintance-ship with the Captain was of the slightest he set no particular store by signs which would have sunk any of John's cronies into the deepest foreboding. He merely said in a disparaging tone: 'Well, I don't know why you should, Soldier. What would anyone want with a cave, except maybe to hide in, and they ain't doing that?'

The sparkle became more pronounced; the eyes were smiling now. 'I don't know. If it weren't for Miss Nell and the Squire, I should call this a capital go! Something must be hidden in that cavern: all I have to do is to discover what!'

'I don't see that neither,' objected Chirk. 'If they've slummed some ken, and prigged the lurries out of it — diamonds and pearls, and silver feeders and such — they wouldn't go putting it into a cavern, not unless they was addle-brained, they wouldn't! They'd take it to a fence, and mighty quick, too! Much good would it do 'em, shoved in a cavern! What's more, Soldier, I'll allow this Henry looks like he's a ramshackle sort of a cove, but it ain't likely as he'd go slumming kens, nor any such lay! That's pitching it too rum!'

'I wonder!' John said. 'No, I should say it wasn't that. Lord, I wish I knew what took him there last night, and what happened to scare him out of his wits! I'll ride over there at first light, and see what I can find. There are at least two deep gorges in the hills, for I saw them this morning.'

'Yes, I suspicioned you would,' said Chirk, with a sigh. 'So did Rose, and what must she do but make me take my dying oath I'd go along with you, in case you was to tumble down, and break *your* leg! Which I'd take it kind in you if you wasn't to do, Soldier, because I've got no fancy for hauling a man of your size out of any plaguey cavern!'

'No, I won't do that,' promised John. 'But come, by all means! We may see some sport!'

'We may see a cavern or two,' said Chirk. 'I don't say as we won't; but as for seeing anything else, I'll wager you an even coachwheel we don't!'

'Done!' said John promptly. 'You'd better sleep here tonight. There's some spare bedding in the room Ben's in. I'll fetch it.'

'Don't you go waking him up! He's a good lad, but there's no sense in letting him know more than is good for him — or me!'

'Wake him up! You don't know him! I might be able to do it if I banged his head against the wall.'

The light of the candle which the Captain carried made Ben stir, and open drowsy eyes, but after muttering something inaudible, he slid back into slumber. The Captain carried a pillow and an armful of blankets into the kitchen, and made up the fire. Chirk, hauling off his cracked boots, said that he had slept on many worse beds.

Turning down the lamp on the table, John bethought him of something, and said: 'Chirk, where's the Wansbeck ford? Do you know?'

Chirk set his boots down carefully side by side. 'No, I can't say as I do. *Which* ford?'

'The Wansbeck. Have you ever heard of it?'

'Wansbeck,' repeated Chirk, a slight frown between his eyes. 'Seems to me as though I know that name, but I can't just think where I've heard it.' He scratched his chin reflectively. 'Blessed if I can place it!' he said. 'I'd say I'd never been there, but I got a feeling — ' An irrepressible yawn broke off this utterance. He shook his head. 'I can't call it to mind, but I daresay it'll come back to me.'

'Tell me if it does!' John said.

He then withdrew to his own bed, and, no one demanding his attendance on the gate, passed an untroubled night.

He possessed the soldier's faculty of waking at

what hour he chose, and got up at dawn to discover that Chirk shared it. The fire was burning brightly, and the kettle was already singing. John at once made tea, and Chirk, finding some cold bacon in the cupboard, clapped a hunk on to a slice of bread, and consumed it, observing that there was no knowing when he would get his breakfast. He then went off to saddle the mare, while John roused Ben, and told him he was off to exercise Beau. Under his father's rule, it had always been Ben's duty to attend to any early wayfarers, and since the dawn-light was creeping in at the little window he raised no demur, merely yawning, and knuckling his eyes.

A few minutes later, the Captain joined Chirk by the hedge skirting Farmer Huggate's field, Beau snatching playfully at the bit, and dancing on his impatient hooves. He had strapped his great cloak to the saddle, but although he had pulled on his boots, he had not chosen to subject his only coat to whatever rigours might be in store, and he wore only his leather waistcoat over a flannel shirt.

'No sense in going by the road,' said Chirk. 'If that high-bred 'un of yours can take a fence or two, we'll edge round by way of the fields.'

'As many as you like!' replied John. 'Or a six-foot wall, coped and dashed, for that matter!'

'What, with you up, Soldier? Come, now, Mollie! We'd best give that big daisy-cutter a lead!'

The mare nipped neatly over the hedge, and Chirk led the way through the spinney to the

223

fields John had seen from the lane. The mist still lay heavily over them, but it was not thick enough to impede the riders' progress. They made their way diagonally towards the lane, and came to it half a mile to the north of the farm on the further side of it. The mare went over the bank cat-fashion, but Beau took bank and hedge flying, which made Chirk say, 'One of these neck-or-nothing coves! And lucky if the prad ain't strained a tendon!'

But Beau was sagacious and the Captain clever in the saddle, and the wheel to the left when he alighted was accomplished without any such mishap. The tumbled mass of the hills could now be seen quite clearly ahead, and, after another quarter of a mile, the lane took a sharp turn, beginning the steep ascent over the pass. The Captain reined in.

'We'll try to the east,' he said. 'That's where I noticed the clefts, and the limestone outcropping. The slope is milder to the west, not so likely, I fancy.'

'Just as you say, Soldier,' responded Chirk amiably.

The bank which had been built up round the farm-lands had come to an end a few hundred yards to the south, and there was only a narrow ditch to be stepped over. Beyond it the land was uncultivated. Birch trees reared up out of a mass of tangled undergrowth, and even found a foothold on the precipitous slopes of the escarpment; and every now and then a boulder sticking up out of the ground showed how thinly the earth lay above the rock. At a walking pace,

John led the way along the outskirts of the bushes, keenly scrutinizing the face of the hill. This was, in many places, very sheer, and there were several deep indentations where the rock showed as naked as though the covering earth had been scraped from it. John said over his shoulder: 'There might be caverns in any of these clefts.'

'Very likely there are,' replied Chirk, 'but it don't look like anyone's been near 'em for many a year. Of course, if you're wishful to push your way through all these brambles, I'm agreeable.'

'No, we'll go on,' John said.

They had not far to go before, rounding a spur, John saw something that caused him to pull Beau up so sharply that the mare, following him closely, nearly jostled him. 'Look!' John said, pointing with his whip. 'Someone has been *here* before us!'

Chirk brought Mollie up alongside, and stared keenly at an unmistakable track, winding through the undergrowth towards the hill. They had reached the big gorge John had seen from the pass; it ran back into the hill, deeply undercutting it; and the rank grass and fading clumps of willow-herb had been trodden down on the rising ground which led into it.

John touched Beau with his heel, saying briskly: 'We will tether the horses round the next spur. Come on!'

A few minutes later, as they dismounted, out of sight of the big gorge, Chirk drew his pistols out of their holsters, slipped one into the capacious pocket of his coat, and thrust the other into the top of his breeches. John, unfastening the lantern from his saddle, noticed this, and said instantly: 'If you start a cannonade with those damned barking-irons, I'll murder you! You're too fond of pulling out a gun! I thought, moreover, that you were sure we should find nothing in the cavern?'

'I daresay we won't,' replied Chirk, setting the second lantern on the ground, and throwing his greatcoat over the mare. 'But, if it's all the same to you, Soldier, now I've seen that track I'll be easier in my mind if I have my pops handy. If that pair from the Manor was to visit the cavern while we're there, maybe they'll save our groats for us!' He waited while John loosened Beau's girths, and covered him with his cloak, and then led the way back to the gorge, steering wide of the bushes until he reached the path through them. He had not gone far along this before he stopped, drawing John's attention to some confused but deep footprints in a patch of softer ground. His face had sharpened, and his quick, frowning eyes glanced about, at the beaten grass, and the bushes encroaching on the track. 'Seems to me, Soldier, there's been several coves here.'

'Several coves,' agreed John, 'and they were carrying something heavy, from the look of these marks. What's more, one or two of these brambles have been lopped back. See?'

Chirk nodded, but said nothing. They went on, the ground steadily rising as it approached the back of the gorge. The hill now towered above them, its rocky face seeming almost to overhang them; and the gorge narrowed rapidly.

A tangle of dead gorse lay ahead, and when they drew nearer to it they saw that it had been arranged to hide a rude fence. As soon as the gorse had been pulled away, the fence was seen to cover an opening in the rock, perhaps six foot high, and almost as broad. Closer inspection revealed rusted iron staples driven into the rock on either side of the opening. To these the rude fence was secured with lengths of twine.

'Fresh,' Chirk said, a little grimly, pulling the knot apart. 'If you ain't had the sense to bring your own pistols, Soldier, you'd better have one of mine!'

'You can give it to me, if we're followed,' replied John. 'That there's no one inside at least we know: you couldn't tie the fence to the staples from inside that hole.' He dropped on his knee as he spoke, setting the lantern he carried down within the cave-mouth, and taking his tinder-box from his pocket.

Both lanterns alight, and burning fairly, Chirk said: 'One of us ought to stay and keep watch.'

'Well, if you've a fancy for sentry-duty, you stay and do so!' recommended the Captain light-heartedly.

'Danged if I will!' said Chirk.

'Then come on!' John said, and, stooping, entered the cavern.

12

Almost immediately, he found himself able to stand upright, and holding the lantern high saw that he was standing in a roughly vaulted chamber of considerable size. Chirk, entering behind him, and looking around, said, with a certain amount of satisfaction: 'Well, there ain't nothing here, that's certain! Queer sort of a place to find in a hill! Was it made natural?'

'Quite natural. Have you never been inside a limestone cavern before?'

'No, I can't say as I have. I've heard tell of them, though. Big, ain't it?'

'Bigger than you think, I fancy.' John walked forward, still holding up the lantern. 'Yes, I thought as much! This is only the antechamber, Jerry.' He walked to the back of the cave, where a narrow opening, like a rude Gothic doorway, led into a passage through the rock. This ran slightly downwards into dense darkness. The lantern-light showed the uneven rock-face gleaming damply; underfoot the ground was soft, mushy with moisture; and the air felt dank. John heard Chirk draw in his breath sharply, and said, amusement in his voice: 'Have your nerves enough steel for this adventure?'

'What you've got bottom for, I have!' Chirk answered through his teeth. 'Go on!'

John went forward, easily at first, but was soon obliged to duck his head, and, in a very few moments, to bend almost double. He could hear Chirk breathing hard behind him, and said: 'Careful! The roof's devilish low ahead: we may have to crawl!'

They were not actually obliged to do this, but by the time they had reached a loftier space they were thankful to pause, and to stand upright. Something grazed John's head as he straightened his aching back, and he directed the lantern's beam upwards, running it over the roof of the chamber. 'By Jupiter!' he said softly. 'That's something to have seen, Jerry!'

'What are they?' asked Chirk, staring upwards. 'They look like icicles to me, and the lord knows it's cold enough!'

'Not icicles: stalactites. They're formed by the dripping of the water — thousands of years of it! I told you this would be a capital go!'

'I don't know when I've enjoyed myself more,' said Chirk sardonically. 'If this was where young Stornaway came, I'm not surprised he caught a chill! Look, Soldier! The walls are streaming wet! What makes 'em so?'

'Water, of course. What's more, it's Carlton House to a Charley's shelter there's a river somewhere below us. There's one in the Peak cavern, and a boat on it: Miss Nell told me about it. Are you ready to go on?'

'I'm within ames-ace of going back!' replied Chirk, with mordant humour. 'Howsever, if we've got to go on, let's cut line and go!'

John had moved cautiously forward, peering ahead. 'Take care!' he said suddenly. 'We're dropping down fast now, and there's a damned lot of loose rubble! Hell and the devil confound it, I wish I hadn't put these boots on! Lord, it's a regular stairway! Look!'

The passage had widened considerably. Chirk, who was standing with his lantern directed on to the rock-face above his head, withdrew his fascinated gaze to glance down the steep descent. Fragments of jutting rock did indeed form the semblance of a stairway, but the drop from one to another was sometimes of several feet, and for the most part the ground was littered with rubble, and treacherously loose stones, some of them of great size. It was not difficult to perceive how Henry Stornaway's father had broken a leg in the cavern. Chirk said so, with some asperity. He then begged the Captain to pause. 'Just you cast your ogles over this devil's work!' he adjured him, keeping the beam of his lantern fixed on the rock. 'Don't you tell me that wicked face came there natural, Soldier!'

It took John a moment to perceive what was holding Chirk chained to the spot. Then he laughed, and said: 'Good God, it's only the weathering of the rock that's done that! If we had the time to waste, I daresay we could pick out a dozen weird faces!'

'Thank'ee, I'd as lief go on!' said Chirk. 'But for the lord's sake take care how you set your feet down!'

The descent, though it was not very long, took time, but close to the walls the rocks were reasonably firm, and after perhaps thirty feet the staircase became a slope, down which it was easy to walk. Occasionally the roof dipped suddenly, making it necessary for them to stoop, and once a long stalactite knocked Chirk's hat off. The cold was intense, and a faint sound of rushing, steadily increasing, did nothing to add to Chirk's enjoyment.

'Hear that noise?' John said, in a satisfied voice. 'I told you there would be a river! Now what have we come to?'

The ground had ceased to slope downwards, and the passage suddenly widened. The sweep of John's lantern failed to discover the walls, and when he turned it upwards it only dimly illuminated the roof.

'We must have reached the main cavern. Jupiter, what a place! Stay where you are. I want to find how big it is, and whether it leads on farther still.' He moved to one side as he spoke, playing the lantern before him. In a moment it lit up the rock-face, jagged and gleaming. Chirk, standing at the entrance to the huge chamber, watched it travel on, and then swing round to light the wall opposite to where he stood. A black cavity yawned, and the Captain said, his words resounding eerily: 'I've found another passage!'

'I see you have,' replied Chirk.

To his secret relief, the Captain moved on, and presently rounded the corner of the chamber, and began to make his way slowly back towards the entrance, his lantern playing all over the rock-face. 'Chirk, this is a wonderful place!' he declared. 'Come over here! The rock's honey-combed with galleries above our heads! I wish we had a ladder! There's no reaching them without one!'

'I don't doubt you'd like to go crawling along a lot of galleries,' said Chirk tartly, walking towards him, and gazing up with revulsion, 'but we've got no call to do so, because if there ain't no ladder here it stands to reason no one — ' He broke off, with a startled oath, almost losing his balance, as his foot came up against some obstacle. He recovered it, and brought the beam of his lantern downwards. His voice changed; he said with careful calm: 'Never mind the galleries! Just you come over here, Soldier!'

John turned. 'What — ' Then he too stopped abruptly, for Chirk was holding the storm-lantern high, and by its golden light he saw a number of corded chests ranged along the side of the cavern. 'Good God!' he ejaculated.

Three or four strides brought him up to Chirk, who, finding one chest standing on end, set his lantern down on it, and said: 'That's a coachwheel I owe you. Lordy, I'd have laid you any odds there'd be nothing here! But what the devil's in them?'

The Captain was on his knee, closely scrutinizing one of the chests. 'Chirk!' he said, rather oddly. 'Unless I'm much mistaken — this is an official seal!'

'*What?*' demanded Chirk, so sharply that his voice seemed to echo round the cavern. He too dropped on his knee, staring at the red seal over the knot of the cord. Then he rose, and ran his eyes over the other chests. 'Six of 'em, and all alike!' he said softly, and whistled. 'Small — ' he

bent and with an effort lifted the end of one
— 'but remarkable heavy!'

'The seal's been broken on this one, and
— yes, the lock's been forced!' John said, pausing
beside a chest which had been set down upon
another. 'Well! — let us see what's inside it!'

He put his lantern down on another of the
chests, and set to work to untie the knot. The
cord fell away, and he lifted the lid. The chest
was packed with neat little bags, and the chink of
metal as John picked one up was not needed to
tell him what these must contain. He untied the
string about its neck, plunged in his hand, and
drew out a fistful of yellow coins, and held them
in the lantern-light, staring down at them.

'*Wansbeck ford!*' Chirk cried, after a stunned
minute. '*That's* why I know the name! Lord,
what a clunch, what a totty-headed dummy!
How *could* I have been such a beetle-head as to
have forgot it?'

John looked up at him. 'What has Wansbeck
ford to do with this?'

Chirk was breathing rather rapidly. 'Don't you
never read the newspapers, Soldier?'

'I do, yes, but not with any particular attention
in these peaceful times. Tell me what I should
have read and did not!'

'A couple o' sennights back — a Government
coach, bound for Manchester!' uttered Chirk
jerkily. 'Took the wrong fork somewhere short of
a place called Ashbourne — matter of
twenty-five to thirty miles south-west of here. It
was after dark, and seemingly a lonesome stretch
o' country. By what I read, it was as clever a

hold-up as I ever heard of! 'Cos what did they do? They — '

'Changed the two arms of the sign-post!'

'You *did* read about it!'

'No. Go on!'

'Well, it's like you said. That's what they did. By God, they had it planned bang-up! There ain't so much as a cottage within half a mile of this ford, and there's a steepish drop down to it, and up t'other side, and woods either side of the lane. The coach was set on when it was pulling out of the stream. There was two guards shot dead afore they could aim their barkers. The driver, and another man with him, which was at the horses' heads at the time, was found gagged and trussed up like cackling-cheats next morning. The coach had been broke open, and not a chest left inside of it.' He paused, and wiped the back of his hand across his brow. 'And you're telling me it was Henry Stornaway and Coate which did it? Lord love me, I don't know when I've been so flabbergasted! But — what do they want to leave 'em here for? There's only one been opened, and there ain't nothing gone from it, by the looks of it! I see it would queer anyone to know where to stack all these chests, but what I *don't* see is why they've took *none* of the gelt away! Well! They say as it's an ill wind as blows no one any good! Here, let's see if there's Yellow Goblins in all these bags!'

'They are not Yellow Goblins.'

Chirk looked sharply at him, struck by an odd note in his voice. 'What? You're not going to tell me they're counterfeit? With *that* seal on the cases?'

'Not counterfeit, but not guineas. Take a look!'

Chirk stared down at the coins in John's hand. He picked one up, to inspect it more closely, and said: 'Danged if I ever see one of them before, but they're gold all right and tight, and new-minted! What are they, Soldier?'

'Do *you* never read the newspapers? They are the new coins — the sovereigns which are to replace the guineas!'

'Are they?' Chirk turned the piece he was holding over, regarding it with interest. 'They're the first I've seen.' He added, with a grin: 'Ah, well, I won't quarrel over the odd shillings! Lord love us, there must be thirty or forty thousand pounds in these cases! And to think if it hadn't been for Rose I wouldn't have come along with you today! No more rank-riding! A snug farm — and never did I think to see the day!'

He thrust his hand into the chest as he spoke, and would have lifted out of it another of the bags had not the Captain caught his wrist, and held it. 'Put that down! You'll take none of this money, Chirk!'

An ugly look came into Chirk's eyes. He said: 'Won't I? Take care, Soldier!'

John let him go. 'If that's the mind you're in, draw your pistol, and add me to the men who have been murdered for this gold!'

Chirk flushed, and growled: 'Ah, have done! You know I wouldn't do that! But you can't stop me taking some of it! There'll never come such a chance again! It's all very well for a well-breeched cove like you to stick to pound dealing, but — '

'Pound dealing! Ay, that's just what this is!' John interrupted, with a short laugh. 'These *are* pounds, not the old guineas! You fool, don't you see why the chests have been stored here, and not a sovereign taken from them? This is the most perilous treasure that was ever stolen! One of these coins would send you to the gallows! Take a bag of them, and try if you can to buy your farm with them! Try if there's a fence alive who will give you flimsies in exchange for them! I'll come to see you hanged! This coinage was only minted this summer: none of it's in circulation yet! *That's* why it has been stored in this place! I should doubt whether it would be safe to touch it under a year.'

Chirk sat down limply on one of the chests. 'A year! But — it could be hid away! just a few bags of it!'

John dropped a hand on his shoulder. 'Listen, Jerry! I didn't tell you, but Stogumber — the man you rescued last night — isn't searching for an estate, as he's tried to hoax us into believing. He's searching for this gold, and for the men who stole it. He's a Bow Street Runner!'

The shoulder stiffened under his hand. '*What?*' Chirk said. 'A Redbreast? A Redbreast which I — *I!* — saved from being stuck in the back?'

'You never did a better day's work in your life. He's not ungrateful, and I fancy I see how he may be made more grateful yet! Don't look so blue-devilled! You'll win your fortune! Why, Jerry, where have your wits gone begging? There will be a huge reward paid to the man who discovers these chests! You told me you wanted no more than a monkey to set you up: if all these cases hold sovereigns and half-sovereigns, as I think they may well, a monkey won't be more than a fraction of what the Government will pay for their recovery!'

Chirk drew in his breath with a hissing sound. 'That's so!' he said, as though a great light had dawned. 'And pound dealing, too! But this Redbreast — ! You're not gammoning me, Soldier?'

'No. While you were holding his head over the sink last night, I picked up the notebook which had fallen from his pocket when we threw his coat aside. Have you heard of Occurrence Books?' Chirk nodded. 'This was one. He doesn't know yet that I've smoked him: I think he has a notion I too may be concerned in this business.'

'Well, he'll soon know you ain't.'

'Not too soon, if I can contrive it! Chirk, you found the gold, and the reward will be yours, but will you trust me to manage the business as will be best for all of us?'

'Ay, but it wasn't me found the dibs!' Chirk pointed out. 'It was you brought me here! I may be a bridle-cull, but I'm danged if I'm a cove as diddles my friends!'

'I may have brought you here, but did I find these chests? All I found was a gallery! I don't want the reward, so let us have no more talk of that! What I want is to keep Miss Nell and the Squire out of this business — and Henry Stornaway, too, for their sakes, though it goes against the grain! I don't know how I may do that, but some way there must be! Sir Peter must not know what you and I have discovered, and I'd give all I possess to keep it from Miss Nell too. How much Stogumber knows already I can't guess: something he must know, for why else should he have come to this district? But not much, surely! If he had proof to bring against Coate or Henry, he would have arrested them; if he knew where this gold was hid we shouldn't have found it here today!'

'What are you wishful to do?' Chirk asked.

'Keep Henry Stornaway's name out of it, if I can. If I can't, get him out of the country before Stogumber knows the whole!'

'And Coate?'

The Captain's jaw hardened. 'No. I'm damned if I will! No, by God! There are two dead men at least to be laid to his account, for I'll swear it was he who shot those guards! He and that man of his, maybe. That's another thing, Jerry! We could reveal these chests to Stogumber, but he wants more than the gold: he wants the men who stole it. What proof is there that Coate was the arch-thief?'

'Well,' said Chirk, stroking his chin reflectively, 'it would look uncommon like he must have done the business — him being at Kellands, wouldn't it?'

'It might look smoky, but unless Stogumber has proof, which I'll swear he has not, it's not enough to warrant an arrest. Lord, I don't know what I am going to do, but give me a little time before you go to Stogumber!'

His wry smile twisted Chirk's lips. 'Didn't I tell you I'd had my orders from that mort o' mine I was to do what you tell me, Soldier? I won't deny that if it was Rose's cousin which had run his head into this noose I'd feel the way you do. I'll stand buff, and there's my famble on it!'

He stretched out his hand, and John gripped it warmly. 'Thank you! You're a damned good fellow! I have one day at least to consider what I can do: I fancy Stogumber won't do much spying today. He'll be feeling as sick as a horse, and will very likely keep his bed. But he's been recognized: we have to bear that in mind! That must have been why he was set upon last night. If Coate were to take fright, and run for it — why, that would solve the thing for us! If he don't — lord, I wish I saw my way!'

'I daresay you will,' Chirk replied. 'I'm bound to say I don't, but that don't signify.' He looked up at John. 'Was Ned Brean in this?'

'I think, undoubtedly,' John said. He glanced round at the encircling gloom, and Chirk saw that the good-humoured expression had quite vanished from his face. 'There was the gate to be passed, and there must have been an urgent need of a strong man to assist in carrying these chests from the lane to this place. There were no wheel-ruts off the lane, nor could a heavily laden vehicle have been dragged across the ditch. The chests must have been carried by hand — and Henry would be useless for such work.'

'What queers me,' said Chirk, 'is how they ever got 'em down that 'regular stairway' of yours! Why, it was as much as I could do to get down holding on to the wall, and any rock that came handy! If I'd tried to carry anything, I'd have foundered, sure as a gun!'

'I fancy they lowered them with ropes. They must have!' John said, picking up his lantern, and walking round the cases. 'Yes, here we are! A couple of coils of stout rope.'

Chirk was frowning. 'If Ned was working with Coate, where is he?' he demanded. 'I remember what Benny said about being woke up by a waggon one night, and Ned going off like he did. What took him off again last Saturday, and where did he pike to? Did he get scared, d'ye think?'

'No, I don't think that. I think — he came here.'

Chirk glanced up swiftly, a question in his face, and then his eyes travelled as swiftly to the one open chest. 'It was him broke that open? Tipping the rest of 'em the double?'

'Trying to, perhaps. He didn't succeed. The chest is full.'

Chirk got up with a jerk. 'Look'ee here, Soldier — ! What's in your noddle, for God's sake?'

'Where is he?' said John significantly. 'Why did the news that Brean had gone away alarm Henry Stornaway so much? Why did Henry come here the night before last? And what did he find here to make him look as though he had seen a ghost?'

240

Chirk passed his tongue between his lips, and cast a staring look about him. 'Maybe — we'd do well to search a bit more!' he said, a trifle thickly. He gave a shiver. 'God, I'll be glad to be out of this place!'

The light from John's lantern was being cast on to the ground, slowly moving in a wide arc. 'If he was surprised here — and killed here, there should be some sign of it.'

'There was no call to kill him!'

'There may have been a fight.'

'Ay, likely enough!' Chirk said, after a moment. 'He'd have fought, Ned would.'

He said no more, and for a few minutes only the rushing noise of water, which seemed to come from deep within the hill, broke the silence. Then the Captain's lantern was lowered, and he knelt, keenly inspecting the ground. Chirk, who had been searching along one of the walls, saw, and trod quickly over to his side. The Captain pressed the palm of one hand on the ground, and lifted it, and held it in the light.

Chirk swallowed audibly, and said in a rough voice: 'Where did they put him? We got to find him, Soldier!'

'Follow the bloodstains,' John replied, rising and moving forward, his eyes fixed to the ground. 'He bled a great deal, Chirk. There was a sticky pool of it where I laid my hand. This looks like some more of it.' He stooped again. 'Yes. And here!'

'Going towards that other passage you saw,' Chirk said. 'I'm for trying that way: they wouldn't have left him here, and the chests being here no one had any call to go farther.'

He walked forward, and his lantern presently found the hole in the rock. It was narrow, and low; more blood was to be detected there; and after one look at it, Chirk went on, John following him.

The passage was only a few feet long; it opened into a far broader and loftier passage, colder than all the rest, and with water dripping from the rock. Chirk stopped short, exclaiming: 'There *is* a river, and we've come to it! Lord, I never saw the like of it! Look at it coming out of that tunnel in the rock! It's quite shallow, though. Do you tell me a little stream like this can flood the whole place?'

'Yes, when the water rises. Look at the slime on the walls! It goes up as far as you can see.' John began to walk along the passage, beside the stream. It plunged into the rock again some fifty yards on, where the passage came to an end, blocked by a mass of loose rocks and rubble, which showed where a part of the roof had fallen in. John set his lantern down, and, his face very grim, began to remove the stones and the boulders from the pile. Chirk came to join him, and in silence followed his example. A choking sound broke from him suddenly, and he sprang back, shuddering. A hand was protruding from amongst fragments of rock, piled up in a rough cairn. In another minute John had uncovered the upper half of a man's body. He picked up the lantern and held it above the body. 'Well? Is this Brean?'

Chirk nodded, his eyes on an ugly gash where

the neck joined the shoulder. 'Knifed!' he said unsteadily. 'His hand — Soldier, it was like a slab of ice, and wet — slimy wet!'

'Do you wonder at it, in this temperature? I don't know how long a body might remain here without rotting: some time, I daresay. That's just as well, for Stogumber must see this! Help me to cover it again! This is what Henry found — and it's my belief he didn't know Brean had been murdered, but suspected it, and came because he suspected it.'

'If Coate did this — '

'Either he, or his man, Gunn. He must have had some inkling of what Brean meant to do. He may even have been watching him at night. It seems certain he followed him here.'

'I don't hold with Brean trying to diddle him, but he didn't have to murder him!' Chirk said, with suppressed violence. 'He's got pistols, no question! He could have held Ned up easy enough! What does he want to stick a damned chive into him for?'

'I should imagine that once he knew Brean was unsafe he meant to kill him. He may have mistrusted his aim in this poor light, and so preferred to use a knife. He seems partial to knives. If it hadn't been for you, I suppose Stogumber's body would have been brought here as well.'

He straightened himself, and went to wash his hands in the stream. The icy coldness of the water numbed his fingers; he wiped them dry on his handkerchief, rubbed them briskly to restore the circulation, and said: 'It's time we were going. We have still to cord up that chest again.'

'I'm agreeable,' Chirk said shortly.

As they tied the last knot presently, he said: 'What's to be done with Benny, poor little brat?'

'I'll take care of that.'

'You ain't going to tell him — what we found there?' Chirk said, with a jerk of his thumb.

'Of course not. I shan't tell him anything yet. Later, he must know that his father's dead, but I don't think he'll grieve much. There, that's done! Let us be off!'

The return journey to the mouth of the cavern was accomplished without very much difficulty. The mist had cleared away, but there was no one in sight. They secured the fence again, replaced the gorse bushes, and went away to where they had tethered the horses.

'I'll brush now,' Chirk said. 'I'll come to the toll-house tonight, though. You know my signal! If all's bowman, open the kitchen-door; if there's any stranger with you, leave it shut!'

'Where can I find you, if I should need you quickly?' John asked, a detaining hand on the mare's bridle.

Chirk looked down at him with a faint smile. 'So now you've got to know the case where I rack up, have you, Soldier? And what's the cove as owns it going to say to that?'

'Nothing, when you tell him I shan't squeak beef on him,' returned John.

'A gentleman like you hasn't got any business to go to flash kens, nor to hobnob with bridle-culls neither!' said Chirk severely. 'If find me you must, take the Ecclesfield road out o'

Sheffield, till you come to a boozing-ken called the Ram's Head, and say to the buffer, *The Whit be burnt!*'

'Much obliged to you! I won't forget!'

'I don't know as I'm so very pleased to know that!' retorted Chirk. He wheeled Mollie round, and said over his shoulder: 'And whatever you do, don't call for a glass of beer! Arms and legs is all they keep there — no body!'

13

Finding that Ben's services were not required, that day, either by the innkeeper or by Huggate, John left him in charge of the pike, midway through the morning, and walked down the road to the village. He was desirous of obtaining news of Gabriel Stogumber; and it was with satisfaction that he learned from Sopworthy that that sturdy gentleman was keeping his bed.

'It's a queer set-out, so it is!' said the landlord, pushing a tankard of his nappy ale towards the Captain. 'He tells me as he was pounced on last night by a couple o' foot-scamperers, but whatever would such be hopeful of prigging on this road? That's what has me fair humdudgeoned! The like has never happened, not in all the years I've lived here!' He perceived a splash of spilt ale on the counter, and wiped it carefully. 'Asked me all manner of questions about you, he did, Mr Staple. 'Course, there was naught I could tell him, excepting you was a kinsman of Brean's — which I done! But what I *would* like to know, sir, — me being a man as likes to keep on the windy side o' the law — what kind of a queer cove is this Stogumber?'

The Captain was spared the necessity of answering this question by the sudden irruption into the tap of Mr Nathaniel Coate, who had ridden into Crowford from the Manor, and now stormed into the Blue Boar, demanding the landlord in stentorian accents. His fancy had prompted him to sport a striped toilinette waistcoat under a coat of corbeau-cloth, and this combination, worn, as it was, with breeches of Angola-cloth and hunting-boots with white tops, so powerfully affected the Captain that for a full minute he sat with his tankard halfway to his mouth, and his gaze riveted upon the astonishing vision. He felt stunned, and looked quite as stupid as he would have wished. Mr Coate, who had looked rather narrowly at him, upon first entering the tap, seemed to be reassured by the fixed stare. 'Well, hempseed!' he said. 'Take care your eyes don't fall out of their sockets! Did you never see a gentleman before?'

'I never see a gentleman like you afore,' drawled the Captain. He shook his head, and took a pull at his ale. 'As fine as fivepence, you be!' he said, in the tone of one who had beheld a marvel.

Mr Coate turned a contemptuous shoulder to him, and addressed himself to the landlord. 'What a clodpole! I suppose that in these benighted parts you never see anyone who is up to the knocker!'

The landlord, who had listened with a wooden countenance to the Captain's sudden illiteracy, followed a lead of which he heartily approved, and replied: 'No, sir. Never! I disremember when I saw Squire himself in such toggery. Slap up to the echo, I make no doubt! And what can I do for you, sir?'

Mr Coate eyed him a little suspiciously, but his hard scrutiny was met with such a bland look of incomprehension that it was impossible to suspect Sopworthy of malice. He gave one of his rough laughs, and said: 'Damme if I was ever in such a backward place! What you can do for me, fellow, is to direct me to the nearest constable! By God, a pretty state of affairs when a gentleman can't step out to blow a cloud, and to stretch his legs, without being attacked by armed ruffians! Ay, you may stare!' He wheeled about, stabbing a finger at John. 'You, there, rustic! You're the gatekeeper, ain't you? Who passed the pike last night?'

John shook his head. 'Didn't see no armed ruffians,' he said.

'Where was you attacked, sir?' asked Sopworthy, staring.

'Why, at the very gate of the Manor! I'm a handy man with my fives, but if my man hadn't come along when he did I might have lost more than my watch and my fobs — ay, and sustained worse injury than a blow on the head which had almost knocked the wits out of me! One of the rascals set upon me from behind: it would have gone hard with him had he faced me, I can tell you!'

He continued in this strain for several minutes, while the Captain, his countenance still schooled to an expression of open-mouthed vacuity, studied him carefully.

To anyone who knew the world it was not difficult to recognize the order from which he sprang. Men very like him were to be met with in any large city, obtaining footholds on the fringes of Society, and earning a tolerable livelihood by decoying gullible young gentlemen of fortune to gaming-hells, or introducing them to horse-dealers who might be depended upon to sell them, at fabulous prices, showy-looking animals which, instead of being the sweet-goers or beautiful steppers which these Captain Sharps swore them to be, turned out to be confirmed limpers or incurable millers.

Such persons were nearly always knowledge-able in all matters of sport, bruising riders and expert dragsmen, and able to give good accounts of themselves in the boxing-ring, for these were accomplishments certain to make a good impression on their prospective victims. They knew as well how to toad-eat as to bully; and since they were almost invariably furnished with reliable racing-tips to impart to patrons, and could be relied upon to discover a really prime hunter, for a valued patron, and to acquire the animal for a ridiculously low price, it was seldom that they failed to attach themselves to several members of the *ton* who tolerated them for the sake of these useful attributes.

To this confraternity, John judged, Mr Coate unquestionably belonged; but there hung about him an indefinable suggestion of force not usually found in the hangers-on of Society. That he was ruthless, John already knew; that he had a brazen courage, he now acknowledged. His policy was declared: the knowledge that a law-officer was on his trail would not frighten him into abandoning his schemes. Since his attempt to dispose of Stogumber had failed, he had adopted a line of conduct which, while it was unlikely to deceive Stogumber, would be hard to counter.

It soon appeared, from the information he was pouring out with such seeming carelessness, that he had whisked Gunn out of the way. He described the man as having sustained injuries which made it impossible for him to fulfil his duties; said with a crack of scornful laughter that he was blue-devilled with fright; and added that he had packed him off to Sheffield, with instructions to return to London by the stage-coach. 'For I'd as lief have no servant as a bleater that thinks every bush a bogle, as the saying is!'

The Captain, having learned enough, did not linger in the Blue Boar, but paid his shot, and slouched off, leaving the landlord to explain to Coate that if he desired to enlist the services of a constable he must ride to Tideswell — a piece of intelligence which provoked him to break into a fury of objurgation, and a declaration that he would be damned if he would put himself to so much trouble only to seek out some gapeseed who, he dared swear, would be of no more use than a month-old baby.

From the circumstance of his having got rid of Gunn, the Captain, so much more acute than he had given Coate reason to suppose, strongly suspected that it must have been Gunn who had recognized in Stogumber a Bow Street Runner. It seemed probable, therefore, that it was Gunn, and not his master, who was known to the officers of the law. Bold Coate might be, but he was not a fool, and for a man previously convicted of crime to remain openly at Kellands, once his presence there had been discovered by the Runner, would have been an act almost lunatic in its foolhardiness.

The Captain reached the toll-house again to find that Joseph Lydd had ridden from the Manor with a scribbled note from Nell. As he broke the wafer that sealed it, he said: 'Lead the cob into the garden, out of sight: Coate is in the village, and will be returning, I fancy, at any minute.'

Joseph unhitched the cob's bridle from the gatepost, but said: 'Is that where he is? I thought he was off to Tideswell to fetch the constable!'

'Not he!'

'Well, it wouldn't do him no good if he did go there,' observed Joseph. 'He says he was set on last night by a pair o' foot-pads. I never heard the like, not on this road, but he swears his watch was snatched from him, and as for Gunn, which Coate says fought off these foot-pads, lord! he looks like a strained hair in a can! I don't know whether it was foot-pads which gave it to him, but he's had a proper melting, that's sure! One of his knees is swole up like a bolster, and he can't hardly walk on it, and he's took a crack on the noddle that's made him as dizzy as a goose. Mr Henry's man was told off to drive him to Sheffield this morning, so that's a good riddance. I'd as lief it had been Coate — though there's small choice in rotten apples!'

He then led the cob round the toll-house to the gate into the garden, and the Captain was left to read his letter. It was not long, and it gave him the impression that it had been written in a brave attempt to convince him that nothing had happened at Kellands to cause him to feel uneasiness. Nell was anxious, she assured him, only about her grandfather. Something which Henry had said to him had affected him profoundly; Winkfield had found him striving to heave himself to his feet; he had collapsed; and the doctor, summoned instantly, said that he had suffered a second stroke, not as severe as the first, but from which it was doubtful that he would recover. He was confined now to his bed, but he seemed to be unable to rest. Nell's dear John would understand that she must not go out of reach: no one could tell when she might be summoned to her grandfather's room for the last time.

Thrusting the single sheet of paper into the pocket of his leathers, John strode through the toll-house to the garden, where he found Ben being given a lesson in horse-manage. He dismissed him curtly, telling him to go back to the gate. Ben, who thought that he had been on duty for long enough, cast him a darkling look, and went off with a lagging step, and an audible sniff.

'He'll make a likely lad in the stables,' remarked Joseph. 'Given he gets the chance, that is. I've told Brean so afore now.'

'Yes, perhaps. Joseph, what is happening up at the Manor? Never mind what your mistress told you to say to me! I want the truth!'

'Squire's mortal bad,' Joseph replied. 'What's more, he ain't dying easy. He's worriting and worriting, and whether it's on account of Mr Henry, or something as he's expecting his lawyer to send him from London, Mr Winkfield don't know. Maybe it's his Will. He would have me ride to Sheffield to meet the mail yesterday afternoon, though me and Mr Winkfield knew there wouldn't be nothing on it, 'cos there wasn't time enough, seeing when it was I carried his letter to the mail. He don't seem to be able to reckon the days no more, though he ain't dicked in the nob — far from it! I'm to go again this afternoon, and I hopes to God there'll be an express packet for him!'

'Miss Nell has told me that the Squire is dying. What she has not told me is what those two hell-born rogues are doing!'

'Now, there's no call for you to fly into your high ropes, guv'nor! Barring Mr Henry's took to his bed, as blue as megrim, they ain't doing nothing. Nor they won't, not while Squire's above ground, and all of us still at the Manor. It's when Squire's dead and buried that the mischief will begin, by what Mr Huby managed to hear Coate saying to Mr Henry last night. He's a cunning old Trojan, Mr Huby is! He saw Coate go up to Mr Henry's room, and he hopped up after him, as spry as a two-year-old, and slipped into the room alongside Mr Henry's. There's a powder-closet between the two of 'em, and into it he creeps, all amongst Mr Henry's fine coats, which is hung up in it, and sets his ear to the door into Mr Henry's room.'

'What did he contrive to hear?' John asked quickly.

'Why, he says as Coate was in a rare tweak with Mr Henry, calling him a paperskulled gabster, and cursing him something wicked for having gone next or nigh Squire. 'Didn't I tell you I wouldn't have no trouble made, you mouth?' he says. Then Mr Henry says something as Mr Huby couldn't hear, and Coate says, 'Wait till he's snuffed it, and the game's our own!' he says. 'You'll send these damned servants packing, the whole curst set of insolent dotards!' — meaning Mr Huby, and Mr Winkfield, and me. 'You won't have no trouble over that,' he says, 'for they wouldn't work for you, Henry, not if you was to offer 'em a fortune for to do it!' Which is true as death,' said Joseph meditatively. 'Myself, I'd as soon drive a hack — or worse!'

'Yes, and then?'

'Well, then Mr Huby heard Mr Henry say, screeching like he was in a fury, yet scared too, 'And what about my cousin?' Coate, he cursed him some more for not keeping his voice down, and he says, 'I'll have to marry the girl, and, damme,' he says, 'I've a mind to, for I'll swear she's a piece as is worth taming!' Which fairly made Mr Huby's blood boil, but there was worse to come. Ay! For Mr Henry says as Miss Nell wouldn't have Coate, and Coate, he laughs, and says, 'Trust me, she'll be glad to have me! And once I've got her to wife,' he says, 'there ain't nothing to be afraid of, 'cos I'll school her to keep her chaffer close, don't doubt me! And once you're master here,' he says, 'me and she will stay long of you, and no one won't think it queer; and when they've called the hounds off, there's a fortune waiting for us!' Then Mr Huby heard a board creak, like Coate had got up out of his chair so he crept away, soft-like. And pitiful it was to see him, when he told Mr Winkfield and me what had passed! Fair napping his bib, he was, to think his strength was gone from him, and he couldn't give Coate a leveller, let alone choke the puff out of him, which he was wishful to do!'

'Let him not weep for that!' said Captain Staple, through his even, white teeth. 'I will settle all scores with this villain, and in full!'

'Well, sir,' said Joseph, with a deprecatory cough, 'seeing as Mr Huby was in such a taking, Mr Winkfield took the liberty of telling him so. Which heartened him up wonderful — if I may say so!'

'Did you tell me you must go to Sheffield today?' John asked abruptly. 'When will you be here again?'

'Oh, I'll be back by six o'clock at latest, sir! The London mail's due at four. It might be a minute or two late, but not above a quarter of an hour, at this season! What was you wanting me to do?'

'Come and take my place here after dark! I must see Miss Nell!'

Joseph nodded. 'I'll come if I can, guv'nor,' he promised. 'But I better be off now — if that Coate has passed the gate!'

He had not, but in a few minutes he came into sight, trotting briskly down the road. John sent Ben out to open the gate; and, after a discreet pause, Joseph mounted the cob, and rode off in his wake.

The Captain then took pity on Ben, and released him from his duties, merely recommending him to eat his dinner before sallying forth to join certain of his cronies on an afternoon of high adventure. Since Mrs Skeffling had left a stew redolent of onions simmering on the hob, Ben thought well of following this advice. He tried to engage the Captain in conversation, but found him to be in an abstracted mood. As his parent, by the simple expedient of clouting him heavily, had trained him not to obtrude his chatter upon unwilling ears, he immediately stopped talking, consumed with startling rapidity an enormous plateful of steak, and slid from the toll-house before his protector could (in the manner of adult persons) change his mind, and set him to perform some wearisome task.

The Captain finished his own meal. In a more leisurely style, and, still deeply considering the problem which lay before him, washed up the crockery. He was wiping his hands on a towel when an imperative voice intruded upon his consciousness.

'Gate! Gate, there!' it called.

The Captain turned his head quickly. The call was repeated, in exasperated accents. The Captain cast the towel aside, and strode out into the road.

Drawn up before the toll-house was a sporting curricle, to which a pair of match-bays was harnessed. The bays were sweating a little, and their legs were mud-splashed, like the wheels of the curricle, but the turn-out was a handsome one, and nothing more point-de-vice could have been imagined than the gentleman holding the reins in one elegantly gloved hand.

He was the model of a nonpareil attired for a journey in rural surroundings, and only the exquisite cut of his coat and breeches, and the high polish on his top-boots, drew attention to his person. His waistcoat was of a sober dove-colour; the points of his collar stiff, but by no means exaggeratedly high; his cravat tied with artistry, but without flamboyance. A beaver hat, of the same delicate hue as his waistcoat, was set at a slight angle on a head of glossy, carefully arranged locks; and cast over the back of the empty seat beside him was a very long and full-skirted greatcoat embellished with a number of shoulder-capes. Upon the Captain's appearance on the threshold of the toll-house, he transferred the reins to his whip hand, and with his disengaged hand sought the quizzing-glass which hung on a black riband round his neck, and raised it to one eye.

For a moment they stared at one another, the fair giant, in leather breeches and waistcoat, and a coarse shirt open at the throat, standing apparently transfixed; and the Tulip of Fashion looking him over from head to foot, an expression on his face of gathering anguish. 'Good Gad!' he said faintly.

'Bab!' ejaculated the Captain. 'What the devil — ?'

'Dear boy — taken the words out of my

mouth! *What* the devil — ?' said Mr Babbacombe.

'Confound you, what's brought you here?' demanded the Captain.

'Just reconnoitring, dear boy!' said Mr Babbacombe, late of the 10th Hussars, with an airy wave of the quizzing-glass. 'No good flying into a miff, Jack! Dash it, no business to write me mysterious letters if you don't mean me to come and see what kind of a lark you're kicking up!'

'Damn you!' John said, reaching up to grip his hand. 'I might have known it indeed, you inquisitive fribble! Did you bring my gear with you?'

Mr Babbacombe removed his driving-coat from the seat beside him, disclosing a bulky package. Indicating this, with every evidence of revulsion, he said: 'Take it! If there had been room for your portmanteaux as well as my own, dashed if I wouldn't have brought 'em! You great gudgeon, we had to smash the locks! I hadn't the keys!'

'Oh, that's of no consequence!' said John, picking up the package, and tucking it under his arm. 'But what's this about *your* portmanteaux? I don't see them!'

'No, no, I left 'em at the inn!'

'What inn?'

'Little place down the road. I don't remember what it's called, but you must know it! It's only a mile away, dash it!'

'You can't stay at the Blue Boar!' John exclaimed.

'Just racking up for the night,' explained Mr Babbacombe. 'Seems a snug little inn. Anything amiss with it?'

'Bab, have you been asking for me there?'

'Wasn't necessary. Fact of the matter is, Jack, I've had news of you for some way along the road. Dashed roadbook of mine ain't to be trusted 'cross country, so there was nothing for it but to ask the way. No, I didn't say a word about you, but it's my belief you couldn't mention the Crowford Toll-gate anywhere for six or seven miles round without being told that there's a queer new keeper to it, the size of a mountain. As for the ale-draper at this Blue Boar of yours, he seemed to twig it was you I wanted the instant I spoke of the toll-gate.'

'Lord!' said John. 'Oh, well! It must be all over the village by now, so there's no help for it! I'm devilish glad to see you, old fellow, but you must brush tomorrow! It won't do if certain fellows here get wind of you.'

'I must what?' said Mr Babbacombe, all at sea.

'Brush! Pike! Lope off!' said John, his eyes brimful of laughter. 'In your own Hash tongue, depart!'

'Yes, I know you're up to fun and gig,' said Mr Babbacombe severely. 'Not but what I must depart tomorrow, because I didn't bring Fockerby along with me, and what with having to see to it that the ostler at the inn I stayed at last night looked after these tits of mine, and being obliged to dashed well stand over the boots this morning — and even now they don't look as they should — *my* boots, I mean! — it's devilish

259

exhausting! Where can I stable the bays? I can't talk to you on the high road!'

'Well, you can't stable them here. You must take them back to the Blue Boar.'

'But I want to talk to you!' objected Mr Babbacombe.

'Of course, but you must see there's no place for a curricle here, let alone a pair of horses! You'll have to walk back: it's not much more than a mile! Oh, lord! here's the carrier! Mind, now, Bab, you've mistaken the road!' He then said, raising his voice: 'No, sir, you should ha' turned right-handed, short of the village!' and turned from the curricle to fetch the tickets from the office.

Mr Babbacombe sat in a trance-like state, listening to an interchange of conversation, during the course of which he learned that his eccentric friend was apparently keeping the gate for someone called Brean. The carrier seemed surprised that this person had not yet returned; Mr Babbacombe was even more surprised to hear that Mr Brean was John's cousin. No sooner had the pike been closed behind the carrier than he exclaimed: 'If you are not the most complete hand I ever knew! Now, Jack, stop bamming, and tell me what the devil you're doing!'

'I will,' John promised, grinning up at him, 'but take that natty turn-out of yours away first! If Sopworthy — that's your ale-draper! — knows you've come here to see me, you may as well borrow his cob: I can stable him in the hen-house.'

'Jack!' said Mr Babbacombe. 'Are you stabling your own horse in a dashed hen-house?'

'No, no, he's in that barn, up there! Now, do be off, Bab!' He watched Mr Babbacombe turn his pair, and bethought him of something, and called out: 'Wait, Bab! — I daresay you won't see him, but if you should meet a fellow at the Blue Boar called Stogumber, take care what you say to him! He was nursing a broken head and a gashed shoulder this morning, but if he gets wind of such an out-and-outer as you, putting up at the inn, he's bound to think it smoky, and very likely he'll leave his bed to discover what your business may be. You'd better tell him you came here to visit Sir Peter Stornaway, up at the Manor, but hearing that he's very ill you've thought it best not to intrude upon the family. Now, don't forget! — Stornaway — Kellands Manor! Stogumber's a Bow Street Runner, but he don't know I've bubbled him.'

Mr Babbacombe regarded him in fascinated horror. 'A Bow Street — No, by God, I'll be damned if I'll go another yard until you've told me what kind of a kick-up this is! Dear boy, you ain't murdered anyone?'

'Lor' bless you, guv'nor, *I* ain't a queer cove!' said the Captain outrageously. 'Nor no trap ain't wishful to snabble me!'

'Dutch comfort! Do you mean the Runner ain't after you?'

'No, he only suspects he may be,' replied the Captain. 'He thinks I'm a trifle smoky.'

'If he knew as much about you as I do,' said Mr Babbacombe, with feeling, 'he'd know you're a dangerous lunatic, and dashed well put you under restraint!'

With these embittered words, he drove off, leaving the Captain laughing, and waving farewell.

Half an hour later he was once more at the toll-house, dismounting from the landlord's cob, which animal he apostrophized as the greatest slug he had ever crossed in his life. The hen-house, he considered, would be a fitting stable; and allowing John to lead the cob away, he entered the toll-house, and was discovered by his friend, a few minutes later, inspecting the premises with interest not unmixed with consternation.

'How do you like my quarters?' John asked cheerfully.

'Well, your bedroom ain't so bad, but where do you *sit?*' enquired Mr Babbacombe.

'Here, in the kitchen, of course!'

'No, really, Jack!'

'Lord, you've grown very nice, haven't you? Were you never billeted in a Portuguese cottage, with no glass in the windows, and a fire burning in the middle of the floor, so that you were blinded by the smoke?'

'I was,' acknowledged Mr Babbacombe. 'That's why I sold out!'

'Don't you try to play off the airs of an exquisite on me, my buck! Sit down! By the way, why the devil didn't you pack up my cigarilloes with the rest of my gear? I've none left!'

With a sigh, Mr Babbacombe produced a case from his pocket, and held it out. 'Because you didn't tell me to, of course. Here you are!'

'Bless you!' said the Captain. 'Well, now we'll blow a cloud together, Bab, and I'll tell you what I'm doing here!'

After this promising beginning he seemed to find it hard to continue, and for a moment or two sat staring into the fire, smoking, and frowning slightly. Mr Babbacombe, his elegant form disposed as comfortably as a Windsor chair would permit, watched him through his lashes, but preserved a patient silence. John looked up at last, a rueful smile in his eyes. 'It all came about by accident,' he said.

Mr Babbacombe sighed. 'I knew that,' he replied. 'You've never been in a scrape yet but what it came about by accident. The thing is, no one else has these accidents. However, I ain't going to argue about it! Why did you send your baggage to Edenhope, though? Been puzzling me!'

'I *was* coming to stay with you!' said the Captain indignantly.

'Well, what made you change your mind?' mildly enquired Mr Babbacombe.

'I'll tell you,' said the Captain obligingly; and settled down to give him a brief account of his present adventure. Certain aspects of it he chose to keep to himself, perhaps considering them to be irrelevant, and although the Squire's name occurred frequently during his recital, the most glancing of references only were made to his granddaughter. But the rest of the story he told his friend without reservation.

Mr Babbacombe, listening in astonishment,

263

and with no more than an occasional interruption, learned with incredulity that the Captain had no immediate intention of divulging to Stogumber the whereabouts of the treasure. He was moved to protest, saying in deeply moved accents: 'No, really, my dear fellow! Only one thing to be done! Tell the Redbreast at once!'

'If you had paid the least heed to what I have been saying,' retorted John, 'you would know that what I am trying to do is to keep young Stornaway's name out of this!'

'Well, you can't do it, and, damme, I don't see why you should wish to! Sounds to me like a devilish loose fish!'

'Yes, a contemptible creature! But I promised his grandfather I would do my possible to keep his name clean!'

'So you may have — though I'll be damned if I see why you should! — but you didn't know then what kind of a business he was mixed up in! I tell you, this is serious, Jack! Good God, it's a hanging matter!'

'Don't I know it!'

'Well, it don't seem to me as though you've the least notion of it!' said Mr Babbacombe, with considerable asperity. 'Dash it, who is this old fellow, and what made you take such a fancy to him?'

This home question brought the colour up into John's face. Avoiding his friend's eye, he was just about to embark on an explanation, which sounded lame even in his own ears, when he was interrupted by a shout from the road. Never more thankful to be recalled to his duties, he apologized hastily to Mr Babbacombe, and went off to open the gate, and to collect the toll. By the time he returned to the kitchen, he was once more in command of himself, and the situation, and informed Babbacombe crisply that he had his own sufficient reasons for desiring to spare Sir Peter as much pain as possible. 'It don't matter why: it *is* so!' he said. 'Just accept that, will you, Bab?'

Mr Babbacombe was conscious of a horrid sinking at the pit of his stomach. 'You're doing it rather too brown, Jack!' he said uneasily. 'The more I think of it, the more I'm sure there's more to this affair than you've told me!'

The Captain looked guilty, but there was a decided twinkle in his eye. 'Well, yes, there is a little more!' he acknowledged. 'No, no, *I* had nothing to do with stealing those sovereigns! don't look so horrified! But — well, never mind that now! The thing is, I've given the Squire my word I'll do my utmost to shield Henry, and I will! Nothing you can say is going to stop me, Bab, so spare yourself the trouble of saying it!'

Mr Babbacombe groaned, and expressed the bitter wish that he had never come to Crowford. 'I might have known I should find you in some damned, crazy fix!' he said. 'If you don't put a rope round your own neck it will be a dashed miracle! How *can* you keep Henry out of it? Now, don't tell me you mean to help t'other fellow to escape as well, because for one thing I know you too well to believe you; and for another, if you *did* do anything so totty-headed, the chances are the Redbreast would arrest you and this highwayman of yours! Stands to reason!'

John laughed. 'Chirk might not be able to prove an alibi, but I imagine I could. But you may be perfectly easy on *that* head! I don't mean to let Coate escape! No, not for anything that was offered me!'

'That's all very well,' objected Babbacombe, 'but you can't have one arrested without the other! The fellow's bound to squeak beef on Henry!'

John nodded. 'Yes, naturally I have thought of that. I wish I knew how deeply he may be implicated! I must discover that.'

This was said with decision, and with a certain hardening of the muscles round his mouth. Mr Babbacombe, looking up at the fair, handsome face, with the smiling eyes that held so level and steady a regard, and the good-humour that dwelled round that firm mouth, reflected gloomily that Crazy Jack was the oddest of fellows. Anyone would take him for a man with as level a head as his frank eyes, and so, in general, he was; but every now and then a demon of mischief seemed to take possession of him, and then, as now, he would plunge headlong into any perilous adventure that offered. It was quite useless to argue with him. For all his easy-going ways, and the kindliness which endeared him to so many people, there was never any turning him from his purpose, once he had made up his mind. He had a streak of obstinacy, and although he had never in the smallest degree resented the attempts of his friends to stand in the way of his will, Mr Babbacombe could not call to mind when the most forceful of representations had born the least weight with him. If you stood in his way, he just put you aside, perfectly kindly, but quite inexorably; and if you swore at him, when all was done, for having done a crazy, dangerous thing, although he was genuinely penitent for having caused a friend anxiety you could see that he was puzzled to know why you should worry about him at all.

'The trouble with you, Jack,' said Mr Babbacombe, following, aloud, the trend of these thoughts, 'is that you're neither to lead nor drive!'

John glanced down at him, amusement springing to his face. 'Yes, I am. Why, what a fellow you make me out to be!'

'Once you've taken a notion into your silly head, one might as well try reasoning with a mule as with you!' insisted Babbacombe.

'Well,' said John apologetically, wrinkling his brow, 'a man ought to be able to make up his mind for himself, and once he's done so he shouldn't let himself be turned from his purpose. I daresay I'm wrong, but so I think. In this case, I know very well what I'm about — and I swear to you I'm not funning, Bab! I own, at the outset I thought it might be good sport to keep the gate for a day or two, and try whether I could discover what was afoot here, but that's all changed, and I'm serious — oh, more than ever in my life! And also I am quite determined,' he added.

'Something,' said Babbacombe, looking narrowly at him, 'has happened to you, Jack, and I'm dashed if I know what it can be!' He paused hopefully, but the Captain only laughed. 'And another thing I don't know is what the deuce there is in this affair to put you into such high gig! I'd as lief handle live coals myself!'

'No, would you? I wouldn't have missed such an adventure for a fortune!' John said ingenuously.

'Wait until you find yourself explaining to a judge and a jury how you came to aid and abet these rogues — for that's what you are doing, dear boy, every instant you delay to tell what you've discovered to the Redbreast, or to the nearest magistrate!'

'Oh, no, I'm not! Now, consider, Bab! If Stogumber knew — if he had proof — that Coate and Stornaway are the men he's trying to catch, he would not be prowling about the district, seeking to come by information. He can do no more than suspect them; it may be that he does not even do that, but has merely some inkling that the treasure is to be looked for here. Of course he would be glad to recover it immediately, but if I know anything of the matter he won't be content only to find those chests. To perform his task successfully, he must also apprehend the thieves. Good God, Bab, there were two guards shot dead at the ford, poor fellows, and the gatekeeper stabbed, and left to petrify in that cavern, and an attempt made to murder Stogumber himself!'

'Yes, and one of these pretty rascals you mean

268

to shield!' struck in Babbacombe.

'Well, yes,' John admitted. 'I must do so, for the sake of — of others, who are quite guiltless, and don't deserve to have an honourable name smirched. If it were not for that I wouldn't shield him! Lord, I'd hand him over to Stogumber, and think the world well rid of him — even though I doubt very much whether he has played any but a minor role in the affair! I am very sure he knew nothing of Brean's death, until he found his body in the cavern, and I'd go bail it was Coate and his rogue of a servant — if servant he is! — who shot down the guards. *His* part in this was to provide the safe hiding-place for those chests, and shelter for Coate and Gunn. Shelter near at hand, too! You may depend upon it, Coate would not go far from where the chests are hid!'

Mr Babbacombe, perceiving that a little ash from his cigarillo had dropped on to his coat, carefully nicked it away, and with some anxiety inspected the superfine cloth. Satisfied that no damage had been done; he raised his eyes again, and said: 'Seems to me, then, that if that's all Stornaway was brought into the business to do, this Coate of yours is paying pretty high for his services! Resourceful sort of a fellow: couldn't he hit upon a hiding-place without using a hen-hearted weasel that would turn King's Evidence at the first hint of danger?'

John looked at him, half frowning. 'I don't know. It might not be so easy, after all, to find a sure hiding-place for six chests of gold! They must remain hidden for many months, remember! Then, too, it had to be near the hold-up — I mean, not so far off that the chests could not be conveyed to it before daylight. Nor yet so close, of course, that it must have been instantly suspected. I fancy that the thirty miles which lie between this place and the Wansbeck ford must have been the extremest limit. I've been thinking about that. This is a wild country, Bab, and if you look at the map of the county, hanging in the office there, you'll see that it would be possible to reach that cavern, from the Wansbeck ford, without passing any toll-gate but this. There is something else that occurs to me. It may well be that when the time is ripe to remove the chests Coate means to dispose of Stornaway, just as he has already disposed of Brean. In fact, I think it very likely. But he dare not murder Stornaway while he still needs an excuse for remaining in this district.'

Mr Babbacombe threw the butt of his cigarillo into the fire. 'Well, if that's the kind of cut-throat villain he is, take care he don't stab you first!' he recommended.

'I'll take devilish good care he don't! But I think he don't suspect me — yet! I've let it be known I'm a discharged trooper, and any flash language I use is due to my having been a bâtman. Rose — she is Miss Stornaway's maid! — has told the woman who keeps this place clean, and cooks for me, that my mother was Brean's aunt, who married a man in comfortable circumstances. It's possible Coate really believes me to be Brean's cousin — though I don't think that. I fancy he don't know yet *what* my — er

— lay is! It don't signify: he'll find me harder to kill than Brean! But I've had some further thoughts on this head, Bab! One of the three confederates recognized Stogumber for a Runner — and I think that one must have been Gunn: he has been got rid of very quickly, which seems to tell its own tale! Now, it seems to me that neither Coate nor Stornaway can have had the least expectation of being known to any law-officer: they would not else be staying at the Manor so openly. It is certainly a bad thing for them that Gunn was known to Stogumber; but I think it was a worse thing for him to have been recognized. He had no expectation of that either, for he has been wandering about the country calling himself an agent of some sort, and that he would not have done had he known that a cracksman with whom he was already acquainted was mixed up in this business. Well, had it not been for Chirk, he must have suffered Brean's fate, and gone to join him in the cavern. But Chirk chased off his assailants, and however much he may suspect that they were Coate and Gunn, he don't know it for certain, since they had their faces muffled in their scarves. But Coate knows that he's a Runner, and fore-warned, Bab, is forearmed!'

'They'll recall him from Bow Street, and send another in his stead!'

'That wouldn't fadge! Any stranger will now be suspect by Coate! I hoped he might take fright, and run for it, but he's a mighty cool customer, and he means to stand fast. That seems to mean that he knows nothing can be brought home to him. Well! Without me, it's possible Stogumber may discover that cavern, and what it contains. But with me, he may be able to arrest Coate also; and I fancy he won't quarrel with me over the means I took to bring that about!'

14

Finding it impossible to turn the Captain from his purpose, Mr Babbacombe allowed himself to be diverted presently into talk of old campaigning days, and an exchange of news about erstwhile companions in arms. Dusk fell, and the two friends still sat on either side of the fire, fortified by tankards of Sopworthy's best ale, and only occasionally interrupted by calls from the gate. By the time the daylight had quite gone, and the Captain went out to hang lamps on the gate, Mr Babbacombe had begun to think of his dinner. It seemed to him a pity that John could scarcely accompany him to the inn, to share it; but when he learned that John had dined at midday he was quite aghast, and perceived that he had had, until that moment, a very incomplete conception of the rigours endured by gatekeepers.

'And I think,' said John, 'you'd best stay here, Bab, and have supper with me. There will be Ben too — if the little wretch comes home in time! — but you won't mind that! I'll give you eggs, and ham, and sausages, and some excellent coffee. The thing is, I am determined to visit the Manor this evening, and I can't leave this place under Ben's charge after dark: he's scared, and won't stay here alone. If the Squire's groom is unable to come to relieve guard, you could remain here till I come back, couldn't you?'

'What, mind the pike?' exclaimed Mr Babba-combe. 'No, I'll be damned if I do!'

'Oh, you needn't do that! Ben will attend to any calls, and I daresay he won't mind, if he knows you're here to protect him.'

'Protect him from what?' demanded Mr Babbacombe.

'Nothing — but he can't be brought to believe that. Damn the brat, I wonder what mischief he's up to? I must go up to attend to Beau. And, now I come to think of it, I never fed the hens, or the pig!'

With these conscience-stricken words, he seized a bucket, into which had been emptied various scraps of food, and went out into the garden. Mr Babbacombe heard him at the pump a few minutes later, and he came in almost immediately, saying, as he dried his dripping hands on a towel: 'I suppose the hens had picked up all they wanted in the garden, for they've gone to roost; but the pig always seems to be starving! You know, Bab, when I started gatekeeping here I'd no notion how much work there was to do! What with the gate, and Beau, and those curst hens, and the pig, and the brat, and keeping my clothes in order, I never seem to have a moment in which to be idle! Confound you, don't laugh! If Ben don't come in soon, you shall have a taste of gatekeeping, for I won't neglect my horse just because you're too high in the instep to take over my duties for me! Besides, I want Beau here, not half a mile away!'

But at this moment the errant Ben slid into

the kitchen from the office, his sharp countenance schooled to an expression of almost angelic innocence. One stocking had descended in rucks about his ankle, and was generously smeared with blood from a badly grazed leg; a rent in his shirt allowed a glimpse of a skinny chest; and every portion of his anatomy, unprotected by clothing, seemed to have attracted grime.

'Disgusting!' said his mentor, after a brief but comprehensive survey. 'Take that shirt off, and get under the pump! No, don't go without the soap, woolly-crown! And if I see one speck of dirt on you when you come in, I'll send you to bed in the pig-sty!'

In any ordinary circumstances, so exquisitely humorous a threat would have drawn from Ben its meed of his broadest grin, but he had by this time perceived Mr Babbacombe. His mouth fell open, and his eyes widened to their fullest extent. Having taken that elegant gentleman in thoroughly, he gave utterance to his feelings with brevity and simplicity. 'Coo!' he said reverently.

The Captain's lips twitched, but he said severely: 'Just so! Be off and make yourself tidy directly! This gentleman can't bear dirty boys!'

'Coo, he *is* a swell cove!' said Ben, accepting reluctantly the bar of soap thrust into his hand. 'What's he come here for, guv'nor?'

'He's a friend of mine. Now, shake your shambles! I want to go up to Huggate's barn!'

'He ain't come to take you away?' Ben cried, with swift suspicion.

'No, no!' the Captain said, pushing him

275

through the door. 'He's come to supper with us!'

'Yes, but I don't think I have!' protested Mr Babbacombe, who had been regarding his friend's protege with disfavour. 'And if you think I mean to spend the evening here with that horrid brat — why, I'd as lief spend it with a Portuguese muleteer!'

'Nonsense! He's quite a good lad. Did you never fall out of a tree yourself, and go home with a torn shirt, and dirt all over you? Besides, the poor little devil's been orphaned!'

'What are you going to do with him?' demanded Mr Babbacombe, looking at him with misgiving.

'Damned if I know!' confessed John. 'I'm bound to look after him, of course. Might hand him to Cocking to train: he's got a way with horses, and will make a splendid groom when he's older.'

'I should think Cocking will enjoy that!' said Mr Babbacombe sardonically.

But when Ben reappeared presently with a well-scrubbed face, and in his other shirt, he admitted that he was not so repulsive an urchin as at first sight he had thought him. Encouraged by this moderate praise, the Captain informed Ben that if Joseph Lydd did not come to the toll-house that evening, Mr Babbacombe would stay to keep him company while he himself went out for an hour. Ben looked dubious, but the Captain said: 'And he's a soldier, too, so you needn't be afraid he would let anyone carry you off! If anyone tried to, he would draw his pistol, and shoot him!'

'No, I dashed well would not!' said Mr Babbacombe. 'What's more, I won't be dragged into this business!'

'Won't stand by me?' John said. 'Bab!'

'Well, what I mean is — No, confound you, Jack, I'm not queer in my attic, if you are!'

'You come and see my horse, old fellow!' said John soothingly. 'Cut some ham, Ben, and put the sausages in the pan! I'm only going as far as the barn.'

Half an hour later, when they re-entered the kitchen, Mr Babbacombe wore the look of one resigned to his fate, and there was a decided twinkle in the Captain's eye. They were greeted by the pleasant aroma of sausages sizzling over the fire, and the intelligence that Joseph Lydd had passed through the gate not five minutes earlier, driving the gig.

'Driving the gig?' John said. 'Where was he bound for? Did he tell you?'

'No. He asked me where you was, and I told him you was up at the barn, and he said as he'd be back presently. And I didn't say nothing to him about the swell cove,' added Ben, with conscious rectitude.

'That's the dandy! Don't you say anything to anybody about the swell cove! Did Lydd leave any message for me?'

But Joseph had apparently not seen fit to entrust a message to Ben. With his assurance that he would be back presently, John had to be satisfied. Leaving Mr Babbacombe to superintend the cooking of supper, he went off to make himself presentable, and to speculate upon the

277

nature of the errand that could have taken Lydd, driving the gig, towards Crowford at such an hour. The doctor, as John knew, lived five miles to the east of the gate; he could think of no other person who might be wanted at the Manor.

He had just arranged his cravat to his satisfaction when the gig returned. He heard Ben go out, and followed him, trying to perceive, in the darkness, who was the man seated beside Lydd. A low-brimmed hat, and a dark cloak, were the only things he could distinguish, until the man turned a little, to look at him, and he saw the gleam of white bands. At the same moment, Joseph spoke.

'You're wanted up at the Manor, Mr Staple. But I got to drive the Reverend back to Crowford presently.'

'I'll come,' John replied curtly. 'Open the gate, Ben!'

He did not wait to see this order obeyed, but strode back into the toll-house, where he found Mr Babbacombe, in his shirt-sleeves, wincing from the savagery of eggs, spitting furiously in boiling fat.

'Bab — I'm sorry, indeed I am! — but I must leave you in charge here!' he said. 'The Squire's groom has just gone past the pike, with the Vicar, driving him to Kellands. I'm needed there — and even if Joseph had not told me so I must have gone! I fear it can only mean that the Squire is dying.'

Mr Babbacombe removed the eggs from the fire, and tenderly licked the back of one scalded hand. 'If that's so, dear boy,' he remarked mildly,

278

'it don't seem to be quite the moment for you to be paying him a visit. No doubt you know best, but I shouldn't do it myself.'

'I think you would. Joseph will come to relieve you if he can, but he will be obliged to remain at the Manor until the Vicar leaves. Ben will attend to the gate, but you'll get very few calls. I'll return as soon as I may — but I might be some time.'

'Very well,' said his long-suffering friend, returning the pan to the fire. 'It's to be hoped Ben likes eggs: there are six here, and *I* never want to see one again!'

'Poor Bab! What a way to treat you! But you will shake the dust of this place from your feet tomorrow, so take heart!' John said, sitting down to pull on his boots.

'Ah!' said Mr Babbacombe. He saw that Ben had come back into the kitchen, and said imperatively: 'Here, boy, come and finish cooking these eggs!'

Ben took the pan, but gave it as his opinion that the eggs were fried hard.

'Then turn 'em out, or fry some more!' recommended Mr Babbacombe.

John lifted his saddle from the top of the beer-barrel, where he had laid it when he brought it down from the barn, and went out into the garden, accompanied by his friend. Mr Babbacombe stripped off the rug from Beau's back, but no sooner had John set the saddle in place than he ejaculated: 'Chirk! I must warn Ben,' and went back into the kitchen.

'If,' said Mr Babbacombe, when he presently

reappeared, 'you're expecting a visit from your High Toby friend, how should I receive him? I don't wish to be backward in any attention, but the truth is, Jack, I never entertained a highway-man before, and I can't but feel that if he did not find me acceptable he might prefer my watch and my money to my company.'

'No such thing! He's an excellent fellow! But I've told Ben to go quietly out to him, when he hears his signal, and to tell him how it is. It won't do to let him in while you're here: he would dislike it — and me too, for having told you about him.'

Mr Babbacombe paused in the act of tightening a girth. 'Do you mean to say I'm not to meet the fellow? No, that's too shabby!' he said indignantly. 'What the devil am I going to do with myself while you're away?'

'Play cassino with Ben!' said the Captain, unhitching his bridle from the fence.

Ten minutes later, he was dismounting in the stable-yard at the Manor, and handing Beau over to Joseph, who said apologetically: 'I'd have come back if I could, sir, but the master don't understand as how you can't leave Ben, and he would have me fetch Parson.'

'It doesn't signify: I've left a friend of mine at the toll-house. Was it your master who sent for me?'

'Ay, and mighty anxious he is you should come, guv'nor. Mr Winkfield says as he's been fretting outrageous, all on account of this letter I had to fetch in Sheffield. But it come by today's mail, and it seems like he's ready to slip his wind now he's got it, for nothing would do but he must have Parson sent for, and you too.' He peered up at John's face in the faint moonlight, and added pleadingly: 'If you *could* set his mind at rest, sir, so as he'll go easy —— '

'You may be sure I will. I'll go up to the house immediately. Where are Coate and young Stornaway?'

'Mr Henry's still abed, and Coate's eating his dinner. There's no fear you'll see either of 'em.'

The Captain strode up the path to the side of the house. The door into the flagged passage was not locked, and a lamp was burning on the chest against the wall. John laid his hat and whip down beside it, and went along the passage to the narrow stairs. At the top, he met Winkfield. The valet greeted him with relief, and with less than his usual impassivity. It seemed for a moment as though he wished to make some kind of a communication. He started to speak, but faltered, and broke off, saying, after a pause: 'I think, sir — I think I had best take you to my master directly!'

'Please do so! Joseph tells me he has been fretting, and you may be sure I'll use my best endeavours to soothe him.'

'Yes, sir, I'm sure — Only it seems as if he's almost taken leave of his senses! If I'd guessed — but he never told one of us! If you should not like it, I hope you'll pardon me! Indeed, I'd no notion what was in his head!' Winkfield said, opening the dressing-room door, and ushering John into the room.

'Why should I dislike it?' John asked, a puzzled

frown in his eyes. 'I collect that he is dying — is he not?'

'I don't know that, sir. I didn't think to see him live the day out, but — but he's in wonderful spirits now! As you'll see for yourself, sir!'

He opened the door into the bedchamber, and announced formally: 'Captain Staple!'

The Captain stepped into the room, and paused, blinking in the unexpected light of many candles. Two great chandeliers stood on the mantelpiece; two more flanked the bed; and two had been set on a side-table, drawn into the middle of the room, and draped with a cloth. Beside this improvised altar was standing an elderly clergyman, whose mild countenance showed bewilderment, disapproval, and uncertainty. The Squire was lying in bed, banked up by many pillows, his eyes glittering, and a smile twisting one side of his mouth. Rose was standing by the window, and Nell at the head of the bed, in her old green velvet gown. Across the room she stared at John, and he saw that her eyes were stormy in her very white face, and her hands tightly gripped together. She said, in a shaking voice: 'No, no! I won't! Grandpapa, I beg of you don't ask it of him!'

'Don't be missish, girl!' Sir Peter said, his utterance slow, and very much more slurred than when John had previously visited him.

'Sir Peter!' said the Vicar nervously. 'If Miss Stornaway is reluctant, I must and I will be resolute in declining to perform — '

'You hold your tongue, Thorne!' said Sir Peter.

'She ain't reluctant. Nothing but a stupid crotchet! Staple!'

'Sir?' John responded, going to the bedside.

'Told me you'd marry Nell with or without my consent, didn't you?'

'I did.'

'Mean it?'

John looked steadily down into those over-bright eyes. 'Most certainly!'

Sir Peter gave a little cackle of laughter. 'Very well! You shall marry her — *now!*'

There was a moment's astonished silence. 'Tell him it is impossible!' Nell said, in a panting undervoice.

'It ain't impossible,' said Sir Peter. '*I've* seen to that! Special license,' he told John, with impish triumph. 'Thorne's got it, but I sent for it! Told you I could still keep my horses together!'

'You're at home to a peg, sir!' John assured him, amusement quivering in his voice. He looked up, and stretched out his hand across the bed to Nell. 'But how is this? Won't you marry me after all, my love?'

'No, no, unthinkable!' she said, wringing her hands. 'You are being forced — *forced* — into marrying me — in *such* a way!'

'Am I? But how unnecessary! I don't even need persuading!'

'Told you so!' said Sir Peter. '*He* don't suffer from distempered freaks!'

'If we are to talk of distempered freaks — !' she exclaimed hotly.

'Yes, but we are not going to talk of any such thing,' John interposed.

'That's the way!' approved Sir Peter. 'Stand no nonsense! You'll do as you're bid, miss!'

'No, certainly not!' said John. 'She will do as she wishes, now and always!' He walked round the end of the bed, and took Nell's tense hand, smiling very kindly at her. 'You shall tell me just what you wish, dearest. I ask nothing better than to be allowed to marry you here and now. Indeed, it seems to me an admirable scheme! To receive you from the hands of your grandfather is just what I would myself have chosen. But I'll drag no unwilling bride to the altar, so if your heart misgives you, my love, tell me so!'

'John, John, not my heart!' she whispered chokingly, her fingers clutching his hand.

'No? Some other consideration, then, which naturally you must explain to me. But we really cannot discuss the matter in public! Let us go into the dressing-room, shall we? We must beg you, Sir Peter, to hold us excused for a short space.'

He drew Nell's hand through his arm, as he spoke, and led her to the door, which Winkfield opened, and held. As he shut it again behind them, the Squire said, on a note of satisfaction: 'Clever in the saddle: he'll handle her!'

'Sir Peter, loth though I must be to disoblige you, I cannot perform this ceremony unless I am fully persuaded that both parties to it are willing!' declared the Vicar, looking more harassed than ever.

'Oh, sir, never say so!' Rose begged involuntarily. She whisked out her handkerchief, and rather defiantly blew her nose. 'He is so truly the gentleman, and so *kind*!' she sobbed.

'Indeed, I must own myself agreeably surprised in him,' acknowledged Mr Thorne. 'I do not perfectly understand why he should be taking Brean's place — in fact, I do not understand it at all! There is something in such eccentric behaviour which one cannot quite like, but I must suppose him to have good and sufficient reason for indulging in what bears the appearance of a mere prank, for there is nothing wild or unstable in his face or in his bearing. But if Miss Stornaway is, I repeat, reluctant, I must decline to perform my office!'

'She ain't,' said the Squire. 'Mere female scruples! She's head over ears in love with the fellow! Winkfield, my cordial!'

In the dressing-room, Nell was folded in the fellow's arms, saying agitatedly: 'John, I cannot, I cannot!'

'Then you shall not,' he replied comfortingly. 'But tell me why you cannot!'

'There are so many reasons — you must perceive! Oh, I couldn't do it!'

'It's too sudden? Of course, you have had no time to prepare for it! What a selfish fellow I am! The thing is that I should like a private wedding so much myself that I forgot that you would wish for something in quite a different style. All girls do, I collect, and God forbid I should deny you anything you want, my treasure!'

This had the effect of making her lift her head from his shoulder. 'No, no! Oh, how can you think me so stupid?' she demanded indignantly. 'As though I care for bride-clothes, or any

285

flummery! Oh, John, how infamous you are!'

He laughed. 'But what else am I to think, unless that you mean to cry off?'

She tried to shake him, gripping the lapels of his coat.

'You know I don't! Cannot you perceive how wrong it would be in me to marry you like this?'

'No,' he replied simply.

'How can I be sure that you did not say you were willing only to oblige a dying man?'

His answer to this left her too breathless to speak, and with a strong suspicion that at least three of her ribs had been broken.

'Have you any more nonsensical questions you would like to ask me, my love?' asked John, a little unsteadily.

'I d-dare not!' she said, between tears and laughter.

'Good! Because I think we should not keep the Vicar waiting, or your grandfather either. And if the only qualms you have are on my behalf there is no reason why we should. Can you wear this signet-ring of mine?'

'John, I am persuaded I ought not to do this!'

'If you feel that I shall turn out to be the devil of a husband, undoubtedly you ought not,' cordially agreed John, sliding his ring on to her finger, and off again. 'This is too loose, but it will have to serve until I can buy a wedding-ring. If, on the other hand, you mean to abide by our engagement, I shall think you have less than commonsense if you cannot recognize the advantages attaching to this charmingly unusual wedding.'

'And if I have less than commonsense I daresay *you* will cry off?' she murmured, snuggling her cheek into the hollow of his shoulder.

'Very likely. Now, consider, my love! If we are to wait until your grandfather is dead, how awkward in every respect must be our situation! You will then scruple to marry me until you are out of your blacks, and what the deuce are we to do for a whole year? Where will you go? How will you support yourself? With so many scruples you would never permit me to do that!'

'No, indeed! I hope I have a little more propriety than that! Perhaps I could take a situation as a governess, or some such thing,' she said doubtfully.

'No one in possession of her senses would engage you,' he assured her. 'Besides, I have a great deal of pride, and it would not suit me to marry a governess!' A stifled gurgle sounded. 'You may laugh!' he said severely. 'But I have some pretty stiff notions of what is due to my consequence, let me tell you!'

'I wonder what can have put it into my head that you had none?'

'There is no telling that. Well, my darling? Shall we go?'

She lifted her head, and looked up at him. 'Yes, John. But afterwards?'

'Are you afraid I mean to carry you off to the toll-house? You will remain here, of course, while you are needed.'

'I must, you know,' she said, a little wistfully.

'Yes, I know. If I were living in a palace, I

would not ask you to leave your grandfather now. But henceforth I shall have the right to protect you. Come, let us go and tell Sir Peter that we are very willing to oblige him!'

The Squire was lying with closed eyes, watched intently by Winkfield, and in pity and doubt by the Vicar; but he roused at the sound of the opening door, and turned his head slightly on the pillow. The Vicar, rising to his feet, and looking anxiously at Nell, was astonished to see that the rigid and decidedly wrathful young Amazon had vanished. She was leaning on the Captain's arm, one hand lost in his larger one, her face softly glowing, and the tenderest of smiles hovering round her mouth as she glanced up at him.

'Well?' said Sir Peter.

'We are very happy to obey you, sir,' John replied.

'Is this indeed so, Miss Stornaway?' the Vicar asked.

'Oh, yes!' she sighed. 'If you don't think it wrong of me!'

'Wrong? Why should he?' said the Squire snappishly. 'Let's have no more time wasted! I'm tired!'

So Miss Helen Stornaway and Captain John Staple were made man and wife in that candle-lit bedroom, watched by a dying man, and attended by a nurse and a valet. The Vicar had to look up to their faces, and thought he had never married a more splendid couple, though the lady's dress was shabby, and the gentleman's leathers were stained. They made their responses firmly; and

288

they looked so happy that Rose (as she afterwards explained) could not help crying a little, and even Winkfield admitted that it was a very touching ceremony.

When it was over, they kissed, and John led Nell back to the bed. Everyone could see that already the Squire's face had altered subtly. The sharpened look had been smoothed, and the eyes had lost some of their unnatural glitter; he looked more peaceful, but when he lifted his right hand, it was with an effort, and it shook perceptibly. Nell hung over him for a minute; he smiled at her; and said indistinctly: 'You'll do now!'

Then he ordered Winkfield to bring wine and glasses, so that the bride's and groom's healths could be duly pledged. 'I feel as though I shall sleep sound tonight,' he remarked. His gaze fell upon the Vicar, and a gleam of amusement shone in it. 'Much obliged to you, old friend! Thought you was here on a different errand, didn't you? You should have guessed I'd surprise you yet! Don't look so glum: I know what I've done, and, damme, it's the best deed of my life, and atones for a deal of past folly! Whatever happens now, my girl's safe. I'll bid you good-night now. I want a word or two with this new grandson of mine before I go to sleep, and I'm tired, very tired.'

The Captain drew his wife a little to one side, and said in her ear: 'Take him away, Nell, and leave me alone with your grandfather! He is very much exhausted, and the sooner he has said what he desires to say to me the better it will be.'

She nodded, and moved away from his side, glancing significantly at Winkfield. In a very few moments, only John was left with the Squire. He returned to the big four-poster, drawing the curtains along the foot of it, to shut off the glare of the candles.

'It wasn't you I forced into it,' Sir Peter said. 'It was Nell. I don't know what it is Henry has done, but it's something damnable. The dog threatened me — threatened *me*! — Said if I would not give orders Coate must be treated with extraordinary civility he and I and Nell would be ruined! By God, I — '

'Let me assure you, sir,' interposed the Captain calmly, 'that there is not the slightest danger of such a thing! Nor does Master Henry's attempt to conjure up bogeys in any way impress me.'

'What are he and Coate doing?' demanded the Squire.

'I'm not in a position to tell you that, though I have some inklings. Henry, I think, is nothing more than a tool, and I have every expectation of being able to bring him off without public scandal.'

The Squire's eyes narrowed. 'You know more than you mean to tell me, eh? Coate will drag Henry into it, if there's a discovery.'

'Not if his mouth is shut, sir.'

'Very likely! And, pray, how is that to be achieved?'

'I think, sir,' replied John, smiling down at him, 'that that is something you had best leave to me.'

One corner of the Squire's mouth lifted a little. 'You do, do you? Know how to do the trick?'

'Yes,' John said.

The deep, imperturbable voice had its effect. The Squire sighed, and seemed to relax. 'I daresay you'll handle it,' he said. 'I've shot my bolt. But I've made all safe for Nell. If Henry's disgraced us, she wouldn't have married you, you know. Forced you into this, of course. If you disliked it — '

'I did not,' interrupted John. He bent over the bed, gently taking the old man's hand, and holding it. 'Indeed, I'm grateful to you, sir, and I swear to you Nell shall never have cause to regret this night's work.' He added, with a twinkle: 'It was, besides, an education to see how a difficult team could be driven to an inch!'

The Squire chuckled. 'Ah, I was a top-sawyer in my day!'

'I should describe you today as a nonpareil, sir,' John retorted. 'I am going to leave you now. May I beg you to think no more of your grandson's nonsense? There is not the least need for you to tease yourself about it.'

The waxen hand feebly returned the pressure of his fingers. 'You came in the very nick of time, you know. Old Mops and Brooms' grandson — ! Send Nell in to say good-night to me!'

The Captain left him with no more words. In the dressing-room he found Nell awaiting him, with Winkfield. He smiled at her, and said: 'Go to Sir Peter, my love: he wishes to bid you good-night.'

She nodded, and went at once into the bedchamber. The Captain, closing the door behind her, said: 'Before she comes back, tell me this! Is Mr Stornaway sick, or is he shamming it?'

'He's sick enough, sir — if you call it being sick to have caught cold! We had Dr Bacup here today, and Mr Henry desired him to go to him, which he did. He was always one to think himself dying for the least ailment, and no sooner did he start sneezing and coughing than he was persuaded he had an inflammation of the lungs. It's no such thing, of course, but his man's been carrying up cans of hot water for mustard foot-baths all day, and he's eaten nothing but tea and toast, because he says his pulse is tumultuous. However, the doctor left a draught for him to take, and I don't doubt he will be more the thing by tomorrow.'

'I see.' John was silent for a moment, frowning a little. 'There is nothing to be gained by my seeing him tonight, then.'

'Seeing him, sir?' Winkfield repeated.

'Yes, and as soon as may be possible. Not before he has left his bed, however — and I myself have certain plans to be made. Where is his room?'

'In the other wing of the house, sir — his and Mr Coate's room too,' Winkfield answered, eyeing him wonderingly.

'Can you describe to me precisely which room it is, and how it may be reached from this wing?'

Winkfield gave a slight gasp. 'Yes, sir, but — '

'Then do so! I am coming to pay Mr Henry a

visit, but since I don't wish Coate to know of it, it will be a nocturnal one — probably tomorrow night, if I can arrange it so.'

'Indeed, sir!' said Winkfield, rather faintly. 'Were you — were you thinking of climbing through the window?'

'Your windows weren't made for a man of my size, I'm afraid. I was rather thinking of entering by the side-door — which you would leave unlocked.'

'That would undoubtedly be better, sir,' agreed Winkfield. 'If you were to proceed along this corridor, you would find yourself on the gallery that runs round the main staircase. Immediately opposite, is a similar corridor to this. The first door upon the right of it opens into Mr Henry's room. Beyond it is a small spare-room, and opposite to that is Mr Coate's room, with a dressing-room beside it.'

'Thank you, that's very clear.'

'If I might venture to suggest, sir — I have been sleeping here, in this room, lately, and if you were to wake me — '

'I think I won't, Winkfield. It is possible that you might not be able to attend to me, or be the only person in this room,' John said bluntly. 'I'm afraid the end is very near now. I've seen men die, and that look is in your master's face tonight.'

'Yes, sir,' Winkfield said quietly, and turned away, as Nell came back into the room.

'Will you go to him now, Winkfield?' she said. 'He is so tired, but — but wonderfully peaceful, and even in spirits!'

The valet went into the bedchamber without a word, his face rather set. Nell looked up at John. 'Do you think — do you think he is better, John?'

He did not hesitate. 'No, dearest,' he replied gently.

'I see.' She went slowly towards him, and leaned against his shoulder as he put his arm round her. 'I couldn't wish it, of course. It is only that there have been just the two of us for so long.'

'I know.'

She put her hand up to touch his cheek. 'And now there is you, and — and so much happiness in my heart that there seems to be hardly room enough for anything else. Am I really married, or is it a dream?'

'You are really married, my wife. It is the strangest wedding ever two people had, but the knot was well and truly tied.'

'I think, even though you would not say so, you must have disliked it very much.'

'No.' He turned her face up, and kissed her. 'Only to be obliged to leave you, my wife. That — I do indeed dislike!'

15

The Captain, having stabled Beau, walked back to the toll-house across the field, and entered it by the back-door. He found Mr Babbacombe alone, seated by the fire, and sipping brandy and water. Mr Babbacombe raised a weary eyebrow, and said: 'What, didn't they offer you a bed? How shabby!'

The Captain grinned at him. 'I beg pardon! Have I been away so long? Where's Ben? Have you murdered him?'

'No, but I found him such a dead bore that I sent him to bed. Pikekeeping couldn't be worse than playing cassino with that bird-witted boy. I only had to open the gate twice — each time to your groom-acquaintance. Happily he knew what the toll was, for I did not.'

'Yes, I met Joseph on my way back,' John said, rather absently. He poured himself out some brandy, while his friend sleepily watched him. He glanced down at Babbacombe. 'Did Chirk come?'

'I imagine he did, since Ben slid from the place in what he no doubt considered to be an unobtrusive fashion.'

'I hope he means to come again tomorrow. If not, I must go in search of him, and I fancy that will mean a twenty-mile ride, if not more.'

'If you're trying to tell me, Jack, that you want me to make a cake of myself, minding the pike while you're away — '

'No, Ben can attend to it during the day. But I don't want you to go back to Edenhope tomorrow!'

Mr Babbacombe yawned. 'Dear boy — not the slightest intention of doing so! *Someone* must carry the news to your mother that you've been taken off to Newgate.'

'You're a devilish good fellow, Bab!' said the Captain gratefully.

'I'm not. Don't choose to have it said of me that I'm the sort of queer fish who leaves his friends in the lurch. Now perhaps you'll tell me what you've been doing up at the Manor? For one who has come from attending a death-bed you've a mighty cheerful appearance.'

'I haven't. At least, the Squire's alive still. I've come from a wedding!'

Mr Babbacombe sat up with a jerk. 'You've come from — *Whose* wedding?' he demanded uneasily.

'My own!'

'Oh, my God!' ejaculated Mr Babbacombe. 'Now I know you're touched in your upper works!'

'Oh, no, I'm not!' John said, the corners of his mouth tilting upwards.

Mr Babbacombe saw it, and groaned. 'If you think *that* is the news I'll carry to your mother, you're mightily mistaken!' he declared. 'It's the girl you mentioned, I collect? Miss Stornaway? So that's why you're so devilish anxious to keep Henry Stornaway's name clean! Lord, what made you do such a thing, you crazy gudgeon?'

'I fell in love with her the instant I saw her,' replied John, with a simplicity that defied disbelief. He smiled, as Mr Babbacombe's jaw dropped. 'Did you think I was indulging in a fit of quixotry? Oh, no! She is — well, never mind that! You will meet her presently, and then you will understand. I am the happiest man on earth!'

'In that case, dear boy,' said Mr Babbacombe, rising nobly to the occasion, 'nothing for it but to drink your health!'

'Thank you! That *is* why I must do my possible to rescue young Stornaway. It ain't that I care *what* sort of a hell-born babe Nell's cousin may be — Good God, haven't we all got relations that are precious loose fish? From anything I've ever heard, Bab, most of our grandfathers were nothing more than a set of Bingo-club boys! — but Nell would! So Sir Peter knew: that's why he got a special license, and had us married out of hand. And that's why I may need you here!' He finished the brandy in his glass, and stood for a moment, thinking. Then he set down the glass, and said: 'The Squire's had notice to quit, and I think it may be only a matter of hours now, and the devil's in it that until I've settled this business with that pair of rogues I can't leave this place, or claim my wife. To let Coate know that she *is* my wife would be to hamstring the only plan I've got. I hardly think that he could be black enough — or foolish enough! — to force his suit upon her while her grandfather is still unburied, but I won't have her subjected to the slightest annoyance! If Henry tries to make it uncomfortable for her, I'll have her away from the Manor instantly, and give her into your charge, until I have finished what I have to do here.'

'Eh?' said Mr Babbacombe, startled. 'Do you mean you want me to take your wife to Mildenhurst?'

'Good God, no! I'll take her to Mildenhurst myself, I thank you! At need, you'll take her to Buxton, and instal her at the best inn there, and take care of her until I come.'

'No, really, Jack!' protested Mr Babbacombe, quite horrified.

'Lord, Bab, don't be such a sapskull! She'll have her maid, and her groom, and her major-domo too, if Winkfield will go with her. All I want you to do is to bear her company, and to see that she doesn't fret. And that puts me in mind of something else! I hope you came here flush in the pocket, because I shall soon be cleaned out, and I must borrow from you.'

Mr Babbacombe thrust a hand into his pocket, and drew forth a fat bundle.

'A roll of soft!' said the Captain admiringly. 'I guessed it! What a thing it is to have a well-blunted friend! No, no, I don't want it now! — only if I should be obliged to send Nell to Buxton!'

Mr Babbacombe restored the roll to his pocket. 'Well, I'd as lief you didn't send her!' he said frankly. 'It ain't in my line of country, Jack, dangling after females! What's more, it seems to me I should be of more use to you if I stayed here, for I can tell by the way you're looking that you've got some dashed dangerous scheme in your head!'

John laughed. 'Oh, no! I think I shall come about safely enough!'

'Well, what *are* you planning to do?' insisted Mr Babbacombe.

'I can't tell you that at present, but — '

'Don't you try to hoax me, Jack!' interrupted his incensed friend. 'If you can't tell me, it means you're bent on some crack-brained dangerous thing you know dashed well I wouldn't hear of!'

'Well, you aren't going to hear of it,' replied John consolingly. 'Oh, don't look so horrified! I don't mean to cock up my toes, I assure you! However, any bold stroke must carry with it a certain risk, and I'm glad you've put me in mind of it. I must make a Will, and you can witness it, and take charge of it. Tomorrow will be time enough for that. Lord, how late it is! Go back to the Blue Boar, old fellow, and don't have nightmares on my account!'

Nothing more could be got out of him, and since he was plainly thinking of something else while he appeared to listen politely to Mr Babbacombe's earnest representations, that ill-used gentleman presently abandoned the losing fight, and departed, freely prophesying disaster. Upon which the Captain went to bed, and dropped into the sleep of one without a care in the world.

He was relieved to learn from Ben, on the following morning, that Chirk proposed to visit the toll-house again that evening, and was able to devote his attention to a more pressing problem. After turning the matter over in his mind while he groomed his horse, he came to the conclusion that his next action must be to reach an understanding with Gabriel Stogumber; and with this end in view he left Ben and Mrs Skeffling to mind the gate between them, and set off down the road to the village.

It was still early in the morning, and he had no expectation of seeing Mr Babbacombe, with whose matutinal habits he was familiar; but when he arrived at the Blue Boar he found the landlord and his wife, the boots, and a flustered chambermaid all anxiously engaged in assembling on several trays a breakfast which it was hoped would not be thought unworthy of the most distinguished traveller the inn had ever housed. Until this Lucullan repast had been conveyed to Mr Babbacombe's bedchamber no one had more than a distracted nod to bestow upon John, so he left the back premises for the tap, and, finding this empty, penetrated to the small coffee-room. Here he was more fortunate. Seated in solitary state at the head of the table, and partaking of a meal which bore all the signs of having been hastily prepared and served, was Mr Stogumber. He was looking far from well, and when he was obliged to use his left arm he did so stiffly, and as though it pained him. At sight of John his furrowed brow cleared a little, and he seemed pleased, bidding him an affable good-morning.

'You see I ain't stuck my spoon in the wall yet, big 'un!' he remarked, adding, with a darkling glance at the muddy coffee in his cup: 'Not but what I very likely will, if that out-and-outer upstairs means to stay here much longer! They tell me he's a friend of the Squire's, but not putting up at the Manor on account of the Squire's being so poorly. I don't know how that may be, but what I do know is that there ain't a soul in this ken as can think of anything else but what he'd fancy for his breakfast, or who's to ride to Tideswell for special blacking for his boots. It's took me the best part of an hour to get the Admiral of the Blue out there to let *me* have anything young Top-of-the-Trees don't happen to want for *my* breakfast!'

'A swell cove, eh?' grinned John.

'Ah! Of course, you wouldn't know him, would you, big 'un?'

John laughed. 'On the contrary! I know him well.'

'Well, now!' said Mr Stogumber, surprised and gratified. 'I disremember that you've ever been so nice and open afore. If it ain't too much to ask, who might he be?'

'Not in the least: there's no secret about that! His name is Wilfred Babbacombe, and he is a son of Lord Allerthorpe. In London, he lives in chambers, in Albany; at this season he may be found at Edenhope, near Melton Mowbray.'

'Fancy that!' marvelled Stogumber. 'Friend of yours, big 'un?'

'A close friend of mine.'

Mr Stogumber, after surveying him with an unblinking stare, pushed his coffee-cup away, and said: 'And you a trooper!'

John shook his head. 'No. I was a Captain in

the 3rd Dragoon Guards.'

'I know that,' replied Stogumber placidly. 'And you lives at Mildenhurst, in Hertfordshire. What I *would* like to know is why you've took it into your noddle all on a sudden to give over trying to flam me?'

'You know that too. I saw your Occurrence Book the other evening.'

'I suspicioned you did,' said Stogumber, quite unperturbed. 'I don't deny it had me in a bit of a quirk at the time, but that was afore I'd had a report on you. I *did* think it might be a longish time before they'd be able, in London, to discover who you was, if they could do it at all, but since you was so obliging as to tell me your true monarch, and the very regiment you was in, it seems there wasn't no trouble about it.'

'Lord, has Bow Street being asking questions about me at the Horse Guards? I shall never hear the end of it!'

'I don't know about that, but by what I can make out nothing you done wouldn't surprise the gentleman which supplied the information,' said Stogumber dryly. '*But*, Capting Staple, I'd take it very kind in you if you was to explain to me why, since it seems you've took to gatekeeping by way of knocking up a lark, you was so careful not to let me think as you'd seen my Occurrence Book t'other night?'

'You're fair and far off,' John replied. 'I didn't turn myself into a gatekeeper for any such reason. Nor did I know, when I saw your book, what had brought you here.'

The unblinking stare was once more bent

upon him. 'Oh! And do you now — if I ain't taking a liberty?'

'Yes, I know now, which is why I've come to see you. You are trying to find a certain consignment of currency, which was stolen about three weeks ago at the Wansbeck ford.'

'How might you have discovered that?' demanded Stogumber, his stare hardening.

'Partly through you, partly through the man to whom you owe your life. You asked me once if I knew the Wansbeck ford. I didn't, but when I mentioned it to — Jerry — he told me what had happened there. He reads the newspapers; I don't. No, he had nothing to do with the robbery: in fact, his ambition is to leave his present calling, and settle down to pound dealing and married life.'

'It is, is it? P'raps he knew where the baggage was hid?'

'He *didn't* know, but he knows this district,' said John significantly.

Stogumber half started up from his chair, and sank back again, wincing a little. 'Are you telling me that bridle-cull has boned the fence?' he gasped.

'If you mean, has he discovered where the treasure is hidden, yes. He tells me it is where no one would ever find it who did not know this district very well.'

Mr Stogumber breathed heavily.

'However,' continued John, sternly repressing a twitching lip, 'the knowledge is perfectly safe with him. He seems to think that this currency is far too dangerous to be touched.' He watched the effect of this pronouncement, and was satisfied. 'What he is anxious to do is to reveal its whereabouts to the proper authorities.'

'Tell him,' said Mr Stogumber earnestly, 'that there's a fat reward for the cove as does that!'

'He knows it. But what he doesn't know is how safe it may be for a bridle-cull to meddle in such matters.'

'Who's to say as he's a bridle-cull?' demanded Stogumber. 'He never gave me no reason to think he was! Come to think of it, I'd say he weren't, because he never took nothing off me, and he might have, easy!' He added, after a pause for thought: 'Besides which, bridle-culls ain't none of my business. I'm a Conductor — sent on this task special!'

'Where's your patrol?' asked John, surprised.

'That's my business, Capting. Don't you fret: I can summon my patrol fast enough, even though I don't see fit to have 'em taking up their quarters in this here village so as everyone can wonder how there come to be so many strangers suddenly wishful to visit Crowford!' said Mr Stogumber, with asperity.

'Well, you won't need them,' said John cheerfully. 'I am going to be your patrol.'

'Thanking you kindly, sir, I don't know as I need trouble you.'

'But I do. Without me, Stogumber, you won't find the treasure, or lay your hands on the man who stole it — and I fancy you wish to do that. Of course, if I'm mistaken, and you're content to recover the currency, I'll tell Jerry to disclose his information to you with no more ado. But if you want the thief as well, then you must leave it to me to bring you to him.'

'Ho! And p'raps, Capting Staple, sir, I know already who stole it!'

'I should think, undoubtedly you must have at least a strong suspicion,' agreed John. 'And I am quite certain that you have no proof, and no possibility of finding proof, unless I take a hand. Would you consider it proof enough if you found the thief and the treasure together?'

'I don't ask no more!' said Stogumber, fixedly regarding him.

'Then nurse that shoulder of yours until you hear from me again,' said John. 'Let it be known that you are a great deal weaker than you are, and in no case to stir out of doors. It would be an excellent notion if you were to put your arm in a sling. You have been recognized: if you are thought to have been too badly hurt to be dangerous, my task will be the easier. I believe I may be able to deliver your man into your hands, but you must let me go to work in my own way. I shan't keep you waiting for long, I hope.'

There was a long silence, while Stogumber wrestled with himself in thought. Suddenly he said: 'Capting Staple, to cut no wheedle, there's two men as I'm after, not one!'

'That is why I didn't, at the outset, tell you that I'd bubbled your lay,' responded John coolly. 'In the position I'm in, the suspicion that you were also after Henry Stornaway made it damned awkward for me! Since then, however, I've been able to satisfy myself that you're wrong in thinking he has been anything more than a foolish catspaw in the business.'

'I daresay you have; but you ain't satisfied me!' said Stogumber. 'I'll tell you to your head, sir, it weren't Coate as led me to this place, but Stornaway!'

There was nothing in John's face to betray how very unwelcome this piece of information was to him. Bent on discovering the extent of Stogumber's knowledge, he shrugged, and said: 'Because the silly goosecap made friends with a rogue?'

'No, sir, because he made friends with a certain party as works in the Treasury, which I ain't going to name, because he's an honest cove, even if he is a gabster, and got to mentioning things he shouldn't ought to have breathed to no one! It was Stornaway which knew when that consignment was to be sent off to Manchester; and the reason young — the other party — talked of it was that it weren't an ordinary consignment, not by any manner of means it weren't! That currency, Capting, ain't been seen yet, because it's the new gold money, which makes it interesting. Ah, *and* dangerous!'

'So that's it, is it?' said John, admirably simulating surprise. 'And because one gabster whispers the interesting news to another, who in his turn passes it on to I daresay every friend he happens to meet, you think he planned the robbery! Perhaps even took part in all the violent deeds performed at Wansbeck ford!'

'I don't know as I go so far as to say he took part in it, but that he was the cove as planned it I got good reason to think!' said Stogumber, a little stung by the mockery in John's voice.

Almost sighing his relief, John retorted: 'Then I fancy you're not acquainted with Henry Stornaway!' He burst out laughing.

'Good God, man, he is the most blubber-headed flat I ever encountered in all my days! Foolish beyond permission — a bleater, created to be nailed by every leg in town! The clumsiest gull-catcher could do him, brown as a berry, only by flattering him a little before pitching him his gammon! Have you seen him? He's a Bartho-lomew baby, and thinks himself a buck of the first head. He wears a driving-coat with fifteen capes, and a very down-the-road man you would take him to be, until you saw him handling the ribbons! It is such pigeons as he who keep the Coates of this world up in the stirrups!'

Suspicion, incredulity, doubt, uneasiness seemed to possess the Runner's mind in turn. He said: 'Ay, but Stornaway ain't well-breeched — not by any means he ain't!'

'Not so well-breeched as he was before he became acquainted with Coate!' replied John, drawing a bow at a venture.

'That might be so,' agreed Stogumber cautiously. 'But what made him bring Coate here, if he didn't know nothing about the robbery?'

'Coate did,' instantly responded the Captain. 'The devil of a fellow is Coate, you know! A clipping rider — and always horses of the right stamp! Never been bullfinched in his life! Hob-nobs with all the Melton men; rattles you off a dozen great names in a sentence; knows every *on-dit* of Society; and will introduce you to what he would have you believe to be the most exclusive gaming-clubs in town! Lord, he had only to hint that he would be glad to rusticate for a space, had always, perhaps, had a fancy to visit Derbyshire, and Stornaway would be so much flattered he would jump at the chance of entertaining such a Blood!'

'I'm not saying that mightn't be so,' said Stogumber slowly, 'but when he found Coate wasn't made welcome at the Manor, and was making up to Miss Stornaway till she was fair persecuted by him — which anyone can learn only by putting his listeners forward in this here village — why would he drive his old grandpa into his coffin sooner than tell Coate to show his shapes? What makes him so set on keeping him up at Kellands?'

'I have my own notion about that,' returned the Captain with ready mendacity. 'It wouldn't surprise me to learn that Stornaway's deep in debt to him. In fact, I'd be willing to lay you odds on it. Now, you thought I had taken Brean's place to knock up a lark, but you were mistaken. I reached the gate after dark last Saturday, and when I found that urchin you've seen in charge of it, and scared out of his wits, and heard that his father had gone out for an hour the night before and hadn't been seen since, I thought there was something damned smoky going on. Well, Stogumber, I have an odd liking for the unusual, and it seemed to me I might find it interesting to discover just what was afoot. It wasn't long before I had learned that

308

both Sir Peter and Miss Stornaway were persuaded that Coate was playing an under-game. They were excessively uneasy, and each of them attempted to convince Henry that his friend was by no means the bang-up Corinthian he thinks him, but a regular Captain Sharp. He didn't believe them. In his besotted eyes, they were a pair of country bumpkins, unable to recognize a choice spirit when they saw one. What, in the name of all that was wonderful, he asked them, could a Captain Sharp find to gain in this sleepy place? They had no more notion than he had: they still have none — but either something has happened to shake Henry's confidence in Coate, or his grandfather's words set up a seed of doubt in his mind. Perhaps Coate's man disclosed *your* presence in the district. I don't know that, but I do know that Henry too has become uneasy. Since he is by far too cowhearted to tell a bully like Coate to pack his trunks, he has taken to his bed on one of the flimsiest excuses I ever heard. In any ordinary case that would certainly be a way of getting rid of an unwanted guest, but this is not an ordinary case, and it has failed. It is time Henry learned just what the case is. If he does not die of heart failure, he will be mighty anxious to prove to the world that although he may have been a dupe he was never a robber or a murderer.'

'Or mighty anxious to warn Coate they've been rumbled!' interjected Stogumber, his eyes never wavering from the Captain's face.

'Coate don't need warning: he knows who *you* are. If Stornaway were in his confidence, he'd know that too. If you are right in your suspicions, neither of them will stir an inch. But if you are wrong, Stornaway will do what he can to save himself from being arrested as an accomplice, and so bringing his name into dishonour.'

'I'll allow he might — if I *am* wrong,' acknowledged Stogumber. 'P'raps you'll tell me, sir, how he could set about convincing me — me not being easy to convince?'

'Yes, I'll tell you,' John answered. 'The hiding-place of your sovereigns would occur only to those who know this country well, remember! Jerry knows it, and it plainly occurred to him very speedily. Well, Stornaway knows it too! He may think I am telling him a Banbury story, but if he is innocent he won't hesitate to go with me to this hiding-place, to discover what truth there may be in my tale.'

Mr Stogumber thought this over. After a lengthy pause, he demanded: 'And how would that bring Coate next or nigh the hiding-place?'

'Stogumber, when you set a trap, do you tell people where it lies, and what you have baited it with?'

'No,' said Stogumber, staring at him. 'I can't say as I do.'

'Nor do I!' said the Captain, with the flash of a disarming grin.

16

Towards midday, Mr Babbacombe strolled down the road to the toll-house. Saturday was a busy day on the road, and he found the Captain very much occupied, and did not for some time venture to approach nearer to the toll-house than the gate opening into Huggate's big meadow, against which he leaned negligently while his friend opened the pike to several vehicles, exchanged bucolic witticisms with a cattle drover, forced the driver of a large waggon to dismount from the back of the fore-horse, and drew the attention of an indignant gentleman to the overladen condition of his cart. During a lull in these proceedings, Mr Babbacombe, deeply appreciative, seized the opportunity to enter the toll-house. He had marshalled some powerful arguments, which he faintly hoped might dissuade the Captain from whatever fell scheme he had in mind, but as his masterly delivery of these was continually interrupted by calls of Gate! much of their force was lost, and he could not feel that the Captain, though amiable, was lending more than half an ear to them. Discouraged, he presently withdrew to the kitchen, where several covered pots, left by Mrs Skeffling round the clear fire, simmered gently, and a large pie, flanked by a fresh-baked loaf of bread and a cheese, stood on the table.

Mr Babbacombe was surveying through his

quizzing-glass these preparations for the Captain's dinner when a footfall sounded in the garden, and a shadow darkened the open doorway. He looked up, and found himself confronting quite the tallest woman he had ever beheld. She was dressed for riding, her whip in her hand, and the tail of her dress caught up over her arm. A startled exclamation broke from her. 'Oh — !'

Mr Babbacombe, showing rare acumen, proved himself instantly equal to the situation. Bowing gracefully, he said: 'Beg you will come in, ma'am! Ah — Mrs Staple, I apprehend?'

Her eyes widened. 'No, I — Why — why, yes!' She blushed, and laughed. 'I beg your pardon! You must think me quite gooseish! The truth is — But if you are a friend of — of my husband's, you must know what the truth is!'

He put forward a chair for her. 'Er — yes! Wilfred Babbacombe, ma'am, entirely at your service! Beg you will accept my felicitations!'

She took the chair, but said, with one of her direct looks: 'I think any friend of Captain Staple's must deplore his marriage — in such haste, and upon such short acquaintance. I know that it was wrong of me to have consented!'

'No, no, not at all!' Mr Babbacombe hastened to assure her. He reflected, and added: 'Come to think of it, wouldn't be Jack if he didn't get married in some dashed odd fashion! Never knew such a fellow! Just the thing for him! Wish you both very happy!'

At that moment, the Captain came in from the office. 'Bab, if you mean to stay to — Nell!' He strode forward, and she rose quickly to meet him, giving him her hands and her lips. 'Sweetheart! But how is this? How have you come here? Have you been evading the toll again?'

'Yes, shall you report me? I left my horse in the spinney, and slipped in through the garden-gate.'

'I perceive I've married the most complete hand! And you found only this fribble here to welcome you! Bab, I must present you to my wife. Babbacombe, my love, is the man I was on my way to visit when I decided instead to become a gatekeeper. He arrived yesterday, trying to nose out my business, and stood guard here last night, whilst I was otherwise employed.'

'Already had the honour of making myself known to Mrs Staple,' bowed Mr Babbacombe. 'Just wishing you both very happy! Feel bound to say I never saw a better matched pair! I won't intrude on you: daresay you have much to say to each other!'

'No, pray don't go away!' Nell said. 'Indeed, I must only remain for a minute!'

'Your grandfather?' John said.

'Oh, John, he — Dr Bacup thinks this sleep he is in is coma. He has scarcely roused since I left him last night, and it may be that he will not again. But if he does — you must see that I cannot stay!'

'Of course. You'll send me word. And particularly if you should need me, my love! Remember, you are mine now! No one can harm you in any way, and it will be very much the worse for anyone who tries to! Oh, confound that gate!' He kissed her hands, and released them. 'I must go. Bab will take you to your horse. But tell me one thing more! Is your cousin still abed?'

'No, I believe not. I have not seen him, however. Don't be afraid *he* will tease me! I am always in my own or Grandpapa's rooms, and Winkfield has forbidden Henry to come into that wing. Since he knocked him down, Henry is a great deal too much afraid of him to make the attempt!'

He was obliged to go, for the shouts from the gate were becoming exasperated; and when he was able to return, Mr Babbacombe had just come back from escorting her to where she had tethered her horse.

The rest of the day passed without incident. Mr Babbacombe did not leave the toll-house until dusk, when he returned to the Blue Boar for dinner; and although he would have gone back to sit chatting to John after this repast, he was not allowed to do so, since John expected to see Chirk as soon as it was dark, and did not feel that he would take kindly to the presence of a stranger.

But it was not, after all, until past midnight that John heard the owl's hoot. He set the door wide, and, as Chirk led Mollie through the wicket, said: 'I had given you up! What the deuce kept you so late?'

'That ain't a question as you should ask a cove of my calling, Soldier!' retorted Chirk.

'Well, stable the mare, and come into the house!'

In a few minutes, Chirk entered the kitchen.

314

He threw his hat on to a chair, but removed his greatcoat with noticeable care. This did not escape the Captain's eye. 'Winged?' he enquired.

'Just a flesh wound,' acknowledged Chirk, with a rueful grin. 'That's what made me late. It ain't so easy to stop one arm bleeding, when you've only t'other to work with. Besides, it made a mess of my coat, so I loped off to have things set to rights. What's the lay tonight?'

'I'm going out, and I want you to wait for me here. If all goes as I hope it may, I shall need you in the morning. I've seen Stogumber today, and he has agreed to stay within doors until he hears from me again.'

'Are you going to tell him where the ready and rhino's hid?'

'No: you will do that! You've nothing to fear from him. I must go now: I'll tell you what I've planned when I come back!'

'Just a moment, Soldier! Where might you be off to?'

'I'm off to have a quiet chat with Henry Stornaway!' grinned the Captain, and left him gaping.

The moon had risen, and a quarter of an hour later, John was walking up the drive at the Manor which led to the stables. Skirting these, he went on to the path across the garden. The house loomed before him, a dark mass silhouetted against the sky. No light shone from any window that he could see, but he trod silently, keeping to the turf beside the path. The door through which he had entered on his two previous visits was on the latch, and on the chest in the passage Winkfield had left the lamp burning low. John paused only to take off the brogues he was wearing. Leaving these beside the chest, he went softly up the stairs. The broad corridor at the top was dimly lit by another lamp, and on the table beside it was set a candlestick and a taper, innocent-seeming objects which had been placed there, John guessed, by Winkfield, for his use. He lit the taper at the lamp, kindled the wick of the candle from it, and stood for a moment, listening. The house was wrapped in a profound silence, but when he came to the dressing-room door, and paused outside it, he thought that he could detect the sound of movement in the room beyond it. He passed on, and through the archway which opened on to the three-sided gallery at the top of the main staircase. Below, the hall was a well of darkness, above, the great beams supporting the roof could be seen like shadows spanning the centre block of the house. John went on, the solid oaken boards under his feet as unyielding and as noiseless as a stone floor. He reached the archway leading to the other wing, and paused again. The silence seemed to press on his eardrums. Two steps brought him to the first door on the right; his fingers closed round the handle, and began slowly and firmly to turn it. The catch slid back so silently that he suspected the efficient valet of having lately oiled the lock. Pressing the door open a few inches, he released the handle, as cautiously as he had turned it the other way. The sound of heavy breathing now could be heard.

The Captain slid into the room, shielding the flame of the candle with his hand. But the curtains were drawn close round the bed, and he saw that they were of worn velvet, too thick to be penetrated by candlelight. He shut the door, and although the tiny click as the catch slid home sounded like a pistol-shot in his ears, it was not loud enough to rouse the sleeper in the four-poster.

The Captain turned, and took unhurried stock of his surroundings. Beside the bed stood a table, with a half-burnt candle on it, the snuffer poised on top of the quenched wick; a gold watch and chain; and a glass containing what appeared to be a paregoric elixir. John set his own candlestick down on this table, and softly parted the bed-curtains. Henry Stornaway was lying on his side, turned away from him, his mouth slightly open, and his night-cap over one eye. John looked down at him, considering him, and then bent over the bed.

Mr Stornaway woke with a convulsive start, and a shriek that was strangled in his throat. A hand was clamped hard over his mouth, forcing his head back against an equally vice-like grip on the nape of his neck. His body plunged, after the manner of a landed fish; his own hands, scrabbling free of the bedclothes, clawed at the one over his mouth, with as little effect as they would have had upon an iron clamp. A deep, soft voice said close to his ear: 'Quiet!'

He could not move his head, but rolling his terrified eyes he caught a glimpse of a face bent over him.

'I am going to take my hand from your mouth,' said that soft voice, 'but if you raise the smallest outcry, it will be the last sound you will ever make, for I shall break your neck. Do you understand me?'

Mr Stornaway, unable to speak, unable to nod, could only tremble, and roll his eyes more frantically than before. He trembled so much that the bed shook, and this seemed to satisfy his captor, for the hand left his mouth. With the best will in the world he could not have cried out; he could do no more than gasp for breath. The grip on his neck had not relaxed; it was not only painful, but it conveyed an exact impression to him of the ease with which this appalling visitor could put his threat into execution.

'Unless you oblige me to, I shan't hurt you,' John said. 'But you will answer me truthfully, and you will not raise your voice! Is that understood?'

'Yes, yes!' he whispered chokingly. 'Pray do not — ! Pray let me go!'

He then broke into a fit of coughing, saw that dreadful hand descending again to cover his mouth, and dived under the bedclothes. While he thus muffled the sound of his paroxysm, John pushed back the curtains on that side of the bed, and sat down on the edge of it, waiting for his victim to emerge again. When the coughing ceased, and Mr Stornaway showed no signs of emerging, he pulled the clothes down, saying: 'Sit up, you hen-hearted creature! Here, drink this!'

Mr Stornaway, struggling up on to one elbow, took the glass held out to him. It clattered against his teeth, but he managed to swallow the elixir. It appeared to revive him a little, for he dragged himself to a sitting position, and looked fearfully at his visitor. The candle now cast its light on to the Captain's face. Stornaway's eyes stared at him; he gasped: 'Who are you?'

'You know very well who I am. Brean's cousin. Did he never tell you that he had an aunt who married into a better order of society than her own? I am the son of that marriage, and I took a fancy to visit some of the relations I had never before seen. But one of them I didn't find, Mr Stornaway. Perhaps *you* can tell me what has become of Ned Brean?'

'No, no, I haven't seen him! I don't know where he is!' Stornaway whispered, white to the lips.

'You're lying. Ned was working for you and Coate. It was you who bought his services. You wanted him to pass a vehicle, heavily laden, through the pike, and afterwards to deny all knowledge of that vehicle. You wanted him also to assist in unloading from it some very weighty baggage. He did these things, but, later, he disappeared.' He saw that Stornaway was watching him with dilating eyes, and continued: 'I think, sir, that you have murdered Ned Brean.'

'*No!* I swear I did not!'

'Keep your voice down! Why should you hesitate to murder him, when you had murdered two others already?'

'No, no, no, no! It's a lie! I did not! I would not! I tell you I had no hand in it!'

'No hand either in attempting to murder a

Bow Street Runner? Do you take me for a flat?'
John said contemptuously. 'Do you take him for
a flat? Let me tell you that he reached the
toll-house, with a knife-slash across his shoulder,
and a broken head, and he knew very well who
had attacked him! When he is recovered enough
to leave his bed, you will be arrested, Mr
Stornaway, and you may try then to convince a
jury that you did not thrust a knife into the
Runner's back. I wish you joy of that task!'

'No, I tell you, no!' Stornaway uttered
hoarsely, drops of sweat starting on his brow. 'I
was not there! I knew nothing about it! O God,
you must believe me!'

'Believe you! I'll come to watch you strung up
at Tyburn! I know more of you than the Runner
has yet discovered. I have been busy while I took
charge of the gate — busy tracing your
movements since the day you left London! Do
not let us waste time! I know that it was you who
laid the plans to steal a consignment of
sovereigns on its way to Manchester. You not
only knew that there would be such a
consignment; you persuaded your friend at the
Treasury to disclose the very date when it would
set out from London!'

'It's untrue! If he said that, he is a liar! I did
not — I never thought of such a thing! It was he
who told me, cup-shot, one night! I didn't plan it
— it was Nat Coate! He saw how it could be
done, but he promised there should be no
killing! He *promised* me!'

'But there was killing, and two men were
guilty of that double murder.'

320

'I was not one! I had no hand in it! On my soul, I had not!'

'You were there, at the ford,' John said implacably. 'I know that, if the Runner does not.'

'You can't prove I was there! I did nothing, nothing! It was Nat, and the Gunns — all of it! Nat and Roger Gunn shot the guards, and Gunn's brother drove the waggon! It was his own, and when — after the gold was taken off it, he drove it away, before daylight. I can tell you where he lives! It's in Yorkshire, not far from — '

'Ah, you are altogether contemptible!' John said involuntarily.

This was not perfectly understood. 'It's true! Nat made me go with them, because I know the roads here! I did not wish to! He forced me, I tell you! I was in his power and could not refuse him!'

'You would not have been for long in his power had you carried the information to Bow Street of what he planned to do,' said John.

Tears began to run down Stornaway's ashen cheeks. 'I wish I had! I wish I were well out of the business! Nat said there would be no danger. I never dreamed he meant to shoot the guards! He swore they should be bound and gagged only!'

'How could two armed men be bound and gagged, you fool?'

'I don't know — I didn't think! I had no hand in it!' Stornaway repeated desperately.

'No hand in it! Was it Coate, then, who knew where the gold could be hidden safely? Or was it you who knew that somewhere in these hills there is a cavern, in which your father once broke his leg? A cavern which has been closed ever since, and is now almost — but not quite! — forgotten?'

If there had been any suspicion in Stornaway's mind that the Captain could not possibly know so much about him as he had alarmingly hinted, this evidence that he was uncannily in possession of the one piece of information which could more effectively than all the rest implicate him in the robbery, effectually banished it. He looked so ghastly that John wondered whether he might be going to swoon; and although he opened and shut his mouth several times no sound came from it.

'As yet,' said John, faintly stressing the words, 'the Runner doesn't know of the existence of this cavern. But I fancy I could tell him whereabouts to look for it. Where had you been, Mr Stornaway, when I encountered you very early in the morning on the lane that leads over the hills? And for what purpose were you carrying a lantern?'

Only a whimper answered him. He remained silent and motionless, waiting. After a long pause, Stornaway whispered: 'What do you mean to do? Why have you come here?'

'I am not perfectly sure yet what I mean to do,' John replied. 'I came to discover the truth from you. *Where is Ned Brean?*'

A shudder ran through Stornaway; he covered his face with his shaking hands. 'Dead!'

'By whose hand?'

'Nat Coate's. I swear that's the truth! If you

knew — if you had *seen* — you would know I'm telling you the truth! He was stabbed! He was a big fellow, and very strong: I *could* not have stabbed him, or have dragged his body — ' He stopped, gulping. 'If I tell you the whole, you'll believe me? You must believe me! When Brean disappeared, I was afraid — but Nat would tell me nothing! So I went one night — because I had to know! I could not bear it! I found Brean!' Another shudder ran through him. 'It was horrible, horrible!' He looked up. 'He will stick at nothing! *Nothing*, I tell you! I wish I had never met him! I wish I had never heard of that curst gold! I wish I were dead!'

'That wish at least is likely soon to be fulfilled,' said John dryly. 'There are three murdered men to be answered for.'

'I killed none of them!'

John looked at him consideringly. Hope gleamed in the pale eyes which watched him so furtively. Stornaway put out a tentative hand, and ventured to lay it on his breeched knee. John could almost feel his flesh creep under the touch, but he restrained the impulse to shake the hand off, and sat still.

'You've no grudge against me!' Stornaway urged, keeping his eyes fixed on that unyielding face. 'If you know what I've suffered! I swear, had I guessed what it would all mean, I would never have joined Nat in the business!' He saw the Captain's mouth curl, not pleasantly, and added hastily: 'It was madness! The gull-gropers are after me, and this place is so encumbered it will do me no good when my grandfather dies! I tell you, I had to get money!'

'Unfortunate that this money cannot benefit you for many a day to come!' interrupted the Captain scathingly.

'No, well — I didn't realize that!' Stornaway muttered. 'I wish to God I had never touched it! If I could be quit of it all — but how the devil can I? I didn't kill those men — no one could be sorrier than I am that they are dead! — but what a fix I am in, what a hellish fix I am in!' He gave a groan, and once more buried his face in his hands.

'Do you want to escape from it indeed?'

'I can't escape from it!'

'If I could be sure that yours was not the hand which killed Brean, I would help you to do so.'

For a moment, the meaning of these words scarcely penetrated to Stornaway's intelligence. The voice which uttered them was so hard that he could not believe he had heard aright. He looked up, staring. The eyes that looked down into his were as cold as sea-water. But the Captain said steadily: 'I could bring you off — if I chose to do it.'

Stornaway passed the tip of his tongue between his lips. A little colour mounted to his cheeks. 'There's a fortune in the cavern!' he said, rather breathlessly. 'Only keep your mouth shut, and you shall have — '

'I do not want your fortune, or any part of it. Nor would it save you if I were to keep my mouth shut. The Runner is not here by chance: he knows that somewhere in this district the gold is hidden. Sooner or later he will find it, make no mistake about that! I'm not here to help you to the enjoyment of a fortune: it goes back to the Treasury. As for you, you may end the affair as a felon and a murderer, or as a mere tool, deceived by a rogue. If you did not kill Brean I have no interest in sending you to the gallows. If you show me Brean's body, stabbed as you have described, and show me also where the gold is lying, I will bring you off scatheless.'

There was a long pause. 'How?' Stornaway said at last, watching him.

'I will tell the Runner that you have been entertaining Coate in all good faith; that when it was proved to you what his reason was for wishing to visit Kellands you realized that it was due to your folly and gabbing tongue that these crimes came about; that in your anxiety to atone for your unwitting share in them you used your best endeavours to discover where the gold was hidden; that you and I went to search for it in one of the caverns with which this country abounds. You will appear a fool, but not a knave.'

Stornaway said suspiciously: 'Why should you do this?'

'I have a reason,' John replied.

'I don't understand! What reason *could* you have?'

The level gaze indifferently scanned his face. 'I shall not tell you that. It is nothing you would understand. But you may trust me to do as I have promised.'

Stornaway's restless eyes shifted. 'You want me to take you to the cavern?' he said mechanically, as though he were thinking of something else.

'Yes,' John replied.

There was another pause. Stornaway looked up quickly, and away again. 'Not now! I am unwell — I cannot go out into the night air! I won't do that! I have the sore throat. I caught cold in that place!'

'In the morning,' John said. 'We will ride there together.'

'In the morning . . . How can I know that you are not leading me into a trap?'

'You will lead, not I.'

'Yes, but . . . '

'I give you my word,' John said deliberately, 'that if you deal honestly with me I will bring you off safely.'

'I'll take you there.' Stornaway's face twitched. He added, with another fleeting look up at John: 'Coate must not know, of course. But he does not rise early in the morning. When — when should we go?'

'When you wish.'

'At — yes, at eight, then!'

'Very well. I will meet you in the lane.'

'Yes. Yes, that will be best.' His voice sharpened. 'The Runner! What have you told him?'

'Nothing that can harm you.'

'But you knew of the cavern,' Stornaway said, suspicion in his face. 'How can I know you have not told him that?'

'You cannot, but I have not.'

Stornaway plucked at the sheet. 'I'll trust you! I have no choice!'

'None,' agreed the Captain calmly.

17

It was three o'clock when the Captain reached the toll-house again. He entered it through the office, and went into the kitchen so quietly that Chirk, who was seated at the table inspecting a collection of small objects laid upon it, was startled, and half leaped from his chair. When he saw who had entered, he sank down again, exclaiming: 'Dang you, Soldier! What call have *you* to go like a cat?'

'I thought you might be asleep.'

'I had a nimwinks a while ago. What's now?'

The Captain was looking at the oddments on the table. He raised an eyebrow at Chirk. 'Tonight's haul? Didn't you tell me you were turning to pound dealing?'

'So I will,' asserted Chirk, scooping up a handful of coins, and bestowing them in his pocket. 'Just as soon as I get my fambles on this reward you tell me about, that is! In the meantime, Soldier, my windmill's dwindled into a nutcracker, so I was bound to make a recover, else I'd have starved.'

John could not help laughing. 'I wish you will not! I could lend you some blunt.'

'Thank 'ee, Soldier, breaking shins is what I don't hold with!' said Chirk, whose morality, though eccentric, was rigid.

John smiled, but said nothing. A handsome gold watch lay on the table, and he picked it up.

'You were fortunate, weren't you? A well-breeched swell!'

'Getting winged ain't my idea of good fortune!' said Chirk tartly. 'If he'd had more than one barker, likely I'd be as dead as a herring by now, for he was a good shot: hit me while his prad was trying to bolt with him!'

'Jerry, was there an exchange of shots?' John asked, a little sternly.

'Ay, but I fired over his head, so you've no call to look at me like that, Soldier! I ain't a man o' violence!'

'You're a very foolish fellow. Don't rob any more travellers! If all goes as I believe it will, we shall finish our business tomorrow.'

'I'd as lief we did,' commented Chirk.

'And I! I am going to tell you just what I have arranged to do, and what your part must be. Everything depends on Stornaway, but I think he will do exactly what I want him to do.'

'I daresay you know what you're about,' said Chirk.

But by the time the Captain had come to the end of a brief account of what had passed between himself and Stornaway, the faintly sceptical expression on the highwayman's face had changed to one of blank dismay. 'And I thought you was a downy one!' he ejaculated. 'Lord, Soldier, you've got more hair than wit, seemingly!'

'Have I?' said the Captain, smiling.

'If you don't see that you'll be queered on that suit, you're wood-headed!' said Chirk bluntly. 'I never clapped my ogles on young Stornaway, but by what Rose has told me — let alone what *you've* just told me — any cove as 'ud trust him an inch beyond the reach of his barker is no better than a bleater! God love you, Soldier, he'll turn cat in pan on you! A cull as'll whiddle on his friends, like he done tonight to you, won't think twice afore he tips *you* the double! P'raps you'll tell me why he was so anxious you shouldn't force him to show you the cavern till it was morning — *if* them windmills you've got in your head don't stop you thinking?'

The smile lingered in John's eyes. 'Oh, no! Not a bit! He wanted time to take counsel of Coate, of course.'

Chirk's jaw dropped. 'He — And you're being so very obliging as to *let* him?'

'It is precisely what I wish him to do. By hedge or by stile, I must get Coate into that cavern. I've been in the deuce of a puzzle to know how to do it — till I hit upon this notion. I believe it will answer: if it doesn't, the lord only knows what's to be done next!'

'Just what *do* you think will happen?' enquired Chirk, regarding him with a fascinated eye.

'Well, setting myself in Coate's place, it's as plain as a pikestaff I must be disposed of. I'm working with the Redbreast; I know too much. It may be dangerous to kill me, but it would be far more dangerous to let me live to tell Stogumber the gold is hidden in a cavern here. Furthermore, Coate knows I came here unexpectedly, and that I'm a stranger to everyone in Crowford, and he might well think that no one would feel any particular degree of surprise if I were to

329

vanish as suddenly as I appeared. I think, then, that Henry will keep his tryst with me, and will lead me to the cavern.'

'So that Coate can murder you there?'

'So that Coate can murder me there,' nodded the Captain cheerfully. 'I do him the justice to believe that he would prefer to have no hand in my murder, but between greed of gold and fear of Coate he will obey his orders — and weep over the harsh necessity later!'

'Yes, I remember as how you said you was going to enjoy yourself!' said Chirk acidly. 'Rare fun and gig it'll be, down in that tomb! Well, I knew when I first saw you that you'd broken loose from Bedlam! You'll find Coate waiting for you, and a nice, easy shot it'll be for him, with you carrying a lantern so as he'll know just where to aim his pop!'

The Captain grinned. 'If Coate is already in the cavern I shall know it, for he cannot fasten the fence from within. But I think he won't be: he leaves little to chance, and even if he took the fence down, and concealed it in the under-growth, anyone must see that a fence or a gate has stood there. He won't wish to make me even a little suspicious. If I am wrong, and find the cavern open, be sure I'll be content to enter with only Stornaway's lantern to light me — and will stay beyond its beam!'

'The only thing as I'm sure of is that you'll be put to bed with a shovel!'

'Oh, not if you play your part, and Stogumber his, I hope!'

'What are you wishful I should do?' asked

330

Chirk uneasily. 'I'll tell you to your head, Soldier, I ain't a-going to help you to make a pea-goose of yourself! I daresay you think it 'ud be a capital go if you was to get your noddle blown off in that cavern, but precious queer stirrups I'd find myself in, if that was to happen!'

'I shouldn't think it a capital go at all,' replied John. 'And whatever may happen to me, *you* will be protected by Stogumber. You have only to do precisely as I bid you, and we shall come about famously.'

'Yes, well, maybe we got different notions about that!' retorted Chirk. 'Seems to me *your* notion o' what's famous ain't by any means mine!'

'Be quiet! A fine rank-rider you are, to turn as melancholy as a gibed cat at the hint of a risk!'

'*Hint? Hint* of a risk?' interpolated Chirk indignantly.

'That's all. Now, you listen carefully to what you must do, and see you don't forget anything!'

'I thought it wouldn't be long before you took it into your head I was one of them troopers of yours,' commented Chirk rebelliously.

'If any trooper of mine ever argued with me as you do, I'd have him under guard before the cat could lick her ear! Stubble it! I've told Stogumber that *you* have found the gold, but that I would not let you divulge the hiding-place to him until *my* plans were completed. I told him also that Stornaway is nothing but a sapskull, and knows nothing of the robbery. Whether he believes that or not is no matter: he *will* believe it. You will tell him that Stornaway, when it was shown to him that Coate had been using him as a mask, readily agreed to use his best endeavours to discover where the treasure had been hidden, and — like you! — suspected the cavern might be the place. You will then tell him that I have baited my trap, and you will take him to the cavern. He can borrow the landlord's cob, and you must both be there a full hour before eight o'clock. You will see fast enough if Coate has entered the cavern. If he has not, take the horses well beyond it, and tether them, and yourselves find cover within sight of the cave-mouth. And then wait! When Coate enters the cavern, which I am persuaded he will do as soon as I am safely inside it, follow him, but not so close that he will see or hear you until he has reached the main chamber. Do you perfectly understand? It will not suit me at all for Stogumber to arrest him before that moment.'

'But of course it wouldn't!' agreed Chirk, with deceptive cordiality. 'Why, if Stogumber and me was to do the trick afore he got into the cavern, you wouldn't be able to play at hide-and-seek in the dark with as nasty a pair o' cut-throat culls as ever I see!'

'Exactly so!' said John gravely. 'But, you see, I have very good reason for what I am doing. Don't forget that I shall be expecting Coate, and so shall not be taken by surprise! Unless he can see me clearly, he won't risk a shot at me, and you know how little light two lanterns afforded us in that place! If it comes to a struggle, why, I fancy I should be able to hold my own against the fellow! Come! Promise me that you'll do precisely as you're bid! If you don't, you may well bring all to ruin!'

After a long pause, and with every sign of reluctance, Chirk gave him the required promise. John gripped his hand, and got up. 'Excellent fellow! I'm off to snatch a few hours' sleep now: I'll rouse you at six o'clock.'

There were several points on which Mr Chirk would have liked to have received some further information, but he had by this time reached a very fair estimate of Captain Staple's character, and he wasted no time in asking questions which, he gloomily knew, would only be fobbed off. Stretching himself out on his improvised bed, he philosophically went to sleep.

In a very few hours' time, he was on his way to the village, slipping out of the kitchen just as Ben emerged, yawning, and knuckling his eyes, from his room.

Upon learning that he must mind the gate during the morning, Ben said that Mr Sopworthy had commanded his services at the Blue Boar. The Captain, knowing very well that he found his work at the inn far more agreeable than pike-keeping, said suspiciously: 'You don't go to Sopworthy on Sunday!'

'It's on account o' the company they got at the inn,' explained Ben virtuously. 'So I tells Mr Sopworthy as I'd go, guv'nor. *Promised* him!'

'Well, I'm sorry for that, but you can't go: I need you.'

'Mr Sopworthy will be in a rare tweak if I don't!'

'No, he won't. I'll make all right with him.'

'But Jem-Ostler says as he'll let me help him groom the swell cove's prads!' cried Ben, much chagrined. 'Coo, they are a bang-up pair!'

But although he laughed, the Captain refused to relent; so instead of beguiling the breakfast-table with artless chatter, Ben ate a hearty meal in cold silence: a form of punishment which suited John's humour exactly.

Since there had been no reappearance of Chirk at the toll-house, the Captain was satisfied that Stogumber must have consented to go with him to lie in wait outside the cavern. He had directed Chirk not to go by way of the road, but to ride across Huggate's fields; and shortly before eight o'clock he himself set forth, walking up to the barn to saddle Beau. Remembering how cumbersome he had found his top-boots in the cavern, he did not wear them; and as he swung himself into the saddle he grinned, thinking of Mr Babbacombe's shocked horror, could he have known that his friend was riding about the country in woollen stockings, much stained breeches, a flannel shirt, and a leather waistcoat.

He reached the lane some minutes before Stornaway put in an appearance, and began to walk Beau slowly up it. It was not long before the sound of a trotting horse made him turn his head. Stornaway came up with him, muffled in his caped coat, and with a thick scarf wound round his neck. That he was extremely nervous, John saw at a glance. He broke at once into speech, complaining of the autumnal chill in the air, and assuring John, who had asked for no assurance, that he had left Coate snoring. John saw him steal several of his furtive glances at him, and guessed from the direction of these that he was trying to ascertain whether or not he was carrying pistols. Rather maliciously, he said: 'No, I am not armed, Mr Stornaway. Why should I be?'

'Armed! I never thought of such a thing! Though, to be sure, for anything I know you may be meaning to murder me in that cavern!' said Stornaway, flustered into unwise speech.

'Why should I?' asked John.

Thrown into worse confusion, Stornaway tied himself up in a muddle of half-sentences, while John reflected that so loose a tongue must effectually have warned him that mischief was intended, had he not been already well aware of it. Stornaway seemed to be incapable of keeping anything to himself; and it was not long before he had presented John with one of the few pieces of information that could interest him. 'You should not call me Mr Stornaway,' he told him. 'I am Sir Henry Stornaway now, you know!'

'I felicitate you,' said John dryly. 'May I know when this happened?'

'Oh, about five o'clock, I fancy! My grandfather's man — an insolent fellow! — did not fetch me, so I've no very precise knowledge. The thing is that *I'm* master at Kellands now, as several people will precious soon discover!'

It seemed to be so much in keeping with his character that he should be looking forward to an easy triumph over his grandfather's servants that the Captain was scarcely angry. He returned an indifferent answer; and the rest of the way was beguiled by Henry's rambling exposition of what he meant to do at the Manor, as soon as his grandfather was buried.

This diverted his mind from his present anxieties, but when he led John off the lane, towards the cavern, these returned to him, and he grew markedly silent, while the fretting behaviour of his horse betrayed unmistakeably how much his nerves were on the jump.

The fence was securely tied across the mouth of the cavern, and the withered gorse bushes almost wholly concealed it. While Stornaway lit his lantern, John stood with his head up, listening intently. He heard no sound of horse's hooves, but he could not suppose that Coate was far behind, and reflected that once he left the lane the rough turf would muffle the noise of his approach.

'Have you no lantern?' demanded Stornaway, still on one knee before his own.

The Captain glanced down at him, slightly shaking his head, a glint in his eyes.

Stornaway looked a good deal taken aback, but said after a moment: 'You should have brought one! It is devilish dark inside, and you might easily miss your footing, not being familiar with the place! You had best take mine, for I should not wish you to break your leg, as my father once did!'

'You shall lead the way,' replied the Captain amiably.

Stornaway hesitated, and then rose to his feet. The entrance to the cave laid bare, he stepped into it, the Captain following him. Except when he warned the Captain to stoop, or to take care where he was setting his feet, he hardly spoke during the descent to the main chamber. John said nothing at all, being fully occupied in listening for any sound of pursuing footsteps. As he climbed down the rough stairway, the rushing noise of the water again assailed his ears, and he realized that it was loud enough, in the confined space, to drown the mere sound of footsteps. This, while it would materially assist Stogumber, would certainly make his own position more perilous, since he would be obliged to rely for warning of Coate's arrival on the chance of seeing the light of his lantern before he darkened it, as he undoubtedly would, on reaching the main chamber. It began to seem as though he might indeed find himself playing at hide-and-seek in the dark, as Chirk had prophesied. However, the imminence of danger had never yet exercised a depressive effect upon the Captain's spirits; it merely sharpened his faculties; and not for a moment did he hesitate to go on.

When they came to the main chamber, Stornaway immediately led John up to the chests, saying jerkily: 'There they are! You may see for yourself that only one has been opened. It was Brean who did that. He came here to steal from us. That's why Nat stabbed him. Now I'll show you where — '

'All in good time,' interrupted John. 'I'll take a look inside the opened chest first, if you please.'

'Nothing has been removed from it!'

'Nevertheless, I will see that for myself,'

replied John, beginning to undo the knot he himself had tied.

Stornaway fidgeted, and protested querulously that this was a waste of time. It was plain that he was anxious to get John out of the main chamber before some reflection of the light from the lantern Coate would be forced to use on the stairway should be perceptible through the rugged opening on to the slope that led to the stair. When he thought John was not watching him, he kept glancing in the direction of the opening; but John, while pretending to be intent upon inspecting the contents of the chest, was watching him all the time, and watching also for any glimmer of light in the darkness beyond him. Suddenly, and after what seemed an æon of time, the darkness was pierced by a flicker of light, as though someone beyond the opening had turned a lantern unwarily. In the same instant Stornaway swung round, interposing his greatcoated figure between the Captain and that glimmer of light, and saying in an unnaturally loud voice: 'There! You see that the chest is full! Do not let us be lingering here! I shall catch my death in this dreadful cold! You made me promise to show you Brean's body, and I will do so. We can cord the chest again later: do, for God's sake, make an end of this!'

'Very well,' said the Captain. 'Where now do you mean to take me?'

'This way!' Stornaway said, going towards the shorter passage which led to the river. 'I wish *you* had brought a lantern.'

His own lantern cast its light only through one

unshuttered side, and the Captain had no hesitation in following him, since the beam of light was thrown ahead, and could not cast his own figure into relief. He trod heavily, allowing his nailed brogues to scrape and clatter on the slippery rock beneath them; and as he went he rapidly considered what had most probably been planned for him. From Stornaway's urgent desire to lead him away from the large chamber, it seemed certain that his murder was not to take place there, but either in the passage beyond it, or where this curved abruptly, and widened into the broader and loftier passage through which the stream ran. Then, quite coolly, he rejected this theory. Stornaway had just taken care to warn his friend that their prospective victim was not carrying a lantern; and Coate would certainly realize that he must depend for his aim on the light Stornaway would cast on to the Captain from his own lantern. But the man who held the lantern would naturally be the leader, and little though Coate might relish having Stornaway as an accomplice he would certainly take care to keep him alive while he was so necessary to the final success of his schemes. He would risk no shot in the confined space of the corridor, John decided, for the slightest deviation of his aim might mean the death of the wrong man. A moment's reflection convinced him that the river-passage would be almost as hazardous a place to choose, for although it was very much broader, the stream, running along one side under the slimy rock-face, took up quite half its width, so that only an uncomfortably small space could lie between two men standing beside it. Had he himself been carrying a lantern, no doubt Stornaway, at a pre-arranged signal, could have cast himself on the ground; but since Stornaway must hold his lantern with its beam fixed steadily upon him this would be an impossible manoeuvre. No one, thought John, would be quicker to realize this, and to provide against such a contingency, than the efficient Mr Coate. Moreover, he doubted very much whether that cool gentleman would, whatever the circumstances, place the slightest reliance on Stornaway's ability to keep his head if he thought himself in the smallest danger of being shot.

I wouldn't myself, thought John, as he entered the narrow passage in Stornaway's wake. So why didn't he darken his lantern, and come down the slope to the main chamber while we were still in it, and he had the light of Stornaway's lantern to guide him?

Then he recalled the rubble and the stones which lay scattered at the foot of the natural stair: Coate must have been afraid of betraying his presence by stumbling over a boulder in the darkness, or kicking some loose stone down the slope, and Coate did not know that his victim carried no pistols.

Very wise! thought the Captain approvingly. If he risked a shot at that range, and missed me, I might, if I were armed, put a bullet into him before he could fire his second pistol. In his shoes, I wouldn't fire the second pistol, except point-blank. In fact, I should do precisely what I fancy he has planned to do: enter the big chamber when I am safely out of earshot and eyeshot, take up a strategic position near the entrance to this passage, and wait for Stornaway to lead me back to the chamber. Not immediately in front of it, for Stornaway's lantern must then reveal him to me, but to the side, out of sight of anyone approaching down the passage. Once clear of the passage, Stornaway will turn, as though to speak to me, *I* shall step into the main chamber, with the light shining full in my face, and Coate will have the easiest shot of his life, and will put a bullet through my temple.

By the time the Captain had reached this cheerful conclusion he and Stornaway had emerged into the river-passage. He halted, exclaiming in well-simulated surprise that he had not known a stream ran through the cavern. But while he marvelled at it, and even bent down to test the temperature of the water, his thoughts raced on.

No rubble in the passage: the rock is slippery, but firm; very little in the main chamber. If I don't make haste, I shall have Stogumber here before I want him.

'For God's sake, never mind the stream!' exclaimed Stornaway, in fretting impatience. 'Look there!'

'Well?' said the Captain, following the beam of the torch to the heap of debris at the end of the passage.

'*That* is where Brean lies buried! You'll find him soon enough!'

'Not I!' said the Captain, with a strong

shudder. 'If that's where he is, you've dragged those stones off him once, and you may do it again! Give me the lantern! I'll hold it for you.'

'I tell you he's there! I won't uncover his body a second time — it's horrible! If see him you must, do it for yourself!'

'No, I thank you!' said John emphatically. 'What makes you so nice all at once?'

Stornaway thrust the lantern into his hand. 'Damn you, take it, then! Do you think I'm lying? Oh, you fool, how can I see what I'm about, if you swing the light all round? Hold it steady!'

The Captain, affecting an awed interest in his surroundings, swept the beam along the wall. 'Hold hard! I've never been in such a place as this!' he said, swiftly calculating the distance from a projecting ledge of rock to the opening into the passage. 'Why are you in such a quirk? A dead man can't hurt you.' He moved towards the ledge he had noticed, and sat down upon it, directing the lantern-light on to the mound of stones and rubble.

'Be quiet, be quiet!' Stornaway said hysterically. He looked over his shoulder, as he bent to lift a rock from the heap. 'What are you doing?'

'Taking a stone out of my shoe,' replied the Captain, who was, in fact, removing his shoes. 'What the devil should I be doing? Brr! How cold it is here! Make haste, and let's get out of this tomb!'

'You're holding the lantern so high I can't see!'

'Is that better?' John asked, setting it softly

342

down on the rock from which he had risen.

'Bring it nearer!' snapped Stornaway.

'Very well. Let me put my shoe on again first, however!' John said, both brogues gripped in his right hand, and his eyes watchful on Stornaway's bent back.

'I wish you will hurry!'

But the Captain returned no answer to this, for he had found the opening into the narrower passage, and was stealing along it, his left hand feeling the wall for guidance, and his stockinged feet making no sound on the rock-floor. He went as swiftly as he dared, for Stornaway had only to look round again to discover his absence, and at all costs he must be clear of the passage before the inevitable alarm was shouted to Coate. The noise of the water, which was here very loud, made it unnecessary for him to worry much over the chances of a stumble, and he knew that there were no alcoves in the walls to mislead him. Ahead of him loomed dense darkness: Coate must have shuttered his lantern.

Well, thought John, if he *is* standing immediately before the opening, and I collide with him, so much the worse for him! I must be nearly at the end of the passage now.

Even as this thought came into his mind, the rough wall seemed to vanish from under his groping hand. He stood still for just long enough to feel the angle of it, as it turned sharply away, knew that he stood on the threshold of the main chamber, and slid straight ahead with long, swift strides. He encountered no obstacle, and the scrunch of a little patch of rubble when he trod on it barely reached his own straining ears above the noise of the water.

He had taken no more than five strides when a high-pitched shout sounded behind him. As though from a long way off, he heard Stornaway's voice calling in panic: 'Where are you? Where are you?'

The Captain's immediate object was to reach the cover of the Treasury chests before Coate could unshutter his lantern, and sweep its light round the chamber. Throwing caution to the winds, he raced forward, knowing that Coate's lantern would not pierce the darkness for a distance of more than a few yards. Again Stornaway's voice shrilled above the rush of the river through the rock. 'Nat! Nat!' Stornaway screamed. 'He's gone!'

The Captain stopped, and faced about, edging his way to his left. A yellow light appeared suddenly at the far end of the chamber, illuminating the entrance to the passage for an instant before it swept in a wide arc towards him. He saw that he was indeed beyond its radius, realized that he must be standing quite near to the opposite wall, and swiftly moved to where he judged the side wall must be. Once he had reached this he would very quickly find the chests, for they had been placed, he knew, close to it.

All at once he was startled by the disappearance of the light, and could not for a moment think what had happened. Then he remembered that only Stornaway knew that he was unarmed, and realized that Coate, ignorant of his exact whereabouts, must be afraid to betray his own position. At that moment, he collided with the wall, stubbing one foot, and grazing one out-thrust hand. He turned again, feeling his way along it, his other hand, still gripping his shoes, stretched out to encounter the chest which had been set up on its end.

A light appeared again, wobbling and wavering. He knew it must be cast from Stornaway's lantern, and was not surprised when he heard Coate say furiously: 'Cover your lantern, fool! Do you want to make a target of yourself?'

'He has no pistols with him!' Stornaway's voice, raised in extreme agitation, seemed to echo all round the roof.

Now for it! thought John, and in that instant found the chests, and dropped to the ground behind them. Beside the first of these, which his hand had brushed, and which he knew to be up-ended, stood two more, one on top of the other; beyond them the other three had been set down side by side, and were not deep enough to afford him any cover. Crouching behind the first chests, he at last abandoned his shoes, and waited for Coate to come within his reach. He heard the hasty tread of shod feet, saw the light approaching, and gathered himself together in readiness. The light swept the wall at the end of the chamber, found the entrance to the slope, and stayed there for a moment: the possibility that he was escaping from the cavern had obviously occurred to Coate. One swift glance over his shoulder showed the Captain that Stornaway was still standing at the far end of the chamber, aimlessly turning his lantern this way and that. While Coate's attention was still fixed on the way of escape, the Captain rose silently to his feet, stepped sideways, clear of the first chest, and, as the beam of light swung towards him, launched himself straight at it. He reached Coate, before the light was focused fully upon him, colliding with him, chest to chest, and flinging one arm round him, pinioning his left arm, holding the lantern, to his side, and grabbing his right just below the elbow.

The lantern fell to the ground with the tinkle of breaking glass; a little flicker of flame ran over the rock, and died; in darkness the two men swayed and struggled desperately, John trying to hold Coate powerless while he shifted his grip on his right arm to the wrist, all the time keeping this pistol-hand pointing harmlessly upwards, and Coate striving with all his might to wrench free from an encircling arm that was holding him in a bear's hug.

He was a shorter man than John, but thickset, and very powerful, as John soon discovered. Hampered as he was by the necessity of maintaining his cramping hold on that danger-ous right arm, he had to put forth every ounce of his great strength to continue holding Coate so closely pressed against himself that he could neither get his left hand to the second pistol John could feel digging into his ribs, nor find the knife which John guessed he carried somewhere about his person. Fractionally, as they struggled together, shifting this way and that over the damp, uneven rock-floor, John was moving his

346

grip nearer and nearer to Coate's wrist. His stockinged feet, holding the slippery ground more securely than Coate's boots, gave him a slight advantage. His toes suffered, but they were by this time so numbed by the cold that he was scarcely aware of being trodden on.

For a minute they battled in complete darkness, but Stornaway came hurrying and stumbling up the length of the cavern, wildly waving his lantern about in an attempt to discover their whereabouts. Its light, vacillating in a way that betrayed how Stornaway's hand must be trembling, fell on Coate's face, and showed it livid, sweat starting on it, the lips drawn back in a grimace like a dog's snarl from clenched teeth. It showed his right arm, uplifted and held by John's grip round it, and his left still trying to work free from the hug which clamped it to his body. In an agony of indecision, Stornaway teetered about the swaying couple, his own pistol in his hand. Once he raised it, and as he did so, the position of the struggling pair altered, and it was Coate's back which was turned towards him instead of John's. His eyes fixed on them, he ventured closer; the Captain saw him, and with a superhuman effort which made his muscles crack swung Coate round, interposing his body between himself and Stornaway. Stornaway, who seemed scarcely to know what to do, retreated a step, and ran round the group. So riveted was his attention that he failed to perceive that another light than the one he carried now illuminated the scene. His change of position had brought him between the combatants and the entrance to the chamber, his back turned to this, and he never saw Jeremy Chirk's arrival. The highwayman, hearing the stamp and scrape of shod feet ahead when he was halfway down the perilous stair, and the unconscious cries Stornaway kept on uttering, abandoned caution, and came down the rest of the steep descent with a reckless speed which left his more ponderous companion far in the rear, and raced down the slope to the opening into the main chamber. There he paused, coolly survey-ing the three men before him, keeping the beam of his lantern steadily upon them.

The Captain's hand had reached Coate's wrist; Stornaway, standing behind him, lifted his pistol, and tried to aim it. His hand was shaking like a leaf, so that the muzzle wobbled lamentably. A deafening report as Coate's gun exploded was succeeded so immediately by a second that this sounded like a sharp echo, reverberating round the vaulted roof of the chamber. A couple of stalactites dropped on to the floor, and Coate's empty pistol fell with a crash, just as Stornaway, who had uttered a queer groan, crumpled where he stood, and collapsed in an inert heap.

The Captain, suddenly releasing Coate, sprang back, his great chest heaving, and his fists up. He met a rushing attack with a left and a murderous right that brought Coate down. He was up again in an instant, a hand fumbling at his waist. The Captain saw the flash of steel in the lantern-light, and hurled himself with such force at him that both men went down together. But the Captain

348

was uppermost, and his hands were at Coate's throat. Mr Chirk, perceiving this, and aware that the panting Runner had reached the entrance, and was standing at his elbow, shifted his lantern, and directed its beam on to Stornaway's still figure.

Mr Stogumber, out of breath, first amazed by the extent of the cavern, and then shaken by a fall on the stair, was feeling a little dazed, and was unable for a few moments to marshal his wits into order. He had heard what sounded like two shots, he had seen Coate's attempt to stab the Captain, and he had seen the two men go down in a wildly struggling tangle of arms and legs. Then they were lost in darkness, and he found himself staring at a dead man on the ground before him. 'Here!' he ejaculated. 'What — How — ?'

Chirk slid a long-nosed pistol unobtrusively into the wide pocket of his coat. 'The poor fellow was shot, trying to help the Soldier,' he said sadly. 'Dropped him like a pigeon, Coate did! Ah, well, it ain't no use crying over spilt milk!'

'Get out o' my way!' Stogumber said fiercely, thrusting him aside, and swinging his lantern to pick up the forms of Coate and the Captain.

Chirk, whose quick, listening ears, had already caught the sound for which he had been waiting, made no effort to stop him, but directed his own lantern towards the spot where he had seen the two men struggling on the ground. The struggle was over. Coate lay spreadeagled, and beside him, on his knee, labouring to recover his breath, his head sunk forward, was the Captain.

'By God, the cull did stick that chive into him!' Stogumber exclaimed, hurrying forward. 'Capting Staple, sir! Here, big 'un, let me see how bad you're hurt! Bring that light closer, you! Catch hold of this lantern o'mine, too, so as I'll have my hands free! Shake your shambles, now!'

The Captain lifted his head, and passed one shaking hand across his dripping brow. 'I'm not hurt,' he said thickly. 'Only winded. Leather waistcoat saved me. Thought it might.'

'Lordy, I thought you was a goner!' said Stogumber, mopping his own brow. He looked down at Coate, and bent, staring. He raised his shoulders from the ground, and let them fall again. 'Capting Staple,' he said, in an odd voice, fixing his eyes on the Captain's face. 'His neck's broke!'

'Yes,' agreed the Captain. 'I'm afraid it is.'

18

There was a long silence. The Captain glanced down into the hard little eyes that still stared unblinkingly at him, an expression in them impossible to divine, returned their gaze dispassionately for a moment, and then turned his head to address Chirk. 'Be a good fellow, Jerry, and fetch my shoes for me! They're behind the chests, and my feet are frozen stiff. Leave me one of those lanterns!'

Chirk handed him Stogumber's lantern, and walked away to where the chests stood. John looked at the Runner again. 'Well?'

'Big 'un,' said Stogumber slowly, 'that cull's neck weren't broke by accident. You done it, and I got a notion I know why! Likewise, I know now why you was so very anxious I shouldn't be in this here cavern when Coate came into it. I never believed that Canterbury tale you pitched me about young Stornaway, and no more I don't now! You broke Coate's neck because you knew he'd whiddle the scrap on Stornaway if I was allowed to snabble him!'

The Captain, listening to this with an air of mild interest, said thoughtfully: 'Well, you may tell that story to your commanding officer, if you choose, of course. But, if I were you, I don't think I should!'

There was another silence, pregnant with emotion. Mr Stogumber's gaze shifted from the

Captain's face to his waistcoat. He made a discovery. 'He *did* stick his chive into you!'

'I felt it prick me,' acknowledged John, 'but I think it scarcely penetrated the leather.' He unbuttoned his waistcoat as he spoke, and disclosed a tear in his shirt, and a red stain. He laid bare the wound, and wiped away a trickle of blood. 'Just a scratch,' he said. 'Not half an inch deep!'

'Ah!' said Stogumber. 'But if you hadn't been wearing that leather waistcoat we'd be putting *you* to bed with a shovel, big 'un! Plumb over the heart that is! I'm bound to say I disremember when I've met a cove as is as full of mettle as what you be! *And* impudence, if you think I'm going to tell 'em in Bow Street that Stornaway never had nothing to do with the robbery!'

'How d'ye make that out, Redbreast?' enquired Chirk, returning with the Captain's shoes. 'When here's me as saw the poor fellow shot down — which *you* didn't, being a long way behind me at the time, and quite took up with tumbling down them stairs.'

'I didn't see it, but two shots is what I heard, and well you know it!' said Stogumber. 'I'm not saying as I blame you, for I'll be bound he was trying to put a bullet into the big 'un here, but it wasn't Coate's pop as killed him: it was yours!'

Chirk shook his head. 'That was the echo you heard,' he said. 'Wunnerful, it is! Was you thinking of clapping clinkers on to me?'

Stogumber breathed audibly through his nose. 'No, bridle-cull, I ain't going to charge you with bloody murder, because for one thing I'm

352

beholden to you, and for another I'd sooner see that sheep-biter laying there than the big 'un! But you don't gammon me, neither of you, that Mr Henry Stornaway wasn't as queer a cull as ever I see, because I knows what I knows, and that's pitching it a trifle too strong!'

'You go stow your whids and plant 'em!' recommended Chirk. 'Seems to me — '

'That's enough!' The Captain, looking up from forcing one bruised foot, not without difficulty, into his shoe, spoke authoritatively. 'We've not reached the end of this yet. I want you first to inspect the chests, Stogumber. Come!'

'One of 'em's open,' said Chirk. 'Did you do that, Soldier?'

'Yes, Stornaway and I opened it to see what was in it. But we didn't break the seals or the lock. Someone had opened it before us, though I don't think any of the bags were stolen from it. Take a look!'

Mr Stogumber, running his eye over the chests, said reverently: 'All on 'em! All six on 'em! Lord, I thank'ee! There don't look to be nothing gone from this one. Quite certain sure it wasn't you as broke the lock, big 'un?'

'Well, may I be snitched!' exclaimed Chirk. 'So now you've took it into that cod's head o' yours that the Soldier's a prig, have you? If that don't beat all to shivers! P'raps you'd like to have me turn out *my* pockets?'

'I ain't accusing neither of you of no such thing,' said Stogumber, carefully closing the chest. 'All I says is that if the Capting *did* break

353

the lock, for to see what was in the chest, it's what anyone might ha' done, even though he mightn't like to mention it. And the only thing as I've a fancy to see out of *your* pockets, queer-cull, is that long-nosed pop of yours!' He began to rope the chest again, adding frankly: 'And I don't know as I've so very much of a fancy to see that neither — things being the way they are! If you didn't break this lock, big 'un, who did?'

The Captain, who had seated himself on one of the chests, said, rather wearily: 'I suspect, the gatekeeper. I told you we had not yet come to the end.'

'The gatekeeper!' said Stogumber, turning it over in his mind. 'By Hooky, you've very likely hit it! Came up here to help himself to the rhino, and — We got to search this place!'

'What a peery cove you are, Redbreast!' said Chirk admiringly. 'No one wouldn't think so, to look at you, neither!'

'You pick up your glim, Jack-Sauce, and come and help me look around this hole in the ground!' said Stogumber.

The Captain rose to his feet again, and followed them, limping a little. The passage leading to the river was soon discovered, and in another few minutes Stogumber, having stared in amazement at the stream, swept his lantern along the chamber, and saw the body of the murdered gatekeeper. It had been partially disinterred, and its appearance was so ghastly that Chirk, who had not expected to see it exposed, gave a sharp gasp, and involuntarily recoiled. Mr Stogumber did not recoil. He walked solidly forward, and in phlegmatic silence surveyed it. 'Knifed!' he said, and looked over his shoulder. 'Does either of you coves know if the corp' is Brean?'

'Ay, that's him,' said Chirk shortly. 'And if it's all the same to you, Redbreast, I'd take it very kind in you if you was to stop shining your glim on him!'

'I'm agreeable,' responded the Runner. He came back to where John was standing, leaning his shoulder against the wall. 'If, big 'un,' he said, 'you seen that poor cove like we see him now afore this — mind, I ain't asking no questions! — all I says is, *if* you did, I don't blame you for breaking Coate's neck, and dang me, I'd like to shake that great famble of yours! Though it goes against the shins with me that I can't bring him to the nubbing-cheat!' he added regretfully, his square hand lost in the Captain's. 'The best thing we can do now is to brush. I got to send for my patrol, and it looks like you're a trifle fagged, Capting Staple.'

'I'm not tired, but my feet are thawing, and one of them's devilish bruised,' said John. 'We'll go back into the main chamber, but we can't leave the cavern like this.'

'God love you, Soldier, ain't you had enough yet?' demanded Chirk irascibly.

'No, I haven't. There's a great deal of untidiness about this business, and I don't like untidiness! I must make all right for Stogumber.'

'I'm obliged to you,' said the Runner heavily. 'I ain't complaining, but the more I thinks on it the

355

more I wonder what they're going to say, up at Headquarters, when they knows that I let you come into this cavern without me, ah, and let you break Coate's neck, 'stead of leaving that to the hangman!'

They had emerged again into the main chamber. John led the way across it, and stood for a moment, looking down at Coate's body. 'I wasn't here at all,' he said.

'Eh?' ejaculated Stogumber, taken aback.

The Captain turned away, and limped to the chests, setting the lantern he had taken from Chirk on the upturned one, and sitting down on another. 'I think I had very little to do with the business,' he said, considering the matter.

'*Little* to do with it?' gasped Stogumber. 'Why — '

'You stow your gab, Redbreast, and put your hearing-cheats forward!' interrupted Chirk. 'If you wasn't here, Soldier, who was it broke Coate's neck?'

'No one,' replied the Captain. 'He fell on the stairs, trying to make his escape.'

'So he did!' said Chirk. 'What's more, I saw him with these very ogles! We'll put him there natural, so as them as Mr Stogumber brings to fetch these here bodies away will find him there, just like he told 'em they would!'

'It *could* have happened that way,' admitted Stogumber cautiously.

'It did happen that way, so don't let's have any argle-bargle!' begged Chirk. 'What I want to know is, who discovered the cavern, and all this rhino?'

'You did. We have already decided on that, so let me have no argle-bargle from *you*! I had my own reasons for bearing a hand in the adventure, and I want no part of the reward. I imagine that will be between you and Stogumber.'

'There'll be plenty for three,' said Stogumber.

'Well, I don't want it, and would prefer to have my name kept out of the business.' He sat frowning into the darkness. 'I wonder what brought Coate here today?' he said.

'If it comes to that, Soldier, it's queering me a bit to know what brought Stornaway here!' confessed Chirk ruefully.

'Well, it ain't queering me!' said Stogumber explosively. 'I've told you already I won't — '

'Stornaway came with you and Stogumber,' said the Captain, paying no heed to the interruption. 'Stogumber could scarcely persuade him to believe that his friend was so villainous. In fact, he wouldn't believe it without the proof of his own eyes. So you brought him here, and showed him both the treasure, and Brean's body.'

'Never saw a cove so goshswoggled!' corroborated Chirk.

'Keep that long tongue of yours still, Jerry!' commanded the Captain. 'Of course I see what must have happened! Stornaway was such a ninnyhammer that he made Coate suspicious that he had discovered the truth. When Coate found that he had left the house mysteriously, he came to look for him here, because it was Stornaway who told him about this cavern in the first place!'

'That,' said Stogumber bitterly, 'is the only

true thing you've said yet, Capting Staple!'

'If ever I seen such a death's head on a mopstick!' exclaimed the irrepressible Chirk. 'Nothing don't please him!'

'Very well,' said the Captain, getting up. 'If only the truth will do for you, let's tell the truth — all of it! You sat at your ease in the Blue Boar while *I* baited a trap for Coate; you didn't call up your patrol because I told you not to; you joined hands with a bridle-cull, and let him persuade you not to enter the cavern until I had done what I had to there; you — '

'That'll do!' said Stogumber. 'There's ways and ways of telling the truth! And while you're reckoning up the things I done, don't you go forgetting who broke Coate's neck, big 'un, else I'd have to remind you!'

'Oh, I won't forget!' promised the Captain. 'I was alone and unarmed — my reserves not having come up! — and I had a desperate fight with a man who held a loaded pistol. If, when we fell together on this rock-floor, his neck was broken, I fancy no one will blame me for it!'

A silence fell. Chirk coughed deprecatingly. 'I ain't never been one for throwing a rub in the way, like this swell-trap we've got here, Soldier, but I'm bound to say I ain't so very anxious you and him should blab *all* the truth!'

The Captain laughed. 'Nor I, Jerry! Come, Stogumber, what's to be gained by blackening that wretched creature's name? You found no proof that he was a party to these crimes, and although you say he would have shot me in the back you don't know that either, for you were

358

not here. He's no longer alive to answer for himself: let him rest!'

Stogumber looked up at him under lowering brows. 'You'd go into the witness-box and swear you knew him for an honest man, wouldn't you, Capting Staple?' he growled. 'On your oath, you would, I don't doubt!'

'Stogumber, what *could* I do but that? His cousin is my wife!'

Chirk gave a long whistle. 'So-ho! To be sure, you been smelling of April and May ever since I met you, but I never suspicioned you was *married*!'

'Two nights ago, in the Squire's presence. He was dying, and I gave him my word that I would keep his name clean.'

Another silence fell. 'If we *are* going to move Coate's body,' suddenly said Stogumber, with some violence, 'why don't we *do* it, 'stead of standing gabbing? As for you, rank-rider, you light the way, and bring the gun along, which he dropped! And if I have any more sauce from you, you'll be sorry!'

Twenty minutes later, they came out of the cavern, and stood for a few minutes, dazzled by the sunlight. Chirk, blowing on his numbed fingers, said caustically: 'There's coves as pays down their dust to go into places like that! It ain't going to break my heart if I never see another!'

'Nor mine,' agreed Stogumber. 'Fair blue-devilled, I was, and I don't mind owning it. We better close it up again, till I come back, with my patrol.'

This done, the Captain left the Runner to tie

the fence to the staples again, and went with Chirk to fetch Mollie and the landlord's cob from where they had been tethered round the spur of the hill. As soon as he was out of earshot of Stogumber, the Captain said sternly: 'Chirk, how dared you do that?'

Chirk did not pretend to misunderstand him. He merely said: 'You'd have had your toes cocked up now if I hadn't, Soldier.'

'Humdudgeon! I daresay he would have been glad enough to have shot me, could he but have summoned up the resolution, but whether he could have kept his hand steady is another matter! Good God, he was as scared as a rabbit! You had only to shout to him to drop his pistol, and he would have done it — and himself with it, in a swoon of terror! You knew that!'

'If you don't beat the Dutch!' remarked Chirk. 'I didn't see you with your fambles round Coate's squeeze, did I? I didn't hear the crack of his neck breaking, did I? Oh, no! but of course I didn't!'

'Yes, I killed Coate, and without compunction!' the Captain said. 'There were three wretched fellows who owed their deaths to him, and an old man whose last days on earth were made hideous by his plots! But Stornaway was no more than a tool in his hands, and that you knew!'

'Well,' said Chirk, quite unperturbed by this severity, 'seeing as you was aiming to marry Miss Nell, Soldier, it seemed to me as you'd be a deal better off without a Queer Nabs like him to call cousins with you!'

360

'I shall be, of course,' admitted the Captain frankly. 'I daresay I should have been obliged, for my wife's sake, to have extricated him a good few times from the consequences of his own folly. But you have made me feel that I've betrayed the Squire's trust, Jerry, and I don't like it!'

'You've got no call to be hipped over that,' Chirk told him. 'By what Rose has told me, Squire would have said I done right. He wouldn't ha' cared how soon his precious grandson was booked, so long as he didn't kick up no nasty dust!'

The Captain, thinking of the Squire, smiled reluctantly. 'I suppose he wouldn't.'

'Besides,' said Chirk, stripping his greatcoat from Mollie's back, and shrugging himself into it, 'while we was about it, it would have been a crying shame not to have made a regular sweep of it! Don't you go napping your bib over that young weasel, Soldier, because the only difference twixt him and Coate was that he was hen-hearted, and Coate weren't!' He hoisted himself into the saddle. 'I daresay the cob won't founder under you, if you throw your leg acrost him,' he observed, handing this sturdy animal's bridle to John. ''Least, not before we get back to the Redbreast, though I wouldn't ask him to carry you further, me being a merciful man.'

'Did you have any trouble with Stogumber?' asked John, mounting the cob.

'Not to speak of, I didn't, excepting how to get him over a hedge, him not being in the habit of it. If it's all one to you, Soldier, we'll take him back by way of the road.' He said over his shoulder, as the mare moved forward: 'He ain't a bad cove — for a trap! Him and me got talking while we was waiting for you and Stornaway, and I'm bound to say he's got a lot of useful ideas in his noddle. We got it settled all right and tight how I come to be mixed up in this business, and a rare Banbury story it is! 'Cos the Redbreast don't want it known what my lay is, and no more I don't neither.' He looked over his shoulder again. 'Lordy, to think I'll be setting up respectable, with Rose, before the cat can lick her ear! When the Redbreast told me how much gelt them chubs in Lunnon will pay down for getting the chests back, it made me feel pretty near as queer as Dick's hatband, 'cos I wasn't expecting it, nothing like it, I wasn't! Seems they pays ten per cent, which is very handsome of 'em, I will say. And I owes it all to you, Soldier, which is why I sent Stornaway to roost, not being able to think of nothing else I *could* do for you!'

This made John laugh; and he was still chuckling when they rejoined Stogumber by the cavern-mouth. That gentleman, receiving his mount from him, said austerely that he was happy to see him in such high gig, and had little doubt that he would find something to amuse him, even if he were on his way to the gallows. 'Which, from what I seen of you, is where you'll find yourself one of these days!' he added, climbing laboriously into the saddle, and groping for his stirrups. 'And I ain't going to pull this nag over any more banks, so mark that!'

'No, no, we'll follow the road!' John said

soothingly. 'Let's be off! I don't know for how long we were in the cavern, but it seems an age since I entered it. I left Ben to mind the gate, too, so I daresay I am quite in his black books by this time.'

But when they came within sight of the toll-gate there was no sign of Ben. An animated group was gathered about the immaculate person of Mr Babbacombe, and it included, besides a spare man in his Sunday blacks, a burly farmer, driving a cow with her calf; a groom in charge of a gig; Rose Durward; and Nell. Most of these persons appeared to be engaged in acrimonious discussion, but the approach, beyond the gate, of a cavalcade, consisting of three riders and two led horses, caused them to abate their strife. They all turned to see who could be coming to the pike in such force.

'What the devil's the matter?' demanded the Captain, dismounting, and pulling open the gate to allow Stogumber and Chirk, who was leading Stornaway's horse, to pass.

An outraged cry broke from the man in black. '*Just* as I thought! How dare you open that gate, fellow? How dare you, I say?'

'Why shouldn't I open the gate?' asked John. 'I'm its keeper!'

'Oh, no, you are not!' declared the spare man furiously. 'You're an impostor and a rascal! And as for that impudent counter-coxcomb there, it's very plain to me that he's a court-card, or worse!'

'Then let me tell you, you nasty, distempered old freak,' struck in Rose, her eyes bright and her cheeks flushed, 'that it's very plain to *me* that you're a vulgar, uncivil make-bait, and if no one else will slap your Friday-face for you, I will!'

'Oh, Rose, pray hush!' begged Nell, between amusement and dismay. 'For heaven's sake, John — !'

'*I'll* slap his face for you, Miss Durward, and glad to do it!' offered the farmer. 'What call has *he* to come here, poking his Malmsey-nose into what ain't none of his business? Threepence for every head of horned cattle! that's what it says on the board, and threepence I paid the gentleman! What's more, I'll pay him threepence more if there's any one of you can find a horn on the calf's head!'

'Damn you, Jack, I *knew* I should catch cold if I let you bamboozle me into staying here!' said the harassed Mr Babbacombe. 'Where the devil have you been? No, never mind telling me! What ought this fellow to be charged for his calf? I'll be hanged if I know! You can't get away from it: not a sign of a horn on its head!'

'Quibbling! Mere quibbling!' cried the spare man. 'You're in a plot to cheat the tolls! Don't tell me!'

'I do believe as he's an Informer!' said the farmer, staring very hard at the spare man. 'Let's take and pitch him in Bob Huggate's duck-pond, guv'nor!'

At this point, the Captain, who had so far failed to make himself heard, intervened. Pushing the gate wider, he addressed himself to the farmer. 'You be off, with your horned cattle!' he said. 'I won't charge you for the calf, though I daresay I'm wrong.'

'You are wrong!' asserted the spare man, dancing with fury. 'My name is Willitoft, sir! Willitoft!'

'Well, don't take on about it!' recommended Chirk, hitching the bridle of Coate's horse to the gatepost. 'No one ain't blaming you if it is!'

Rose, who had been gazing at him for the last few minutes as though she doubted the evidence of her eyes, exclaimed faintly: 'It *is* you! Whatever *are* we coming to?' and sat down suddenly on the bench behind her.

'Willitoft!' repeated the spare man. 'I represent the Trustees of the Derbyshire Tolls!'

'Oh, lord!' ejaculated the Captain ruefully. 'Now the cat's in the cream-pot!'

'Yes, fellow, it is! Indeed it is!' said Mr Willitoft. 'How dare you let these persons through the pike without payment? Two led horses as well! Three ruffians — ruffians, I say! — and — '

'Give them a couple of tickets, Bab!' said the Captain.

'You keep your tickets for them as may need 'em!' interposed Stogumber, who was still bestriding the landlord's cob. 'I'm employed on Government business, and I don't pay tolls, not in any county!'

'I don't believe you!' declared Mr Willitoft, bristling with suspicion. 'You're a hardened scoundrel! I knew you for a rogue the instant I laid eyes on you!'

'Ho!' said Stogumber. 'You did, did you? Then p'raps you'll be so obliging as to cast your wapper-eyes over *that* afore you says something as you'll be sorry for!'

Mr Willitoft, reading the information inscribed on the grubby sheet of paper handed down to him, looked very much taken aback, and even a little daunted. In a milder tone, he exclaimed: 'Bow Street! God bless my soul! Very well, I demand no tax from you! But this fellow here is another matter!' he added, looking with dis-favour at Chirk.

'He ain't neither,' said Stogumber. 'He's working for me.'

'Miss Nell,' said Rose, in a hollow voice, 'I am going to have a Spasm! I can feel it coming on!'

'Oh, don't do that!' said John, who, having tethered his horses, had limped up to them. He took Nell's hands, and held them in his firm, comforting clasp. 'My poor girl!' he said gently. 'I wish I might have been beside you when it happened!'

'You know, then? I came to tell you, and to ask you what I should do now. Just at the end, he knew me, and smiled, and, oh, John, he *winked* at me, and with *such* a look in his eye!'

'Did he? What a right one he was!' John said warmly. 'He made up his mind he would live to accomplish one task, and, by Jove, he *did* accomplish it! You mustn't grieve, my darling: he knew all was well, and he was glad to be done with his life.'

'That's what I've been telling her, sir,' agreed Rose. 'Not even Mr Winkfield wished him to drag on longer! Oh, for goodness' sake, sir, whatever is my Jerry doing, as bold as brass?

Such palpitations as it's giving me I shall very likely go off in a swoon!'

'No need for that: he's turned respectable, and is about to set up as a farmer. Mrs Staple and I are coming to dance at your wedding.'

'Oh, Rose, I am so glad!' Nell said. 'But is that man indeed from Bow Street, John? What were you doing in his company, and why are you limping? Good God, can it be — John, what does it mean?'

'Nothing disagreeable,' he assured her. 'It's too long a story to tell you now, but you have no longer anything to dread, my brave girl! I'll tell you later, but I think I had better first get rid of this waspish fellow who wants my blood, don't you?'

An involuntary chuckle escaped her. 'Poor Mr Babbacombe tried his best to fob him off, and I did, too, but there was no getting him to listen to a word we said. And then Tisbury came, with his cow, and they quarrelled over him! Mr Babbacombe told Willitoft that if he knew so much about tolls he might mind the pike himself, and welcome! I thought Willitoft was going into convulsions, he was so angry!'

Mr Willitoft appeared still to be in this condition. As John limped back to him, he stabbed an accusing finger at him, and said: 'You have no right here! You are an improper person to be in charge of the gate! You have no authority! You are an interloper, and an impostor, and I shall have you arrested!'

'Well, I have no authority,' admitted John, 'but I don't think I deserve to be arrested! I haven't robbed the trustees, you know! In fact, if you like to take the strong-box I'll fetch it out to you.'

'Look 'ee here, Mr Willipop!' said Stogumber severely. 'I wouldn't advise you to say no more about improper persons being in charge of this here gate, because your trustees took and authorized a cove as was very highly improper indeed to mind it for 'em. He's snuffed it now, but p'raps you'd like to know as he was hand-in-glove with them as committed a daring robbery in these parts not so long ago — *which* I shall set down in my report!'

Mr Willitoft looked quite dumbfounded by this intelligence, but having stared first at the Runner, then at John, and lastly, and with loathing, at Babbacombe, he said that he should require proof of the accusation. 'And I fail to understand what that may have to do with my finding that *dandy* here! I won't permit him to remain, I say!'

'Well, I don't want to remain,' said Mr Babbacombe. 'And if you call me a dandy again, you antiquated old fidget, I'll dashed well take off my coat, and show you how much of a dandy I am!'

'Officer!' cried Mr Willitoft. 'I call on you to witness that this fellow has offered me violence!'

'Well, you hadn't better,' responded Stogumber. '*I* never heard him offer you no violence! Nice thing if a cove can't take his coat off without a silly nodcock calling on us Runners to stop him!'

'That's the barber!' said Chirk approvingly. 'Dang me if you ain't a great gun, Redbreast!'

'Insolence!' fumed Mr Willitoft.

Stogumber jerked his chin at John, who went to him, a good deal of amusement in his face.

'We don't want no trouble with this Willipop,' said Stogumber, in an undervoice. 'You leave me take him up to the Blue Boar, Capting! I'll have to tell him what made you stop on here like you have done, but you won't care for that, I daresay.'

'Not a bit! I shall be much obliged to you if you take him away. He's a tiresome fellow!'

Mr Stogumber nodded, and addressed himself to Mr Willitoft. 'It's me as is answerable for the Capting here staying to mind the pike, and very helpful he's been. If you was to come along o' me to my temp'ry headquarters, which is the inn up the road, I'll tell you what'll make you take a very different view of this business, Mr Willipop.'

'My name,' said the incensed Mr Willitoft, 'is not Willipop but Willitoft! And I will not under any circumstances permit this person to remain in charge of the gate!'

'If you mean me,' said the Captain, 'I can't remain in charge of it. I'm leaving it today — immediately, in fact!'

This unexpected announcement threw Mr Willitoft off his balance. 'You cannot walk off and leave the gate unattended!' he said indignantly.

'Not only can, but will,' said John cheerfully.

'But this goes beyond everything! Upon my soul, such effrontery I never thought to meet with! You will stay until the trustees appoint a man in Brean's place!'

'Oh, no, I won't! I'm tired of gatekeeping!'

John replied. 'Besides, I don't like you, and I don't feel at all inclined to oblige you.'

'Oblige — Well — But *someone* must stay here!'

'That's all right, old bubble!' said Chirk. '*I'll* mind it for you! But don't you waste no time sending a new man, because it wouldn't suit me to stop here for long. Gatekeeping is low, and I'm a man o' substance!'

'Now I *am* going to suffer a Spasm!' uttered Rose.

Mr Willitoft did not look to be any too well satisfied with this solution to his problem, but since nothing better offered he was obliged, however ungraciously, to acquiesce. He then mounted into the gig, and was driven back to Crowford. Stogumber, pausing only to tell John that he would be returning later, followed him; and Mr Babbacombe was at last free to deliver himself of his free and unflattering estimate of his best friend's character.

'Well, of all the infamous things!' protested John. '*I* never asked you to look after the gate today! Why the devil didn't you leave it to the boy? Where *is* Ben?'

'You may well ask!' said Mr Babbacombe. 'All I know is that he was here when I arrived, over an hour ago! I went in to wait for you, and he must have gone off then, for I hadn't been in the dashed place above fifteen minutes when some fellow out here started shouting gate! By the time he'd shouted it a dozen times, I could have strangled him! Told him so. In fact, we had a bit of a turn-up.'

'Do you mean to tell me you've been fighting everyone who wanted to pass through the gate?' demanded John.

'No, not everyone. I planted that fellow a facer, but that's all.'

'Except for telling the doctor's man that you had something better to do than to keep on opening the gate,' interpolated Nell, with a mischievous look. 'And I made that right! I'm afraid Ben seized the opportunity to play truant, John.'

'Young varmint! He probably slipped off to help the ostler groom your horses, Bab. That's what he wanted to do, when I made him stay here.'

'What?' ejaculated Mr Babbacombe, in lively dismay.

'Oh, don't be afraid! He's very good with horses. With all animals, Huggate tells me. I shall have to try if I can induce one of my tenant-farmers to take charge of him until he's old enough to work under Cocking,' John said, wrinkling his brow. 'I wonder — '

'If it's all the same to you, Soldier,' interrupted Chirk, 'seeing as his dad's hopped the twig, and his brother ain't likely to want him, even if he was to come home, which I daresay he won't, *I'll* take young Ben, and bring him up decent. He's a likely lad, and if it hadn't been for him opening the door to me the very first night I see you, Soldier, I never *would* have seen you, and, consequent, I wouldn't be setting up for myself respectable, nor marrying Rose neither. So, if Rose ain't got no objection, we'll take Benny along with us.

'Certainly we will!' Rose said, a martial light in her eye. 'Many's the time, since his mother died, I've wanted to give him a good wash, poor little fellow, and mend his clothes, and teach him his manners!'

'Well, he may not relish that overmuch,' said John, grinning, 'but there's no doubt he'd far rather be with Jerry than with me.'

'John,' said Nell, who had been frowning at the horses, 'why have you brought those two horses here? That brown belongs to my cousin, and the bay is Coate's!'

'Well, yes, dearest! The thing is — but let us go into the house! At least, I must stable Beau first!'

'I'll do that,' said Chirk. 'And since I'm going to stay here, I'll take Mollie too.'

'Perhaps,' suggested Nell, 'Rose should go with you to explain the matter to Huggate.'

'I think she should,' agreed the Captain. 'And then come into the house, Jerry, so that we may drink both your healths!' He ushered his wife and his friend in as he spoke, and when he had them both safely inside the kitchen, said bluntly: 'There's a great deal I shall have to tell you presently, but for the moment only one thing of importance! Both Coate and Stornaway are dead.'

Nell could only blink at him, but Mr Babbacombe was in no mood to submit to such treatment, and said, with a good deal of asperity: 'Oh, they are, are they? Then you may dashed well tell us how that came about, and what you had to do with it, Jack! I can tell only by looking at you that you've been up to some harebrained fetch, so out with it!'

'Oh, later, later, Bab!' the Captain said, frowning at him. 'What I need is beer!'

'Very well,' said Nell, removing from his grasp the tankard he had picked up from the shelf. 'I will draw you some beer, but not one sip shall you have until you do as Mr Babbacombe bids you! He is very right! And if you suppose, sir, that you can walk in with a graze on your forehead, blood on your waistcoat, and a lame foot, without explaining to me how you came by all these things, you will very soon learn better!'

'Good God, I've married a shrew!' said the Captain, playing for time, while he mentally expunged from his story certain features, and materially revised others.

'John, how did my cousin come by his death?'

'He was shot when Coate's gun exploded.'

'Did you kill him?'

'No, Nell. On my word as a gentleman I did not!'

'I shouldn't have cared a button if you had,' she said calmly. 'Did you kill Coate?'

'Coate broke his neck — falling on a natural rock-stair. I wish you will let me have my beer!'

She looked enquiringly at Mr Babbacombe. 'You know him much better than I do: do you think he did kill Coate?'

'Of course he did!' said Mr Babbacombe scornfully. 'Knew it the instant he told us the fellow was dead! Probably didn't kill your cousin, though. Didn't seem to have any such notion in his head when he talked to me about it.'

She gave the Captain his beer, and, taking his free hand, lifted it to her cheek. 'I *wish* Grandpapa had known!' she said simply. 'He would have been so delighted! Now tell us, if you please, John, just how it all happened!'

We do hope that you have enjoyed reading this large print book.

Did you know that all of our titles are available for purchase?

We publish a wide range of high quality large print books including:
**Romances, Mysteries, Classics
General Fiction
Non Fiction and Westerns**

Special interest titles available in large print are:
**The Little Oxford Dictionary
Music Book
Song Book
Hymn Book
Service Book**

Also available from us courtesy of Oxford University Press:
**Young Readers' Dictionary
(large print edition)
Young Readers' Thesaurus
(large print edition)**

For further information or a free brochure, please contact us at:
**Ulverscroft Large Print Books Ltd.,
The Green, Bradgate Road, Anstey,
Leicester, LE7 7FU, England.
Tel: (00 44) 0116 236 4325
Fax: (00 44) 0116 234 0205**

COTILLION

Georgette Heyer

The three great-nephews of cantankerous Mr Penicuik know better than to ignore his summons, especially when it concerns the bestowal of his fortune. The wily old gentleman has hatched an outrageous plan for his stepdaughter's future and his own amusement: his fortune will be lovely Catherine Charing's dowry if she marries one of his great-nephews. To the spirited Kitty, the conditions of her guardian's will before she can inherit a tuppence are intolerable. But while the beaux are scrambling for her hand, Kitty counters with her own inventive, if daring, scheme: a sham engagement that should help keep wedlock at bay . . .

ARABELLA

Georgette Heyer

Arabella, daughter of an impoverished country parson, dreams of a new life in London. But her beauty and charm will only get her so far — and when she embarks on her first London season armed with nothing but a benevolent godmother, she quickly runs afoul of Robert Beaumaris. He's the most eligible bachelor of the day, with a personality as strong and combative as hers. Arabella cannot abide him thinking of her as just another pretty girl after his wealth, so she allows herself to be provoked into a game of deception — one that could have unexpected consequences . . .

SPRIG MUSLIN

Georgette Heyer

Sir Gareth Ludlow has decided he'll never fall in love again — but Fate has other ideas ... A chance encounter with Amanda, a young and devastatingly pretty runaway, inspires him to set her on a path towards a good life, despite the fact that she is determined to keep her identity a secret. But Sir Gareth has been neck-deep in a life of debauchery and hedonism ever since his fiancée's death, and Amanda's startlingly lively imagination proves to be more than he bargained for. As they match each other lie for outrageous lie, will the truth eventually prevail?